# My Soul To Take

Suzannah's stomach tightened. 'Are you talking about the implant?' she asked.

'Yes,' he said, his expression almost fierce. 'The microchip. I want you to take the ghastly thing out of my brain.'

Suzannah stared at him, her mind reeling. 'Take it out? You can't be serious.'

'Oh, but I am.'

She felt a heaviness in her chest, compressing her lungs, making it hard to breathe. How could this be happening? Andrew Dugan was trying to drag her back in time, to a place she must never go again.

Steve Morgan, who has been praised for his depiction of strong characters and authentic medical background, has a PhD in clinical psychology. His other books include *Before I Wake*, *Painkiller*, *Hellstone*, and a science fiction trilogy. He and his wife live in Arlington, Virginia.

STEVE MORGAN

# My Soul
# To Take

ARROW

Published in the United Kingdom in 1994
by Mandarin Paperbacks

1 3 5 7 9 0 8 6 4 2

Copyright © Steven Spruill 1994

The right of Steven Morgan to be identified as the author
of this work has been asserted by him in accordance
with the Copyright, Designs and Patents Act, 1988

First published in the United Kingdom in 1994 by William Heinemann

Arrow Books
The Random House Group Limited
20 Vauxhall Bridge Road, London, SW1V 2SA

Random House Australia (Pty) Limited
20 Alfred Street, Milsons Point, Sydney,
New South Wales 2061, Australia

Random House New Zealand Limited
18 Poland Road, Glenfield
Auckland 10, New Zealand

Random House (Pty) Limited
Endulini, 5a Jubilee Road, Parktown 2193, South Africa

The Random House Group Limited Reg. No. 954009

www.randomhouse.co.uk

A CIP catalogue record for this book is available from the British Library

Papers used by Random House are natural, recyclable products made from
wood grown in sustainable forests. The manufacturing processes conform to
the environmental regulations of the country of origin

Printed and bound in Great Britain by
Bookmarque Ltd, Croydon, Surrey

ISBN 0 7493 1445 1

*To John Anthony Spruill,*
the best big brother
a guy could have.

## Acknowledgements

I thank the following people for helping me with this novel: Katie and Jay Baker, Maureen Baron, Joe and Claire Cockrell, Bill and Marcia Eggleston, Jeanne Kamensky, Genie and Steve McBurnett, Mary Ann and Dick Setton, Dolores and John Vaughn and Mary Wilson.

My special thanks to MDs Pam Blake and Paul Wilson for their expert assistance with the medical aspects of the novel.

And, as always, I thank you, Nancy, from the bottom of my heart.

# 1

Fighting to keep her eyes open, Dr Suzannah Lord watched the monkey. Rain drummed on the roof of the lab, steady, monotonous, turning the warm, humid air heavy on her eyelids. The monkey blurred . . .

Suzannah heard a whisper of sound behind her. Snapping fully awake, she turned and peered at the rear of the lab. Filing cabinets loomed in the shadows, flanked by boxes of old study protocols, the vital notes on experiments and treatments. Her heart pounded, pumping cool aftershocks through her veins. She replayed the sound in her mind – soft, stealthy, like a shoe gliding across the floor. But no one was back there. It must have been a gust of wind, rising above the drone of the rain.

Suzannah turned back to the monkey, but an edgy sense of the space behind her lingered. Fine – it would help her stay awake. Already she could feel the fatigue creeping back. She rubbed at her eyes and patted her cheeks. The clock above the door read seventeen past midnight, which made it thirty-six hours, and counting, on duty. Still, she shouldn't be this whacked, not with the three hours sleep she'd grabbed in her on-call room before rounds yesterday morning. Must be that last operation over at DC Memorial – standing on the hard flooring for six hours backing up Sid.

Suzannah stood and swung her arms, stamped her feet,

watching the monkey. Seymour sat motionless in his chair, his eyes hidden behind the twin TV screens of his headset. Was he dozing off too? She checked the electroencephalograph beside the computer. Seymour's brain scratched green, saw-toothed waves across the dark grey screen, ten cycles per second. Good – Seymour was awake and watching, keeping at his task. It was nice to see him so calm tonight, but she needed to stay alert anyway. If he panicked, took fright, one hard jerk of his head could tear the implant loose inside his brain and she would find herself fighting for his life.

Suzannah poured a coffee from her thermos. It tasted strong and bitter, just right. She drank it down and took a turn around the lab, keeping her blood moving by tidying up the stack of circuit boards on one of the long, black counter tops. A light sweat formed on her face. It must be eighty in here. Clearly, the air conditioning had broken down again too late in the day to fix. Actually, the humidity and warmth felt rather nice. After a week cooped up in hospital air conditioning, she'd almost forgotten it was summer. How long since she'd grabbed that day at Ocean City with her sister and nephew? Only two weeks but it felt more like two months. Suzannah smiled. So much more happened when you didn't sleep.

She took the picture from her wallet. It wasn't bad for an automatic photo booth down by the shore. At eight, J.D. had the towheaded cuteness she remembered in kid pictures of his mother. Juli kept saying he took after his father Wesley, but it wasn't true. Looking at the photo, Suzannah could almost smell the hot tar of the roadways, the wonderful, greasy fragrance of french fries. It had been a magical day – the always-difficult Wesley away on business, just she, her sister and her nephew at the beach. She remembered how

J.D. had kept crowding her in the photo booth to make sure they could both be in the picture. In one shot, he'd 'horned' her with two fingers. She'd felt his wrist brush the back of her head as he'd done it but had let it go, not wanting to spoil his fun.

Looking at her own face, Suzannah felt a curious contentment. She had not always liked her face, but now she did. Her jaw line and cheekbones, honed by the rigours of hospital life, had an ascetic but pleasing sleekness. Her dark hair, cut into a pageboy, glinted with red undertones. It showed no sign of the surgical cap that mashed it down for hours every day. The grin that had once seemed too restrained was free and open. She liked the direct, brown eyes, the dusting of freckles the sun had brought out in just an hour on the beach. She was not gorgeous, like Juli, but the face in the photo was pretty enough, the face of a neurosurgeon.

Suzannah put the photo away, careful not to bend it. It proved there was life outside this period of residency – family, people you loved. In a few more years, she would have all that, not just a few precious days a year but as much as she wanted. But first she had one or two more things to learn.

Her mind went back to this afternoon in surgery, the awful moment when Sid's clip had popped off the aneurysm. She grimaced, flexing her fingers, remembering how her hands had almost cramped as she tried desperately to suction the gushing blood from the torn blood vessel. Three units gone in a horrible red flash, the patient plunging into shock, starting to fibrillate. Give Sid credit for staying cool, though. If he hadn't hung in there, fishing through the blood, somehow getting the clip back on, the patient would be lying in the morgue right now instead of the recovery room.

I would have set that clip better in the first place, Suzannah thought, then wondered. How could she know, with Sid taking the lead all the time? Not just for aneurysms; everything but the easy spinals. As a third-year resident, he had the say, but when was he going to give her the reins on a challenging case? She'd learned all she could about sawing skulls, working the suckers, and closing.

Maybe I should talk to Dr Lancaster about it, she thought, then realized it was a bad idea. She couldn't go over Sid's head like that, especially to the chairman of neurosurgery. Some of the other residents had already hinted that Dr Lancaster had given her this second lab slot because she was a woman. Mike Fachet, his other lab assistant, was a senior resident and apparently both slots were usually filled by R-4s. Suzannah felt herself flushing. It made her mad to think anyone believed she'd got lab unfairly. If being a woman got you ahead in this field, why was she Lancaster's first female neurosurgery resident in seven years?

No, she'd won the lab slot through hard work and lots of it. I get in on every operation I can, she thought. On rounds, I'm one of the few junior residents Dr Lancaster hasn't had to chew out for sketchy histories or inadequate physicals. I never gripe when the chief resident dumps arteriograms and myelograms on me – though I'll admit I've been tempted. I even take private practice rounds for the staff physicians so they can sleep in for an extra hour. And I'm organized. Dr Lancaster knows he can count on me to show up in lab when I'm scheduled – and even when I'm not.

I earned this, Suzannah thought.

I'll just have to talk with Sid again, she decided. Lean on him harder about giving me some aneurysms and tumours. All the male residents yell at each other when they're fed up. I can do it too, if I have to. And if that fails, *then* I'll tell Sid I'm

4

taking it to Lancaster and he can come along if he wants.

A movement flickered at the corner of her eye.

Straightening, she scanned the lab. The stack of boxes in the shadows against the rear wall drew her gaze again. Two stacks, actually, reaching nearly to the ceiling, with a narrow alley between. In her mind's eye, she saw someone slipping through the rear door, sneaking up on her and ducking between the stacks when she turned. She groaned. Now that she'd imagined it, she'd not be able to sit with her back to those boxes until she checked. She sidled up to them, inching her head into the dark, narrow gap between. Smells of mildew and dust. No one hiding.

Behind her, Seymour clicked his teeth. Suzannah felt a rash of goose bumps on her arms. Monkeys did that when they were agitated or excited. Had Seymour heard something too? She took another long look around the lab. It appeared as empty as before. She listened, wishing the rain would stop so she could hear better. She found herself edging over towards Seymour, taking care not to step on the channel of wires that led from his brain back to the computer. She saw he was gripping the armrests now, leaning forwards slightly. He did that when he was especially absorbed in what he was seeing on the headset. Seymour had heard nothing.

She relaxed, feeling foolish. The lab was locked. The hospital had good security. Why did she keep getting the creeps? Must be the caffeine. She'd been pounding coffees and Cokes all day and it had made her jumpy, that was all.

She became aware of Seymour's smell, strong and gamey but not unpleasant. As long as she was up, she might as well do the exam. She checked the soft cuff restraints on the armrests, making sure they were not holding Seymour's forearms too tightly. Peering through the hole in the top of Seymour's helmet, she inspected the shaved spot on his skull

5

where she and Mike Fachet had implanted the socket. It looked clean and free from infection, no sign of inflammation on the shaved skin. The plug was firmly seated. Stepping back, she checked the pulse and blood pressure monitors. Pulse a little high, blood pressure normal. She finished up with the gross exam. Seymour's weight looked good. His delicate fingers showed none of the nicks or cuts that would indicate stress. His coat, soft and bushy, gleamed under the fluorescents. Nikki must have been brushing him again, bless her. Suzannah shook her head: personal physician to a Macaque monkey. It wasn't exactly what she'd envisioned when she entered medical school.

In fact, it was the chance of a lifetime.

She reached out to stroke his back, then stopped. When he was so engrossed by the headset, any touch would startle him.

What *was* he looking at that had him so fascinated?

Suzannah walked back to the computer and flipped on the TV link. The screen lit with a jungle scene, the camera moving forwards between the boles of towering trees, draped with green vines. Ahead, a brown river glinted through the thick vegetation. Suzannah stared, caught by surprise. This must be the new footage Dr Lancaster had talked about adding to the experiment. He'd persuaded a study group from pharmacology to take the camera rig along on their expedition to the Amazon. Had they returned already? Suzannah bent and checked the cabinet under the computer. Yes, there the rig was, back in its place. A withered strand of vine clung to the crosspiece that yoked the two videocams together. She felt a surge of interest. No wonder Seymour was transfixed. After weeks of looking at weird 3-D movies of apples and bananas and boxes rotating on a platform, this must be like a trip to the beach for him.

6

Looking at the monitor again, Suzannah wished she could see both tracks of the new tape in 'visual stereo' the way Seymour could. It was one thing to view 3-D images of simple objects and quite another to find yourself deep in an Amazon jungle that looked entirely real.

Maybe this tape would put the computer over the top.

Suzannah felt a mixture of hope and doubt. Everything she'd read on visual research said Dr Lancaster was wrong to show the monkeys such complex vistas. None of the other researchers in the field had even gone 3-D yet. They were still showing their lab animals simple flat designs projected on a screen.

Of course, those researchers were just gathering information, bit by bit, in the time-honoured way of science not trying to crack the brain's code for vision all at once. They hadn't ventured beyond single hand-held electrodes, and they were still exploring cell response relatively close to the eye, where the brain had only started its analysis. Lancaster, on the other hand, used a multi-electrode implant and placed it deep at the key bottleneck where complex images, thoroughly analysed by the visual cortex, crossed between halves of the brain.

And now he was upping the ante again.

Suzannah admired his boldness. At the rate other researchers were going with their single electrodes, it would take another fifty to a hundred years just to map the visual system of a monkey. Analysing the painting on the Sistine Chapel one brushstroke at a time would be child's play by comparison. Roland Lancaster did not have that kind of patience. It was all or nothing for him. With his typical blend of drive and arrogance, he had taken on the whole problem at once. Huge hurdles faced him. He was smashing them down, one by one, with bold head-on genius. First he'd had to find a way to show the monkeys moving 3-D images rather than static, flat ones; you couldn't expect the computer to crack the code for vision if the images you fed to the eyes did not trigger the millions of brain cells that perceive depth and motion. Lancaster had got wind of the budding and largely unknown technology of 'virtual reality' and had adapted its experimental 3-D equipment to solve his problem.

But he wasn't stopping with 3-D. Going from simple rotating objects to this complicated jungle scene was the boldest stroke of all. The computer hadn't yet even been able to solve what happened in Seymour's brain when he looked at an apple. But instead of holding back, Dr Lancaster was now pushing it. He was gambling that the image of an apple wasn't too *hard* for the computer but too *simple*, that it activated too little response in the brain for the computer to identify the overall patterns in the visual code.

This new footage would pour a tidal wave of data through the CM5 computer. The exotic CM5 'Connection Machine' was of the most powerful breed of computers available for recognizing patterns. It boasted sixty-four thousand central processing units – each one the heart of a computer in its own right – hooked up in parallel rather than in series, which was how the human brain itself analyses information. At this moment, the CM5 was monitoring the millions of impulses coursing through Seymour's brain as the monkey watched the jungle. The computer was programmed to find *patterns* in that deluge of neuroelectricity and then *link* those patterns to the specific images Seymour was seeing.

So far, week after week, the computer had failed.

But if Lancaster's gamble with this new footage paid off, tonight might be the night.

A nerve throbbed in the pit of Suzannah's stomach. She imagined what would happen if the CM5 broke the code. It would be stupendous, one of the greatest breakthroughs in the history of science. If a computer knew the code for vision, an implant could be devised to enhance the data from damaged or diseased eyes and restore perfect vision. It would be wonderful! Victims of diabetic retinopathy, severe glaucoma damage, progressive myopia ... thousands of people, effectively blind, would be able to see again. Roland Lancaster would be hailed as the Jonas Salk of neuroscience. As one of his residents and a member of his research team, she would gain too. Doors would open for her all down the road, doors that might otherwise stay closed, especially to a woman. When her residency was over, she would be able to treat the most difficult and challenging cases. She could get grants herself, to work on whatever her mind could devise. A surgical cure for epilepsy, perhaps. Or a way to arrest, even reverse, Alzheimer's.

Suzannah realized she was grinning. She was glad no one was around to see her. Residents, the slave labourers of medicine, weren't supposed to get this excited about their work at one o'clock in the morning after thirty-six straight hours on duty.

Suzannah dug into her medical bag, taking out her Walkman and slipping the earphones over her head. She popped in a Keith Jarrett tape and turned the volume up high in case sleep tried to steal back over her. Jarrett's complex jazzy rhythms boosted her natural high. Watching Seymour, she drummed her fingers on the arms of the chair in time with the music. I am the luckiest person in the world, she thought.

A hand came down lightly on her shoulder, fingers squeezing. She screamed and jumped, but the hand held her gently down in the chair. Her earphones rose up from her head, tugging strands of hair along.

'Sorry,' said a deep, male voice behind her.

9

Dr Lancaster!

Suzannah swivelled around under his hand, feeling her heart hammer. 'You startled me!' she said.

'Sorry.'

She waited for him to lift his hand so she could stand, but he kept it on her shoulder with a companionable pressure. It was a large hand for a man only five feet seven, the fingers strong from years with the drill and bone pliers. His red hair, peppered with white, looked freshly combed and he'd shaved recently, even though it was after midnight. His white shirt looked fresh. He gave her a rueful smile, transforming the patrician sternness of his face.

'I thought I was making plenty of noise, scuffing my feet,' he said, 'but I guess you had the volume way up. Trying to stay awake?'

'Yes, sir.' His palm was warm on her shoulder. She began to feel uncomfortable.

As if realizing it, he released her and pressed one of the earphones against his ear. He raised a disdainful eyebrow and she remembered a diatribe he'd launched last month on 'modern music'.

'What brings you to the lab so late?' Suzannah said. Her heart was still pounding. She was annoyed with herself for screaming. A male resident would not have screamed.

'Had a head wound emergency,' he said. 'Bullet didn't exit. It was very close to the optic nerve. Took me longer than I expected. Just got done, in fact. No point driving out to Fairfax County when I've got rounds in five hours. Thought I'd stop in, see how you and the monkey were doing.'

Suzannah felt flattered.

And a little uneasy. Was he checking up on her?

Dr Lancaster glanced over at Seymour, then returned his gaze to her.

'He really likes that new tape you got,' she said.

'All of them do. You look a little tense, Dr Lord.'

Suzannah realized her shoulders were up. Embarrassed, she let them drop. Dr Lancaster walked around behind her again. 'Here, I know just the thing,' he said, putting his hands on both her shoulders now, squeezing gently, kneading the tight muscles, letting one hand work its way up the back of her neck. It felt good, but she could feel each muscle knotting up again as soon as his fingers moved on. She could smell him suddenly, a lilac scent like hair tonic. She tried to think of something to say. 'Was it a drug shooting?'

'Domestic,' he said. 'Man popped his brother-in-law. Bullet went right here.' He tapped her head gently, his finger lingering. 'You know, you have the most beautiful hair.'

'Uh, thank you.' She felt his nose brush the nape of her neck, heard him inhaling. Her skin seemed to freeze.

'You're a lovely young woman,' Lancaster said. 'Easily the loveliest resident I've ever had.' He chuckled.

Foreboding filled Suzannah. Those male residents who thought she'd got into the lab because she was a woman – she realized suddenly how she had minimized it, avoided what they were really saying: because she was an *attractive* woman. Was that it? Did Lancaster have the hots for her? How could I have missed it? she wondered. Her mind raced back over the months she had known him, looking for signs she might have ignored. He seemed to hold eye contact with her a lot during rounds, but surely he did that with the male residents too. He'd put his hand on her shoulder before, but only in a fatherly way. Or had she deliberately defused his touch in her mind, not wanting to deal with it?

Suzannah felt an ache in the pit of her stomach. She had to stop him, before things got out of hand.

But she mustn't be too obvious about it.

'Would you like some coffee?' She tried to bend over and pick up her thermos, escape his kneading hands. He held her in place.

'Don't fight it, Suzannah,' he said.

Her heart sank. 'I . . . Dr Lancaster . . .'

'Every time I look at you,' he said, 'I imagine what it would be like to feel your lips on mine, my hands on your lovely breasts.' He bent close, nuzzling her ear.

Panic surged in her. She pulled away and stood, turning to face him. 'You – we can't do this,' she said.

He smiled, an easy, knowing half smile. 'Of course we can. What's the matter, Suzannah? You want a bit of romance first, perhaps? I take you to dinner, we discuss the theatre, take a picnic lunch to Sugar Loaf or the tidal basin? I'd like that too, but *that* we truly cannot be seen doing – even if either of us had the time. We have chosen a difficult life, you and I. We don't have the luxuries other people have. But we have got to know each other the only way we can. You are impressed with me, or you would never have applied for this residency. And I'm impressed with you. Have been from the start, or you wouldn't be here.'

Suzannah heard a slight emphasis on the last words. Fear struck through her like a cold knife.

'I'm crazy about you, surely you know that? What man wouldn't be? You don't have a husband, so . . .'

'But you have a wife.'

He coloured slightly. 'Let's leave Martha out of this.'

'How can we? You're a married man.'

'So?'

'So I don't want to be the one to threaten that.'

'Don't you find me attractive?' He smiled; no one could possibly fail to find him attractive.

Suzannah swallowed, trying desperately to think, to

negotiate her way through this minefield. One wrong word now and she could lose everything. 'Of course you're attractive, sir–'

He smiled again. 'We can drop the "sir" for the moment. Call me Roland.'

'I think it's better if we–'

'I want to make love to you, Suzannah. I'm very good at it, you'll see. No one's here, no one will know. Life is short. I need you and I want you, now. And you need me too, whether you know it or not.'

He was in here earlier, she thought, chilled. The sounds I heard. He sneaked in and was watching me.

Roland Lancaster reached for her. She put her hands between his, fending his arms off. She had the odd dissociated feeling that she was looking at a stranger. This was not Dr Roland Lancaster. This was an imposter. I'm having a nightmare, she thought. She shook her head, but Lancaster was still there, still moving in.

She pushed his hands away again.

His face darkened. 'Suzannah, do I need to spell it out for you? You are here because I took you on. I can end that any time I choose, as easily as I began it. Just think about your position a minute.'

Suzannah stared at him, appalled, unable to look away.

'Now, will you do as I say?'

'Please–'

He lunged at her, grabbing her shoulders, pulling her to him, mashing his lips against hers. She went rigid, feeling his teeth, praying he would stop. Undeterred by her passivity, he thrust a hand inside her blouse, groping her breast. She shoved him. He tripped over the edge of her chair and sat down hard.

Oh, dear God, she thought. She stepped forward to help

13

him up. He batted her hand away. Getting up on his own, he glared at her.

'Please, Dr Lancaster, you're tired, that's all. You didn't mean this. We won't ever mention it again. We'll just forget it happened.'

'We will?' His voice was cold as ice. He straightened his jacket and walked to the door, opening it with his key. Turning, he stared at her for a long time. 'Remember what I said, Dr Lord: any time I choose.'

He stepped out, closing the door softly behind him.

Suzannah's knees buckled. She grabbed for the back of her chair, circling it, sitting down. She felt cold, distant, as though she were watching a movie of someone else. What did I do? she wondered. Did I do something to encourage him? Did I do look at him wrong, say something?

She was surprised to find tears pouring from her eyes. Her hand shook as she wiped them away.

*Any time I choose.*

What was he going to do? Would he fire her tomorrow, cancel her residency?

Suzannah felt her stomach heave. She clapped a hand over her mouth, bending over in the chair, waiting for the nausea to ease. I'll go somewhere else, she thought, get into another programme.

And then she realized she couldn't – not without a recommendation from Roland Lancaster. She felt the panic again. Not to be a neurosurgeon? She could not conceive of it. She had hoped for it, planned and worked half her life for it. She couldn't stand to lose it now. Please God, don't let him do this.

Straightening, she took deep breaths. Calm down, she thought. He won't do it tomorrow, or even next week. If he's really going to do it, he'll wait until what he tried tonight can't be linked with his dismissing me. And while he's waiting, he'll watch me for mistakes, anything he can use to justify firing me.

Or maybe he'll cool off. If I can just get through the next few weeks, maybe he *will* forget about it.

In the meantime, I'll work harder. I won't make any mistakes . . .

Suzannah heard Seymour click his teeth again, a sound that now seemed full of derision.

# 2

**Georgetown, 14 January 1993:**

Suzannah stood at the edge of the gallery crowd, sipping champagne, missing Jay. He should be here watching the opening with her, his arm around her waist, offering some dry Texas witticism about finger foods or cummerbunds, all the while looking stunning in his own tux.

Cut it out, Suzannah told herself. You're the one who kept encouraging him to visit his family. Sure, it would be great if you could share this with him, but it's going to be wonderful anyway. A new showing by Andrew Dugan! Nothing can stop this from being a fantastic evening.

She made her way to the gallery's high arching windows. The panes shone like black gems against the night, etched at the corners with frost. On P Street below, tyres crunched through the snow, making a frigid counterpoint to the tropical warmth of the anteroom.

Actually, she was glad Jay had gone to Texas. Getting away will be good for him, she thought. His book is driving him crazy. Maybe a few days of not thinking about it will help him over his writer's block.

Maybe he'll even unbend enough to let me try and help. Something about that book is bothering him. If he'd just stop acting as if everything were fine and *talk* to me, we could work on it together.

Suzannah felt a touch of uneasiness. How long had she and Jay been dating? Over five months. For the first few, it seemed that every time they were together they drew closer. But the relationship had levelled off a bit. At a very nice place, true. But the plateau had begun around two months ago, right about the time Jay had taken a leave of absence from the *Post*. It was starting to come between them, this book.

But I won't let it, she thought.

Resolutely, she turned from the window and scanned the gathering crowd. The room was filling up fast. Mostly uppercrust Georgetowners, by the look of them; slim, cosmopolitan women in designer dresses, well-groomed men who wore their tuxes with the ease of practice. That tall man over in the corner: she'd seen him on TV just last week, on *MacNeil/Lehrer*; he was – what? – an Assistant Secretary of State. And there was the elegant Cokie Roberts with her adorable husband, Steve. What a great smile he had. Did Jay know them? Probably. She'd love to be introduced some time.

Watching the urbane crowd mingle, Suzannah was glad that her sister had caught her going out of the door in her wool suit and made her change. Juli's black dress with the flared collar and her pearl necklace were good choices. Clearly, this stratum of the art crowd dressed to the nines, even on Thursday nights.

'Hors d'oeuvres, miss?' A red-coated waiter held out a tray of breads, meats, and glazed fruits on little swords.

'No, thank you,' Suzannah said. She was too excited to eat, full to the brim with anticipation. A showing by her favourite artist – who, four years before, had been virtually blind! It was fabulous, like the discovery of a tenth Beethoven symphony or an unknown Hemingway novel. She wanted to see the new paintings right now, push through the crowd and try for a glimpse through the french doors that still sealed off the gallery proper. If she could not go in soon, she would burst with curiosity. What effect would the visual implant have on Andrew Dugan's work?

*Roland Lancaster's implant.*

Suzannah had a sudden mental image of Lancaster's arrogant patrician face. She felt her jaw clench and forced it to relax. It would be difficult, but she was *not* going to think about Lancaster tonight.

With an effort she focused her thoughts on Dugan again, remembering his paintings from before the surgery. While glorious, they had mirrored his deteriorating eyesight. More and more, his compositions had featured thick black boundaries around colliding blocks of colour, as though Dugan had been trying to fight off his failing vision by putting brilliant, fortified edges on everything. How desperate he must have been then, feeling what little was left of his eyesight growing steadily worse, plunging him into a quasi-blindness of colour and light without form.

What would his work be like now that he could see perfectly?

'Hey, Doc!'

Suzannah turned, surprised and delighted to find Sharon Harrad and her husband, Jeff. Sharon wore a loose silk dress with a beaded stained-glass motif, perfect for a modern art showing. Meandering seams of black silk showed between the dress's hand-sewn patches of colour, complementing her long raven-black hair.

'Hey, Doc, yourself,' Suzannah said. 'You look beautiful. Hi, Jeff.'

'Suzannah. Good to see you. Where's Jay?'

'Visiting the family ranch in Texas, probably eating barbecue with his fingers after a day of punching cattle with his daddy, Billy-Jim-Bob.'

Sharon laughed, a rich, easy chuckle. She seemed so happy, so relaxed. Suzannah was glad. Looking at Sharon now, it was hard to believe that only a few years ago she'd been tense and wary, a woman trying to shake an inner demon. Sharon rarely talked about her past, but apparently she had been desperately poor and it had been one long struggle. When they'd first met two years ago, Sharon was a third-year resident in psychiatry, about to marry Jeff. Suzannah could remember moments of pain in her eyes, occasional distant silences. Those seemed entirely gone now. Jeff was a dream of a guy, boyishly handsome, a newly minted neurologist from a well-to-do family. Sharon's Oleg Cassini dress suggested that her med school debts had been paid off, and then some. More important, she looked radiantly happy.

'We're all anxious to read Jay's account of the Gulf war,' Jeff said.

Not as anxious as he is to write it, Suzannah thought. She said, 'I didn't know you were an Andrew Dugan fan.'

'My parents have a couple of his early paintings, *Canterbury* and *Reflexions*. Sharon and I are interested in whether the surgery has changed his style.'

'Aren't we all. I've been in love with his work since I was in high school.'

'Just his work?' Sharon's green eyes twinkled.

Suzannah was exasperated to feel herself blushing. 'I think he's the finest American artist alive today.'

'I don't know about that, but he's certainly the best looking.'

19

'Ladies, ladies!'

Sharon laughed. 'Just throw some ice water in our faces, Jeff, we'll be all right.'

'Interesting timing, this showing,' Jeff said. 'The pilot study on the vision microchip is almost up and I understand the Federal Drug Agency is in the final stages of approving it for general use.'

Sharon cleared her throat. Jeff glanced at her without comprehension and continued, 'Dugan is the most famous test subject in the pilot group. If his painting has improved, it will give Roland Lancaster an even greater –'

Sharon nudged Jeff gently in the ribs, but not so gently that he didn't wince slightly. Poor Jeff. For all Sharon's slimness, she pumped iron, and that sharp elbow had probably stung. *Sharon hasn't told him how I feel about Lancaster*, Suzannah realized, impressed at this new token of her friend's discretion. Most women – even psychiatrists – with a husband as nice as Jeff would share such a juicy titbit and swear their mates to secrecy. Of course, some mates might then forget, but not Jeff. He was as tactful as Sharon was discreet.

Sidetracked, Jeff gave his wife a baffled look. Mercifully, someone called his name. He excused himself and moved away. Sharon gave a little grimace of apology. Suzannah squeezed her hand. There was really nothing to apologize for.

'I almost called you at the hospital today,' Sharon said. 'I got a consult call down to Emergency – some guy wanting to commit himself. He hinted that he was a CIA man.' Sharon hesitated. 'Do you know anyone at the CIA?'

Suzannah searched her mind. 'I don't think so. Juli has met a few CIA men through her work in naval intelligence, but she's never introduced any of them to me, that I remember.'

'The man I'm talking about is fifty, short, very white hair, pale complexion.'

'Doesn't ring any bells.'

'Strange,' Sharon said. 'This guy knew you worked at the hospital and asked if I knew you. When I said yes, he kept subtly bringing the conversation back to you.'

Suzannah shook her head, baffled. 'That *is* strange. Why did he want to commit himself?'

'Not clear. He seemed very tired, but he denied sleep loss. At first he talked about seeing things, then he switched gears and said he was thinking of killing himself. When I started to follow up on that, he stepped past me and pulled the curtain aside. He looked out for a minute. A cop had walked into the department. My patient excused himself to go to the bathroom, and that's the last I saw of him.'

'Sounds like he was on the run. Don't you get criminals from time to time who fake symptoms, hoping they can hide away on the ward until the heat is off?'

'Sure, but a CIA man?'

'Maybe he wasn't really CIA.'

'Maybe. But I was curious enough to check his insurance. Unless he'd stolen his card, from the prefix he was a fed of some kind.'

Suzannah did not know what to say. It was strange and a bit troubling. Why had the man asked about her?

Sensing movement in the crowd, she turned in time to see a gallery employee open the french doors with a flourish. At last! she thought.

'Oh!' Sharon said. 'I'd better find Jeff. Want to do the tour with us?'

'No, you go on. I'll catch up with you later.'

Sharon nodded and hurried off. Suzannah gulped the rest of her champagne and handed the glass to a waiter, letting the wake of the crowd pick her up and draw her into the gallery.

Her first glimpse made her breath catch. Each painting hung on its own wall, in a blazing pool of light, separated from the others by the dark corners. It was very dramatic.

But only four paintings?

She felt a twinge of disappointment. It had been four years since his surgery. She had expected more, at least twice that number.

Ah, well, it was quality, not quantity that counted.

She worked her way to the first painting. It was magnificent. Its umber centre had the dense magnetic weight of a black hole. A vortex of light ringed the centre in clamouring shards – searing yellows and brilliant whites, bending to the pull of the dark core. Looking at it roused butterflies in her stomach. It wielded an incredible power, making her think of the retinal showers of eyes pinched shut in ecstasy.

Suzannah moved on to the next painting. It was gentler, a sandy surreal plain stretching away to a distant horizon. A single fantastical creature, manlike but with an odd-shaped head, scampered towards the painting's horizon in a leaning, loopy run. The head was a trifle ominous – it looked almost like a hammerhead shark's – but there was a contrasting delight and exhilaration in the figure's wild abandon that seemed as playful as one of Miro's.

The paintings drew her around the walls. Her awareness of the crowd receded. The brilliant colours, the persistent dashes of detailed realism amid the joyous chaos, touched her, speaking of an artist reborn. The tiny microchip inside his brain was not just enhancing the faulty signals from his eyes, it was giving him back his life. She was not a critic, not schooled in art beyond her own inept if persistent efforts, but the paintings spoke to her with great power.

She turned away from the light and colour of the walls, needing to catch her breath. In the midst of the crowd, she saw Jeff and Sharon gazing, hand in hand, at one of the paintings. Their closeness touched her. She wished again that Jay were here. He was not especially fond of art, but these paintings would move him, she was sure.

Suzannah plucked another glass of champagne from a passing waiter. Sipping it, she readied herself mentally to make a second tour of the paintings.

Then she saw Andrew Dugan, standing against the far wall.

She felt her heart skip a beat. He was dressed all in black, tall and broad-shouldered and gorgeous. He must be mid-forties by now, but he looked younger. His Irish-black hair had grown out into a fantastic mane. Dear God, look at his eyes – what a change! She remembered the glasses he'd worn to surgery that day four years ago. They had been thick as magnifying glass, shrinking the eyes behind them into tiny pinched blurs. Without his glasses, his eyes were striking, making her think of the dazzlingly handsome actor Pierce Brosnan.

Suzannah watched Dugan, intrigued. At the moment, he looked distracted, nodding as his coterie of admirers vied for his attention but not really giving them his full concentration. Was it her imagination, or did he need rescuing? After all, she had met him several times, during the course of helping Lancaster implant the microchip. She considered it, feeling a scrape of nerve in her stomach. He probably wouldn't remember her. How could she just walk up and start talking to one of the premier painters of the twentieth century?

More people moved in on Dugan, and, feeling a little deflated, Suzannah was about to turn away when he looked at her. He straightened against the wall as if he were just waking up. He moved the man who had been talking to him aside and walked towards her as the surprised man stared after him.

'Dr Lord,' Dugan said, offering his hand.

It was huge and warm. She felt a small thrill. This was the hand that had created the glorious paintings that surrounded them now. She groped for something to say. 'I'm surprised you remember me.'

'Remember you? Yours was one of the first faces I saw after the surgery. It is a pleasure I will never forget.' His eyes, those remarkable eyes, bored into her. She realized he was looking at her, not talking, just looking at her in a strange, intense way. She felt an eerie tingle along her skin, knowing his eyes were still as impaired as ever. What had changed lay behind the eyes.

As he continued to gaze at her, she felt the silence stretch awkwardly. *Say something.* 'I think your paintings are wonderful.' I'm gushing, she thought with dismay. Surely I can come up with something better than that.

'Yes, thank you,' he said almost curtly, then seemed to catch himself. 'I'm delighted that you like them.'

'They're fantastic. The second one, there—'

'Ah, Andrew dear, there you are.' A short chunky woman of about sixty in a stunning red Oscar de la Renta gown swept up and slipped her hand into the crook of Andrew's arm. She gave Suzannah a warm smile, then gazed at her with frank curiosity. Her wrinkled, rosy-cheeked face was alive with mischief.

'Dr Lord,' Andrew said, 'may I introduce my agent, Grace Gorchakova.'

'Pleased to meet you,' Suzannah said.

'And I am pleased,' Grace said, 'to meet so beautiful a young woman. A doctor, eh? I'm impressed. It's a noble profession, not like ours, eh, Andrew?'

Suzannah smiled, not knowing quite how to answer. She found herself liking the woman at once and realized Grace reminded her of Miss Szabo, her old piano teacher. Miss Szabo used to march back and forth, tapping her young students on the backs of their heads with a pencil to help them keep time. If you hadn't practised she would bawl you out royally. But we all loved her, Suzannah thought.

Grace turned to Andrew. 'Listen, *chudozhnik* – forgive me, Dr Lord, but there are some filthy rich people from New York who, though they are trying to hide it, are desperate to buy one of Andrew's wonderful paintings. If he will just come over and meet them, they will break down completely and I will be able to go to Paris for a month and live like a czarina on my commission. Could you spare him a moment?'

'Of course,' Suzannah said.

'In a minute,' Andrew added.

'Aha!' Grace said eyeing Andrew. 'You are serious about this young woman. Good, good! But she will still be here in a minute, only sixty seconds older and just as beautiful. Come on.' She squeezed his arm and moved off a few steps.

Andrew bent closer to Suzannah. 'I can't talk now,' he said, 'but I need to see you.' He glanced around at the crowd, his expression wary, almost fearful. 'If you don't mind hanging around till the end of this, we could go for coffee.'

Suzannah hesitated, flattered and taken by surprise.

'Please,' he urged before she could answer. 'I know this must seem strange, but I really need to talk to you. I've tried

Lancaster and he won't help me – won't even listen any more.'

Suzannah's stomach tightened. 'Are you talking about the implant?' she asked.

'Yes,' he said, his expression almost fierce. 'The microchip. I want you to take the ghastly thing out of my brain.'

Suzannah stared at him, her mind reeling. 'Take it out? You can't be serious.'

'Oh, but I am.'

She felt a heaviness in her chest, compressing her lungs, making it hard to breathe. How could this be happening? Andrew Dugan was trying to drag her back in time, to a place she must never go again.

'You don't understand,' she said. 'I can't take the microchip out. I'm . . . not a neurosurgeon.'

# 3

After the glowing warmth of the gallery, the freezing night air hit Suzannah like a plunge into a frigid pool. An icy wind blew up P Street, driving needles of snow into her face. She pulled her collar up and leaned into the wind.

'The cafe's just in the next block,' Andrew said apologetically.

'No problem,' Suzannah mumbled through numbing lips.

'Must be an Arctic front.' Andrew seemed to relish the raw wind, pushing his face into it, striding along in his flaring greatcoat like a sea captain pacing his quarterdeck.

'Another day or two of this and people will be skating on the Potomac,' Suzannah said. A sense of unreality gripped her. I'm going out with my idol, she thought. I should be excited out of my mind. And all I can think about is the microchip. What could be so terrible that he would prefer near blindness?

'Here we are,' Andrew said.

The inside of the cafe door was damp with condensation. Suzannah pushed it shut, revelling in the warmth, savouring the rich smell of coffee. The place was cozy, dark oak floors, half a dozen check-cloth tables, all empty at that hour. Behind a rear counter, an old woman in a baggy cardigan sorted through order stubs. The only food in sight was a cheesecake under glass on the counter. Andrew led Suzannah to a corner table, settling across from her with his back to the wall. He said, 'Thanks for waiting out the showing.'

'I couldn't have refused if I'd wanted to. What you said about the microchip –'

Andrew held up a cautionary hand as the woman shuffled over, pen poised with wordless economy over her pad.

Suzannah said, 'Just coffee, please. Black.'

'For me as well,' Andrew said.

He waited until the woman was gone, then leaned forward, his expression intense, mystified. 'Not a neurosurgeon? How could that be?'

'It's a long story, Mr Dugan.'

'Please, call me Andrew.'

Suzannah felt a pleasurable lift in her stomach. He was so handsome, with those striking dark eyes, the thick hair. Even with the bombshell he'd dropped on her, she found herself imagining what it would be like to feel Andrew's arms around her, that wonderful masculine mouth on hers.

He gave her a slight smile. 'A long story, eh? Why do I get the feeling you are avoiding the question?'

'Andrew, the important thing is this. When the microchip is implanted, its electrodes intertwine with the nerves, in effect melding with them. When we tried removing the chip from our lab monkeys, it blinded most of them. Even if it did not blind you, you would return to having the severely impaired vision you suffered before the implant. Remember, the microchip does not just interpret signals from your eyes. Your own visual cortex was already doing that. The whole point of the microchip is that it takes very poor visual signals and enhances them by many orders of magnitude.'

'Is there any chance at all that the battery alone could be removed?'

'No. To make the microchip small enough, the battery had to be fully integrated.'

'Then I want you to take the whole thing out. I don't care about the risks.'

She shook her head, exasperated. 'Even if it were medically correct to remove the chip, I couldn't do it.'

'Come on. You were a neurosurgery resident for – what, two years? You helped put the microchip into my brain in the first place. And as a general surgeon you are licensed to operate.'

'Not on brains.'

Andrew sat back, gazing at her with a sad, baffled expression. 'What happened, Dr Lord?'

'Suzannah. I decided to switch to general surgery.'

He waited expectantly. When she stayed silent, he arched a black eyebrow. 'That's it? That's your long story?'

Suzannah heard the door to the cafe open behind her; a draft chilled her neck. Andrew immediately looked past her, his eyes tracking whoever had come in. His quick response, the sharp concentration in his eyes, made her wonder if he had taken this corner table so he could keep an eye on the room. Glancing over her shoulder, she saw a man in a blue woollen overcoat standing at the wall phone just visible in a narrow side hall to the toilets. He dropped change into the phone and began talking. His voice murmured indecipherably across the small cafe. He turned slowly as he talked, glancing at her, then turning away again. From the corner of her eye, Suzannah saw that Andrew was still watching the man.

'Someone you know?'

'No.' Andrew returned his attention to her. She felt his gaze like a touch, gently searching her face as though trying

29

to find a way into her mind. It was quite exciting to be the focus of his gaze.

'It was Lancaster, wasn't it?' Andrew said. 'He did something to discourage you.'

The words, so uncomfortably close to the truth, shocked her. She felt a few drops of hot coffee spill down her fingers. Blotting her hand with a napkin, she found her voice. 'We had a serious disagreement,' she said.

'What did he do, Suzannah?'

'Let's just leave it at that, shall we?'

'You're right. It's none of my business.' He looked down at his coffee, then peered over her shoulder again. His eyes tracked something, the man at the phone leaving, perhaps. Looking at her again, he said, 'It's just that you seemed so dedicated, so in love with your work. I find it incredible that anything could turn you away from it.'

Suzannah had a sinking feeling. She fought the memories with all her strength, but they forced their way in. Against her will, she remembered the night Lancaster had tried to force himself on her. For the first few days afterward, she had been terrified. And then the CM5 computer had deciphered the visual code.

Suddenly it was not so easy for Lancaster to do without her. It would take months to train another resident to her level of knowledge on the experiment. And he was a very impatient man. So days stretched into weeks and weeks into months, her fear receding, her hopes that all would be forgotten rising. Work on a vision implant accelerated to a frenzied pace. Lancaster drove himself, her, and his other assistant, Mike Fachet, mercilessly. He did not try to touch her again. He was cold and distant, except to give orders. She could live with that a lot better than his questing hands. He gave her permission to cut back hours at the three hospitals in the residency programme so that she could devote more time to the lab. He mumbled vague assurances that the time could be made up later; he would extend her residency another year, if necessary.

*I will extend your residency.* What a golden promise that was. I should have made him put it in writing. It was a bitter thought she had had so many times before.

Except that he wouldn't have.

Eight months after the CM5 had translated the visual code in Seymour's brain, she and Lancaster and Fachet had replicated the result with human subjects and had secured FDA approval for a pilot study. Andrew Dugan was among the first of the fifty volunteers who passed screening by the National Institutes of Health, the federal agency that supported all medical research. For the next three weeks, they performed two to three implants a day.

The day after the final one, Roland Lancaster dismissed her from her residency.

She would never forget his cold smile, his deadly words: 'You have neglected your hospital work, the most important part of a neurosurgery residency. I have determined that you have neither the stamina nor the proper mentality to become a neurosurgeon. I cannot, in good conscience, recommend you to any other neurosurgery programme.' He hesitated, watching her, and she knew he was drinking in her misery. 'Of course, general surgery is much less demanding,' he went on. 'I'm sure we can find you a suitable programme in that field.'

Though to the internship committee it would look like mercy, it was not meant that way. Lancaster was casting her adrift in a lifeboat without water. She was facing death by thirst and he was telling her to drink sea water. There was no appeal against his sentence: life outside neurosurgery.

Suzannah felt a pain in her fingers and realized she was gripping the coffee cup with murderous force. With an effort, she relaxed her hand. 'I am a general surgeon,' she said to Andrew Dugan, 'and a very good one. I am happy with that. The brain is only one organ, and the one we know the least about. Maybe I just didn't want to spend the rest of my life trying to see the dark side of the moon.'

'The dark side of the moon.' Andrew tilted his head back, as if savouring the words. 'Tell me, Suzannah, have you ever painted?'

She felt a jolt of surprise. How could he guess that? If she admitted it, would he want to see one of her paintings? She imagined being alone with him, showing the canvas she was working on now, feeling the touch of his hand as he took it from her. The thought both titillated and terrified her. Her painting was terrible. She must never let him see it.

And this was all fantasy, anyway.

'Andrew, why do you want the microchip out?'

He settled back, blowing out a breath. 'The microchip, yes. When I said that, I didn't realize you couldn't help. If I had, I never would have brought it up. Maybe that's the way we should leave it.'

Suzannah looked at him, incredulous. 'Why? You can't just let this drop. In my own small way, I helped Lancaster develop that chip. If it's giving you trouble, come out with it. The test period is almost over. A Food and Drug Administration ruling on the microchip is only weeks away. What the FDA says *goes*, in all things medical, and everyone expects approval. In a few months it won't be just you and the forty-nine other pilot subjects, it will be all the thousands of people who are lined up waiting to have their vision given back to them.'

'Don't you think I've considered that? There are things you don't understand.'

'So tell me.'

Andrew's expression turned grim. 'You liked my paintings tonight.'

'You know I did.'

'What if I told you the most recent work in that exhibition was finished over a year ago?'

She felt surprise and confusion. 'Why didn't you have the exhibition then?'

'I was working on a series. There were supposed to be two more, but I couldn't paint them. I . . . could not paint them.' His voice was suddenly harsh.

'Why?'

Andrew straightened. Suddenly he was looking not at her but through her. His eyes widened a fraction and she could see the pupils shrinking though there had been no change in the room's light. A chill went through her. What was it, a trance? A seizure coming on, perhaps? She reached across and jogged his shoulder. He blinked.

'Andrew, what's wrong?'

He stood. 'I'm sorry, but I've got to go.'

She looked up at him, startled. 'What? Why?'

'That man who came in to use the phone. He was at the showing tonight, watching me, but he didn't come up to speak to me. I thought I recognized him, but I couldn't place him. Now I remember him. He's . . . he's put on weight, and he's got a moustache now, but he's a . . . private detective. I think my ex-wife hired him before the divorce when she was trying to get some dirt on me.' Andrew looked pained. 'It's not a very attractive story. I'm sorry, but I've got to go after him, find out what he's up to.'

Suzannah got up too. 'Andrew, we need to finish this business about the microchip.'

'Later.' He did not look at her, staring instead out the window of the cafe. 'Look, I apologize, but I do have to go. I'll be in touch.'

Before she could say anything else, he dropped a ten-dollar bill on the table and hurried out. She stared after him, uneasy and not sure why. His excuse seemed weak. Why should he care if his ex-wife's private detective walked in to use the phone? And if he did care, why not just call him up later and ask him? Surely a private detective was in the phone book.

That was not a private detective, Suzannah thought. It was someone else, someone Andrew has reason to fear.

Was it connected with the microchip?

Puzzled and frustrated, she pulled on her coat and left the cafe alone.

# 4

Shivering in the midnight cold, Suzannah paid the cabby and hurried up the steps to her house. As she shut the door behind her and turned the dead bolt, a sense of security flooded her and she realized how on edge she'd been. She stood in the warm darkness, listening to the familiar hum of the refrigerator in the back of the house.

All right, she thought, if the man in the blue overcoat wasn't the former Mrs Dugan's private detective, who was he? And why was he watching Andrew?

The total darkness of the house registered; Suzannah realized with disappointment that her sister had gone to bed. She had been hoping to find Juli waiting up. Oh, well, Suzannah thought, I need to get to bed too. Bed and a nice dream: Andrew Dugan takes me to the Old Ebbitt Grill. We drink martinis and discuss art, tropical cruises – anything but Roland Lancaster and the microchip.

And then, she added, Jay comes home and I file my evening with Andrew Dugan under one-time thrills.

Shrugging from her coat, she tiptoed through the darkened living-room to the closet at the foot of the stairs. Through the open french doors, hot embers ticked in the den fireplace, making faint red mirages of the couch and chairs. She hung up her coat and was easing the closet door shut when her mind registered something amiss in the den. She whirled back, goose bumps skating along her arms.

'Juli!'

'WHA–?' Juli bolted upright on the couch, rubbing at her eyes.

Suzannah sagged in relief. 'You scared me!'

'*I* scared *you*? At least *you* were awake.'

Suzannah felt a surge of warmth for her older sister. She had waited up after all – or tried to. Suzannah reached for the light switch.

'No, wait,' Juli said. 'OK.' Keeping her eyes shut against the flood of light, she sat up on the couch and adjusted her bathrobe. Suzannah looked at her with a sense of wonder. It was past midnight, Juli had just been jarred awake, but already she had recovered her poise. She looked very sophisticated in the lavender Christian Dior silk. Even those silly bunny slippers looked good on her, though they'd probably not be the choice of most Commanders in the US Navy. Suzannah felt a sudden sadness. The chic dress she was wearing was Juli's, bought for a special occasion that never seemed to come. Instead, Juli spent long days at the Pentagon in her severe navy officer's uniform, and rarely went out at night, preferring to stay home with young J.D. It was almost as though Juli had forgotten how attractive she was. Replace her stodgy glasses with contact lenses, fluff out that blonde bob, dash a little make-up on that flawless skin, and she would be glamorous enough to anchor the evening TV news.

She put on her glasses and knelt by the fireplace. 'Let me turn this log, get the fire going again. Then I want to hear all about your evening.' She rolled the charred log with a poker and blew on the embers. When they flamed up, she turned out the light. The room flickered in a pine-scented glow. 'Ahhh, that's better.'

Suzannah sat beside her. Toeing her shoes off, she pointed her feet toward the fire, luxuriating in the warmth.

'So how did it go?' Juli asked.

'I had an interesting evening,' Suzannah said. 'The paintings were wonderful, glorious –'

'Forget the paintings. Did you get to see Andrew?'

'He took me out for coffee afterwards.'

'Get out of here!' Juli looked at her, wide-eyed, then held her palm out. Suzannah slapped it lightly.

'Where did you go?'

'A little cafe down the street from the gallery. I didn't notice its name.'

'I guess I wouldn't have either. I saw Dugan's picture in the *Post*. He's a real hunk.'

Suzannah groaned. 'How can you call the premier artist in America a hunk?'

'What would you call him?'

'Swoon city.'

Juli laughed, then sobered. 'Careful, Suzannah. Men that handsome can be trouble.' Her face clouded, and Suzannah knew she was thinking about Wesley. Three years since their divorce had become final, and she still wasn't over him. Wesley was a vain, disloyal rat, Suzannah thought, and you're better off without him. She touched her sister's hand.

Juli brightened again. 'So you walk up and say hi, and boom! he takes you out. He must think you're swoon city, too.'

'It wasn't like that.'

'Come on, Suze, what happened to that cast iron surgeon's confidence of yours?'

'He just wanted me for my scalpel. He asked me to remove the microchip.'

A look of disbelief crossed Juli's face. 'You're kidding. But that would be like . . .'

'Yes.'

'Why?'

'I have no idea. When I started pressing him, he left.' Suzannah told her about the man in the overcoat, Andrew's hurried exit.

'Weird.' Juli pushed her glasses up on her nose and stared reflectively into the fire. It was her professional face: Commander Lord of Naval Intelligence working on a problem. 'The fire's burning down,' Juli said. 'Let me get another log, and then we can take this again from the top.'

'Do those bunnies go outside?'

'Hey, they were born out there.'

Juli went through the kitchen out of the back door. A wave of fatigue swept Suzannah, and she leaned back into the soft cushions of the couch. Sheba, J.D.'s sleek tortoiseshell cat, walked in, stretched, then jumped up on the couch. Suzannah patted her absently. Andrew *was* attracted to me, she thought. I could see it in his eyes. She felt a little thrill at the thought. If she and Jay weren't . . .

But they were. Andrew might be handsome and famous and her idol since she was in high school, but he was also – even after tonight – a man of fantasy for her. Jay Mallernee was real, their relationship solid and exciting and aggravating in all the ways of real life.

As for handsome – her tall blond Texan wasn't exactly a dud himself.

The back door shut with an odd gentleness and Juli hurried in. Dropping a log on the hearth, she went over to the curtains of the bay window, opening them a crack.

Suzannah sat up. 'What's the matter?'

'There's a man in the Sydecki house. I saw a flashlight for just a second in an upstairs window. He was wearing dark clothes.'

Suzannah felt a pang of unease. 'Come on, Juli.'

'I am not joking.' Juli turned back to the window.

'Maybe it's Mr Sydecki.'

'He retired to Florida last month, remember? An estate agent comes around to show it, but not at one a.m. with no lights on. There, I saw him again.'

Sheba jumped down from the couch and stalked out with a nervous 'neeow-weep'. Feeling a shiver of apprehension, Suzannah walked to the window and held the curtains open a crack.

'You watch the windows,' Juli said. 'I'll call the police.'

While Juli went to use the phone in the kitchen, Suzannah peered out between the curtains. The Sydecki house loomed in the darkness about sixty feet away, a brick colonial separated from their house by the back yards. The rear of the place was dark, but Suzannah could make out the three upstairs windows. The drapes on two windows were open but she couldn't see anyone inside.

Juli came back into the den. 'The police say they have a stakeout in the Sydecki place to try and catch a burglar. Someone reported a car driving by Sydecki's a number of times and slowing down in front. There have been some break-ins of empty houses on the south side of Arlington Forest lately, so they put a man in there.'

'Then it was a cop you saw?'

'That's what they say.'

Suzannah let the blinds close again and looked at Juli. 'You sound sceptical.'

'Stakeouts are expensive. It doesn't seem reasonable that

the Arlington PD would run one just because someone reported a car slowing down in front of a house. At most, they'd just drive by every few hours.'

Suzannah perched on the edge of the couch then stood again, jittery with adrenaline. 'So what *is* going on?'

'They're after bigger game.'

'Here?'

Juli nodded. 'Much as we like the small-town feel of Arlington Forest, you've got to remember we're only six minutes from Fort Myer, eight from the Pentagon, and twelve from the White House. A lot of federal workers and military personnel live in our quiet little neighbourhood, and you can be sure I'm not the only one with a top-secret clearance.'

'What are you saying?'

'Maybe they're after a spy.'

'A spy? Come on, Juli, the cold war's over.'

'So? Listen, Suzannah. Keep this to yourself, but just last month the FBI quietly arrested a cipher clerk who worked in DIA signals, one corridor away from me. They got a tip on him and bugged his phone, followed him, staked out his house – the whole nine yards. They caught him passing codes. Fortunately, it was to the Mossad, the Israelis. But it could just as easily have been Syria or Iraq. The cold war may be over, but all that means is we have a harder time knowing what dangers we're facing.'

'Fine, but why would the police lie about being over there?'

'To cover for the FBI. When the FBI moves in, they usually alert the local police, who then run interference for them.'

'I thought it was the CIA who looked for spies.'

Juli gave her a patient smile. 'Only in foreign countries.

40

They're expressly forbidden from operating in the US. What's the matter?'

'Nothing.' Suzannah hesitated, remembering sudden what Sharon Harrad had told her about the strange man in Emergency who'd claimed to be CIA. The man had asked about her, then slipped out when he saw the police. 'It's just an odd coincidence.'

'Tell me,' Juli said.

Suzannah did. 'Sharon thought the guy might have been faking symptoms in order to get himself committed.'

'What I'd like to know,' Juli said, 'is why he was asking about you.'

'I have no idea. I don't know anyone from the CIA. I'm sure it's just a coincidence.'

'Maybe,' Juli said, 'but it's odd. Very odd. He could be on the run. If the FBI is after him and they know he's interested in you, he could be the reason they staked out Sydecki's place.'

'That seems pretty far-fetched.'

'I see things more far-fetched than that every day,' Juli said soberly. The worried note in her voice increased Suzannah's anxiety. She went to the window and peered out at the house again. The upstairs windows gave an excellent view across the adjoining yards. Anyone up there could zero right in on their bay window. There was no trace of the man, but he was there watching, she could feel it.

'Listen,' Juli said. 'I don't want to scare you. Even if it is FBI and they're keeping a lookout for this guy, it doesn't mean the guy wants to hurt you. He's probably some harmless loony, and if he shows up here they'll nail him.'

'Nail who?'

Suzannah turned to see J.D. standing between the french doors. His blond hair stuck up on one side in a cowlick. In the fading light from the fireplace, he seemed thin and vulnerable, the right height for thirteen but fragile-looking, his hands and feet too big for his bony limbs. Happy to see him, Suzannah went over and gave him a hug.

'Nail who?' J.D. repeated.

Suzannah glanced back at Juli.

'What are you doing up, guy?' Juli said, taking the offensive.

'I heard you talking.'

'Well, we're finished now, and it's after one. I don't want you dragging out of bed late and missing the bus.'

'After one?' J.D. held up a woman's watch and peered at it. 'This says it's only twelve sixty-five.'

Suzannah realized the watch was hers. 'You scamp! You took that right off my arm when I hugged you!'

J.D. grinned and handed her the watch.

'Where did you learn that?' Juli asked disapprovingly.

'It's for the class play,' J.D. said. 'I told you, I'm playing Fagin. He's a pickpocket and it has to look real. Aunt Suze has been helping me practice so I won't get my hand stuck in the guy's pocket in the play.'

Juli turned to Suzannah. 'And just where did you learn to pick pockets?'

'Nowhere,' Suzannah said, feeling sheepish. 'We've sort of been discovering it for ourselves.'

'I'm living with a pair of juvenile delinquents,' Juli said with mock exasperation. 'Now go on, J.D., up to bed with you.' Juli goaded J.D. back upstairs, pinching at his heels. His deepening voice broke into a squawk as he fended her off. Suzannah felt a wistful pang. He was growing up so fast. Another year and he'd sound more like a man than a child. She put her watch back on, marvelling. With those hands, he'd make a good surgeon. Better than she, maybe – after weeks of practice, he still caught her half the time when she picked his pocket.

Stooping before the fireplace, she broke up the remains of the log and scattered the pieces. In the darkness, she felt her way downstairs to her apartment on the lower level. In her bedroom, she trudged over and gazed at the print that hung beside her bed. Andrew Dugan, circa 1987 – a print of one of the last canvases he'd done before his vision became so bad he could no longer paint. The chaotic colours swirled before her eyes as though her own vision were fading.

Tired. Go to bed.

*Why does he want the microchip out?*

It seemed inconceivable. It would almost be like plucking out his own eyes.

The image made her shudder.

A man watching Andrew, Suzannah thought, and now – maybe – a man in Sydecki's house watching me. Why would someone from the CIA be asking about me?

Suzannah made herself relax. It was probably nothing. Let the man in Sydecki's house – cop, FBI, whatever he was – worry about it.

She undressed and got into bed, pausing with her hand on the lamp switch to take a last look at the painting.

In the morning, she thought. I'll figure all this out in the morning. She turned the light off.

Her dreams were of a tall, handsome man watching her with empty eye sockets from a distant window.

# 5

Suzannah silenced her bleating alarm clock. She made herself roll out of bed. Taking slow, deep breaths, she stared at the dial: 5 a.m. She was pleased with herself. Six mornings in a row. She turned the other two alarm clocks on her nightstand off. Finally, a year out of residency, she had weaned herself down to one clock. Amazing what four-plus hours of sleep a night could—

*Andrew, staring at her with no eyes.*

A chill ran up her spine as she remembered the macabre dream. She sat for a moment trying to decide whether to jog this morning. She'd missed several runs because of the cold weather. One more won't hurt, she decided. In the shower, she inched the hot tap around until steam swirled around her and thought about last night and Andrew's shocking request. There were only two possibilities. Something was wrong with the microchip. Or something was wrong with Andrew . . . with his mind.

He'd called the microchip 'ghastly'.

The smell of coffee lured her out of the shower. Wrapping herself in a towel, she tiptoed up into the dark kitchen, homing in on the faint light of the coffee-maker's program panel. She filled her mug to the brim and sipped off the top inch as she went back downstairs.

In her bedroom, she studied her prized Dugan print again.

His last work before the microchip. The original hung downtown in the Hirshhorn Gallery. People came from all over the country to see it. It had been hailed in the normally restrained *New Yorker* as 'a compelling work of great genius'. Yellow and magenta swirls dominated the painting's centre, showing a fierce, organized power. Over the years, she had seen many different things in it, but today it made her think of a mind laid bare – a neurochemical typhoon at the instant of inspiration. Maybe it was a self-portrait. Maybe Andrew Dugan, in a world melting away from him, had painted the self he could still see, the one behind his eyes.

He'd said he'd been unable to paint for a year. Frustrating, but surely he understood that without the microchip he would *never* paint again. Vincent Van Gogh had cut off an ear. How much deeper Andrew Dugan's pain if he longed to cut out his own eyes?

She threw the towel down, then retrieved it and hung it on its rack. I'm letting this get out of proportion, she decided.

Dressing, Suzannah thought about how unbearable it must be to be an artist unable to paint. Or, like Jay lately, a writer unable to write. Thank heavens surgery was not a creative art. The day never came when she could not operate.

Jay was coming back on Monday. Just three more days. His plane was due around four. She hoped he would come straight to the hospital. She'd be seeing patients but could keep an eye out her office window. She thought of the other times she'd watched him pull into the hospital lot, looking forward to seeing his Jeep zoom again into the first available space. Just as it seemed it must crash into the grille of the car parked nose-on, the Jeep would stop sharply. A cowboy-booted foot would pop out from the driver's side. Then the rest of him would emerge, tall and lean in jeans, his worn leather flight jacket and his prized Orioles baseball cap. He would stride across the lot . . .

Amazing, his energy, especially lately. He had to be depressed over the book, and depression usually showed in the way people carried themselves. But Jay never gave in to it. He would come back from Texas bubbling over with new jokes and tall tales. She loved his voice. It was warm and energetic, usually a bit loud because of his bad ear, but never shrill. She ought to talk to him again about a hearing aid. 'I'm only thirty-one,' he'd protest, as if that had anything to do with it. Suzannah shook her head, vexed. The hearing loss was either hereditary or he'd shot off too many guns when he was little. Either way, there was nothing she could do about it if Jay wouldn't let her; just like his Gulf War book. He could be stubborn. It was so frustrating, loving him, wanting to help him, and not being able.

Suzannah felt a sharp pang of loneliness. We'll go to Joe Theismann's restaurant, she thought. He likes their draft beer. We'll hold hands while we talk.

Who knows, maybe he'll come back ready to write.

Suzannah went back upstairs, moving quietly in the darkened kitchen, not wanting to wake Juli and J.D. She ate a yoghurt and a bran muffin, standing in the den with the lights off, gazing out the back bay window. The Sydecki upper window returned her stare with blank patience. She couldn't see anyone in the shadows beyond the glass, but the eerie feeling that someone was there remained. At least he could not see her either.

Unless he was using one of those night scopes.

Suzannah felt a chill as she realized she might be flooded in the cold, green light no normal eye could see. He could be watching her, smiling at her fruitless stare. She jerked the blinds shut. Time to stop spooking herself. In one hour, she would be starting a thyroidectomy on Mr Delancy, cutting into his throat, and she did not want even the slightest tremour in her hand.

Suzannah reached pre-op as they were rolling in her last scheduled patient. 'How are you, Mrs Cardenas?'

'I'm fine, doctor.' Mrs Cardenas looked relieved to find her surgeon ready and waiting for her.

Suzannah was glad too. Mr Delancy's thyroid tumour and Lacy Dubois's lump had both been benign. As a result, Mrs Cardenas wouldn't have to wait, growing more and more anxious. Things were on schedule and going smoothly. She gave Mrs Cardenas's hand a gentle squeeze. 'Just think – when you wake up, no more feeling sick to your stomach.'

Mrs Cardenas smiled. 'I can't wait.'

'Good. Your anaesthetist will give you a shot now, and you'll go to sleep and I'll take out those gallstones. I'll see you afterwards, when you wake up. You just relax and leave everything to us.'

'I will.'

By the time Suzannah had finished the long ritual of scrubbing, Mrs Cardenas was asleep in Operating Room number 4, her abdomen draped, the exposed area painted orange with Betadine. Suzannah greeted Earl, the assisting surgeon, and Mary Jo and Frieda, the scrub and circulating nurses, and took a quick look around. Everything looked right. Frieda had the TV monitor set up where she liked it, to her right towards the foot of the trolley. The cardiac monitor murmured to itself, a steady reassuring bleep. She held her hands up for Mary Jo to pull the rubber gloves on them, then turned while the nurse tied her mask and gown. 'How's Johnny?' Suzannah asked.

'Much better. The eardrum didn't break and he's back in school.'

'Good.' Suzannah waved at Jane Donelly, the anaesthetist, half hidden behind the raised surgical drape. 'Ready to go rock collecting?'

'Yup.'

Suzannah held out her hand and Mary Jo pressed a trocar against her palm. She pushed the razor-sharp point through the skin beside Mrs Cardenas's navel. Gauging the resistance of muscle and fascia, she kept up the pressure until she felt the point slip through the tough wall of the peritoneum into the abdominal cavity. A small bright circle of blood welled up like a drain backing up. She withdrew the trocar, leaving the plastic cylinder behind to keep open the portal into the patient. She nodded at Mary Jo, who blotted up the blood with a sponge.

'Fill her up with regular,' Suzannah said to Earl. She waited while he threaded a tube through the portal and inflated Mrs Cardenas's abdominal cavity with carbon dioxide gas. As he withdrew the tube, she pressed the stomach lightly, making sure the portal's valve was working, holding in the gas. Then she threaded the long tube of the laparoscope through the portal. Shifting her attention to the TV monitor, she saw Mrs Cardenas's stomach gleaming in the white light from the eye of the scope.

Suzannah felt the day's stresses dropping away. Eagerly, she steered the eye of the scope down and down past the pink coils of the small intestine, watching on the screen, feeling like a diver exploring a fascinating reef. There was the uterus, perched on the flat plane of the bladder like a plump pink fish on bottom sand. It looked fine. She nosed around it with the camera, checking the fallopian tubes and ovaries. They too appeared normal. The red appendix dangled from the cecum above like a stalactite of coral. It was normal size with no sign of inflammation. Continuing, she examined the colon, looking for any suspicious bulge that might indicate a tumour mass. Mrs Cardenas had no family history of bowel cancer, but you didn't go in without checking. Everything looked good.

Suzannah remembered what an inelegant operation this used to be. Six years ago, when she was a first-year resident rotating through general surgery, gall bladder operations were still done mostly by feel. She recalled the way Rick Thiel, her supervisor and chief resident on the rotation, would hack through the abdomen. The hole had to be large enough to admit his hand. Then he would grope blindly through the abdominal cavity. In the aftermath, the patient would require serious pain medication and a one- to two-week stay in the hospital. Now she could see each organ, the arteries and ducts, the tubes and sacs. The patient would go home tomorrow with BandAids over the small cuts. The laparoscope was truly a miracle of science.

*But not as miraculous as the microchip.*

Suzannah put the comparison from her mind, applying herself to searching the spleen. No nodules, good. She checked the wall of the stomach. Nothing out of order. Zeroing in on the liver, Suzannah found the gall bladder under the massive right lobe and worked the camera into a good viewing angle. In the light from the scope, it was a pretty blue, almost the colour of a robin's egg. She could see some scarring around it from the stones.

Suzannah felt pleased. Mrs Cardenas was, indeed, going to feel much better in the weeks and months ahead. No more pain, no more nausea.

'Hold it right here for me, will you, Earl?' she said, turning the scope over to the assisting surgeon. Mary Jo was ready with three more trocars. Quickly, Suzannah pushed them through above and to the right of the navel. Mary Jo handed her the needle-nosed forceps. Suzannah slipped it through and, watching on the monitor, clamped the tip of the gall bladder. Next, she entered the other two portals with the scissors and cauterizing wire. She separated the gall bladder from the fold of peritoneum that held it under the liver, following up with the cauterizer to seal off bleeders. Switching back to the forceps, she pulled the gall bladder away from the liver. Now only its artery and duct stood in her way. She withdrew the cauterizer and re-entered the portal with a thin catheter, draining the gall bladder into a jar that Mary Jo held for her. Once it was collapsed, she clamped the artery, stapled and cut it, then did the same to the duct. Taking the forceps in hand again, she pulled the severed and deflated gall bladder out through the portal. She prodded the limp sack, feeling several large stones. 'Earl, how's the gravel holding up on your driveway?'

'That's all right,' he said, 'you can have 'em.'

Frieda held out a stainless steel tray, and Suzannah dropped the bladder into it.

She debated briefly whether to check for stones in the duct between the liver and intestines. It would mean a delay of twenty to thirty minutes while she pumped some dye into the duct and waited for the portable X-ray machine to get her some pictures. The pre-op lab reports had showed normal alkaline phosphatase, and the duct from the gall bladder had looked too small to pass any stones that wouldn't easily pass on through the larger duct. Delay for a cholangiogram meant a longer time under anaesthesia. Anaesthesia was the largest risk factor in gall bladder surgery, especially since Mrs Cardenas was forty-nine and overweight.

No cholangiogram, Suzannah decided.

And if I'm wrong, she gets jaundice.

I'm not wrong.

Suzannah opened the laparoscope and vented the gas from the abdominal cavity. 'That's it,' she said. 'Want to close?'

Earl nodded. 'Might as well earn my twenty per cent.'

Suzannah found Mr Cardenas in the waiting-room and assured him his wife would be fine. Back in the surgeon's lounge, she dropped into a chair. Her scrubs were soaked, her hair, where it had been bound up under her cap, plastered to her head. She should get in the shower, enjoy the afterglow. A good day's work – five operations.

And all of them routine.

The thyroidectomy on Mr Delancy, two benign breast tumours, a diverticulectomy, and the lap GB she'd just performed. She could do them in her sleep.

She was working the visible side of the moon.

Come on, she thought. It isn't always routine. Sometimes the lumps are not benign and you have to fight to save the woman. Or you get a call to Emergency and sew arms back on or put someone's insides back inside. That's not routine. One tiny slip close to the recurrent laryngeal nerve this morning, and Mr Delancy could have lost his voice permanently. People die. You can never take what you do for granted. A lot of people live, and live better, because of you. That should be enough for anyone.

Suzannah wondered why she was even having these thoughts. It *was* enough. She had not questioned herself in years. Granted, those first months after Lancaster forced her out had been hellish. A lot of second-guessing about whether general surgery would be enough for her. But she'd dug in and worked hard and found the fascination in it. She was not going to let that slip away now just because Andrew Dugan had summoned up her past last night. She was going to put the microchip – and Andrew – out of her mind.

*And if something really is wrong with the microchip?*

Suzannah realized she was rubbing her fingertips with her thumb. She could feel a thin sweat building up. The gesture took her back five years, to those intense moments when she would stand over an opened skull, poised to put her fingers into a living human mind.

She pushed up angrily from her chair and stalked into the showers. Damn the microchip! It and the man who had made it were not her problem any more.

At five o'clock, Suzannah ushered Mr Clift, the last patient of the day, out of her office and told Marjory, her receptionist, to go home. She was about to do the same when she noticed the haughty face of Roland Lancaster staring up at her from the stack of magazines on the waiting-room table. Her stomach clenched. What was this? The new issue of *Newsweek*. She swept up the magazine and threw it in the waste basket.

No, she couldn't leave it there. Marjory would just retrieve it.

Suzannah picked it out of the basket, trying to avoid the caption, feeling her gaze drawn to it anyway.

'DR ROLAND LANCASTER, HEALING THE BLIND'

Suzannah groaned. She took the magazine back into her office. It was almost dark outside. She closed the vertical blinds.

She ran a feather duster over her corn plant.

She opened the blinds again and gazed down at the parking lot.

All right, Roland Lancaster *was* brilliant.

He was also, behind the noble patrician face, a vile human being.

Oh, God, I still hate him so much, she thought.

I don't want to hate him. I don't want to feel anything about him. I don't even want to think about him. But suddenly, everywhere I turn, I'm reminded of him.

Unable to resist, she sat down at her desk and started the *Newsweek* article. 'Since the late 1980s,' it began, 'implants at the margins of the brain have restored hearing to the near deaf. And now, taking that same principle a quantum jump further, Dr Roland Lancaster is entering the brain itself on behalf of the blind. His implant, actually a tiny self-contained computer referred to as "the microchip", has already restored vision to fifty people who were nearly blind. These people constitute a four-year pilot study on the microchip that is now drawing to a close. For the past eight months, the FDA has been conducting an exhaustive review of the medical data on these fifty people.'

Suzannah remembered Jacob Fiore, the first human subject. His daughter, Tricia, was nearly blind from macular degeneration, a disease of the retina that severely degrades the signal the eye passes along to the brain. Jacob had bravely volunteered to have his skull opened, to have a transducer placed inside, to sit for hours in front of the tiny twin TVs while the CM5 'Connection Machine' watched the same scenes and read his microvoltages. The massively parallel computer, already 'educated' by its experience with the monkey, took relatively few sessions to sort out microvoltage patterns and link them to what Jacob was seeing. Everyone in the lab had celebrated. It was a fantastic accomplishment. But they had not yet reached their final goal. Next they must try reversing the flow, to see if feeding Jacob's microvoltage patterns back into the brain of his daughter would cause her to see.

What an incredible moment that had been, that first test.

'Oh!' Tricia had exclaimed, bringing her hands up to her eyes as if to shield them. 'Fireworks!'

Suzannah remembered how her heart had sunk. All of them knew what the computer was feeding Tricia, and it was not fireworks.

But as Lancaster was about to switch off the feed, Tricia's mouth had dropped open. 'The seashore!' she exclaimed. 'I can see the gulls!'

Bedlam broke out in the lab.

Suzannah realized she was smiling. Blocking Lancaster from her mind had cost her some very good memories as well. How hard they'd worked to get to that point. But there had still been one critical step left: the computer must now be taught to read the partial signals from Tricia's own impaired eyes, compare them to the patterns it had stored, and use that information to enhance the impaired signals from her eyes.

At first, Suzannah remembered, Tricia could see no better with the computer hooked up than without. After a few weeks, everyone became quite tense. Then, all at once, the computer cleared that final hurdle. Suzannah remembered it as though it were yesterday: Tricia staring around the lab with a dejected look. Suddenly, her expression cleared. She looked at her father, standing beside her. She cradled his face in her hands. 'You cut yourself shaving,' she said. Her smile was the most beautiful thing Suzannah had ever seen.

I was there, she thought. Lancaster can never take that away from me.

She picked up the magazine again, flipping through, skimming for substance. A passage near the end caught her eye: 'Ironically,' the reporter wrote, 'for all his brilliance, Roland Lancaster has not actually learned the visual code. A computer has. Indeed, the code consists of billions of bits of information – too much for any human to grasp fully. But in a way this only makes Dr Lancaster's feat the more remarkable. Bypassing understanding, he has cut straight to the results. Long before the modern age of medical science, physicians found that chewing the bark of the willow tree could relieve pain. Even now, many years later, the workings of aspirin are not fully understood medically. Perhaps, in time, scientists will come to understand exactly how the tiny self-contained computers interact with the human brain. But fortunately for the fifty people already able to see and the thousands of others who will soon emerge from their blurred worlds, mankind need not wait for understanding. FDA officials, following their usual policy, will make no comment on their pending decision. But according to Dr Lancaster, during frequent follow-up testing and interviews not one of the fifty pilot subjects has reported any problems, so it seems almost certain the microchip will soon be approved for general use.'

Not one of the fifty? Suzannah thought.

Hadn't Andrew told her he'd gone to Lancaster and that Lancaster had refused to help him?

She put the article down, disturbed. If Andrew had, in fact, complained about the chip to Lancaster, then Lancaster had lied to the interviewer.

There was one way to find out. Ask Lancaster.

Suzannah's stomach felt suddenly hollow. To stand in the same room with Roland Lancaster again, to look at that smug face and try to talk to him as if he had not tried to ruin her life?

She threw the *Newsweek* against the wall and stood, gripping the back of her chair. No, she thought. I can't.

But I have to do something. Either Andrew Dugan or Roland Lancaster is lying.

55

So talk to Andrew.

At once Suzannah felt better. Yes, she would call Andrew and arrange, if possible, to meet him tonight or tomorrow.

Before Jay returns.

And then that had to be the end of it.

# 6

John Stockwell worked on the lock with growing frustration. His ID card was thin enough to slip easily between the jamb and the bolt, but when he tried to slide it up and out, the bolt resisted. It didn't help that his fingers were numb from the cold.

Hold on, starting to get it—

The badge slipped out of his hand, falling into the crust of snow at his feet. He cursed and bent to pick it up, feeling a sharp twinge in his arthritic shoulder. Too old for this. And he'd never been on the operations side anyway. He was probably doing it all wrong. No doubt there was some hidden trick to picking locks with bits of plastic.

Stockwell heard a sound around the corner of the building, the crunch of broken glass – someone coming up the alley from the street. He went rigid with fear. Had Grayburn found him?

The glass crunched again and Stockwell remembered the line from the old John Wayne movie: 'If you saw them, they weren't Apaches.' A laugh caught high in his throat. No, that wasn't Grayburn's men out there. He picked up his ID card and stood, forcing it with furious strength into the slit between door and jamb, prying again at the bolt. The rumbling roar of an accelerating Metrobus pounded down the alley, drowning out lesser sounds. Noxious diesel exhaust invaded his throat and lungs. *Someone* had stepped on the glass out there. It was a rough neighborhood. He had to get inside out of sight.

There!

The bolt slid back and he yanked the door open, slipped inside, eased it shut again, and threw the bolt. A second later, the door pulled against the bolt as someone tried the handle from outside. Stockwell heard a muffled curse and relaxed. Definitely not one of Grayburn's men.

He heard footsteps shuffling away in the snow outside. Relieved, he turned to find himself in a short hall. The floor was bare cement, cracked in places. A faint mélange of urine and mediciny sweetness reminded him of a hospital ward. Bare light bulbs shed a yellow anti-bug glow on the empty hall. Not much in the way of decor, but at least it was dry and warm. A hell of a way to spend Saturday night.

Stockwell put his back against the cinder-block wall and slid down to his haunches, then eased his legs out straight. God, what a day – and he was still no closer to Dr Lord. Every move he made, they seemed able to block him. How did they know?

Archer Montross, that's how. He knows every move I'm going to make, Stockwell thought bitterly. The man's not human. Archer is living proof I made the right decision. What would I be like now, if I'd let them put the microchip in my brain?

Stockwell felt a clammy sweat breaking out on his forehead. He'd rather be running for his life than be like Archer. But he should have played along, planned better. He should have known that, once they approached him, they wouldn't just let him refuse and walk away. He should have stalled them.

Except Archer Montross would have known.

Stockwell felt his teeth clenching as he remembered how close he'd come to death the first night after he'd refused them. If he hadn't taken the precaution of staking out his own house, they'd have nailed him for sure. He would never forget the ugly fear that had gripped him as he'd watched Grayburn's men going in.

Up until then, he'd had his doubts. The pitch from the Adept leadership had seemed too incredible to be true.

Never mind, he thought. Just keep trying to get to Dr Lord. Her name was on the National Institutes of Health grant paper to Lancaster. She was in on the development of the microchip. She'll know enough of what I'm talking about to believe me. And she's not on their side . . . I hope.

Stockwell went over his options. Try again to get to Dr Lord through her psychiatrist friend at the Emergency Room? No. The police had got there minutes after him. They could have been there for some other reason, but he couldn't afford to assume that.

He must also assume they'd have Suzannah Lord's phones tapped. If he tried calling her, they would cut him off at once – and they would know exactly where he was.

And they were no doubt watching her house as well. A younger man, spryer, cleverer, might have a chance at night, but only a slim one.

Stockwell felt a burning frustration.

Maybe he should try contacting her through her boy-friend, Jay Mallernee. The trouble with that was, Mallernee was also a top reporter for the *Washington Post*. Such people were more than curious, they were relentless once they smelled a story. And this would be the story to end them all.

Perhaps literally.

Stockwell closed his eyes and thought: could he pass a

message to Dr Lord through her boyfriend that she would understand and he would not? *The Lancaster process is* – No, he mustn't mention Lancaster. That alone would get Mallernee sniffing. *Your work is being misused* – No, not much better.

Stockwell clenched his hands, feeling the press of time. Whatever he did, he must hurry. The very fact that he was trying to reach Dr Lord put her in danger, too.

Should he try the Pentagon again?

No, he'd never make it.

The door rang under a hammer blow. Stockwell scrambled to his feet, his heart pounding. The blow came again, and then a volley of them, someone knocking in a fury on the steel door.

'C'mon, Tatum, open up. I lost my damn key.'

Stockwell held still, pressing himself against the wall. Go away, he prayed fervently.

'Well, why don't you let him in?'

Stockwell looked up the short hallway. A huge black man dressed in jeans and a leather jacket was studying him with apparent composure.

'I didn't think it was my place,' Stockwell said, amazed at how cool he sounded.

The big man smiled. 'No, this isn't your place, all right.'

'C'mon, Tatum. You don't let me in, I'll jus' take my business over to Jamal's,' yelled the voice outside the door.

Stockwell stared at Tatum, who raised a finger to his lips.

'All right, then!' The door rang with a final blow. Silence. Stockwell stood still, waiting for Tatum to do something.

'So, you the heat or what?' Tatum said at last, his voice mellow.

'Or what.'

Tatum smiled again and ambled towards him. 'I think I'd

like you to be a little more specific.'

Behind Tatum, a head poked around the corner, so low that Stockwell thought it must be a midget. Then he realized the man was sitting and had leaned just his head around.

'Wha's happenin'?' The voice was slurred, dreamy.

'Nothing,' Tatum said. 'Everything's cool.'

Drugs, Stockwell thought. I've walked in on a shooting gallery. 'What's the going rate?' he asked Tatum.

'For what?'

'You know.'

'I know I'd like to see your ID, little old pasty-faced white man.'

Stockwell suppressed a groan. 'I'm not from the police.'

'Then what *are* you from?'

'I'm in intelligence.'

Tatum laughed. 'I'm starting to like you. You've got a sense of humour, and you're not scared of me.'

Oh, yes, I am, Stockwell thought, but he didn't say it. He handed his ID to Tatum. Tatum looked at it, turned it over, sobering. 'This is real,' he said thoughtfully.

'Yes.'

'So what are you doing, Stockwell? Drugs in-country aren't your territory.'

'You're very well informed.'

'You mean educated?' Tatum gazed at him. 'Some of us do get educated, you know. I, for example, have a master's degree in history from Howard University. Unfortunately, I do not have a job.'

'So you run a shooting gallery. You're the friendly community pusher.' Stockwell was amazed at himself. He should not be standing here, having this conversation. He should be back in his house, drinking a glass of wine, watching *Mystery* on public television.

Tatum looked pained. 'Yes, I run a shooting gallery. No, I'm not a pusher. I just see that the brothers and sisters are safe, that no one rolls them, and that they get to the hospital if someone forgot to step on their blow enough times.'

Stockwell gazed at the big man, wondering whether to believe him. He sounded very sincere. 'So you're a Samaritan?'

'They pay me. Twenty dollars a head for my services.'

'I'll pay you.' Stockwell reached into his coat and pulled out his wallet, sorting through the twenties, pulling one free. When he looked at Tatum, he saw a new hardness in his face.

'And what, little elderly white man, is to stop me from taking the rest of it?'

Stockwell reached back into his coat and pulled out the pistol. 'Would this be satisfactory?'

Tatum groaned and rolled his eyes at the ceiling. 'Oh, man. A twenty-two? That thing wouldn't even go through my jacket.'

'Don't count on it.'

Tatum reached into his jacket and froze as Stockwell pointed the twenty-two at his forehead. 'You forgot to put a jacket on your head. Take out whatever you have in there with your left hand and put it on the floor.'

Tatum sighed and, moving slowly, pulled a compact automatic weapon from his coat and deposited it gently on the floor. Straightening, he said, 'You aren't going to harass my customers, are you?'

'No. I just need a place to sit and think for a few hours. I'd give you all the money, but I'm going to need it.' Keeping an eye on Tatum, he stooped, pulled the gun to him and ejected the clip. Putting it in his pocket, he motioned with the twenty-two.

Tatum sat down, put his back against the wall and rested

his forearms on his knees. He looked amused. 'You've got some nerve.'

'I'm learning,' Stockwell agreed.

'So what is a vanilla like you doing on Fourteenth Street, home of the pimps and whores and pushers, just a few lovely blocks from the White House?'

Stockwell could think of no way to answer him.

'You spying on your own kind? I believe that's allowed.'

'No.'

'Wild horses couldn't pull it from you, right?'

'There's no way to explain.'

Tatum shook his head. 'I knew I should have gone on for my doctorate.'

Stockwell tried to smile; couldn't. 'It's too dangerous to explain.'

Tatum eyed him, more seriously. 'Pardon me for saying this, but you don't look like a man used to dealing with danger. I mean, you're doing pretty well on the spur of the moment, but –'

'So now you're patronizing me.'

Tatum shrugged. 'Sorry.' He shook his head. 'Let me ask you something.'

'Go ahead.'

'Does your outfit ever hire guys with master's degrees in history from Howard University?'

'Yes, they do.'

'I don't suppose you'd consider recommending me, inasmuch as I didn't shoot you.'

'What do you mean? I have the gun.'

'Safety's on. You never would have made it.'

Stockwell looked at the safety catch and was mortified to realize that Tatum was right. He stuck the gun in his pocket. Tatum made no move to get up and retrieve his own gun. He shook his head, a sad expression stealing over his face. 'They say the races should talk more,' he said. 'Is this what they had in mind?'

Stockwell smiled. It felt strange on his face. 'Maybe it is,' he said. 'If I can, I'll recommend you for a job.'

Tatum cocked his head. 'If you can?'

'I'm in a spot of trouble right now.'

'No kidding.'

And then they shot the lock off and came in, two of Grayburn's men, and John Stockwell felt the first bullet plough into his leg as he reached for his twenty-two and remembered to flip the safety.

# 7

Suzannah felt a little rush of pleasure as the *maitre d'* seated her across from Andrew at an intimate corner table. The cozy parlour-like room seemed to glow with promise. Candlelight shimmered in the wine glasses. Behind Andrew's shoulder, a bay window with ornate wood mouldings framed the brownstones across Q Street. I'm having dinner with Andrew Dugan! she thought, enthralled.

Fine. Just remember why you're here.

She wondered if she'd been wise to let Andrew turn their meeting into a Saturday-night dinner engagement. Exciting, yes; flattering, surely, but all the harder now to press him about the microchip.

'What do you think?' Andrew asked.

'I like it. Very much. But you didn't need to.'

'I wanted to. Very much.' He looked mildly startled, as if the last two words had slipped out. Glancing away, he surveyed the other diners. She watched him, her heart thumping inside her. Her breath seemed caught in her chest. *Very much.* He really likes me, too.

Suzannah eased her breath out, taking a sip of water as she studied Andrew over the rim of her glass. He was so gorgeous it was hard to take her eyes off him. He had settled sideways in the big chair, elbows on the armrests. His hands, laced together, seemed to float against the soft blackness of his turtleneck and Armani jacket. The wind outside had tousled his thick black hair, and he hadn't thought to comb it. His lack of vanity impressed her. Gradually she became aware that he wasn't just glancing around the room, he was making a study of it, his alert eyes drinking in every detail. He was not a man who missed much – an asset for an artist.

'I've always liked this place,' Andrew mused. 'You can tell it was a private home. In fact, the same architect designed my townhouse over on Thirty-fourth Street. These old buildings fascinate me. All their curlicues and flourishes, the elaborate stonework . . . You look surprised.'

'I guess I shouldn't be. Baroque touches sometimes show up in your paintings – even the abstract expressionist ones.'

He tilted his head back, studying her. 'Really?'

'The brushstrokes in the darker parts of *Hyperion*. The elaborations around the edges in *Engine Joe*.'

A finger untwined, pointing at her in acknowledgment. 'You never read that in any review.'

*I've impressed him,* she realized, and felt absurdly pleased.

'I was very rude,' he said, 'after the showing. I hope you've forgiven me.'

'You were upset, I could see that. Did you catch up with the . . . detective?'

'Alas, no.' He sat forward, studying the coat of arms sewn to the pocket of her blazer. 'I like your jacket. So many reds in the world, but this one is pure, no taint of yellow or blue. Very beautiful.'

'Thank you.' *Drop it,* she thought. *The man he went after is none of my business. What matters is the microchip.*

The waiter came. At Andrew's urging, she ordered the

Chassagne-Montrachet, pleased to find it available by the glass. Andrew asked for a Jim Beam bourbon, neat.

As the waiter left, she felt her shoulder muscles tightening. Sitting together, as if they hadn't a care in the world, was very nice and she did not want to spoil it, but she had to get this over with. 'Andrew, I asked to meet you because I wanted to talk about the microchip.'

'Of course.'

'We did leave things up in the air on Thursday night.'

'Yes.'

'Even though I'm not willing to remove the microchip, I can't just let this drop. Obviously, you can see all right. Is there something else wrong with the chip? Something that might endanger the health of people waiting and hoping to get the implant?'

'Suzannah, I should never have brought it up.'

'Were you serious about wanting me to take it out?'

He hesitated. 'I was . . . in a black mood that night. As I mentioned, I've been unable to paint for a while. It's all in my head, of course.'

The waiter brought their drinks. Suzannah sipped the chilled wine, savouring its dryness, the hint of pear. 'Roland Lancaster told a *Newsweek* reporter that not one of the fifty pilot subjects has had any complaint. And yet, you told me he had refused to help you.'

'You don't miss much, do you?'

'Did Lancaster lie to the *Newsweek* reporter?'

'I'm sure he felt he was telling the truth. It's a matter of interpretation.'

'I don't see how. Either there's something wrong with the microchip, or . . .'

'Or there's something wrong with me, yes. Lancaster is sure something's wrong with me.'

'So Thursday night was just a bad mood?'

Andrew raised an eyebrow. 'Yes – like quicksand is just wet dirt. Thursday night I was in up to my chin, grabbing for branches.'

She tried to read his face.

'You're still sceptical,' he said.

'You don't miss much yourself.'

He seemed about to say something. Instead, he picked up his bourbon and downed it. His eyes watered briefly. Before she could pursue it, the waiter reappeared. She realized she had not even glanced at the menu. She scanned it, ordering gingered grapefruit, fillet of sole with grapes, and a ratatouille. After some consideration, Andrew ordered an avocado pear with vinaigrette dressing, a potato omelette, and carrots Vichy. He declined the waiter's offer of another bourbon.

'You're a vegetarian?' Suzannah asked.

'Only when I eat.'

She laughed, feeling relaxed for the first time that evening. A huge weight was inching off her shoulders. Andrew had just said there was nothing wrong with the microchip. And why shouldn't she believe him; just enjoy the rest of the dinner? It would be something to tell Juli about.

'Suzannah, are you married?'

She felt startled, as if he'd just tuned in to her thoughts. 'No.'

'Boyfriends?'

'Singular,' she said. 'He's a reporter for the *Post* – Jay Mallernee. You may have seen him on TV during the Gulf War. He was interviewed by CNN a couple of times.'

'Mallernee.' Andrew nodded. 'The handsome fellow in the

Orioles baseball cap who kept talking as if nothing were happening while the scuds flew in and the camera jiggled like crazy.'

'That's him. The cameraman really yelled at him after that one. Evidently the guy was desperate to run but he couldn't, not with Jay standing there so coolly.'

'A brave man,' Andrew said approvingly.

'That – and a little hard of hearing.'

Andrew laughed. 'How about you? Why did you decide to become a physician? Are either of your parents doctors?'

'No. Mom and Dad were both from poor families and didn't get to college. But they both had this tremendous, almost overblown respect for it. The other thing they believed in was that you should serve your country – humankind. They were always preaching that. So my sister is a naval officer and I'm a doctor.'

Andrew looked interested. 'Is she a daredevil, too?'

'What do you mean, too?'

'Come on, Suzannah. You're a surgeon. You cut into people. Sometimes those people are dying and you have only seconds to save them. One wrong move and you could kill them instead. Don't you think that's pretty daring?'

Suzannah considered it. 'I don't think of it that way. It's . . . it's what I do, that's all.'

Andrew smiled. 'When you were little, you liked to go to summer camp.'

'Sure. Doesn't everybody?'

'Actually, no. But you'd have gone all summer if they'd let you.'

'It was fun.'

'You were the first one into the water, even when it was cold.'

Suzannah smiled. 'Usually, yes.'

'And at the amusement park, you liked to sit in the front of the first car of the roller coaster.'

'Of course. Where do you sit?'

'You were begging your dad to let you drive when you were twelve.'

'Oh, before that.'

'And when the family went to the Grand Canyon, you stood close to the edge.'

Suzannah laughed. 'All right, all right.'

'Hey, I don't mean to give you a hard time. I think it's wonderful. You mentioned a sister. Any brothers?'

'No. Mom and Dad, Juli and me. Dad's grandmother also lived with us for a little while when I was a girl. Great-grandma Thompson was Cherokee from down south, where Dad grew up. I remember her well. She was very brown. She had a sweet smile and a cute button nose. She wore four or five full skirts at once and snorted snuff and told tall tales. Her maiden name was Mary Kansas. She saw her people walk the trail of tears, and yet she harboured no hatred for whites – or I wouldn't be sitting here tonight.'

Andrew gazed at her with fascination. For a second, his eyes grew distant, and she could tell her story had triggered something in his mind. Excitement played across his face and was gone. 'No,' he murmured.

'Andrew?'

His eyes focused on her again. 'Your mentioning your great-grandma gave me an idea for a painting. But it won't work.'

She sensed a sudden darkness in him, anger or sadness, maybe both. She had the urge to reach across and touch his hand, but both hands were still locked lightly together. 'How do you know until you try?'

He started to say something and stopped, looking uncomfortable.

'Listen to me,' Suzannah said, embarrassed. 'What do I know about painting?'

Andrew smiled. 'Quite a bit, I have a feeling.'

The waiter appeared with their appetizers. Suzannah spooned up the juicy sections of grapefruit, enjoying the mix of tart and spice. Andrew poked his avocado around the plate.

Suzannah said, 'How did you decide to become an artist?'

'I didn't decide. I began drawing as soon as I could hold a pencil. Painting when I was nine or ten. My paintings were terrible at first. I just couldn't seem to do what I wanted to do. The colours would smear together; everything would be too dark. It was damn frustrating.' He did not look frustrated. He looked happy at the memory. Then his face clouded.

I should stay off the subject of painting, Suzannah realized. She tried to think of another topic.

'Let's talk about *your* painting,' Andrew said.

Startled, Suzannah returned the last spoonful of grapefruit to her plate. 'What makes you think I paint?'

'Just guessing. Your remark about the brushstrokes in *Hyperion* was quite astute.'

'You guess well. But I'm not sure you could call what I do painting.'

He leaned forward. 'Why?'

'It's terrible. I have no talent.'

'What has that got to do with it?'

The question took her aback. She groped for an answer.

'Why are your paintings terrible?' Andrew asked.

'I can't get what I want. I can *feel* the right colour, the right brushstroke, but then it comes out all wrong. Somewhere inside I think I might have the instincts of a painter. Unfortunately, I don't have the skills. Actually, I don't know why I keep at it. It aggravates the hell out of me.'

Andrew gave her a strangely tender smile. 'Maybe that's why you keep at it.'

The waiter reappeared with their main courses. The sole was wonderful, garnished with paprika pepper and dressed in a light sauce. The ratatouille was perfectly cooked, the eggplant and zucchini soft but not mushy.

As Andrew dug into his omelette, he told her about how, early in his career, a *New York Times* critic had called his paintings 'a disastrous mishmash of styles devoid of any serious content'. At first he had been furious. But then he'd realized the man had a point. He'd written to the critic to say so. After his letter appeared, curious collectors had swamped the gallery and someone bought the painting for a large sum. It was the critic's turn to be incensed, thinking Andrew had slyly and deliberately shown him up. Now they were such good friends the critic had to excuse himself from reviewing Andrew's work.

Suzannah was glad to see Andrew relaxing moment by moment, starting to really enjoy himself. They shared a lemon souffle for dessert. Over snifters of Hennessey, he said, 'I'd like to see you again.'

She felt her heartbeat surge. 'I'm flattered. But I'm not sure it's a good idea.'

'Mr Mallernee?'

'We're serious about each other.'

'He's a lucky man. You're a beautiful and fascinating woman. What if we keep it to business, after a fashion.'

'Business?'

'We're both painters. I know a good art supply store on Sixteenth Street. They have some excellent books on fundamentals. Perhaps I could take you there, introduce you to the owner.'

'I'd like that,' Suzannah said.

'Good.' He reached across and touched her hand. At that precise instant, her beeper sounded.

They both burst out laughing. 'Excuse me,' she said. Taking the beeper from her bag, she recognized the number – the Emergency Room at the George Washington University medical centre. Andrew pointed her towards the phone at the back of the dining-room. She punched in the number and waited patiently through ten rings.

'ER, Roberta speaking.' Something crashed in the background.

'This is Dr Lord.'

'Oh, yes. We've got a multiple gunshot coming in, including a heart and a head wound. Dr Simon's here, but he's in the middle of a bad aneurysm. Can you make it?'

'I'm in Georgetown. I can come, but if anyone's closer –'

'Nope. And the paramedic says the victim asked for you before he lost consciousness.'

'What? Who is it?'

'Male, around fifty, that's all I know. Sorry.'

'I'll be there as soon as I can.'

Suzannah said a hurried goodbye to Andrew and ran to her car. The engine turned over sluggishly in the cold and then caught. She felt a mixture of excitement and anxiety. A head wound – she'd be working inside the brain.

But it might be a friend. She went through the list of fiftyish men she knew. Most of them were colleagues.

She pulled into the emergency bay behind an ambulance. The back door was open, the engine idling. A trail of blood led through the sliding glass doors. Suzannah leapt out and ran in. Roberta met her. Suzannah pulled off her coat and blazer, tossing them on the counter of the nurses station, holding up her hands for the gloves. Roberta tugged them on and tied a mask on her. 'We've got two lines in. He's had an amp of bicarb.'

Suzannah nodded and followed her at a run to the surgery booth. A small crowd ringed the trolley – several nurses and two residents, one of whom she recognized: Rudy Stratton, a junior resident. She called his name. He stepped back with a grateful expression and she plunged into the gap. The man was naked from the waist up, his shirt and coat cut away and hanging in tatters. Blood dripped on the floor on both sides of the trolley. Suzannah saw two chest wounds, one very close to the heart, and knew from the dripping blood that the bullets must have exited through his back. One trouser leg, sliced away, revealed another bullet wound, but it was the least of his problems right now. A neat hole in his forehead to the left of his left eye leaked a small trickle of blood. His white hair stuck up in wild tangles. His face and chest were the colour of dough.

She did not recognize him.

The head wound could be bad or not; in any case, the heart would have to be first. 'Get another line going,' she barked. 'Use the femoral.' She checked the man's pupils. The bullet in his brain was surely causing some swelling. 'A hundred milligrams of Decadron, stat,' she said. 'What's his pressure?'

'Ninety over fifty,' said one of the nurses.

'How much in?'

'Four units.'

'Keep it coming.'

Suzannah glanced at the cardiac monitor, saw the jittery signal of V-fib.

'Isuprel,' she said. Roberta handed her a filled syringe

74

fitted with an intracardiac needle. She plunged it into the heart and injected, watching the monitor. The fibrillations eased for a few seconds, then worsened.

'I'm cracking the chest' she said. 'Let's go!' A nurse handed her the knife and she made quick, deep incisions, peeling back skin as the second resident positioned the spreaders over the ribs and cranked until the heart lay exposed. It jerked, spilling a spurt of blood from a tear in the left ventricle. 'Clamp,' she said. Grabbing it, she placed it partially across the aorta. She began suturing the hole in the heart, thinking ahead to the brain. 'Get the drill ready,' she said.

'No heartbeat,' said Rudy, who was now handling anaesthesia.

Suzannah's scalp tingled. She dropped her needle and grabbed the heart, massaging it. The muscle twitched spasmodically. 'Defibrillator!'

She placed the paddles on the exposed heart.

'Two hundred,' she said. 'Stand back.'

Everyone backed away from the table.

'Go!'

The heart jerked under the paddle, then stopped.

'Again!'

The heart jerked again, then lay still. Suzannah saw that the fluid pouring from the torn ventricle was clear. All the blood had run from his body. He was bleeding out the plasma and other fluids. He was dead.

She stood back, feeling a dull pain in her throat. 'That's it,' she said. 'He's gone.'

The flurry of activity around the trolley stopped. Everyone looked at her. 'You did all you could,' she told them. 'There was no chance.'

She turned away from the table, ripping off her mask and

gloves. An intense disgust filled her. She hated losing a patient. And to murder. So senseless.

She remembered the man had asked for her. She turned back to Roberta. 'Did you ID him yet?'

'He had nothing on him. But the guy who rode in with him said his name is – was – John Stockwell.' Roberta hesitated.

'What is it?'

'The man thought Mr Stockwell might be CIA.'

'Where is this man? I want to talk to him.'

Roberta turned towards the waiting room. 'He's the big black guy in the – wait a minute. He's gone.'

Suzannah felt a surge of frustration. 'Did he tell you anything else?'

Roberta looked at the ceiling. 'Let's see, he said he and Stockwell were talking when two men in ski masks broke in and started shooting. Stockwell shot back, wounding one of the attackers. According to the big black guy, it was all over before he could move. Apparently, the unwounded gunman grabbed Stockwell's ID and wallet, then dragged out his wounded accomplice. Listen, I'm sorry for calling you in. If I'd known he was that far gone . . .'

'You did the right thing,' Suzannah said.

Roberta nodded. 'Thanks. I'll have Rudy make out the death certificate. Oh – here are the cops.'

'Can you keep me out of it for a minute?' Suzannah said. 'I have to make a call.'

'Sure.' Roberta hurried off.

Suzannah picked up the phone at the station and dialled Sharon Harrad's number. While it rang, she glanced down at her white shoes. They were spattered with blood, already turning brown as it dried.

'Hello?'

'Sharon? Suzannah.'

76

'How you doing, kiddo?'

'I've been worse. Listen. I've got a question for you. That man you saw in Adams's ER, the one who asked about me. Can you tell me his name?'

Sharon hesitated. 'What's up?'

'I think I may have just worked on him. He's dead. Multiple gunshots.'

'I see,' Sharon said soberly.

'Was the man you saw named John Stockwell?'

'Yes,' Sharon said. 'That's right.

Suzannah blew out a breath.

'What's going on?' Sharon's voice was suddenly full of concern. 'Suzannah, are you in some kind of trouble?'

'I don't know. And I really wish I did.'

# 8

Archer Montross felt good as he walked across the frozen snow-flecked lawn of the Agency's psychiatric hospital on Sunday morning. He found himself enjoying the fog, the slippery feel of it on his skin, the way it cooled the left side of his face. He didn't even mind that the blurry grey images reminded him of life before the microchip.

Of course, the real reason he was in such a good mood was Suzannah. By rights, he should be worried about the problems she was causing, but all he could think about was her. Her dark eyes, her creamy skin –

Enough. Plenty of time for that later. He needed to clear his mind. In moments, he would watch Suzannah's ex-colleague, Dr Michael Fachet, operate. Watching, he would prime himself to answer the crucial question: was Fachet capable of improving as a surgeon? It was essential that more of the Adept operations succeed. A forty per cent success rate wasn't good enough. Only a few people had the training and knowledge to become the kind of Adepts the Agency needed. Each time the operation failed, the incredible potential of one of those people was wasted for good. Fachet refused to move a microchip once it was implanted, insisting that it would blind the subject.

Archer felt a cold pleasure at what he was about to do. He

was, by training, a psychologist, not a physician. He had only an intelligent layman's understanding of the microchip surgery. And yet today he would look down on the high and mighty Dr Fachet with the power to decide his future. Because the question of whether Fachet stayed or went had a great deal less to do with his medical skills than with hidden aspects of his personality, character, and nerve.

Hidden aspects to other men, Archer thought, but not to me. I will watch him, and I will *see*.

A chilly breeze cut through the fog. Bypassing the psychiatric hospital, he walked toward the pine grove. The grass slapped at his trouser turn-ups, soaking them through with a wet dusting of snow. Too bad they couldn't put a sidewalk through here. But a sidewalk would invite traffic, draw attention to the small outbuilding hidden in the trees.

Archer grimaced as he thought about how close Adept had come to being blown wide open. If John Stockwell had got to Suzannah or spilled his story to the Pentagon . . .

But he hadn't. Grayburn's men had done the job on him. Old John had given a pretty good account of himself for a desk man armed only with a twenty-two. In fact, he actually *had* got to Suzannah, though he was well past saying anything by that point. If they had consulted me before they tried to recruit him, Archer thought, I would have seen the risk. They won't make that mistake again.

The trees that hid Station Three emerged from the fog. Archer followed the winding path through the grove, enjoying the faint gin-like scent of the spruce needles. Above him, a cardinal chirped. Stopping, he located the blob of red in the green. He focused in on it until he could make out the finely etched lines of feather and beak. Walking on, he came to the gate at the perimeter fence. A sign read: '*Station Three, Toxicology Unit, US Fisheries*. DANGER: TOXIC CHEMICALS.

ABSOLUTELY NO ADMITTANCE'. Archer liked the sign, a perfect mix of boring and browbeating. Who would risk his neck for a peek at diseased fish?

The guard stepped out of his shed. His face was red with the cold, the collar of his overcoat turned up, his breath puffing out in grey clouds that merged with the fog. His hand rested on the butt of his combo pistol. All the guards were in love with the combos. The latest thing in high tech, they fired two yoked darts. One was a taser dart on a wire, which would shock an intruder into instant immobility. The other was a conventional tranquilliser dart loaded with Versed, an anaesthetic that would knock the intruder out before he could recover from the paralysing shock. Versed tended to cause short-term memory loss, muddling the victim's recall of the twenty minutes before injection. So if an intruder stumbled across the facility by chance and tried to get past the guard, he wouldn't even remember it when he woke up.

'Cold enough for you, Lefty?' Archer said.

'Good morning, Mr Montross.' Lefty dropped his hand from the combo and gave Archer a nervous smile. Cold people had very little sense of humour. Archer was tempted not to give Lefty today's code. It was stupid anyway. Was there another man in the whole world who stood six-foot-six, looked like an Olympic weight lifter, and had a face half covered with red scar tissue? Two out of three wasn't good enough. To fool Lefty – or any other guard they put out here – an imposter would have to severely burn his face. Who would do that just to get into a small 'fisheries' facility?

Archer decided to have mercy. He gave Lefty the code.

Lefty checked his wrist, where he no doubt had inked the numbers, although it was against regulations. 'All right, Mr Montross,' he said. 'Have a good day.' The guard scurried back into his bunker. A second later, the gate slid back.

Archer went down the rocky path to the building where, using his plastic card key, he opened the steel door. Warm air smelling of antiseptic and floor wax accosted him. He unbuttoned his overcoat as the door slid shut behind him and walked down the centre of the empty corridor to the Operating Room, entering the balcony. The room felt excessively warm. He shrugged out of his overcoat, blotted the good side of his face on his sleeve and seated himself in the front row of the balcony. David Mahoud was already prepped and sitting in the special surgical chair used by neurosurgeons. He was hooked up to the heart monitor and the TV screen that would help the surgeon place the microchip. A male nurse was assisting Dr Michael Fachet with his gloves. Fachet turned and stared up at Archer, his masked face unreadable.

Archer gave him a pleasant nod.

'What are you doing here?' Fachet asked.

Archer felt his mind focusing. 'Do you object, doctor?' He didn't care about the answer, but the way Dr Fachet gave it would no doubt be grist for the mill.

'This is a very delicate operation,' the surgeon said. 'I don't need any distractions. I'm afraid I'll have to ask you to leave.'

'I'll be very quiet, doctor. You won't know I'm here.'

'I'm sorry, it's out of the question.'

Archer began to enjoy himself. He leaned back in his chair, spreading his hands in a gesture of reason. 'I'm afraid that's not your decision.'

The strip of skin visible around the surgeon's eyes flushed angrily. 'This is my Operating Room, and I'll say who's in it. If you insist on staying, the operation's off.'

'You would make us find another surgeon?'

The doctor gave a harsh laugh. 'There *is* no one else.'

'That's not entirely true, is it?'

Dr Fachet glared at him for a minute, then turned back to the table. 'All right, stay. But you're putting needless pressure on me. You'd better take that into account in any judgments you make.'

'Just forget about me,' Archer said mildly, 'and take good care of David, here.'

Leaning forward, Archer braced his arms on the balcony rail. David Mahoud, sitting in the special chair with his head clamped in the headrest, rolled an eye up at him. Archer gave him the thumbs up sign and Mahoud sent back a drowsy barbiturate smile. Even from where he sat, Archer could see the sweat on Mahoud's face below the green draping of surgical towels. The target area on the top of his head had already been shaved by the scrub nurse. The patch of skin, deadened by local anaesthetics, glowed red-orange with Betadine disinfectant. The anaesthetist sat back on his stool beside Mahoud's chest, his work done for the moment. Mahoud was as relaxed as drugs could make a man who knew his head was about to be drilled.

Dr Fachet looked at the monitor beside the surgical trolley. 'Angle that light away,' he snapped at someone who was out of sight beneath the balcony. There was a soft hum, and the bright surgical light tilted slightly away from the monitor. With the glare eliminated, Archer saw that the screen was on but blank.

With a blue marking pen, Dr Fachet drew a square on the exposed patch of skull, outlining where he planned to cut. He then drew a scalpel along the lines he had made. Blood welled up. The nurse vacuumed it up with a dangling tube called a sucker. Archer watched, fascinated. He had read the closely guarded surgical protocols outlining the operation. He'd experienced it. But this would be the first time he'd actually seen it.

Dr Fachet picked up a stainless steel power drill and set the point against Mahoud's head. Archer felt the skin on his neck contract. 'I'm going to start now,' Dr Fachet said. 'You might feel a slight pressure, but it's nothing to be alarmed about.'

'All right, doctor.' Mahoud's voice was slightly slurred. The bit turned slowly, biting with exquisite care into the CIA man's skull. Shavings of bone curled up from the drill, tumbling down the draped towels to the floor like hair from a barber's clippers. The sound of the drill set Archer's teeth on edge. He recalled that sound vaguely from four years ago, but then he'd been full of dope, hardly caring. It had made his nose itch, he remembered.

Dr Fachet drilled four holes at the corners of the rectangle he had drawn. Then he sawed between the holes with a small circular saw, connecting the dots. The saw cut through the bone with an irritating insect's whine. A smell like singed wood reached Archer. Dr Fachet gripped the sides of the rectangle of bone in a plier-like device and popped the rectangle of bone free of the skull. He set it aside in a tray. When he was done, he'd put it back in to plug the hole.

The tube went to work again, suctioning off blood.

Leaning forward, Archer saw a dark pink membrane, the dura mater. A sense of wonder swept him. Beneath that pink tissue, crisscrossed with blood vessels, lay the brain itself. A brain that was about to change forever.

If Dr Fachet succeeded.

The thought made Archer anxious. Mahoud was more than promising, he was a top expert on the Baath party and had lived in Iraq for several years. He was almost as skilled at reading the Iraqis as John Stockwell had been. Better, he'd jumped at the chance Stockwell had so foolishly thrown away – along with his life. If Dr Fachet squandered Mahoud, it would be a real setback.

The surgeon cut an X through the dura mater with a scalpel and peeled the four resulting triangular flaps back to the scalp, putting a stitch in each to hold it there. He could now see straight down on the midline of David Mahoud's brain. Archer saw Dr Fachet glance at the cardiac monitor. It made him aware of a sound he'd been hearing, a deep gurgling rhythm, the noise of Mahoud's blood flowing through his heart. With Mahoud sitting up, there was a greater risk that air might enter the bloodstream.

The male nurse handed Dr Fachet a metal device consisting of narrow parallel strips about five inches long. Dr Fachet lowered it through the hole in Mahoud's skull, sliding it carefully down between the cerebral hemispheres and then screwing the two strips apart until he'd separated the hemispheres enough to provide a channel down to the corpus callosum. The surgeon lowered the microchip, attached to the end of the wirelike fibrecope, into the channel. Archer leaned forward, wishing he could see better. On the monitor, greyish-pink brain tissue lapped over the silvery edges of the spreader channel. As the probe descended, the bottom of the crevice between hemispheres came into view and there lay the corpus callosum, central crossroads of the brain. It looked like stitching, a close pattern of white threads crisscrossing the bottom of the crevice. Cut those threads and you literally split the brain, leaving the two halves unable to communicate. As Fachet moved the scope, the tail end of corpus callosum swam into view on the monitor. Here, Archer knew, visual signals passed between the halves of the brain. To work, the microchip had to be placed at such a crossroads – the visual cortex was spread over too large an area for the tiny chip to access all of it directly. Fortunately, the neural traffic from both eyes converged at two places, the optic chiasm and the corpus callosum.

Archer was very interested in why Lancaster had chosen the corpus callosum. Why not the X-shaped optic chiasm? It lay just behind the eyes. All visual signals were known to converge through it. In contrast, the corpus callosum was known to exchange only part of the traffic from each eye between hemispheres. However, because the corpus callosum came into play much later in the visual process than the chiasm, the signals it did pass were much more fully organized and interpreted by the brain. Lancaster knew that his choice of implant site might well determine whether the microchip succeeded or failed. His reasoning in choosing the corpus callosum seemed almost too simple – that it is easier to identify the picture in a puzzle after seeing a few fully assembled sections than if you see all the individual pieces lying in a heap.

Archer shook his head. Genius often looks simple in retrospect. Gazing at the corpus callosum now, he felt awe. Lancaster's decision to place the microchip here had been more inspired than he could have imagined. Linked with the microchip, this cradle of crisscrossing nerves could do more than exchange visual information. Oh, yes, much more.

Archer watched as Dr Fachet leaned close to the monitor and peered at the image of Mahoud's brain. Fachet said, 'David, I want you to close your eyes now. Keep them closed until I tell you to open them. In a minute, you should see some flashing lights. The instant that happens, I want you to tell me.'

'Yes,' Mahoud said.

Dr Fachet's shoulders hunched. This was the hard part,

the part that only three people in the world could have any hope of managing. A millimetre off in any direction, and the microchip would still enhance visual signals perfectly but the secondary effect would never emerge. Archer felt a sudden intense sympathy for Mahoud. Mahoud did not need the microchip to see. If Dr Fachet blew this operation, Mahoud could walk out of here and go back to the life he had been living as an 'expert' on Iraq. Mahoud was an ambitious man, a volunteer, and he would be disappointed.

The leader of Adept would be even more disappointed.

'Lights!' Mahoud said. 'Reddish orange.'

'Are they flashing or steady?'

'Steady.'

Dr Fachet moved the stiff tube slightly, watching the monitor. Archer saw a sudden darkening of sweat around the rim of his surgical cap.

'Now?'

'Still steady,' Mahoud said. 'but they look bluer now.'

'Good. Do you see any bars?'

'Yes.'

'David, you must tell me exactly what you see at once – *everything* you see.'

'Sorry, doctor. I see . . . vertical bars . . .'

Dr Fachet made a minute adjustment, turning the tube of the scope in his fingers.

'The bars are leaning over now,' Mahoud said. 'They're lying flat and flashing. They're dark blue, the colour of cobalt. Oops! Now they're red again – no, blue.'

Dr Fachet relaxed visibly. 'Good. Just relax, keep your eyes closed.'

'Now I see a river! No, a train. Incredible!'.

'That's fine.' With infinite care, Dr Fachet pushed the release button at his end of the scope. On the monitor,

Archer saw the tiny rectangle of the microchip release, sinking its transducers into the net of nerves like a spider clutching its web. He shuddered. The microchip was so fragile looking. What an effort it must have taken to make it so small. It was essential, of course. Even if infection were not a problem, people could not go around with wires trailing out of their heads attached to an outside computer. The battery was by far the biggest part of the chip, and the part that worried Archer. What if it wore out? He would go blind.

He would lose his special abilities.

Archer shook off a spasm of fear. He was being irrational. The microvoltages of vision were so small, the demand so slight, that the battery would last a hundred years. When I'm in my grave, Archer told himself, there will still be life in my brain.

Dr Fachet withdrew the tube from Mahoud's skull. He unstitched the flaps of dura mater, tucked them back and sewed them together, then put the rectangle of bone into the opening he had made. Finally, he sutured the red-painted skin together over the hole, shutting it.

'That's it, David,' he said.

Mahoud made a sleepy sound deep in his throat. The scrub nurse loosened the clamps of the headrest and removed it. The anaesthetist, looking bored, got up and walked out of the room. Dr Fachet turned and peered aggressively up at Archer again. 'Well?'

'Well what, doctor?' Archer said innocently.

'What did you think of it? Did you see what you came to see?' Dr Fachet persisted.

Not yet, Archer thought. But I will. 'Thank you very much, Dr Fachet. It was very interesting.'

Fachet turned away, yanking off his gloves and stalking out of the Operating Room. Archer watched him until he was gone, then sat back, relaxed, as the nurse wheeled Mahoud out. The surgical light winked out. Clinks and thumps – the circulating nurse cleaning up. That nurse left, too, dialling the lights down as he walked out.

Archer sat in the cool near-darkness, waiting. He saw nothing about Fachet's prospects. It might be hours or days. It would come.

Archer continued to sit, comfortable in the padded chair, listening to the murmur of forced air that carried bacteria away from the centre of the room, pinning them to its walls.

He let his mind go back to Suzannah. He felt a stir of sexual longing. What were you doing at the gallery, Suzannah? Did Andrew ask you to take the chip out?

Or are you in love with him?

The thought brought a curdling taste deep in Archer's throat. Even in college, she had idolized the artist. If that's what you could call a man whose paintings usually didn't look like anything. Archer gave a wry smile. Still jealous, still in love with her, and she had never even known it.

It did not matter whether it was romance or the microchip. Adept needed Suzannah. All it would take was a bad report from him on Fachet, and they would need her more than ever. And they would get her, ensnaring her like a beautiful butterfly.

How would it be, that first moment between them? She would look him full in the face, as always. Would she still pretend to feel no repugnance?

It would be good to be around her again, stand close, smell her perfume, hear her voice. He remembered the way he had once had to steal touches – the quick comradely hand on her back or pat on the shoulder. He remembered the feel of her skin, firm and warm, the light brush of down her arm gave his fingertips. It would be good to touch her again.

Perhaps he would more than touch her.

If she refused Adept – and she would – they would leave it to him, her old friend, to persuade her. And I will persuade her, Archer thought with grim resolve. Whatever it takes. Because she is too young and beautiful to die.

# 9

Suzannah waited at the steel door to the room known as Seclusion until Sharon Harrad came out. A huge young psych tech followed her. Suzannah recognized him from Emergency, which had no techs of its own any more and had to call one down from psychiatry when needed. 'Hello, Curtis,' she said.

'Hi, Dr Lord.' Curtis gave her a bashful smile.

'Suzannah,' Sharon said. 'Good to see you.' She waved Curtis off, releasing him to amble away down the long hall, keys jingling.

'Glad that's over,' Sharon said, glancing back at the locked door of the padded cell.

'A difficult patient?' Suzannah asked.

'He bit one of his ward mates,' Sharon said.

Suzannah grimaced. 'Nasty.'

'I had to shoot a million two hundred thousand units of penicillin into one of our edgiest needle phobics.'

'Why did he bite?'

'Why? Let's see, the long answer involves toilet training, the Oedipus complex, or bad reinforcement history, depending on your school of thought. The short answer is he's faked taking his meds for who knows how long. He likes feeling wild and crazy.' Sharon looked thoughtful. 'Come to think of it, I might like it too – better than Haldol.'

'Vitamin H.'

Sharon sighed. 'Yeah. My least favourite "vitamin". But what's the choice? After he bit his ward mate, I told Count Dracula he didn't have to take his meds if he wanted to stay in Seclusion, where there was no one to gnaw on. "That sounds fine," he says. Today, he's not so sure. I'm hoping he'll come around by this evening, agree to medication, and I can let him out. I hate locking people up. Sometimes I wish I were a surgeon.'

'Only sometimes?'

Sharon gave a wan smile. 'I'm not kidding. You cutters, you see a tumour, you take it out; a gash, you sew it up.'

'Last night,' Suzannah said, 'I tried to sew up a man with four well-placed bullets in him. The padded box he's going into is a lot smaller than Seclusion and he's not coming out again.'

Sharon touched her arm. 'I know. Rough.'

'Sorry. I wasn't trying to one-up you. I just hate losing them, even when there's no chance.' Suzannah realized she'd spoken through clenched teeth. She made a toss-away gesture.

'Want to talk about it?' Sharon nodded down the hall towards her office.

'Actually, I do. But not the way you mean. What can you tell me about John Stockwell?'

'Not much, I'm afraid. But if you want to come down to Emergency with me, I'll dig out my work-up, such as it is. He ran out in the middle of it.'

'Thanks, I'd appreciate that.' Suzannah checked her watch. 'Any chance we could do it now? Jay's due in another hour, and I have hopes of getting out of here.'

Sharon smiled. 'Ah, romance on a Sunday afternoon. More tempting than psychotherapy any day of the week.'

Holding on to Jay's hands, Suzannah skated backwards. He moved in perfect time with her, shoulders swaying as he gazed into her eyes. She listened to their blades cutting the ice together, a sound she loved – *skritch, skritch, skritch*. A cold wind scoured her face. She could smell the snow in it, feel the answering hot sting of blood in her cheeks. Beyond Jay's head, she caught glimpses of the crowd around the rink and, in the far background, the Washington Monument rising into the heavy black sky like a massive icicle. It felt great to exercise after all the morning runs she'd been skipping lately. Breathing the clean, crisp air, she felt better than she had in days, since Jay had gone to Texas, in fact.

'You do this very well,' Jay said. 'One might even think you grew up in the frozen north.'

'Michigan is full of lakes,' she said. 'In winter, everyone skates. I used to love it. Under the moon, ice glows like quicksilver. Gliding over it, you feel so free . . . I missed you. I'm glad you came home a day early.'

'I got tired of sleeping with Tallulah.'

Suzannah raised her eyebrow. 'Excuse me?'

'My daddy's Irish setter. She hogged all the covers and she has terrible morning breath.'

'May all your other women be so charming. So you had a good time?'

The long dimples in Jay's cheeks creased in a gentle smile. 'It was real nice to be home. Next time, you've got to come with me. They all want you to visit.'

'I'd like that.' Suzannah thought with affection of Jay's father, Dick, a respected Austin lawyer, greyer and heavier than his son but almost as vigorous, and his mother, Joan, a refined and lovely Texan who had once held classrooms of volatile adolescents in the palm of her hand. Joan and Dick had flown east at Thanksgiving just to meet her. When they were leaving, Jay's mother had told him, 'If you don't marry this woman, I'm going to adopt her.'

'About what we were discussing at dinner,' Jay said, 'maybe I can make some inquiries at the *Post*. See if the morgue has anything on this hombre Stockwell.'

'That would be good.'

'I wouldn't worry too much about it, though. It's probably just what the police figured – he was down on Fourteenth Street to hustle some poontang and got shot in a robbery.'

'But why was he asking Sharon about me a few days before?'

Jay spun her around smoothly so that now he was skating backwards. 'Maybe he'd been hanging around the hospital, saw you in Emergency and took a shine to you. I'd say that was highly credible.'

'Hanging around why?'

'Listen, Suze, I've interviewed lots of intelligence types. Most of them are pretty sharp old boys. Some of them are also as crazy as a bull in tight shorts. There can be a lot of strain in that job. Stockwell could have made several trips to Emergency, trying to screw up his nerve to get himself committed. You're down there enough that he could easily have seen you ... I love you in this cute little shorty dress. You have legs that would turn a man's Stetson around.'

'That's because I'm wearing four pairs of pantihose to keep from freezing.'

'Want to go in?'

The way he said it brought a pleasant heat to Suzannah's stomach.

'Your place?'

He hesitated. 'How about the Hay-Adams Hotel? It's only a few blocks from here.'

'A *hotel*?'

'*The* hotel. Grandest and most respectable in all of Washington. It would be fun. Have room service send up a bottle of Dom and some little chocolates.'

She heard the plea in his voice and realized he did not want to go back to his apartment yet. He did not want to be in the same room with the blank, accusing screen of his word processor. It troubled her. But now was not the time to talk about it.

'All right,' she said.

Thirty minutes later, she sat soaking in a big ornate bathtub and listening to Jay humming in the bedroom. The place was everything he'd said it was, with its high ceilings and ornate moldings, its plush carpet and Louis XIV chairs, its hush of old money and Washington secrets. She liked it, but she could not help wondering if Jay had brought other women here. And what if he had? she thought, nettled with herself for being jealous. That's history. This is us.

And besides, wasn't that you at dinner last night with another man in a fancy Georgetown restaurant? You haven't mentioned that to Jay yet, have you?

Jay walked into the bathroom wearing only his jeans. His chest looked hard and tanned. 'You put bubbles in,' he complained. 'I was going to get in with you.'

'Well, come on.' She patted the side of the tub.

'And smell like lilies of the valley? No thank you, ma'am.'

'You can at least wash my back.' She leaned forward, and

he knelt beside the tub. His hands were very gentle, rubbing circles on her back, massaging her spine. She felt a nice glow spreading through her. Lying back in the tub, she gazed up at him.

'Front?' he said, the wonderful dimples showing again. His eyes were so blue, like a Texas sky in summer.

She nodded, watching his eyes as his hands, slippery with the bubble bath, found her breasts, cupping them gently, sliding her nipples between his fingers. She felt his hand sliding down over her ribs, rubbing the creases between them, descending to her stomach. The warmth there grew. She gasped as his hand slipped below the water. He bent so that his face nuzzled her cheek.

'I love you, Dr Suzannah Lord.'

'Oh!' she said, unable to think. 'Oh-h-h – Jay!'

His lean arms, ropy with muscle, slid under her knees and shoulders to lift her from the tub. Carrying her into the dressing-room, he pulled a big towel from the rack. She watched, smiling, as he spread the towel on the thick carpet with a sweep of one arm and lowered her onto it. He lay down and she rolled onto her side, finding the zipper on his jeans, pleased and excited by the bulge beneath. She pulled the zipper down slowly, releasing him. He tugged his jeans and undershorts off and turned in to her, kissing her gently. She kissed back, finding his tongue. It tasted salty-sweet. He rolled across her, making his body slick with the bathwater. He slid into her easily, cradling her ribs with his forearms. He sucked her nipples lightly, sending little shocks of pleasure inward to her heart. She found his thick hair, twining her fingers into it, pulling his mouth against hers as he moved, ever so gently, then more insistently.

She felt the heat descend, then spread throughout her

body as his wonderful hardness struck pleasure deeper and deeper into her.

'Oh, Jay. Oh! God, Jay!'

Distantly, through her own harsh gasps, she heard him coming with her, a long groan of ecstasy.

He held her tightly, kissing the hollow of her neck. The heat of lovemaking lingered with the warmth of the bath. She felt him drying her, tenderly, gently, and then he lifted her to the bed, drawing the covers up, sliding in beside her as the room faded into a warm, comforting darkness. She fell asleep with his arm across her.

Deep in the night, she awoke, the faint honk of a cab echoing in her mind. For a moment, she could not orient herself, then she remembered where she was. Outside the tall windows of the bedroom, the night lights of Washington glimmered faintly in the darkness. She could hear Jay breathing softly beside her. She reached across to touch his chest, letting her fingers play in the thick hairs. She felt wonderful, happy . . .

And just the barest bit uneasy.

The microchip.

What if Andrew wasn't telling me the truth last night, she thought. Does he really believe his problems with the microchip, whatever they are, are all in his mind?

He went to Lancaster. But now he won't talk about it.

Has anyone else gone to Lancaster with problems, one of the other pilot subjects?

Suzannah really did not want to get into that. But her mind, perversely, had just served up a perfectly easy thing she could do. She could call some of the other pilot subjects. Ask them if everything was all right. If it was, fine; she could drop this once and for all.

If not . . . well, she'd deal with that if it happened.

Satisfied, Suzannah rolled against Jay, hugged him, and drifted back to sleep.

She did not get a chance to make any calls until Monday evening. Surgery took up the morning, then a call down to Emergency: a Catholic U student had fallen from his dorm window. Splenectomy, collapsed lung and twelve broken bones, including a compound fracture of the femur, for which she'd called in orthopaedics. She was late getting to her office patients, later still when a lab report came back positive for breast cancer and she spent an hour trying to reassure a sobbing young woman who shouldn't have had to face such a terror so soon.

She made it home around seven. Juli had held supper, pasta primavera, her favourite. J.D. complained good-naturedly. How was he going to grow big and strong on only noodles and vegetables?

After dinner, Suzannah called Jay. He wanted to go back for another roll in the Hay-Adams tonight. Laughing, she told him to get to work on his book – and to ask her again later.

She knew she should go downstairs, find the names of the pilot subjects, and start calling, but she didn't want to. She watched Juli and J.D. start up a game of Attack Sub 688 on the computer in the den instead.

Go on, get it over with.

Downstairs in her bedroom, she began burrowing through her pile of diaries in the bottom drawer. The ones for 1988 and 1989 should contain the names of most of the pilot subjects. Suzannah picked up the one for 1989. Unlocking it, she thumbed through, stopping whenever she saw a name from the pilot study – someone who had made it into her diary because of a sense of humour, orneriness, or some other characteristic she did not want to lose from memory. Each time she found a subject's name, she wrote it on a sheet of paper.

Picking up the 1988 diary, Suzannah's fingers slowed of their own accord as she neared the page for 13 July, the night when Roland Lancaster had come back to work and slipped into the deserted lab with her. A dull ache started up in her stomach. She had written nothing on that page, but somehow its blankness oppressed her more than words could have done.

*You smug, arrogant bastard. Do you ever think of what you did?*

She stood, taking a deep breath.

Sitting again, she pushed the diaries aside and looked at her list. Seven names, enough for a start. Using the phone book, she started making calls. She got hold of Lori Fishbein first. Lori was fine, Lori remembered her well. No, there were no problems from the operation. She could see perfectly. It was the best thing that had ever happened to her.

Same for Brandon Tate.

Same for Sherri DeLong.

Mike Anzeloni wasn't home.

Suzannah looked at the remainder of the list, losing steam. Why was she doing this?

Because Andrew Dugan wanted someone to take the *ghastly* thing out of his brain. The same thing that, starting in a few weeks, would be implanted in the brains of thousands of other people.

Suzannah dialled the next name on her list, Tricia Fiore. Tricia the schoolteacher, the first to receive a microchip.

'Hello.'

The voice was low, relaxed.

'Tricia?'

'Yes. Who is this?'

The detached serenity in the voice made Suzannah uneasy. 'This is Suzannah Lord, from the pilot study four years ago. I was one of Dr Lancaster's assistants.'

There was a long silence.

'Tricia?'

'Yes. I remember you. What do you want?' Despite the brusqueness of the words, Tricia's voice was still relaxed. Drugs? Suzannah wondered. No. There was no slurring of words, just a strange tranquillity.

'I've been calling test subjects as a follow-up—'

'I heard you'd quit the study, that you hadn't become a neurosurgeon.'

'That's right,' Suzannah said reluctantly, seeing any hope of co-operation flying out the window. But was this really Tricia? What was wrong with her?

'Then you can't help me,' Tricia said.

Suzannah felt the ache in her stomach again, sharper this time. 'Help you? Is something wrong?'

Tricia gave a soft grunt. 'Everything's wrong. I should never have had the operation. I should have gone blind. But then I wouldn't have been able to work with the children. Dr Lancaster won't help me. And now he's having me watched.'

Suzannah felt the skin drawing tight on her scalp. 'Tricia, I'd like to talk to you in person. May I come over?'

'It doesn't matter.' There was no strain in her voice to go with the words. 'They'd like to kill me,' she went on passively. 'I'm going to die. I see it all clearly.'

'Stay right where you are!' Suzannah said. 'I'll be there in twenty minutes. Tricia? Tricia, do you hear me?'

'Thank you for calling, Dr Lord.'

The line went dead. Suzannah ran upstairs, afraid for Tricia, afraid that, to Tricia, twenty minutes was the same as eternity.

# 10

Suzannah called 911 and gave them Tricia's address. The dispatcher said all units were at a fire, but they'd send one as soon as they could. Suzannah wanted to shout at the dispatcher that this was more important.

But it wasn't.

Tricia had made no actual threat, after all. It was just a hunch, her voice, that chilling serenity.

Suzannah grabbed her medical bag and car keys and raced upstairs. Juli and J.D. were still playing Attack Sub 688 on the computer.

'I've got a patient in trouble,' Suzannah said. 'Rescue's tied up with a big fire.'

Juli stood. 'Need help?'

'I might, but what about J.D.?'

'He can go to Joe and Claire's.'

'Hey,' J.D. said. 'Take me with you.'

'Not this time,' Juli said.

'Jeez, I can handle it. You'd think I was just a kid or something.'

'Suze, make sure Father Time here gets over to Joe and Claire's, and I'll start the Porsche.'

Suzannah started to protest that she could drive, then realized the Porsche would be better. They needed speed, lots of speed, and her old Chevy didn't even like to start in cold weather. As she ran across the street with J.D., she slipped into one sleeve of her coat and tried to tug on the other one. The frigid air bit at her face. She heard the Porsche start up with a throaty rumble at the kerb behind her. Hurrying back, she finished pulling her coat on, slid in beside Juli, and read off the address she'd torn from the phone book.

The Porsche leapt from the kerb with a squeal of tyres. Suzannah prayed for the light at Route 50 to be green. Yes . . . oh, no, turning yellow! The tyres squealed again as Juli sped around the little traffic circle and careened through the intersection. Once they'd made the highway, Suzannah forced herself to lean back in the seat and take a deep breath. There was nothing to do now but hope she was wrong about Tricia, or, if she was right, that they'd be in time.

'This woman – Tricia Fiore – is not actually my patient,' she said to Juli. 'She was our first implant subject in Roland Lancaster's pilot study four years ago. Can this car go any faster?'

Juli shot her a snide look and trod on the gas. Suzannah felt the car lunge forward, pressing her back into the seat. The big oaks and poplars fronting the homes on Route 50 flashed by. Juli had no trouble weaving in and out of the sparse traffic as the speedometer hit seventy-five. She slowed to turn onto Route 7, then speeded up again. 'So what's up?' Juli asked. 'Tricia take an overdose?'

'Not yet.'

'But she threatened it?'

'Well, no – not exactly.'

Juli looked surprised but kept her eyes on the road. 'Then what makes you think she's in trouble?'

'Her voice was wrong for what she was saying. She should have sounded either anxious or depressed. Strain in the voice is good, means the person is fighting. No strain when there should be strain is a bad sign.'

'How do you know she's not just a cool customer who thinks she has her crisis under control?'

'That's just it, I think she *does* have it under control. Not just under control, solved. Her solution is that she's going to kill herself.'

'How do you know?'

'I can't explain it. It's not a guess exactly. More a hunch, a very strong hunch. I heard her voice and something in my subconscious kicked in and I *knew*. Last year I had a patient with terminal liver cancer. Mr Widner. I spoke with him on the phone one afternoon and he sounded just like Tricia tonight, very much at peace. That night, he went out to his garage, ran a vacuum hose from his exhaust into his car, and sat in the front seat. They found him the next morning, dead, his hands on the steering wheel. I could be wrong about Tricia, I *hope* I'm wrong, but I don't think so.'

Juli said, 'I don't believe this. I'm driving my Porsche almost eighty miles an hour because my sister's subconscious kicked in.'

'No,' Suzannah said, 'you're driving almost eighty because you trust your sister's hunches. Now try actually going eighty.'

Juli pushed her glasses up her nose and leaned forward, tightening her grip on the steering wheel. The Porsche sped into Falls Church. Shops and restaurants flashed by on either side, separated from the highway only by a narrow sidewalk. Suzannah sucked a breath as Juli ran a red light. Brakes screeched in their wake, horns honked, and then Suzannah heard a siren cranking up behind them. Her heart sank. Twisting in her seat, she saw a black and white Fairfax

County police car, gaining very slowly but gaining. The cycling bleat of the siren hiccuped with two louder whoops.

'Want me to lose them?'

'No, pull over. I'll take care of it.'

Juli gave a wild laugh. 'Take care of it? You don't know these guys. They're not our nice polite Arlington police. We'll be lucky if they don't drag us straight off to jail.'

'Come on, pull over.'

'OK, OK.'

Juli braked steadily, pulling the Porsche to the kerb in front of a darkened hardware store. 'Just wait here,' Juli said. 'They'll come to you.'

Suzannah fished in her purse for her hospital ID from Adams Memorial. Turning back, she saw the two cops just sitting in their cruiser. 'What are they waiting for?' she fumed.

One of them got out and approached the Porsche with maddening slowness, his hand on the butt of his gun. Unable to stand it any longer, Suzannah jumped out, feeling Juli's hand grab at her coat.

The cop drew his gun and aimed it at her in the classic two-handed crouch. 'Stop right there!'

Suzannah felt a kick of fright. 'I'm a doctor,' she shouted, holding up her ID, amazed at how calm and strong her voice sounded.

The cop stayed in his crouch, staring at her.

'This is a medical emergency,' Suzannah said. 'I'm going to walk to you, show you my ID, and then we'll need you as an escort.'

The cop straightened, motioning her over with a curt jerk of his hand. She hurried to him, showed him the ID. He stared at it, his face red, a muscle in his jaw jumping. 'What's the emergency?'

'A possible suicide. If she took pills, we can still save her.'

'Are you a shrink?'

'Surgeon.'

The cop frowned. 'This better be on the level.'

Juli's questions flashed through her mind. What if they went crashing into Tricia's house and Tricia said, 'What seems to be the problem, officers?'

'We're wasting time,' Suzannah said.

'All right, but you were going over ninety. If it turns out this ain't a suicide, it's going to be your funeral.'

Suzannah gave him the address and jumped back in the Porsche as the cruiser pulled out past them, siren screaming. In minutes the cruiser slowed, swinging into a subdivision of West Falls Church. Suzannah leaned forward, peering at the houses, looking for numbers. Tricia's house was a small Cape Cod, well back from the street. Suzannah grabbed her medical bag and led the way, sprinting up the long slope of front lawn. The window of the front door shone with a pale light. Two big azaleas guarded the door, their leafless branches sticking up like bared nerve endings. Suzannah hammered on the door, thinking, I only hope it *is* my funeral.

No answer.

She felt the cops at her back. 'Break it down,' she said.

The officer who'd pointed his gun at her gave his partner, a big overweight guy, a pained look. 'You sure?'

'No, I'm not sure. How could I be sure?'

The bigger cop cleared his throat. 'All right, Jase, you heard the lady. Let's break it down.'

The man called Jase braced his back against the back of the big cop. The big cop cocked a leg and slammed his booted foot into the door, just above the knob. The jamb splintered and the door flew inward. Suzannah hurried in, turning a corner through the living-room, into the kitchen.

No sign of Tricia.

Suzannah found the bedroom in the back of the house, the bed neatly made, the bathroom dark. She flipped on the light, heart pounding, terrified that she might see Tricia lying in a bloodied bath.

The tub was empty, a dry clean white.

Running back out, Suzannah bumped into the big cop. 'The basement,' she said, looking for the door, finding it at the rear of the kitchen. The light was already on. Filled with foreboding, she ran down into an unfinished room.

Smell of mildew, ducts and pipes lining the ceiling. Tricia's body, turning slightly, hung from a pipe in the corner, the stool at her feet overturned.

For a second, Suzannah stared, shocked. Five years ago Tricia had been rather plump. Now she was bone thin. The body was dressed in a pink nightgown. A flip-flop lay under the overturned stool. The rope seemed absurdly thick, a stout braided thing that could have held up a ton. Suzannah ran to Tricia, grabbing her wrist. Still warm . . . but no pulse.

Setting the stool upright, Suzannah started to climb onto it.

Feet thundered down the stairs behind her. 'Hold it, doctor!'

She turned and saw both cops, rooted in place, staring with distaste at the dangling body. Juli descended into sight behind them. 'Come on,' Suzannah shouted, 'we've got to get her down!'

The big cop's jaw dropped. 'She has a pulse?'

'No, but maybe we can get one.'

'If she's dead, we're not supposed to disturb the evidence –'

'Dammit, get over here.' Suzannah clambered up on the stool, hugging Tricia, lifting the thin body to take its weight off the rope. 'Get the noose off,' she said. 'Now!'

The cops shook off their paralysis and ran over to help her hold the body. Juli, white-faced, pried the rope away from the deep groove in Tricia's neck. Suzannah cradled Tricia's head as the cops laid the body out on the floor. Then she snatched a syringe from her bag and fitted an intracardiac needle to it. What would Tricia weigh? About ninety-five. Suzannah drew epinephrine into the syringe, hoping Tricia's neck wasn't broken or the cartilage in her throat crushed.

Thumping an air bubble from the syringe, Suzannah banged the epinephrine straight into Tricia's heart. She felt a furious energy pumping through her. She grabbed the endotracheal tube from her bag and ripped off the sealing paper. Making room for one of the cops to straddle Tricia, Suzannah started chest compression.

As Suzannah tried to insert the trache tube, Tricia's swollen tongue got in the way. Suzannah poked it flatter, easing the tube down, hearing the faint wail of a siren through the thick basement walls. The tension in her shoulders eased a fraction.

'Go meet 'em,' she said to Juli. 'Tell them asphyxiation – oh-two and defib.'

Tricia's body jiggled as the cop thrust, grunting, at her sternum. The trache tube still didn't want to go down. Suzannah fought a surge of impatience. Was she hitting the esophagus? Or maybe the rope had crushed the cartilage too much. She checked the ugly groove left by the noose and saw it was filling in slightly, a good sign. The tube slipped down suddenly, forcing Tricia's airway open. Suzannah bent, blowing into it. The cop stopped to let her ventilate, then resumed. She fell into a rhythm with him – his five pushes, then her breath. Footsteps pounded down the stairs, and Suzannah got up to move aside for the paramedics. One of them connected a canister of oxygen to the end of the trache tube. Suzannah caught Tricia's limp wrist, groping for the pulse. The vein fluttered faintly against her finger. She felt a rush of hope. Come on, come *on*! For a moment there was nothing more; then a slow erratic beat started up.

'I've got a pulse!' Suzannah shouted.

Tricia's body twitched.

'She's breathing,' one of the paramedics said. He gave Suzannah a gap-toothed grin and held one thumb up. The cop named Jase got up, standing away from the body. He was grinning, too. Suzannah felt Juli's arm across her shoulder. She lost her balance, falling against her sister. The room dimmed, then firmed up again. She hugged Juli, feeling a wild elation.

'You did it!' Juli said. 'You saved her.'

'I know,' Suzannah said, her exhilaration fading, 'but the problem is, she *wanted* to kill herself.'

*Either that, or someone wanted it to look that way.*

# 11

Suzannah stood at Tricia Fiore's bedside the next morning, trying to muster some optimism. Tricia didn't seem to be in a full-fledged coma. That was hopeful. But she wouldn't wake up either. That was *not* hopeful. A little movement, a flicker of the eyelids, would be nice.

Suzannah studied Tricia's unconscious face. Both eyes were black and blue. The rope mark made an ugly purplish weal across her throat. Suzannah looked at the EEG and tried to understand. According to this printout, Tricia was showing considerable brain activity. The blood toxicology values were encouraging too. And yet she continued to lie there with that utter disheartening stillness. Baffled, Suzannah slipped the EEG back into the chart at the foot of Tricia's bed. She was conscious of Ed Gaspard standing behind her. She was glad Ed was on the case; he was the best neurologist at Adams.

'So what do you think?' Ed asked.

Suzannah held up a finger, signalling Ed to wait. She walked to the head of the bed and leaned close to Tricia's face. She could see Tricia's eyes moving, the slight bulge of the cornea jerking beneath the lids, as though Tricia were watching a furious tennis match.

'Tricia?' Suzannah said sharply.

No response.

She took Tricia's limp hand. 'Tricia? It's Suzannah Lord. If you can hear me, give my hand a squeeze. Squeeze my hand, Tricia. Come on, squeeze.'

The hand remained limp in hers.

Behind her, Ed cleared his throat.

Suzannah watched the eyes another moment. The rapid, furious movement stopped. Suzannah felt a sudden chill. She motioned Ed out of the room.

In the hall, he said, 'What, you think she's listening to us?'

'It's possible.'

'I think it's the start of a persistent vegetative state,' Ed said.

'You're the neurologist.'

'Sure. But I didn't do my residency under Lancaster.'

'Part of a residency,' Suzannah corrected, then wondered why she felt it necessary to be so scrupulously accurate.

Ed looked away down the corridor. Suzannah followed his gaze to a couple of nurses, who were joking in loud voices at the station. A man with a bandage over half his head shuffled towards them, gripping his walker, his eyes blank. Suzannah felt a sudden, sharp sense of loss. This should be her domain. She had worked for it, trained for it, and through no fault of her own –

*Stop it.*

'I'm not trying to hedge,' Suzannah said. 'It's just I have no idea how long her air had been cut off when we got there. The EEG is a good sign that it wasn't more than four minutes. She's breathing on her own, so the brain stem is bouncing back, thanks to her light weight.'

'Do you think the microchip could be a factor?' Ed asked. 'Keeping her from waking up somehow?'

'I don't see how.' The question made Suzannah uncomfortable. A week ago, she'd have thought she knew everything about the microchip. Now she knew she did not.

'We can assume she was depressed,' Ed added, 'or she wouldn't have done this.'

*If* she did it, Suzannah thought. Because that was the big question, and they weren't going to know the answer unless Tricia woke up. The police had found no evidence of foul play, but they probably hadn't made a thorough investigation. And why should they, when the first thing they'd heard from her was that a woman might be committing suicide? When Suzannah had told the detective about Tricia's remark on the phone – 'They want me dead' – he'd nodded and written it down. Then he'd asked her if she knew who might want to kill an elementary school teacher. She'd had to say she did not know.

But I'm going to find out, Suzannah thought. She checked her watch. Ten minutes to twelve. If she was going to eat lunch, she'd better do it, before her office appointments started at one. 'Ed, I've got to run.'

'Thanks for stopping in,' he said. 'I guess the next thing is to call her shrink.'

Suzannah stopped and turned back to him. 'Her shrink?'

'Yes. We talked to people at her school to get whatever history we could. Seems Tricia's been on a leave of absence because of "nerves". Her best friend, who teaches second grade, says she's been seeing a Dr Munley in Fairfax.'

Suzannah felt some small relief. If Tricia had been seeing a psychiatrist, she might really have been suicidal – depending on her diagnosis. Before lunch she could call Munley, try to get an appointment. Psychiatrists often saw patients in the evening. She had a dinner date with Jay at seven, but, with luck, Munley could work her in either before or afterwards. 'See you later,' she said to Ed. 'I'd appreciate it if you'd keep me posted on her.'

'Sure.'

Back in her office, Suzannah found Munley's number in the phone book and was about to dial when Marjory buzzed her from the receptionist desk.

'Dr Lord, you have a call from a Mr Dugan.'

Andrew! Suzannah's heart skipped a beat. 'I'll take it.'

'Suzannah?'

'Hi.'

'Are we even now?'

'What?' She searched her mind. 'Oh. The way I ran out on you. I apologize.'

'No apologies necessary. I hope you were able to save the man.'

'No.'

'I'm sorry.'

He did not rush on or say anything else. She liked that. 'It happens. You learn not to think about it too much.'

'It's lunchtime. I have made two sandwiches from dark pumpernickel bread and Italian fontina cheese, and I have a bottle of Evian. We could eat it at Bob's.'

'Bob's?'

'The art supply store I told you about at dinner. To the uninitiated Bob is known as Guy Robert Lyon.' He pronounced it Gee R-r-robair Leeohn. 'It's only five minutes from the hospital.'

'But where are you?'

'In the phone booth in the hospital lobby.'

Suzannah laughed. 'Why didn't you just come up?'

'Hospitals terrify me. And so does rejection. From here it

takes only seconds to dash in front of an onrushing automobile.'

'In that case, I'd better go along with you. But I have to be back at one.'

'I give you my word. Come right now, will you. I have a cab waiting.'

'All right.' I'll have Marjory call Dr Munley, Suzannah thought as she hung up. She grabbed her coat, amused and a bit nettled. Right now, indeed. Confident, wasn't he? And why shouldn't he be? He must have become used to women throwing themselves at him, beautiful actresses, rich society women, all craving the attentions of a dark handsome prince of the art world. This is totally different though, Suzannah told herself. I'm not rich and I'm definitely not an actress.

Bob's was an ancient narrow-fronted shop on Sixteenth Street, ten blocks north of the White House. It was narrow inside, too, and deep, with whitewashed walls and a stairway in the back that led to a cozy mezzanine full of books. The alluring smell of the place – old paper, turpentine, and wood polish – grew as she climbed the steps behind Andrew. Above her she saw a wonderful old ceiling made of moulded tin. Four rows of bookcases ran from almost the back wall to the wrought iron rail of the mezzanine. Andrew led her into a warm shadowy lane between two of them and sat cross-legged on the oak floor. After a moment's hesitation she joined him. No one else seemed to be on the mezzanine; she wondered if Bob had put a chain across the stairs after he'd ushered them up.

Andrew handed her a sandwich. He looked every inch the dark prince in his black turtleneck and wool slacks. He had not shaved lately and his jaw was darkened by a soft stubble shot through with silver. She liked men to shave, but somehow he did not look untidy. His hair was clean, brushed back into a thick black helmet. His dark eyes held a hint of sadness at odds with his smile. 'I'm glad you could make it,' he said.

'As long as we're back by one. I've got patients.'

'So little time,' he murmured.

She took a bite of the sandwich. It was delicious, the bread thick and heavy, the cheese soft and rich. 'This is fabulous,' she said. 'Where did you get it?'

'My oven.'

'You baked this?' she said, surprised and impressed.

'I had no choice. I got hooked on it growing up. It's my old man's recipe, and none of the bakeries can match it. Here.' He poured her a plastic cup of water.

'Evian,' she said. 'Pretty fancy.'

'Pretentious, you mean. If I didn't like the stuff so much, I'd have to give it up.' Andrew eyed her. 'I hope I'm not becoming a nuisance.'

'Don't be ridiculous. I've admired you since I was twelve.'

He groaned.

'Sorry.'

'Next you'll tell me I'm old enough to be your father.'

'Not true. I'm thirty-one and you're forty-five.' Suzannah felt herself blushing. She'd let slip that she knew his age. Now he'd think she'd studied him, like some teenager poring over biogs of her rock idol.

He gazed at her. 'Why did you come with me today?'

'You're going to show me that book.'

'Is that all?'

'I like you.'

Andrew pinched the bridge of his nose lightly, as if he had a headache. 'So little time,' he repeated.

She sensed the sadness again. 'What do you mean?'

He looked at her, as if her face held the key to something vital. 'It's difficult to explain. But since I met you at the gallery, I've been unable to get you out of my mind. I've thought about you constantly, seen your face in my mind, heard your voice – that confident, crisp voice, so full of life. Only a few days, but I feel as if I've known you much longer.'

Suzannah felt her head spinning. This was a fantasy coming true. It excited and, in an odd way, aggravated her. Fantasies did not come true. Only real life came true. She said nothing: waited.

'I don't want to come between you and someone you love,' Andrew said. 'I just want to see you, be with you, as much as I can.'

Coming from him, the words had an incredible power. He was no ordinary man, he was one of the geniuses of the twentieth century. A man she had worshiped from afar. And now they were near and he wanted her. She could feel his desire, his urgency, and it aroused her tremendously. She wanted him too, but . . .

Suzannah dusted the crumbs from her fingers, finished her water and stood. 'Where's this book you're going to show me?'

He stood too, taking her hands. 'You have such pain,' he said softly.

'Do I?' Her voice was a bit unsteady.

'"You learn not to think about it too much." I believe that's what you said.'

With absolute certainty, she knew he was talking not about a surgical patient she'd lost but about Lancaster, and what Lancaster had done to her. It was almost as if he knew the details. He couldn't know them, but he had felt them, had seen inside her somehow. Her throat constricted. 'Andrew –'

'No, please. It must stay buried. I understand that. If I could just know how you do it.' His voice was tight with his own pain.

'The microchip,' she said. 'It is doing something terrible to you.'

He gave a very slight nod.

'Will you tell me what?'

'I . . . no, I can't do that.'

'But why?'

He shook his head mutely. 'I've got to learn to live with it. Teach me.'

An intense discomfort seized Suzannah, the feeling of dark things trying to break loose inside her. 'I can't. I'm not a psychiatrist. I'm a surgeon. I do what I do. I don't think about it. It's just the way I am. I can't teach it.'

'You're so beautiful. So much pain, and yet you enjoy, you laugh, you live.'

Suzannah knew she should pull her hands away, but she could not. 'Another member of the pilot study has had trouble, did you know that?'

Andrew's jaw tightened. 'I'm not surprised.'

'It appears she tried to kill herself last night.'

His hands tightened on hers. 'Suzannah . . .' His eyes lost their focus, staring through her, beyond her. Seconds crawled by. Suzannah began to feel alarmed. It was happening again as it had that night in the cafe, some sort of fugue state. Had the microchip created some strange form of epilepsy in Andrew? But why would he try and hide that from her?

'Andrew?' she said sharply, growing alarmed.

Abruptly, his eyes focused on her again. 'Have you noticed anyone watching you lately?' he asked.

'No.'

'Men watching your house?'

She felt a small shock. 'Yes. There's a stakeout in the house behind mine. But—'

'I should never have approached you,' Andrew said.

'What do you mean?'

'You must be very careful now,' he said.

'Andrew, what are you talking about?'

'I can't tell you more. There's a chance it's not too late and you'll be all right. But you've got to forget about the microchip. Just put it right out of your mind. And we can't see each other again. I'm leaving now, out the back way. You wait a few minutes and then go too — back to the hospital, back to your patients who need you.'

'Andrew—'

He turned to the bookcase and pulled out a thin volume entitled *Light and Shadow*. 'This is the book,' he said. 'My gift to you. Light and shadow. Without both there is neither. I've got to go.' He gazed at her another moment, then pulled her to him and kissed her gently, quickly on the lips.

He walked away. She watched him go, mystified and a little afraid. There *is* something wrong with the microchip, she thought. And Lancaster knows it. Or would if he would listen. But he is not a man who listens — not to Andrew or to Tricia or to me. All he cares about is himself.

A savage determination filled her. You arrogant bastard, she thought. Something's wrong with your crowning achievement and you'd let thousands of people suffer rather than admit it. I'm coming after you, Roland old boy. This time you're going to be the one who suffers. I'm going to nail your hide to the wall.

# 12

Suzannah sat in Joe Theismann's restaurant, sipping coffee and listening to Jay's story about getting lost in the Pentagon basement during his early days on the Defense Department beat. The garden room was pleasantly warm, filled with the hearty smells of steak and fries. Hanging ferns offered an amusing contrast to macho paintings of Joe and his football team-mates. Suzannah glanced over Jay's shoulder at the dark mahogany bar, three steps down. The usual group of singles stood around, pressing together in a double row, thirtyish women in flashy dresses and too much make-up, forty-something men in suits, smoking nervously. They had that slight edge of tension, continually scanning, too conscious of themselves and each other. Suzannah was glad she was not down there alone, looking and hoping.

Jay finished his tale and she laughed, wondering if he would ever run out of stories. Maybe when they had grown old together, he would start repeating himself. She wouldn't mind that.

Suzannah smiled at herself. Neither of us has even talked about getting married yet, she thought.

Jay ordered another coffee and she checked her watch. Eight-thirty. Darn! She'd have to break this off soon to keep her appointment with Tricia Fiore's psychiatrist, Dr

Munley. She had intended to ask Jay about his writing but hadn't found the right opening yet. She'd better just forget about openings and ask.

'So, how's it going with the book?'

His face sobered. 'Fine. Just fine.'

She felt a small hope. 'The first chapter, is it working out all right?'

'Yes.'

'How long is it?'

'Well, I haven't exactly finished the draft yet. But I think I've finally got it organized in my mind.'

Suzannah hid her disappointment. That's what she was afraid of; it was exactly what he'd said before he went off to Austin. And for four weeks before that. His reluctance to talk about it frustrated her. She only wanted to help him – without pushing, of course.

'First chapters are rough,' she said.

'Don't I know it.'

'Especially the first few sentences. I was reading an article about writing in *Book World* last Sunday. The author said he had to skip the lead sentence until he'd written the chapter. Otherwise, he'd never get past it.'

'Uh-huh.'

'I'd probably be that way,' she said. 'Too perfectionistic.'

Jay smiled. 'It's OK to be perfectionistic, as long as you're not too perfectionistic.'

'English majors.' She sniffed. 'You know what I mean.'

'Yes.'

'It's not a bad idea. Just write down the parts that come to you now, then organize them into a book later.'

'Suzannah,' he said softly, 'I appreciate what you are trying to do, really. But it's hard to understand if you weren't there.'

'I've never had appendicitis either, but I've cured a hundred cases.'

'This isn't something you can just cut out of me.'

She looked at him, stung.

'I'm sorry. That was uncalled for.' He reached out and covered her hand.

'You're such a good guy,' she said. 'Always ready to help me. But when I try to help you, you push me away. It hurts, Jay.'

'I don't mean to be pushing you away,' he said. 'I know you want to help, but this is just something I have to deal with myself.' He picked up her hand and kissed it.

He's comforting me, she thought, for being unable to comfort him. She felt stymied. She thought about Andrew at lunch today, asking for her help: *I've got to learn to live with it. Teach me.* How powerfully his need had drawn her to him.

And I turned him away, Suzannah thought guiltily. I'm saving my help for Jay, and he doesn't want it.

She leaned across the table and gave Jay a quick kiss. 'I've got to go.'

He looked at his watch. 'I wish you didn't. Is it something important?'

'I'm hoping it is. I have to talk to Tricia's doctor and this is the only time he could see me. I'll call you tomorrow.'

Dr Vincent Munley pumped Suzannah's hand. 'I'm so happy to meet you, Dr Lord. It would have been a great loss if Tricia had killed herself. What you did for my patient – well, it was heroic.'

Suzannah felt a bit put off by his enthusiasm, but she smiled. 'Thank you, Dr Munley.'

'Please call me Vince.'

'And I'm Suzannah.'

He cocked his head. 'With a z?'

'Yes.'

'Excellent.'

Munley was a rather homely man of around fifty, completely bald and a bit plump around the middle. He looked very tidy in a tweed jacket, sweater and wool slacks. His bow tie was knotted perfectly. Her overall impression of both him and his office was of painful neatness. The big bookcase along one wall was a model of order, every spine lined up precisely with the next. The flowerpots on the windowsill behind him had been arranged according to the height of the plant.

Munley motioned her to a seat. Pulling another small armchair from beside the window, he paused to look out at the towering business complex across from the Leonard M. Weyl Medical Building. The steel-and-concrete horizon of Bailey's Crossroads glowed with a thousand lights against the night sky. He drew the chair close to hers and sat, shaking his head. 'It's the last decade of the twentieth century,' he said. 'And what have we come to? People are writing books about how to kill yourself. Doctors are making machines to help people do it. My profession does its best to fight it, but I'm afraid we're falling behind. At least you won one.'

'I just hope Tricia Fiore will be glad,' Suzannah said. 'I appreciate your taking the time to see me. Dr Gaspard requested an informal consult from me on the Tricia Fiore case.'

Munley nodded energetically but looked a little uneasy.

'Ed called me in because I was a resident in neurosurgery,' she explained, 'before I switched to general surgery. Both Ed and I feel that the psychiatry of this situation is at least as important as the neurology.' Suzannah knew she was flattering him now, but he looked like the type who needed it.

'I see, I see.' Munley seemed reassured. He gazed at her with frank interest. 'Neurosurgery and then general surgery.' When she did not explain, he said, 'Where did you do your neurosurgical work?'

'NIH and Washington General.'

'Under Roland Lancaster, by any chance?'

'Yes.' Suzannah began to feel impatient. She wanted to talk about Tricia Fiore, not herself or Roland Lancaster. Munley is just curious, she reminded herself. Perfectly natural.

Munley tapped his thumbs together, gazing at her with obvious respect. 'Did you work on the visual implant?'

'Yes, I did.'

'Ah. I was wondering how you happened to be talking to Tricia just before she made the attempt, but you must know her from the pilot study.'

'Yes.'

'You've kept in touch, then?'

'Not as much as I would have liked.'

Munley studied her. 'Is the microchip your interest in this? You think maybe it caused Tricia to attempt suicide?'

Suzannah realized she must be careful. This was the perfect opening to ask the questions most on her mind. But she had no idea whether Munley was discreet. She had come here to find the truth, not start rumours about the microchip. 'I can think of no physical reason why the microchip should be involved,' she said. *Except that it is planted in the brain and only the computer knows exactly how it works.* 'Of course, you're in a better position to assess any effects of the microchip on Tricia than I am. Did *she* feel it was causing her any problems?'

Munley waved his hand dismissively. 'Oh, from time to time, but it was a delusion, of course. Poor woman. She was suffering from schizophrenia with prominent paranoia, so it was quite natural for her to believe the microchip was at fault. A victim of schizophrenia feels his mind slipping and wants desperately to believe there is some outside agent at work. They complain about radio signals in their heads, wrap their ankles with foil to keep out the rays, et cetera.'

'Were there any unusual features to her schizophrenia?'

Munley tipped back in his chair, staring at the ceiling a moment. Suzannah noted that the chair didn't let out a single squeak. She pictured him down on his knees oiling it every day, after he checked the plants for height. 'Can't think of anything unusual,' Munley said. 'She was under pressure at school and she decompensated, started hearing voices and so on. Towards the end, a lot of depression got mixed in. In fact, a few weeks ago I hospitalized her at Lee General, here in Fairfax. I feared suicide.'

'Did she threaten it?'

'No. But she seemed so down, I thought it best. She showed a marked improvement, and I could hardly justify keeping her there any longer. Then–' Munley gave her a bleak look, spreading his hands– 'I wish now I hadn't discharged her, of course.'

'Dr Munley – Vince – it would be very helpful if I could take a look through her file.'

'That would be fine if I'd kept any notes on her case.'

Suzannah looked at him, surprised. 'No notes? How about tapes?'

'Nothing. I'm a bit paranoid myself when it comes to putting my patients' lives down on paper. The courts can subpoena that stuff, you know, and your doctor–patient confidentiality goes right out the window. No, no. I used to keep rudimentary notes, but I even gave that up. Harder for me, but safer for the patient.'

Suzannah glanced at the filing cabinet behind his desk. Munley had draped it with a geometrically aligned table-cloth. A potted geranium sat in the precise centre of the cloth. She found Munley gazing at her and knew he'd caught her implication. He said nothing.

Why didn't she believe him? Maybe because he was so organized. It would be very hard for a man like Munley to let Tricia's words in therapy disappear into thin air week after week. He would want a record, probably a very detailed and comprehensive record.

If she was right, why would Munley lie?

Up to now he'd seemed completely forthcoming. What might be in Tricia's file that the good Dr Munley didn't want her to see?

She said, 'So you would say Tricia is a paranoid schizophrenic with severe depression. There was nothing unusual about her case, and the suicide attempt was not unexpected.'

'That about sums it up. I have been in to see Tricia, of course, and I'm looking forward to working closely with you and Dr Gaspard on the case. Adams Memorial is a fine hospital for neurology.'

He's politely brushing me off now, Suzannah thought. She weighed her options. Tricia had said, 'They want me dead.' Paranoid fantasy or reality? If she could just have five minutes with a comprehensive psychiatric write-up on Tricia, she would know. Should she confront Munley, press him?

No. There was nothing she could do short of accusing him of lying. Where would that get her? He'd given every appearance of co-operating fully.

Suzannah stood. 'I appreciate your time.'

'Glad I could help. If you have any questions, just call. I'll be around to see Tricia regularly, of course.' He ushered her to the door, a hand lightly on her back. 'Goodbye, Suzannah.'

'Goodbye, Vince.'

Suzannah drove home from Vincent Munley's office feeling irritated and impotent. She was convinced something was wrong with the microchip but could think of no way to prove it. Tricia couldn't talk, her psychiatrist was happy to talk but wouldn't say anything.

And Andrew Dugan *would* not talk.

Suzannah thought of the strange interlude with Andrew. It was starting to worry her. *So little time.* He'd said it twice. He was in great inner pain. She did not know enough about him to know if he could kill himself, but she mustn't ignore the possibility – especially after Tricia's attempt. And she wasn't ignoring it. She had called his house every chance she'd had this afternoon between patients. But his phone just rang endlessly; not even an answering machine spoke to her. It gave her a bad feeling. She kept imagining Andrew lying sprawled in his bed, a bullet hole in his temple, the phone only a few feet from his hand ringing and ringing.

She felt pain in her knuckles and realized she was gripping the steering wheel with all her strength. She forced her fingers to relax. There was one more thing she could do. She could go to his house, now. Pound on the door. If Andrew didn't answer, she could at least check for lights on, music playing inside, sounds of movement. She could look for broken windows, any sign that something was wrong.

Suzannah drove past Arlington Forest and continued east on Route 50, heading for Washington. She took the Fort Myer exit, circling back and over Route 50, then down through the steel and glass canyon of Rosslyn. Key Bridge loomed in front of her, arching across the dark Potomac like a jewelled bracelet. In Georgetown, she turned right off the bridge onto M Street. Despite the cold, the sidewalks were full, people in leather coats and furs hurrying between the restaurants, jazz clubs and theatres. Suzannah drove uphill into the residential heart of Georgetown, picturesque, tree-lined blocks of old town houses and apartments, stately and quiet under the soft wintry glow of streetlights. She slowed, trying to see the numbers on the dark fronts of the houses. There it was, a brick-fronted place with elaborate stonework around the door and under the eaves. Stone lions guarded the front steps.

There were no lights on inside.

Suzannah stared at the darkened house, uncertain. The place looked so peaceful. I've come this far, she thought; I'm not quitting now. She looked up and down the street for a parking space. There was none; of course not. This was Georgetown. The second time around the block, she noticed someone sitting in a blue Ford right across the street from Andrew's house. She stopped beside the car and tried to get the driver's attention, hoping he might be about to pull out. After a sidelong glance, he turned away from her, busying himself with something on the car seat. A car behind her honked and she was forced to move on. Finally, she found a space four blocks downhill from Andrew's.

As she hiked back up the hill, she began to shiver in the cold. She hurried up the walk between the stone lions to a magnificent double doorway of carved oak. On each massive door, brass rings dangled from eagle's beaks. She banged one against its plate, watching her breath stream out, trying to control her shivering.

No answer. She kept knocking. The house remained dark

and silent. Turning, she saw the man in the blue car watching her. Again he turned away.

He's staking out the house! Suzannah realized.

She walked down the sidewalk and away, taking care not to look at the man in the blue Ford again. Her mind raced: Andrew had asked her if people were watching her house. And now it appeared someone was watching his. Did that mean Andrew was in there? Possibly, or the man might be keeping a lookout in case he came back.

Suzannah walked uphill another block, turned down the street behind Andrew's, and peered through the trees in people's back yards until she located the back of Andrew's place. If Andrew's there, she thought, he might need help.

I'll have to break in.

Her heart began to pound. She felt a strange excitement. This was crazy, but it felt right. At least she was doing something.

At the house that backed onto his, she headed up the narrow driveway as if she belonged there. The driveway ended at an ancient wooden garage so narrow it could only have been built for a Model T. An alley, steeped in shadow, ran back between it and a high brick wall that encircled the back yard next door. Suzannah stepped sideways into the gap, trying to see ahead to the back of Andrew's house. It was very dark in the alley. She edged deeper, eyes straining, feeling the brick wall angle in against her shoulder. A crust of snow sliced at her ankles. She smelled urine. A cat or dog, she told herself firmly. A man wouldn't fit in here.

Just when it seemed the brick wall would converge with the rear corner of the garage, she squeezed through into Andrew's back yard. She crouched against the rear of the garage, scanning the yard. If they had a man out front, there might be one watching the back, too. She made herself hold still, searching along the brick wall that surrounded the yard, looking for a mist of breath, any sign of movement. Her teeth began to chatter. If someone *was* back here, he would have frozen to death by now.

She crept along the wall into the narrow crease between Andrew's house and the next, feeling a little safer. Now no one could see her unless they looked straight up the alley. Small windows, grimy with the residue of the last snowfall, looked out from Andrew's basement. She pushed at the sash of one. It wouldn't budge, probably hadn't been opened in years. Taking off her scarf, she wrapped it around her feet and sat with her back against the foundation of the neighbour's house. Planting her protected feet against the edges of the glass, she slowly straightened her legs. The window resisted, then popped inward. She heard the muted tinkle of glass below.

Scrambling forward, she used the scarf to clear the remaining glass from the window frame. She crouched on the cold ground and backed through the opening. Her feet landed on something solid that moved an inch or two under her – a table or bench. The basement was pitch black. She felt her way down from the table. Her heart pounded in fear and exhilaration. She had done it, broken in.

Now if she could just see her hand in front of her face.

She heard a sudden *whoosh* and jumped, startled, then realized it was the furnace kicking in. The pilot had lit the burners, sending a weak blue light into the room. In the dim glow, she could make out steps across the basement from her. She hurried up, through a door, into a small kitchen. It was dark, but nothing like the basement. Light from the street filtered back dimly through the house. She walked quietly towards the front of the house, passing through a large dining-room. After a quick search of the downstairs, she started up the house's central staircase.

Upstairs, a floorboard creaked.

Suzannah froze. 'Andrew?' she said softly. 'It's me, Suzannah.'

Silence.

She looked up the staircase into darkness. Shapes swirled in its soft depths, like the things you saw inside your eyelids when your eyes were closed. The silence seemed to breathe, a pressure on the eardrums halfway between hearing and imagination.

Giving herself no time to think, Suzannah mounted the stairs. She edged down the hall, looking into a library and a bathroom, both empty. The next-to-last door opened onto Andrew's studio. Four skylights, invisible from the street, flooded the room with the silvery night-bounce of Georgetown's lights. Suzannah inhaled the oil and turpentine fragrance of the room with a feeling close to reverence. This was where he had done the glorious paintings at the showing the other night. It was like seeing Gershwin's piano or Steinbeck's typewriter. There was his easel, in the middle of the room. It held a large canvas up to the eerie light. The canvas was blank.

A final door awaited her at the end of the hall. It must be Andrew's bedroom. Was he lying in there, hurt or dead? Dread rose in her as she opened the door and stepped through. In the weak glow of a nightlight, she could make out a huge four-poster bed.

Andrew was not on the bed.

An open suitcase was.

Relieved and mystified, she sat down on the bed, running a hand along the case. It was expensive leather, completely empty. Beside it, the spread bore the imprint of another case.

On the bed table, Suzannah saw a framed photograph. She took it to the nightlight and examined it. The photo was of an attractive woman with short dark hair. Her intense eyes peered directly, almost aggressively into the camera. Her smile was bright and confident. Across an upper corner was scrawled, *Love always, Darcy*. Suzannah remembered reading about the Dugan divorce in the style section of the *Post* several years ago. None of the details came back to her. But she sensed, looking at Darcy's photo, that the woman had not written 'always' lightly.

Suzannah noticed that the glass in the frame was smudged, as though Andrew picked it up often. For the first time, she felt like an intruder.

Carefully, she put the photo back in its place.

A car passed in the street below, the faint wash of its headlights illuminating the far wall of the bedroom. Suzannah went to the window, easing her head past the curtain until she could see the blue Ford across the street.

Its driver stood beside the car, staring at the house.

Suzannah jerked her head back, startled. Was he going to come in? She would be trapped upstairs. Maybe he was just stretching his legs.

She risked another quick peek.

The man was headed across the street. Suzannah ran out of the bedroom and hurried down the stairs. At the back door she grappled with the knob, opening the door just wide enough to slip through, then easing it shut before racing across the snowy back yard. When she got to the street behind Andrew's again, she let herself slow to a trot.

As she drove out of Georgetown, she watched the rearview mirror for the blue Ford. It did not appear. Her fear eased at last. That was close. Crossing the bridge back into Virginia, she felt calmer. All right, think: a man staking out Andrew's house, waiting for him to come back. Who? The same people who were watching her own house?

Andrew had said, *You must be very careful now.* Despite the warming blast from the Chevy's heater, Suzannah shuddered.

# 13

Jay Mallernee stared at his word processor, burning with frustration. The dark blue screen sat becalmed before him like the Gulf during the war, mined and treacherous. He was disgusted with himself. Coming back from Austin, he'd really believed the block was broken, that he'd be able to get going.

Though Suzannah hadn't actually come right out and said it at Theismann's last night, she'd been thinking it and she was right: he was royally stuck.

He raised his hands from his lap, unclenching his fists, wiggling the stiff fingers. I am a professional reporter, he thought. I write thousands of words a day. I have been sitting here all damn day without writing a single decent sentence.

He pounded out a new paragraph about life in the press pool out in the Gulf. It was horrible, flat and dead. He wiped it out letter by letter, jabbing at the delete key.

Pushing back from the computer screen, he stalked across his apartment, cracking his knuckles. His face felt tight, as though someone had grabbed the skin on the back of his head and pulled all the slack out of it. He could smell his own sweat, feel his T-shirt clinging wetly to him even as the bitter January wind rattled the den's picture window. He gazed across Twenty-first Street at the drab brick facade of the

University Hall apartment building. Most of the curtains were drawn over there, but in one window a short man leaned on his own desk, sorting through some papers. Probably a George Washington professor, plotting tomorrow's lecture.

Jay thought about trying to call Suzannah again. She'd been tied up all day – a big car crash, her secretary had said, that had pushed all her operations back. Which, of course, rippled down the line to her office patients. At eight, she was still at the hospital – an emergency appendectomy. That makes a hundred and one, Jay thought, remembering her remark at the restaurant. Suzannah was a brilliant woman, but she just didn't understand about writing. It must be wonderful to have your work walk into your office, or roll into your Operating Room; to not have to drag it out of thin air.

Jay checked his watch. Ten p.m. Surely she'd be home by now.

Write one acceptable sentence, one, he told himself. Then you can call her. He stared out of the window. Just start at the beginning, he thought.

Instead, he remembered the end, going into the apartment building in Kuwait City with the triumphant Kuwaiti soldiers. They were supposed to rendezvous with a leader of the underground, a man who had funnelled intelligence to the Allies. Jay could recall precisely what he had felt going in: the pride of being one of the first American reporters into the city, mixed with a gut-tightening fear that Iraqi soldiers might still be around. There had been shooting earlier, just down the street.

The Kuwaiti with the sergeant's stripes and a Foreign Legion-style cap waved him in behind his squad, shouting, 'Come on, no problem, no problem.'

He ran in. Even inside, the air was hazy with thin black

smoke, raw with the stench of flaming oil. The long Persian carpets in the hall had been desecrated with hundreds of filthy boot prints. Iraqi graffiti defaced the gleaming ceramic tiles of the wall. An old man limped towards them down the dim corridor, talking rapidly to the sergeant, pointing back behind him. The sergeant's face darkened.

'What's he saying?' Jay asked.

'Torture. In a room at the end. The Iraqis raped and tortured – I mean, Kuwaiti women. Come, come.'

Jay followed the men down the hallway, feeling a dragging stiffness in his legs. Suddenly he did not want to be there. The sergeant burst into the room at the end of the hall. His squad followed, shoving each other to get in the door. Jay had a sense of unreality, as though he were watching the Keystone Kops. But there was nothing funny in it. These men, like the oil wells outside their city, were burning, their mouths charred with adrenaline, their eyes bloodshot from smoke and fury and tears.

Jay slipped through into the room behind the squad. One of the men pointed at blood on the floor, shouting at him in Arabic. The brownish bloodstains were everywhere, twisting patterns smeared across the tiles. Jay's eyes swam in the stinging haze. The soldier shouted more vehemently.

'He wants you to – I mean, write the blood down,' the Kuwaiti sergeant said.

Jay took out his notebook and scribbled a few words: *I try not to see the corpses that are no longer here – the bodies that bled these stains.*

The soldier grinned at him and nodded.

A man stepped into the room. He was tall. He wore the *keffiyeh*, the traditional headcloth, banded by a red *akal*. His face was deeply tanned, but his eyes were a dazzling Nordic blue. Jay remembered Peter O'Toole in the movie *Lawrence of Arabia.* The Kuwaiti sergeant stiffened into an approximation of attention, and Jay realized the man was the underground contact they had come to meet. The soldiers backed away a bit, their faces respectful. Jay felt the man's blue gaze centre on him. There was something very disturbing in his eyes.

'My name is Mallernee,' Jay said, 'from the *Washington Post.*' He prepared to counter the man's objections to his being present, marshalling assurances that he wouldn't report names or give any identifying physical characteristics or the location.

The man said nothing.

Surely he speaks English, Jay thought.

At that instant, two Kuwaitis ran into the room dragging with them a thin Arab boy dressed only in fatigue pants . . .

And the memory ended, as though a black curtain had descended over it. Jay was standing again in his apartment, gazing out of his window at the night. 'No,' he said. His voice felt raw in his throat.

The phone rang, jarring him. He leaned his face onto the windowpane, feeling the shock of cold glass against his feverish forehead. The phone rang four more times, then it cut off and there was a moment of silence while his taped message ran. The phone beeped, and Suzannah started talking. 'Jay, if you're there, please pick up.'

Jay pushed away from the window and hurried to the phone. 'Well, hello there!'

'Oh, good,' she said, her voice filled with relief. 'I was wondering if I could drop by.'

Jay felt a bright cleansing rush in his head. 'Of course. Come right over.'

'Thanks. I'll be there in twenty.'

Jay waited until she hung up, then put the phone gently

back into its cradle. He stood for a second, wondering about the undercurrent of strain in Suzannah's voice.

Never mind, he would find out soon enough.

He ran into the utility room, no time for a shower. Tearing off his sweaty undershirt, he stuck his head under the spigot of the laundry sink and lathered up with shampoo. He rubbed briskly, scrubbing his face and underarms with the shampoo, then stuck his head back under the rushing water, thinking that the mess in the kitchen must be first, then the newspapers all over the living-room floor, did he have any wine, what about shaving? Yes, he must shave.

Towelling off, he brushed his hair back, squirted a dollop of Barbasol onto the stubble on his chin. He flicked away with the razor, wondering about his shirts.

Ouch, *damn!*

He finished up, rinsing, sticking toilet paper on the bleeding cut. Old Spice under his arms, a splash of Polo on his face. He replaced the soggy blood-soaked bit of toilet paper, then ran into his bedroom to pull the blanket up over the bed and kick his fallen clothes into the closet.

The cotton sweater, good. He pulled it on, careful not to mess his hair. Dashing through the living-room, he side-kicked the week's pile of newspapers across the parquet and out of sight under the low couch. Grabbing up the two Lone Star empties, he loped into the kitchen, stuffed the beer bottles and pizza box into the trash, dumped the pile of encrusted dishes willy-nilly in the dishwasher, wiped the bread crumbs off the counter into the open door then slammed the dishwasher shut. He shook two spearmint Tic Tacs from the little plastic box in the silverware drawer and, sucking hard on them, took another turn through the living-room, scanning, straightening throw rugs.

Suzannah was under stress; he'd felt it in her body when

they'd made love at the hotel, and he'd sensed it again at dinner last night. She wasn't just worried about him, she was worried about herself. Useless to push her until she asked for help, which she rarely did. He hoped she would do so now. Take his mind off his own troubles.

Back into the bathroom, just to make sure, but it sparkled, thank goodness – the one room in the house that he couldn't bear to let slide.

What had he forgotten? Something, he was sure of it.

He strode to the CD, picked out some Charlie Byrd, and pushed *play*. Mellow guitar started up as the door buzzer sounded.

He walked to the door, his mind racing.

The toilet paper!

Carefully, he eased the blood-crusted patch off the shaving cut, wadded it into a tiny ball, and stuffed it in the pocket of his jeans as he pulled the door open.

Her face was pink from the cold. The wind had fluffed her dark brown hair into a thick wild mane. Her eyes, the neat strong jaw, the full mouth, were all set with determination. He could smell her bath oil, a soft musk. The fake fur collar braced her hair from beneath.

Jay leaned into her, kissing her on the mouth. A moment of stiffness, then Suzannah joined in fully. He held it until he needed to breathe, pulling back.

She gave him a half smile. 'May I come in?'

'Of course,' he said, feeling foolish. He helped her off with her coat. She sat on the leather and chrome couch. As he was about to sit beside her, he realized he wanted to look at her. The rocker his grandaddy had carved faced the couch. He settled in it.

'Sorry to barge in on you so late,' she said.

'Don't be silly.'

She glanced at the computer screen, which was still on. 'I hope I didn't interrupt your work.'

'Time for a break, anyway.' He smiled, hoping he was not being too transparent, got up, and walked over to turn off the computer.

He returned to the rocker. 'How about a glass of wine? Or a Coke and bourbon?'

'No, thanks. So how's it coming?'

'Fine, just fine.'

'There's so much material, so many ways to organize it, I imagine it's hard to pick one. Maybe if you went through your old columns, lined them up according to date –'

'It's going fine. Don't worry.' He realized he'd sounded irritated and smiled again to cover up. 'But something is on *your* mind.'

Suzannah gazed at him a moment longer, her mouth tight. He knew she wanted to help him, but there was nothing she could do, and he didn't want to dump on her anyway. She had enough trouble with all the medical crises and dying patients and telling people they had cancer. She didn't need to grapple with his demons too. He got up and sat beside her, taking her hand. It was cold, as though she'd been outside for an hour rather than just running up from her car. Sitting close to her, he could feel his heart pounding. She was so beautiful, so bright, the essence of everything he wanted. The longing he felt for her made an aching hollow in the centre of his chest. 'Tell me what's bothering you, Suze.'

She took a deep breath, blew it out. 'I think something's wrong with the microchip, and Roland Lancaster is refusing to admit it.'

Jay felt his mind focusing. 'Lancaster.'

'Yes.' Something in her voice warned him that she did not want to talk about Lancaster. She never wanted to talk about him. She'd told him about her crushing disappointment, just once, and after that discouraged every attempt he'd made to discuss it.

'I think it may go beyond Lancaster,' Suzannah said.

He listened with growing uneasiness as she told him about Andrew Dugan and Tricia Fiore and the man watching Andrew's house. Andrew's warning that she must forget the microchip. Part of him was alarmed for Suzannah. But he felt a quickening in his stomach too, the old reporter's reflexes, dormant for months, giving a little kick. It might be a hell of a story.

But he already had a hell of a story, and he couldn't seem to put down the first word of it.

'Every time I try to get some hard answers,' Suzannah said, 'I run into a brick wall or another mystery. Jay, Andrew's furnace was still running, but there was luggage on his bed—'

'Wait a minute,' he said, startled. 'You were *inside* Andrew Dugan's house? How, if he wasn't there?'

'I broke in.'

Hell and damnation, Jay thought. She had real steel in her. She had the kind of nerves he'd trust to shoot a rattler off his boot – provided she'd ever give in and let him teach her how to shoot. 'You should have called me.'

'I didn't go over there expecting to break in. It was a spur-of-the-moment thing.'

'I'll wager it was.'

'The point is, it appears he packed and left in a big hurry. Whoever that was outside his house, Andrew is afraid of him. I think there's more here, even, than a problem with the microchip.'

'You're probably right.'

She turned towards him on the couch, taking his hands

again. She started to say something, then hesitated. Her cheeks turned a shade pinker. 'I imagine as a reporter you've probably had to do some pretty, uh, creative things in your time in order to get a story. I remember reading about a *Post* reporter who picked the lock of a publisher's warehouse to get at the advance copies of some memoirs. Nixon, I think, or maybe it was Reagan.'

'Suzannah, stop beating around the bush. What are you getting at?'

'I think Tricia Fiore's psychiatrist was lying when he said he kept no notes on Tricia.'

'And you want me to help you break into his office.'

'Right.'

Jay grinned. 'Well, what are we waiting for?'

# 14

A fierce tension gripped Suzannah's neck and shoulders as she watched Jay work on Dr Munley's office door. She glanced up and down the long hall. Still empty. Recessed ceiling lights glowed on the earth-tone carpet, making the building seem sleepy and peaceful. But any second a night watchman could step into the hall.

'Can't you hurry?' Suzannah whispered.

'Sure,' Jay whispered back. 'But not if you want me to pick this lock.'

Suzannah had a sudden powerful urge to laugh. It purged her of some of the tension. She gazed fondly at Jay. What would she do without him?

'Got it,' Jay said softly. He pocketed his set of files and picks and pushed the door inward an inch. 'You sure about this?'

'I'm sure,' she said. 'But if you're not . . .'

Jay pushed the door the rest of the way open. She moved in front of him into Munley's waiting room, relieved to be out of the hallway. A lamp on one of the tables gave a soft light to the row of chairs. The magazines had been squared up with the edges of the table. She could imagine Vince Munley doing it on his way out each evening. She felt a twinge of regret at what she was doing. Aside from the fact that Munley had told her nothing, he seemed a decent, likeable man. She was invading his office, not his home, and she would not use anything she might find against him, but still it made her feel shabby. *Yes, Judge. I broke into Dr Munley's office, but I didn't enjoy it.*

Jay bent to examine the lock on Munley's inner office. 'Whoa, Nellie,' he murmured. 'That's odd.'

'What?'

'This lock is top of the line – much better than the hall door. Usually, the inside doors are pushovers.'

'Just how much practice have you had at this?'

'Before I answer that, can you be forced to testify at my trial?'

'Jay . . .'

'Sorry. Bad joke.'

'Can you open it?'

'I think so.'

Jay knelt in front of the lock. His body went very still, the broad shoulders barely moving as his fingers worked at the lock. How delicate his touch was. She was not surprised. She had felt those gentle hands on herself.

Jay pushed Munley's door open.

'Bravo!' Suzannah said. She followed him into the office. Closing the door behind them, he turned the bolt. The room's obsessive neatness struck her again, the books all perfectly aligned on the shelves, the clean desktop.

Come on, Munley, she thought. You keep patient files, and we both know it.

She went straight to the oak filing cabinet with the plant on top. Without moving the plant, she rolled the tablecloth up away from the drawers. 'We've got to be very careful,' she explained. 'Our guy is obsessively neat and clean. If we don't leave everything exactly as we found it, he'll know.'

Jay nodded. The cabinet lock seemed not to challenge him at all. He pulled the top drawer open and moved away. Lying down on Munley's Freudian-style couch, he laced his hands behind his neck, the picture of total relaxation. Suzannah looked in the drawer. There were only three manila folders, too few to be Munley's patient files. She glanced through them quickly. They contained financial records, clippings from psychiatric and psychological journals, and a pack of Rorschach cards.

All right, the bottom drawer then. Hoping, Suzannah slid it out.

It was full of coupons.

Hundreds and hundreds of coupons. The stale smell of ancient paper drifted up from the drawer. She sifted through the coupons, not knowing whether to laugh or cry. Here was one for ten cents off a package of Bisquick. It had expired in 1987. Another one offered a nickel off on Fizzies. Fizzies? She must have been four years old when they had gone off the market. 'What's the opposite of Bingo?' she asked.

'Oshit,' Jay said.

Suzannah looked around the room. There was nothing else remotely resembling a file. They could check behind the receptionist's counter on the way out, but Munley was unlikely to keep confidential files there. So much for my hunches, Suzannah thought, discouraged.

'I'm afraid we broke in here for nothing,' she said. She plunged her hand into the coupons again, stirring them around. Her fingers closed on something that was not a coupon. She lifted it through the mass of paper, a flat plastic tab like a credit card, except that it was blank. A strip of magnetic tape ran along the lower edge. Her spirits lifted. 'Look, what's this?'

Jay took the tab from her. 'I've seen one of these.' He turned it over, eyes narrowing in concentration.

Suzannah heard a soft click from the waiting room. Alarm shot through her. 'Did you hear that?' she whispered.

Jay nodded, staring at Munley's office door.

Someone must have come in from the hall, Suzannah thought. The night watchman? She scanned the room, looking for a place to hide. Jay eased the file drawers shut and dropped the tablecloth back in place. Suzannah fought panic. There was no good place to hide, except behind the desk. She got down behind it, pulling Jay down with her, knowing it wouldn't save them if the watchman did more than stick his head in.

Seconds crawled by. The night watchman did not stick his head in. Suzannah's nerves stretched to snapping point. She wanted to bolt, run out the door, anything to have it over. As if he sensed it, Jay draped a cautionary arm across her back.

Small ticking sounds filtered through the lock on Munley's inner door. Suzannah realized it wasn't the night watchman. Someone was trying to pick the lock – someone else!

'I just figured out what this bad boy is,' Jay whispered, looking at the plastic tab.

'Shhh.'

He rose from behind the desk and went to the bookcase, bypassing the rows of perfectly aligned volumes to prod at the plate of a light switch beside the case.

The scratching sound continued to trickle through the lock. If the man on the other side of that door was as good as Jay, it would open in seconds. Suzannah's mouth went dry. She would rather face a night watchman than a burglar, possibly armed and panicky. She rose and went to Jay's side.

He was digging at the switch plate with his fingernails now. What on earth?

The plate slid aside, revealing not an electrical switch box but a metal plate with a slot down the middle. Jay slipped the plastic card into the slot.

The bookcase slid silently three feet to the right.

Suzannah stared, dumbfounded, into a small hidden room. Inside it, a soft light winked on as the bookcase completed its slide. At the same instant, a television monitor set into the room's back wall winked on.

The handle on the door rattled.

Suzannah switched off the office lights and hurried into the hidden room, pulling Jay in after her. Jay reached out to rotate the switch plate back into its normal position. The bookcase rolled back the other way, hiding them just as the bolt on Munley's office door slid open with a loud snick.

Suzannah's heart pounded. That was too close!

Jay nudged her and pointed at the TV screen. It showed a tall man with a nylon stocking drawn tight over his head walking across Munley's office. He went straight to Munley's file, lifting the tablecloth back, just as they had done a moment earlier. Suzannah stared at the monitor with a mixture of dread and fascination. The nylon stocking gave the man's face a horrid alien look. The contrast with his expensive suit, white shirt, and tie somehow made it even worse. The man pulled the unlocked file open. He looked through both drawers with quick efficiency. Settling back on his heels, he stared at the mass of coupons, his expression unreadable beneath the smear of nylon.

After a moment, he stood and scanned the room, his body rotating slowly in place, robot-like. For a second, the awful face stared straight at the hidden camera, straight at her. Then he moved on.

Despite her fear, Suzannah felt excited. Clearly, the masked intruder was after Munley's therapy notes too – presumably, Tricia's file.

The man on the screen shook his head and slipped from the office, closing the door carefully behind himself.

Who was he? Suzannah wondered. If he *was* after Tricia's file, best guess is he wants it because of the microchip. Which would mean we're on the right track.

'Fortunately,' Jay said, 'the camera doesn't appear to be hooked up to a video recorder. Otherwise, ol' Doc Munley could sit back and watch us on his home movies tomorrow. He sure did go to a lot of trouble, setting up this cozy little hidey-hole. Kind of makes you wonder why.'

Suzannah saw a cabinet in the corner, a twin to the one outside. 'I don't know,' she said, 'unless there's something awfully important in there.'

Jay walked over and pulled the top drawer open. Suzannah held her breath, hoping. An odd expression crossed his face as he looked inside.

'What?' Suzannah said.

He pulled a pair of black lace panties from the drawer, dangling them from a finger. Then he pulled out a corset, a garter belt, and a big bra, also in black. Two large falsies fell out of the bra and bounced on the floor. Jay gave her such a thunderstruck look that she burst out laughing. Reaching into the drawer again, Jay pulled out a flaming red wig and a pair of man-sized high-heeled shoes. 'Well, damn my eyes. It looks like hoarding coupons isn't Doc Munley's only secret.'

Suzannah tried to wipe the smile from her face. 'It's not funny.'

'Nope,' Jay agreed solemnly. 'It's hilarious, that's what it is.'

'It's sad. I wish I hadn't seen this.'

146

'I wish I hadn't seen what this makes me imagine,' Jay said.

'Maybe they're not Munley's. Maybe he got a patient to give them to him.'

'I imagine that must be it, all right.'

'Put them back.'

Carefully, Jay tucked the transvestite gear back into the open drawer. 'I'm almost scared to open the bottom one,' he said.

'Just do it, will you?'

He pulled it open. It was packed with manila folders.

Suzannah knelt at the file and winnowed through the folders. They were alphabetized, of course. With a feeling of triumph, she pulled out Tricia Fiore's file. It wasn't very thick. She scanned the pages of close, neat handwriting. According to Munley's notes, Tricia Fiore had been in therapy with him for just under four months. Her presenting complaint was that she was seeing visions. Suzannah felt the chill of the words through Munley's antiseptic prose. It was a possible sign of schizophrenia, but, from what she remembered of her first-year psychiatry rotation, visual hallucinations were much rarer than auditory ones. Certain drugs could make people see things, but Tricia Fiore, a devoted grade school teacher, was hardly the type to be experimenting with LSD or PCP.

Suzannah read quickly through Munley's diagnostic notes, making sure he'd gone through the proper steps to rule out drugs as a cause. He had; he had come up with the tentative diagnosis of either schizophrenia or a brain tumour. He then tentatively ruled out tumour with a CT scan. He put Tricia on Haldol, 1.5 mg b.i.d., and started a course of psychotherapy.

Interesting. From what Sharon Harrad had told her, most

psychiatrists did not believe one-on-one psychotherapy was very useful with schizophrenics. Did Munley still harbour some doubts about his diagnosis?

Suzannah turned her attention to the therapy notes. From the first session, Tricia made it quite clear that she felt her 'visions' were being caused by the microchip that had been implanted in the 'vision centre' of her brain by Dr Roland Lancaster in a pilot study four years earlier. She freely acknowledged that the microchip had corrected her vision perfectly and, for the first three and a half years, caused her no problems whatsoever. She had been delighted with the microchip during that time, not just because it made her teaching so much easier but because she loved being able to see her pupils' faces clearly for the first time. She could join in their games at recess. She no longer suffered the severe headaches that holding their homework inches from her eyes had caused when her eyesight was so poor. Tricia Fiore was a happy woman.

Then the visions started.

Four months ago, Tricia was brushing her teeth as she got ready for bed when suddenly, as clearly as 'a movie running in her head', she saw one of her students, Larry Washington, being badly beaten by two older boys. The boys beat him until he didn't move anymore. She saw him lying on the pavement, eyes closed, blood running from his battered nose.

The extreme vividness of the vision startled and unnerved Tricia. After a few hours, though, she'd been able to convince herself that it was due to weariness. She'd been working too hard, that's all.

The next morning, as she was sitting in her empty classroom getting ready for the day, an assistant principal had come in with the news that Larry Washington was in the hospital. He had been mugged by two older boys. Tricia was deeply shaken. The administrator, seeing her reaction, called in a substitute teacher. Tricia went at once to the hospital. Larry's eyes were swollen almost shut. His nose had been broken.

Holding the boy's hand, she kept thinking, I saw this! The knowledge made her almost frantic for a while. She knew no one would believe her. So in the next days and weeks she tried to put it out of her mind. But then she began to have other 'visions'. Tricia admitted that actual events varied in minor details from the visions that preceded them. But even these minor discrepancies began to fade. Tricia insisted in therapy that her visions, in all important details, were coming true. Therefore, she was not going crazy. The only other thing she felt could explain it was the microchip. So she went to Dr Roland Lancaster, who had implanted the device. The meeting with him obsessed her. In therapy, she kept coming back to it, complaining over and over about how cold Dr Lancaster had been. She even accused him of threatening her.

Suzannah felt the notes curling in the furious grip of her fist. She forced her hand to relax.

Munley wrote, 'I conferred with Dr Lancaster and am satisfied that his conduct with my patient was exemplary. He stated he did his best to allay Tricia's fears, assuring her that there was no neurological foundation for her complaint and none of the other test subjects had reported her symptoms. In his remarks to me, Dr Lancaster agreed completely with my theory that Miss Fiore is suffering from a psychosis unrelated (except, possibly, psychosomatically) to the microchip. This psychosis has, as one of its features, a confusion regarding time. That is, the events Miss Fiore believes she is seeing in advance have, of course, already taken place. She recalls them vividly and then, because her sense of time and the chronology of events is distorted by her psychosis, mistakes these recollections for prophetic visions. Delusions of this sort are not unheard of in schizophrenia, and it is certainly not credible, on the face of it, that Miss Fiore could be having actual prophetic visions. Moreover, her most persistent vision, in which she sees men watching her, are of a classic paranoid nature. She admits that she has not been able to verify this particular "vision" with actual evidence of any surveillance.

'It might be added that Dr Lancaster would certainly have some reason to be upset by Miss Fiore's charges about his remarkable visual implant since, if made public, they could present a wholly unfounded barrier to the hopes of thousands of people for having normal vision restored to them. I assured Dr Lancaster I would do all I could to help Miss Fiore contain her psychosis.'

Suzannah closed the file. So that was why Munley had denied he took any notes. Roland Lancaster had co-opted him. She could imagine it: the great man – the Jonas Salk of neuroscience, certain to become a Nobel laureate – takes into his confidence an undistinguished psychiatrist in private practice. *I agree with your diagnosis completely, Dr Munley. Tricia Fiore is obviously a paranoid schiz with severe time distortion. Very good call. I'm glad she's in your care. I know I can depend on you.*

Suzannah opened the file again, a bitter taste in her mouth. There was no time for reaction now; she had to finish and get herself and Jay out of Munley's office. She scanned the rest of Tricia's file. Lately, Tricia had become steadily more agitated in sessions. Though she insisted she was still taking her medication, she said it was doing no good. Munley increased the dose, with no better effect. Finally, when

Tricia kept insisting that men were watching her, the psychiatrist arranged for her hospitalization. After two weeks at Lee General, all Tricia's symptoms cleared up. Munley was greatly encouraged.

She pretended she was well to fool Munley, Suzannah thought. She knew she had to act as if her symptoms had cleared up if she wanted to get out of the ward.

A final note said that Tricia had been given a three-day pass. Under this note, Munley had written, *Suicide attempt, 22 Dec. Hosp. Adams Memorial*.

How cryptic Munley suddenly had turned. Suicide, the great rebuke.

Suzannah closed the file, deeply disturbed by what she had read. The microchip was designed to enhance vision, not *visions*.

Was there any way in the world it might be doing both?

The idea seemed crazy, and yet how much did anyone really know about the microchip? It worked as intended. That startling, wonderful fact had obscured another fact: how it worked was a secret locked inside the microchip and the big CM5 computer that had fathered it, a secret too complex for human comprehension.

The file felt suddenly slick and Suzannah realized her hands were sweating. She put the folder back in the cabinet and closed the drawer.

'Well?' Jay said. 'Do you think she tried to kill herself or did someone do it for her?'

'I don't know,' Suzannah said, feeling a growing dread. 'I do know this: if what Tricia told Dr Munley is true, the microchip is destroying her, just as it must be destroying Andrew Dugan. We've got to make sure that Roland Lancaster's crowning achievement does not go into one more human brain.'

# 15

Tricia Fiore's eyes, under their lids, were still. Suzannah knew it meant only that she was not presently dreaming, but she could not shake the ominous feeling that Tricia was slipping away. Thursday – three days now and, though she was breathing fine on her own and yielding close-to-normal EEGs, she still would not wake up.

Suzannah checked the feeding tube, feeling helpless, wishing she could do something. She pushed a damp strand of hair back from Tricia's forehead. What secrets lay trapped in that comatose brain? Could Tricia really see things before they happened? It seemed incredible.

The file she'd read last night had blamed the visions on schizophrenia. Then why hadn't Haldol controlled them?

No scientist would argue that visions didn't exist. PCP and LSD were known to induce hallucinations. Dreams were a form of vision. So was imagination, where you saw something in your 'mind's eye'. The root word of imagination was 'image'.

Suzannah rubbed at her forehead. Her mind seemed to quicken as the implications began to flow together into a coherent focus: the unconscious did generate images. The question was, might the nerve impulses of those images be so similar to the ones for normal vision that they fooled the microchip? Neuroanatomists knew where the visual cortex was located in the brain, but no one knew which anatomical part – or parts – of the brain generated the 'unconscious mind'. The microchip was not located in the visual cortex. It was implanted deep in the corpus callosum, the neural crossroads of the brain. Had the microchip inadvertently been put in position to pick up images not just from Tricia's visual cortex but from the uncharted regions of her unconscious? If so, it would turn those mental images into visions as surely as it did the outside world that flowed in through Tricia's damaged eyes. Tricia would, quite literally, have the ability to see into her own unconscious.

And what was her unconscious showing her? The future.

But how could it be? The unconscious mind was supposed to be irrational, disorganized. How could it yield coherent, accurate images of anything at all, much less the future?

Suzannah's mind whirled. If she was on the right track, the implications were staggering. She gazed down at Tricia's sleeping face, amazed at where her own mind was taking her.

'Ah, Suzannah.'

She turned to see Ed Gaspard, Tricia's neurologist, standing in the doorway. With an effort she let go of her racing thoughts and focused on him. 'I think that's supposed to be "*Oh*, Suzannah", Ed.'

He smiled and motioned her over to the door. 'I'm glad you're here. Got any brilliant suggestions for me?'

What could she tell him? The microchip *was*, somehow, behind this; she felt surer of it every hour. But until she understood how, she could not suggest a treatment.

'I'm afraid not,' she told Ed.

Ed looked back at the still form in the bed. 'Poor woman. She was very close to her father, but he died of a heart attack two years ago. Only person's been in to see her is another teacher from her school. According to her, Tricia is – was – the best teacher at Swanson Middle School. All the kids really love her, and she loves them. After her dad died, they've been her family.' Ed's expression was almost stony. He was trying to harden himself, Suzannah knew, to the deeper sadness it was dangerous for doctors to feel too often.

'How long can you keep her?' Suzannah asked.

'Only a couple more days, unless she shows a change. Then we'll have to farm her out to a veggie ward somewhere.'

Suzannah did not wince, though she felt like it.

'Fortunately for her, she's got good insurance,' Ed continued. He poked his head through the curtains of the bed next to Tricia's. A chart clicked against the foot of the bed, then Ed came out. 'Gotta run. Catch you later.'

Suzannah watched him hurry up the hallway, feeling her own sense of urgency. She had to find the missing pieces of this puzzle – and soon, before Food and Drug Administration approval let the microchip loose on thousands of people.

I've got to talk to Roland Lancaster, she thought.

The very idea repulsed her. Tricia and Andrew had already talked to him, and it hadn't done any good. What made her think she could do better? I'm not his protégée any more, she thought, but I *am* a physician. Maybe he'll listen to me. I've got to try.

She walked down the corridor to the nurses' station and used the physician's phone on the counter.

'Dr Lancaster's office.'

'This is Dr Beverly Crusher,' Suzannah said. 'I'd like to talk to Dr Lancaster about a referral.'

'Hold on, please, Dr Crusher.'

Suzannah held on, her stomach churning. Her fingers gripped the phone receiver with painful force, pressing the warm plastic into her ear. She could feel her teeth clenching.

'Dr Crusher?' His voice was just as she remembered it. Smooth, condescending.

'No, Dr Lancaster, this is Dr Lord. I need to talk with you.' She listened to the slight hesitation on the other end.

'Is this your idea of a joke?' he said stiffly.

'Would you have taken the call if you'd known it was from me?'

'I can't imagine what we have to talk about.'

'We can start with two of your pilot study subjects. They appear to be suffering severe side effects from the microchip.'

'Where are you now?' he snapped.

'I'm standing at the nurses' station on the neurology floor at Adams Memorial Hospital.'

'For God's sake, don't say irresponsible, totally unfounded things like that where people can hear you. You're completely out of line.'

'I want to see you today.'

'Impossible.'

Suzannah heard the fear in his voice, savoured it. 'In fact,' she said, 'I want to see you in your office in twenty minutes.'

'I'll be leading rounds then.'

'No,' Suzannah said in a patient tone, 'you'll be in your office meeting with me. I'm sure one of your trusted residents can lead rounds.' She hung up before he could say anything else. She looked at her hand. It was trembling. She jammed it into the pocket of her medical coat.

I hate him, she thought. I hate him so much.

But I can't let that matter. This is too important.

Roland Lancaster's office was much as she remembered it, except the *Newsweek* cover had been framed and added to the twenty or so other honours, degrees, and certificates on one wall. He was a touch greyer at the temples but still slim and fit looking.

The mere sight of him made her angry. She could feel the cold fury sliding inside her like a glacier breaking loose.

His slight smile lasted just long enough for his secretary to close the office door. Then he leaned forward, knuckles down on his desk, and glared at her. She remembered how she had respected this man, hung on his words, basked in the slightest word of praise from him, felt awful when she disappointed him. Being in his presence again was worse, even, than she had imagined.

'I don't care to see you,' he said, 'so let's make this quick, shall we?'

*You* don't care to see *me*? Suzannah thought. Outrage flamed up in her.

No, she must remain calm, stick to the issue. 'Andrew Dugan says he came to you and asked to have the microchip taken out.'

'And I refused, yes. I've no desire to blind the man.'

'Did he tell you why he wanted it out?'

Lancaster stared at her. 'What he told me is between the two of us.'

'He's having visions, isn't he.'

'Ridiculous.'

'And the visions are coming true.'

Lancaster shook his head slowly, staring at her. 'How could you ever imagine such a thing?' he said. 'I was righter than I knew to terminate you.'

Suzannah pulled a slow, even breath. *The bastard.* 'The past is irrelevant,' she said. 'I am going to get to the bottom of this. I am not going to allow you to drive patients to suicide.'

'That's absurd,' Lancaster sputtered. 'What makes you think you can do a better job of protecting patients than the FDA?'

'Maybe you've convinced yourself there is no problem. But unless you share all the facts with them, they can't make an informed decision on the microchip. Clearly, you should at least ask the FDA to delay their decision for a while.'

Lancaster paled. 'Delay? You really have no idea what's at stake here, do you? If approval is delayed, no matter how close-mouthed FDA is, some reporter will dig out the reason. I can see the headlines now: Microchip Makes People Insane. Totally untrue, but there is no way the procedure could live down such an inflammatory suggestion. Thousands of people will be denied vision because of a totally scurrilous charge.'

'What is happening to Tricia Fiore and Andrew Dugan is profoundly disturbing to them, but I'm not convinced they are insane.'

Lancaster stared at her. 'You can't be serious, Suzannah –'

'It's Dr Lord to you.'

'If you can't see they are insane, *Doctor* Lord, then you're an idiot who should go back and repeat her first-year rotation in psychiatry.'

Suzannah felt furious. With a huge effort, she controlled her voice. 'You will not speak to me that way,' she said quietly.

Lancaster's face turned red. 'I'll speak to you any way I please, you silly bitch.'

'You did not choose me to be one of your residents because I am silly, an idiot, or, for that matter, a bitch. If what I have come here to tell you is incorrect, convince me with science and logic. If you can't, then maybe you should listen to me.'

Lancaster made a visible effort to get control of himself.

He sank into the chair behind his desk, motioning Suzannah to a seat in front of it. She remained standing, staring down at him.

'Surely you can see,' he said, 'that Andrew and Tricia must have been neurotic to begin with, and now they're in full-blown hysterical crises. We should have screened them better, that's all. A person with psychosomatic leanings might, over the years, come to suspect that something implanted in his brain was responsible for all his imaginary ills. For decades we've known that patients can have irrational psychosomatic reactions to artificial limbs, heart implants, you name it. We knew from the beginning it would be a risk in our pilot study.'

'Yes, and we screened every subject carefully. None of them, including Tricia and Andrew, showed any signs of psychological problems.'

'Screenings aren't perfect. Andrew Dugan is an artist. We know they're more neurotic–'

'That is not true. Studies have shown–'

'I don't care. Even if it isn't true in general, there is no other possible explanation for Tricia and Andrew. Now listen here, I've strengthened the precautionary recommendations in the final protocols now before the FDA. Those recommendations plainly state that potential implant recipients must in every case be screened for prior history of mental illness or neurosis. That should satisfy you.

'Tricia Fiore saw that one of her students was going to be mugged by two boys.'

'Nonsense. She'd probably seen them bullying him on the playground the day before and worried about it. But worry is not the same as visions of the future. For God's sake, the future has not happened yet. No one can see something before it exists.'

'We see into the future all the time,' Suzannah said.

Lancaster rolled his eyes towards the ceiling.

'Half the time the "future" we see is wrong, doesn't happen,' Suzannah said, 'but we do it, whenever we hope for something or visualize a coming event. What is visualizing but a form of seeing inside our own minds? Sometimes it happens when we're not trying to make it happen. An image flashes into consciousness. We have a hunch.'

'A hunch? Be reasonable.'

'I am being reasonable, as reasonable as I know how to be without ignoring the facts. In one sense, the difference between Andrew and Tricia and us is huge, and in another it is only a matter of degree. I had a hunch Tricia was going to kill herself, and I got there in time to save her. A day later, I had almost the same hunch about Andrew – that I would find him dead – and I was wrong. Andrew and Tricia are having hunches – no, they are *seeing* their hunches – and they are *not* wrong. It is tearing them both apart. I don't yet know how it happens, but there is evidence –'

'Evidence? You haven't a shred of proof.'

'Dr Lancaster. You hooked a tiny computer into a very big computer, the human brain. The tiny computer boosts and clarifies visual signals. We don't know a hundredth of what the big computer does. We don't know a thousandth of what it's capable of. But it's beginning to look like it has hooked up with the little computer – the microchip – in a way we never anticipated.'

'Forty-eight people have had no problems whatsoever,' Lancaster said.

'Are you sure? Tricia and Andrew, in particular, are extraordinarily sensitive people. They may be only the first to feel the effects.'

'Sensitive people!' Lancaster snorted.

'Are you going to listen to me, or am I going to have to go to the FDA myself?'

Lancaster glared at her. 'You want revenge. That's what this is really about, isn't it?'

'No, it is not.'

'I see. You are immune to normal human motivations, incapable of revenge.'

'Why would I want revenge on you?' Suzannah said. 'Did you wrong me in some way?' Lancaster held her gaze a moment, then looked away. Tears of rage rimmed her eyes. Fiercely, she held them back.

Suddenly, Lancaster looked very tired. 'If you try to make trouble for me,' he said, 'I'll make worse trouble for you, believe me. Do you honestly think anyone will take your word against mine? Who are you, after all? An obscure general surgeon, bitter because she didn't have the stuff to become a neurosurgeon.'

With a tremendous effort, Suzannah held back her fury. 'I had the "stuff", and you know it. Tell me something, Dr Lancaster. When I wouldn't let you force yourself on me sexually, were you even a little bit disgusted with yourself for trying?'

Lancaster gave her a cold half smile. 'You're raving. I don't even find you attractive, and I never did. Apparently you have harboured some fantasy to excuse yourself. If I had wanted to have sex with you, which I didn't, I'm sure you'd have agreed.'

'What a disgusting piece of trash you are. Do you really think being brilliant excuses it?'

Lancaster looked at the wall of degrees and certificates, the framed *Newsweek* cover. 'If you come after Roland Lancaster, if you try to stand between thousands of people and their right to see, I guarantee you you'll lose. Now get out.'

Suzannah felt the room telescope around her until only Lancaster's face filled her vision. She said, 'Tricia Fiore was afraid someone was going to kill her. Who was she afraid of, Dr Lancaster? Who is watching Andrew Dugan's house? Why has Andrew disappeared?'

Lancaster gave a faint laugh. 'Get a grip on yourself. Do you realize how you sound?'

Suzannah walked to the door, turned. 'It's not how I sound that counts,' she said. 'It's whether I'm telling the truth.' As she closed the door on Roland Lancaster, she saw a slight doubt cross his face.

It was enough.

# 16

Archer Montross stood in his office in Station Three, US Fisheries. Looking out of his window, he studied the spruce trees. The feathered layers of their needles were complex and beautiful. After a lifetime of squinting at objects eight feet away, it was good to see pine needles at twenty yards, to make out the delicate patterns frost had traced on his window.

Archer thought of Suzannah. Three wonderful years he'd had with her at Georgetown U. They'd just been friends, but she was the most beautiful woman who had ever paid even a little attention to him. That hadn't made it any easier to watch her go out with her various boyfriends. Sometimes he'd see her and a guy strolling across the campus, hand in hand, and he'd feel a terrible burn high in his stomach. Not all her boyfriends had been handsome, but all had been better looking than he. Before the auto accident, before the burns, he had been handsome too . . .

Archer touched the side of his face. He looked a little better now, after the skin graft the Agency had paid for. But not better enough.

At least Suzannah had never really fallen for any of her campus boyfriends. But in a way, that had been cruel, keeping his hope alive when there was no real hope. For the last two years at Georgetown, he and Suzannah had gone from friends to close friends.

But never close enough.

And now look at us, Suzannah. We still haven't found anyone, have we?

The window and woods wavered, and Archer *saw* Suzannah. I'm having a vision, he thought. For a few seconds, she was superimposed on the window; he could see through her to spruce grove. He felt the usual chill down the back of his neck as the two images fought for dominance; then the window and woods dissolved.

Suzannah was standing in a frozen field. Patches of snow dotted the brown mud. On a distant ridge, he could see skeletal trees. The sky was grey. She was wearing her long coat and a white scarf. Someone was with her, a tall lean man with blond hair. Archer recognized him from Agency photos: her boyfriend, Jay Mallernee, the *Post* reporter.

Archer felt slightly breathless. He groped for the window sill, knowing it was there even though he couldn't see it. The edge of the sill bit into his hands as he stood, keeping his eyes fixed on Suzannah. She and Mallernee were looking at something, but it was outside Archer's vision.

Archer waited with rapt attention, watching as they walked across the field. They seemed to be strolling rather than walking towards something.

'We've got to find him,' Suzannah said. 'He's the key to all this. With Tricia still unconscious, he's the only one who can stop approval. We've got to get him to tell his story.'

The scene faded with wrenching abruptness. Archer blinked, startled by the sudden light pouring through his window. His hands stung from the knife edge of the sill. He jerked them back, taking deep breaths. Sinking into his chair, he massaged away the angry red creases on his palms. He waited until his breathing evened out, then picked up his phone and dialled.

'Exec one,' said a woman's voice.

'Angie, Archer Montross. Is Mr Pederson here today?'

'Yes, he is.' Her voice was several degrees cooler now she knew who it was. Archer realized she never said his name, as though it would pollute her mouth. Angie did not approve of him. Or maybe she was scared of him – his size, his burned face. Or she thought he could see through her clothes or something.

Stupid woman.

'I need to see Mr Pederson right away,' Archer said.

'Just a minute, please.'

Archer pursed his lips, aiming a mocking kiss at the receiver.

'Mr Pederson can see you now.'

'Great, thanks. I'll be right down.'

Archer hurried down past the computer room and ciphers to the office that Station Three held open for the Deputy Director. He said hello to Angie in the anteroom, and she said hello back but still didn't use his name. Inside the dim inner office, George Pederson rose from behind his desk, waving him to one of the chrome chairs that Archer hated. They were too low-slung. He sat down, resigned. His knees stuck up ridiculously. From where Archer sat, the DDI's oversized head seemed to balance on the front edge of his desk, the half glasses perched on the end of his nose, white hair wreathing his head like the Wizard of Oz.

'How are you doing, Archer?'

'All right.'

'Happy in your new office?'

'Yes, thanks. I like the window and the view.'

The head nodded, lit eerily from beneath by the bounce of the desk lamp. Why did Pederson live in perpetual night? His office at headquarters was larger, but he kept it just as dark. I'll know someday, Archer thought. The more I see of him, the more I'll know.

'So,' Pederson said.

'I've just seen Dr Lord,' Archer said. 'In my vision, she is looking for Andrew Dugan; clearly, she hasn't given up since she went to his house. And she has – or will have – company. Her boyfriend.'

Pederson frowned. 'Damn!'

'Yeah, the *Post* reporter. I saw them out in the country somewhere,' Archer said. 'There was a field with a stand of trees.'

'The country? You're sure it wasn't a city park or something?'

'The ground had been ploughed, though not recently.'

Pederson nodded. Archer could hear his pen scratching, taking notes. 'No sign of where it was; Virginia, Maryland?'

'Sorry.'

'But it must be buried somewhere in your mind, right?'

Archer shrugged. 'The actual location might be somewhere in my mind – a projection I haven't consciously recognized yet or two pieces of information I haven't put together.'

'Well, I wish you could put them together for us.'

'So do I, but you're talking about thinking now, not *seeing*. I'm not an analyst any more, George. I know that's what you recruited me for three years ago, but that was before the visions.'

'You weren't bad at it. In fact, you were quite good.'

'Thank you. But it's the visions that count now. Let your other analysts go on working on where Dugan is hiding.

They're as good, and as bad, at it as I am.'

Pederson sighed. 'Maybe you'll see it in your next vision.'

'Maybe. I can't control that.'

'No.' Pederson looked at him curiously. 'I'm wondering how you could know that she'll keep going after Andrew.'

Archer suppressed a twinge of impatience. 'I *saw* it.'

'Yes, yes,' Pederson said, 'but the visions do seem to depend in part on what the Adept knows. You knew Dr Lord well at one time, but that was a while ago, wasn't it?'

'I still know her,' Archer said. 'People don't change that much.'

Pederson nodded. 'That sounds rather cynical coming from a man with a master's degree in psychology, but I think you're right, Archer my friend.'

Archer wondered what Pederson would do if he called him 'my friend'.

'Forget the visions for a moment. From your *knowledge* of this woman,' Pederson said, 'would you predict she'll keep pursuing this?'

'For what it's worth, sure. But I can't forget the visions. As I told you yesterday, I already *saw* her talking to Lancaster.'

'But that, by itself, doesn't prove—'

'She plans to find Andrew and use him to stop us from proceeding with the microchip. Today's vision makes that clear.'

Pederson grimaced.

'One way or another,' Archer said, 'sooner or later, she'll know enough to move against us. Unless we can get her to join us.'

Pederson got up from his desk, came over, and sat down beside Archer in one of the low slung chairs, something he'd never done before. The move put Archer on alert. Pederson hooked his veined hands around his knee, looking sidelong at Archer. 'Are you sure about this?'

'George, you're looking for Andrew Dugan. If you had a bloodhound and you let him smell Dugan's shirt, and he went running across some field, you would follow the dog, right?'

'You bet.'

'Suzannah is my shirt. Only we're not talking about a dog's nose now, we're talking about an Adept, your first and best Adept, Archer Montross. I'm telling you, I can *see* her, plain as day, going after Andrew Dugan.'

'Does she find him?'

'I haven't seen that yet. But if she finds him, she could move against us; you don't have to be an Adept to see that. We should bring her in now. Especially since there's a chance we could use her.'

Pederson nodded gravely. 'Forgive me, Archer. I didn't mean to sound like I doubted you. It's just reflex, I guess. I'm an old hound dog myself. I've been in this business for twenty-seven years. For most of those years, I've listened to analysts tell me what they think might be likely to happen. Always, they've covered their behinds – *always*, Archer. If one of them were here now, and he'd made a careful lifelong study of Dr Suzannah Lord, he would be telling me, she might do this, or she might do that. That's not much use, Archer, and I've had an endless flood of it – intelligence data that were neither intelligent nor data. Reports as fat as novels that the analyst could have put in five pages if he had just pulled the trigger and chosen among the possible outcomes.

'You're always sure. I love it, Archer. You have no idea how much I love it. Especially since you're always right.'

Despite his wariness, Archer felt warmed by Pederson's

praise. The old man had a way with people, no question.

'I wish we knew how you do it,' Pederson mused.

Archer shrugged. 'I don't do anything. All I do is *see*.'

'Like Daniel in Babylon,' Pederson mused. '"*Mene, mene, tekel, upharsin:* Thou art weighed in the balances and found wanting?" And sure enough, Nebuchadnezzar lost his mind and went out into the fields and ate grass like a cow for seven years.'

Archer nodded, wondering if it was a joke. He had no idea what Pederson was talking about. Babylon – wasn't that in the Bible? Archer almost smiled at the thought of George Pederson reading the Bible. But that last part, about losing his mind, made him too uneasy to smile. George Pederson never said anything without a reason, layers of meaning within meaning. Had that pompous jerk Fachet tried to undermine him with Pederson, make Pederson think he might be mentally unstable? It would be one way for Fachet to protect his ass, Archer thought, in case I give Pederson a bad report on him.

My mind is perfectly fine, Archer told himself; but he felt a worm of fear in his stomach.

'So you think we should bring her in?' Pederson said, eyeing Archer again.

'I do.'

Pederson nodded. 'Well, perhaps we'll do that.'

'No, sir, you won't.'

Pederson frowned. 'What was that, Archer?'

Archer nerved himself. There was no backing away now. 'After I leave here,' he said, 'you call in Mr Degas and Mr Holer. You confer with them, and the three of you decide to let Dr Lord look for Dugan while you keep a real close watch on her. You decide he likes her and might let her find him. You think you can be right behind.'

Pederson gazed at him, utterly still.

Archer was pleased to find that he was not afraid of Pederson, not even now. 'It's a dangerous game, George. Look, you are *analysing* the situation. You're thinking about it, weighing all the alternatives, the probabilities. You're a smart man, a very smart man, but analysis is the old way, like you just got through saying. George, I've *seen* her striking out at us.'

'Yes, but you didn't see when, did you?'

'Not yet, but she'll do it.'

'If we permit it,' Pederson said. 'I think we have a little play here, a day or two to work with before we have to act against her. Andrew Dugan is hiding from *us*, not her. She has a much better chance of finding him than we do, and we have to use that.'

Archer felt a rising impatience. 'George, what do you want me to say? That your plan sounds reasonable? Fine, it does. I don't think there's a thing wrong with it. But we're not dealing with what I think. We're dealing with a part of my brain a hundred times smarter than the Archer Montross you're talking to right now. A part that never forgets *anything* it sees or hears, that puts the remotest pieces of information together in a way that transcends normal human logic. The only direct and unerring access we have to that part of my brain is through these visions. You can leave Dr Lord out there as long as you want, but remember this. The minute I have a vision of a *Washington Post* headline that says "*Brain Implant Causes Accurate Visions of the Future*", it will be too late.'

'All right, Archer.' Pederson got up and went behind his desk again. 'We'll put her on a *very* short leash. One move in the wrong direction, and we'll grab her.'

Archer sighed. 'It's your decision.'

'How long have you been having visions of me and my meetings?' Pederson's voice was carefully neutral.

Archer felt a rush of blood to his muscles, like the first instant when his arms surged up against the brutal weight of a bench press. 'This is first time. I'm sure you must have expected it.'

Pederson nodded.

'I knew it might upset you to hear it, but I told you anyway because there's no way you can trust me unless I tell you everything you need to know. I will always do that, George. Of course, if you don't want to hear things that concern you personally . . .'

'No. You did right. It's a little unnerving, but I'd rather know.'

Archer nodded. He realized Pederson was still standing. The meeting was over. Archer pushed on the armrests, heaving himself up from the chair. He left, feeling Pederson's eyes on his back. As he walked to his own office, he weighed what he had done, decided he'd been right. He had put a new note into Pederson's voice – fear. Pederson didn't like his bloodhound tracking its keeper along with the prey. Pederson's fear could be to his advantage or it could be dangerous. But if it got dangerous, it was likely he would *see* that – probably before Pederson himself did – and could take appropriate steps.

Maybe he would even end up sitting behind Pederson's desk – including the big one at headquarters.

Archer felt a surge of anticipation, barely noticing the way people stepped to the side a little so he wouldn't touch them as he passed. Soon he would be with Suzannah. After what he had told Pederson, the man wouldn't dare delay much longer.

Besides, Archer thought, I've seen it. It *will* happen.

Suzannah and me together again. Bright, beautiful Suzannah, who never really looked at me, never saw my true self behind the scars.

Archer felt a smile pull against the scar tissue on his face. Back in college, he'd been Suzannah's big buddy. She'd never seen him as a man, with a man's desires. He would prove to her that he was a flesh-and-blood male.

He would prove it with or without her co-operation.

# 17

Suzannah felt a surge of last-minute nerves as she sat down across from Dr Theodore Salter of the FDA. It was such an important meeting. Was she ready? A delay in approving the microchip would be best, but if she could just get the FDA to question Lancaster about Tricia and Andrew, that would be a start.

She sized up Dr Salter. He looked about sixty, portly, with a slight hypertensive flush. His thick glasses kept sliding down his nose and he kept pushing them back up with an irritable jab of his finger. Suzannah wished they'd given her someone with twenty-twenty vision.

And someone with more clout.

Salter was a group director in the neuro-ophthalmology section of FDA, working on the Lancaster protocols. He no doubt had some authority, but she'd have preferred to talk with someone further up the chain of command. Oh, well, it was a start.

'Thank you for seeing me,' she said.

'No problem.' He jumped up, circling behind her to adjust the blinds on his window. Suzannah swivelled in her chair, trying to keep eye contact. She saw the sky had turned a leaden grey while Salter had kept her waiting in the windowless reception area. The tall arc lamps in the vast FDA parking lot flickered as their photocells lost purchase on the failing light. Only a few minutes until dark. It must be near Salter's quitting time. Suzannah felt a growing sense of urgency. She wished he would stop puttering.

'As you know,' she said, 'I'm here about the Lancaster microchip.'

'Yes.' Salter sat down again but gazed past her out the window.

'I was one of Dr Lancaster's assistants during the implantation phase of the study four years ago.'

'Yes, yes, I know.'

His brusque manner began to annoy her, but she controlled her impatience. 'I've come because of concerns about possible side effects,' she said. 'I've spoken with two of the test subjects. Both reported problems to Dr Lancaster. The problems are so severe that both have considered having the microchip removed, even though it would mean a return to near blindness. The nature of this side effect –'

'Dr Lord,' Salter said, 'are you aware that three to four per cent of all people who go to a physician are suffering from some form of emotional problem?'

'I hadn't heard that figure, but it sounds reasonable.'

'I'm glad you think so. Two subjects out of fifty is four per cent, on the nose.'

'These people were carefully screened.'

'As carefully as possible,' Salter agreed, 'but there are limitations. Remember, the subjects had all suffered years of failing vision – together with all the emotional stress that would cause.'

Suzannah realized with a sinking feeling what must have happened. 'Lancaster called you up and talked to you about this.'

'Yes, I've spoken with *Dr* Lancaster.'

'When?'

Instead of answering, Salter riffled through a manila folder. 'Tricia Fiore and Andrew Dugan. Both claimed to be suffering from disturbing visions of the future. Dr Lancaster recommended them to psychiatrists, as well he should have done. The eyesight, incidentally, of both subjects continues to be perfect.' Salter stabbed his glasses back up and looked squarely at her for the first time. 'I'm curious, Dr Lord. Why would you give any credence to claims that one can see into the future?'

'Dr Salter, I'm curious too. I haven't even presented my evidence, but it seems you've already made up your mind. Perhaps I should talk to your supervisor.'

'What evidence are you talking about? I tried to contact Miss Fiore and found out she is comatose after a suicide attempt. Andrew Dugan is not answering his phone. Do you have taped depositions from either one of them?'

'No.'

'The truth is, you don't have any evidence at all, do you?'

Suzannah returned his stare. I saw Tricia's therapy notes, she thought. But I can't tell him that. 'I don't understand your attitude, Dr Salter. This is not a court of law. The FDA is supposed to be making an exhaustive evaluation of a radical new device.'

'And that is exactly what we are doing, rest assured.'

'Really? Then why are you so unwilling to at least consider my report? I'm a physician in good standing who helped develop the microchip.'

Salter sat back, giving her a small smile. 'Yes. And you were thrown off the project, weren't you?'

Suzannah felt the blood rising to her face. 'Dr Lancaster and I had a difference of opinion.'

'About what, Dr Lord?'

'I don't think that has a bearing here.'

'Isn't it true that you tried to seduce him, and when he'd have no part of it you threatened to blackmail him with charges of sexual harassment?'

'No, it is not true,' Suzannah said, outraged. She pushed to her feet. 'Did Dr Lancaster tell you that?' Of course he did, she thought. That incredible bastard. She was wordless with fury. Lancaster had a right to call FDA and give his version on Tricia and Andrew, she thought, but not this, not *this*. He's done it to me again. She looked at Salter's smirking face and felt a vast despair. I have to keep trying, she thought.

'I believe the microchip might be reading neural impulses that do not originate in the eyes,' she said. 'Impulses from the brain's internal imaging capability.'

Salter stood and looked at his watch. 'We have already investigated that possibility and found no evidence for it. Now, if you'll excuse me.'

'No, I will not excuse you. You have taken the unsupported word of a man who has everything to lose against the word of a physician with nothing to gain but the safety of patients. I cannot accept that.'

'Nothing to gain, eh? How about revenge? Shame on you, Dr Lord. Trying to pull down a good man with unsubstantiated allegations. Well, I have no time or patience for that. And I suggest you think very seriously before you try to peddle your ridiculous notions anywhere else. That is, if you really care about the people who can benefit from Dr Lancaster's microchip.'

'Won't you at least postpone approval while you look into this?'

'*Good day*, Dr Lord.'

# 18

Suzannah found herself in the parking lot with little memory of how she'd got there. She headed across the huge lot, leaning into the icy wind. Despite the cold, her face burned. Lancaster, you bastard, you *bastard!* She got into her Chevy and slammed the door. She started the car and turned on the heater, then stared out at the parking lot. She had a powerful urge to scream. She took deep breaths, trying to pull herself together.

Dark now. She checked her watch: five-thirty. In forty-five minutes she was supposed to be playing racquetball with Juli. Barely enough time to drive from Rockville to the Pentagon Officers Athletic Center. The last thing in the world she wanted to do right now was play racquetball.

No. Actually, it was exactly what she needed. She wasn't jogging much these days and she could use the exercise. She would smash the ball until it exploded.

Suzannah guided her Chevy through the remains of the evening rush hour, forcing herself to drive carefully, to signal all lane changes, to stay a proper distance from the car ahead. The window kept fogging from the heat of her breath. Her foot itched to mash the accelerator. *Isn't it true that you tried to seduce him, and when he'd have no part of it you threatened to blackmail him with charges of sexual harassment?*

When she walked into the Pentagon Officers Athletic Center – known, in inevitable Pentagon-speak, as the POAC – Juli was already on Court 2, warming up. Suzannah changed hurriedly and ran down, feeling a hunger in the muscles of her arms and legs.

'Hi,' she said, ducking through the door onto the court.

'Suze,' Juli said, slapping her outstretched hand. 'I hope you feel lucky today.'

'Oh, I do,' Suzannah said. 'I certainly do.' She put all her fury into her first serve, driving the ball into the front wall. It hit too high and sailed back past her, a perfect plum for Juli. For an instant nothing happened and Suzannah realized Juli was waiting to take it off the back wall. Suzannah tried to get ready without giving herself away. Right corner, she thought, holding herself still until the last moment, then lunging right as Juli smashed the ball into the right corner, close to the floor. It caught the sidewall on the rebound and shot back, a low scorcher. Suzannah, already diving for it, blocked it back into the end wall an inch from the floor. It rolled back out, unhittable, a perfect kill.

'Lucky guess!' Juli said.

'Pure skill.' Suzannah grinned fiercely.

Beyond Juli, behind the Plexiglas rear wall, a couple of guys with marine haircuts and USMC T-shirts stood watching. The POAC wasn't posh like the private racquet clubs, but it did have one distinct advantage: lots of handsome young officers to look at. One of the marines gave her a little wave. Suzannah nodded and turned back to serve, trying to concentrate on where to hit the ball. Instead, her mind stuck on what Juli had said: 'Lucky guess.' But it was more than a guess, wasn't it? She had played racquetball over and over with Juli. Not only did she know how the ball would bounce off the wall in almost every shot now – something that had often thrown her at first – she also knew Juli.

Suzannah realized Juli was waiting for her to serve. She smacked the ball at the left third of the service wall and set herself for the return. After a second, she realized Juli must have missed the return. Turning, she watched Juli walk, muttering, after the rolling ball.

'I can't believe it,' Suzannah said. 'I aced you.'

'That's right, gloat.'

Suzannah won the next seven points, before letting Juli to the service line. Juli lunged so hard for the ball her glasses flew off and skittered across the floor. 'I can't read you today,' she complained, retrieving them. 'You're really mixing up your serves, outthinking me.'

'Actually, I'm not thinking at all.' Not about my serves, anyway. *Shame on you, Dr Lord. Trying to pull down a good man with unsubstantiated allegations.*

With a fierce diving lunge, Suzannah won the service back. Juli battled hard, but she couldn't get the edge. Not today. Suzannah served. Juli, cheating to her left to cover her backhand, sprawled flat trying to lunge back. 'That was your fourth serve in a row to my forehand,' Juli said.

'It was?' Suzannah said, surprised.

Juli put her hands on her hips in mock aggravation. 'Give me a break. How'm I supposed to figure out your strategy if you don't even have one?'

Suzannah took the ball from her. 'My plan,' she said, 'is to have no plan. What's the score, anyway?'

'Fifteen to seven, your favour.'

'Really?' Suzannah was astonished. She almost never beat Juli. And she hadn't done it today – yet.

Juli made the classic choke sign and smiled evilly.

Suzannah grinned back. Not this time, big sister. She

would imagine that Juli was Roland Lancaster or that smug bureaucrat Salter.

Suzannah won three more points, then Juli took back the serve and ran her around from corner to corner, front wall to back. It felt good to run, to tear after the ball with everything she had. She dived for low shots, smashing the ball hard every time she could. She scraped an elbow diving for a shot. She banged into walls. The sweat began to pour off her. She saw that the two men were still watching and played even harder. The bell rang just as she was serving for the second game. She smashed the ball back along the left wall, catching the crease perfectly. Juli dived for it, fluffing the ball back into the centre of the front wall. Suzannah ran up, dropping the ball into the corner with a soft tap. The bell was still ringing.

Juli got up and offered her hand. 'Good game!'

'Thanks,' Suzannah said. 'Sorry about that dump shot.'

'Yeah, I can tell. Actually, I'm proud of you, kiddo. That's the first time you've beaten me in six weeks, let alone twice in a row. And I was giving it all I've got.'

Suzannah patted Juli's shoulder, feeling better than she would have thought possible two hours ago. She was not finished with the FDA yet. They wouldn't listen, they thought she was just some vengeful female? She'd find proof they couldn't explain away and stick it in their ears!

She followed her sister off the court, yielding it to the two marines. When she entered the women's locker room upstairs, Suzannah was surprised to find it almost empty, no sound from between the rows of lockers. 'Where is everybody?' she asked Juli.

'They're not fools like us.'

'What do you mean?'

'There's no hot water today,' Juli said.

179

Suzannah stopped. 'No hot water? Not again!'

'Didn't I tell you?'

'You sadist!'

Juli laughed, dialling her combination lock and pulling her locker open. 'There's a sign at the desk. You must've missed it. A cold shower will be good for you, get your blood moving.'

Suzannah followed her into the communal shower, steeling herself, turning the tap on gingerly. The water hit her like a sheet of ice; they must have taken it straight from the frozen Potomac. She danced and yelped, letting the frigid water scour the sweat off her. At the next shower, Juli stood stoically in the icy stream, lathering up as if she were standing under a tropical waterfall. All her muscles showed. She looked strong and fit, not an ounce of fat on her. Suzannah felt proud again at beating her today.

She fled the shower ahead of Juli. Towelling off, she thought about what she should do next. She had gone in to the FDA too soon, armed more with logic than with proof. Now, she must find the proof. Andrew Dugan was that proof. He was the only implant recipient who could back up what she was saying. She felt a surge of exasperation. All along, Andrew had been the key. His reticence about the microchip bothered her. To say the least, he was suffering serious complications from it, and yet he did not want to warn the public. Everything inside her told her he was a responsible, caring man. Didn't he feel some obligation? All he had to do was go to the *Post* or *Newsweek* and he could torpedo the microchip, keep whatever he was suffering from being inflicted on thousands of others. Why hadn't he?

Juli walked in from the shower, towelling off briskly, her skin pink from the cold shower. 'Ah, that was good.'

'Liar.'

Juli laughed. She hung her uniform on the door of her locker and got into her underwear and slip. Then, instead of putting her uniform on, she sat down on the dressing bench and looked at Suzannah. 'So what is it?'

'What do you mean?'

'That wasn't my kid sister on the court today. That was a lean, mean fighting machine. What made you so mad?'

Suzannah told her about her visit to Lancaster and her fears, based on Andrew Dugan and Tricia Fiore, that something might be dangerously wrong with the microchip. She stopped short of mentioning that she'd broken into Andrew's home and Dr Munley's office.

'So to hell with Lancaster,' Juli said. 'Go straight to the FDA.'

'I did, this afternoon, and I shouldn't have.'

'Why not?'

'Because I don't have proof. Tricia is still unconscious. She shouldn't be, but she is. And Andrew is God knows where. He never actually told me why he wanted the microchip removed. Even if he had, the FDA would want to hear it from him, examine him with their own doctors. I've got to have proof. FDA will make a decision any time now. It could still be stopped after that, but if I know Lancaster, he'll begin operating as soon as he can. I've got to find Andrew Dugan.'

'You're really serious about this, aren't you?'

'I don't see that I have any choice.'

Juli nodded. She stood and put on her uniform. 'Is there any way I can help?'

'There might be. Naval Intelligence has pipelines into other intelligence services – DIA, CIA – right?'

'To an extent. Why?'

'Remember, we thought the guys staking out Sydecki's

house might be feds of some sort. Someone was after Andrew that night in the restaurant, and possibly after me too. I . . . drove by Andrew's place, and a guy in a late-model blue Ford was staking it out.'

'Interesting,' Juli said. 'Langley has a fleet of those. But, except in very rare circumstances, the CIA isn't supposed to be doing domestic surveillance. What are you saying: that one of the intelligence services might have an interest in the microchip?'

Suzannah thought about Tricia, seeing what was going to happen in the future. 'Yes, I do.'

'Why?'

'It's very complicated. Do you have some time right now?'

Juli shook her head. 'I've got to walk back over and make sure my secretary got my charts and graphs folded into a report; my admiral called a meeting at eight tonight. Admirals really hate to see us go home.'

'That's all right. I'll tell you the whole story when we get time. But can you start checking into it? Any possible signs of interest in the Lancaster procedure among any of your colleagues.'

Juli gave her a long probing look. 'I'll do what I can.'

'Thanks – and thanks for listening.' Suzannah gave her a quick hug.

Juli straightened her tie. 'I was supposed to take your nephew to the circus tonight,' she fretted. 'J.D.'s going to be real disappointed.'

'I'll take him.'

Juli brightened. 'Would you? That would be great. He's really been looking forward to it. I'll call and tell him.' She hesitated. 'Something's been bothering him, and I can't get him to tell me. Maybe he'll talk to you.'

'I'll give it a shot.' Suzannah felt comforted at the

prospect. Forget Lancaster, she thought. Just for tonight. I have a life, people I love and don't see enough of. Maybe I can take Jay along. We'll all forget our troubles at the circus.

'Well, I've gotta run,' Juli said. 'See you later.'

Suzannah waved her out. She realized she was still wrapped in her towel from the shower. Better get moving.

The emptiness of the locker room began to weigh on her as she dressed. She tried to dismiss her unease; the POAC was a very secure place. Its members were civilian employees of the Pentagon, military officers, and their families. There was nearly always a POAC employee at the desk at the entrance, and a magnetic ID card was required to get past the entry turnstiles.

I'm perfectly safe here, Suzannah thought. She pulled her blouse on quickly and stepped into her skirt.

She heard a sound behind the next row of lockers, the slight gritty scrape of a shoe.

The hairs stood up on her neck. 'Hello?' she called.

No answer.

'Is anybody there?'

She heard another faint sound, further down the other side of the row. She pulled her skirt on quickly, buttoned it, swept up the rest of her clothes, and hurried in the opposite direction. As she rounded one end of the row, the heel of a man's shoe disappeared behind the locker at the other end. Suzannah felt a shock of alarm. Her heart pumped furiously. She ran barefoot between the next two rows of lockers. Halfway down, she stopped to listen. She heard his footfalls, light on the indoor/outdoor carpet, a whisper partially masked by drips from the showers. She edged to the end of her row and looked back and forth, ready to jump either way.

The man stepped into view at the other end of her row. She got a quick impression of a stockinged face, a tall man in a suit, and then she saw his gun. As she lunged away, she heard the soft thump of the silencer. Metal screeched as the bullet whined along the faces of the lockers.

Suzannah screamed. She ran along the row ends, listening for footsteps. If he ran up towards her, she could slip down a different row and run for the exit. His steps slapped the carpet at the far end. He was staying down near the door, cutting her off. Peeking around the edge of a locker, she saw him watching her. She jerked her head back just as he fired. The gun made a soft *thttt*. The bullet rang off the tile walls. He ran towards her. She screamed again and ran toward the door. Halfway down, she knew she wouldn't make it out before he rounded the end and fired on her. So she jumped up on the dressing bench and threw her weight into the row of lockers, furious with fear. The row tipped and then straightened. She flung herself into it again and the whole row crashed over on top of the man. He cursed. She dashed towards the exit.

Another *thump*, and plaster showered out of the wall beside the doorframe as she ran through it. Pounding down the steps, she headed back towards the racquetball courts. One of her shoes fell out of her hand, and she missed the bottom step as she grabbed for it. She tripped and sprawled right at the feet of one of the marines from the court.

'Help me!' she shouted.

The marine reached a hand out, then looked beyond her. The man in the stocking mask was pointing his gun at her. The marine officer jumped in front of her. The man turned and ran in the opposite direction. When the marine started after him, Suzannah tackled him from behind and he went down with a crash. He twisted around, giving her a dumbfounded look.

'He's got a gun,' Suzannah said apologetically. 'Let's quit

while we're ahead, shall we?' Suzannah heard someone cough behind her and realized she was lying on the floor with her skirt up to her neck, holding onto the gym shorts of an officer of the US Marine Corps. She rolled off, blushing furiously.

The marine's racquetball partner stood, looking down at them. 'And to think,' he said, 'I was against women in combat.'

The Pentagon police did their best to be reassuring. A woman sergeant in the Federal Protective Service made Suzannah comfortable in an office used by the army general in charge of the POAC. An Arlington police detective arrived quickly and took her statement while his partner and two uniformed men collected evidence in the locker room. The detective was even more reassuring than the FPS police. He told her about a flasher who had been invading women's locker rooms in private health clubs in the area. The man wore a stocking over his face and was the height and build of the one who had shot at her. He typically struck when the locker rooms were almost deserted and escaped through a rear fire exit, as the man had this evening.

There was only one discrepancy. Like most flashers, he had never been known to carry a gun, let alone to fire at anyone. But there was a first time for everything.

'Don't worry,' the detective told her. 'He doesn't even know who you are. And now that he's getting violent, the captain will put two teams on this case around the clock. We have some ideas who this guy might be. With the extra manpower, we'll tail him and nail him.'

Suzannah wanted desperately to believe them.

The FPS escorted her to her car and made sure she got away safely. She headed straight for Jay's apartment. She needed to feel his arms around her. She'd stay there tonight, safe in his arms. Tomorrow morning, she'd call the detective, see if he'd rounded up the suspect –

J.D.! she thought. I got so rattled I forgot. I promised Juli I'd take him to the circus. He's waiting at Joe and Claire's, and I'm late.

She thought about finding a pay phone and calling him to cancel, but she hated to disappoint him. She'd have to tell him why. It might frighten him, give him nightmares.

I'll take him, she decided, and go to Jay's afterwards.

By the time she reached Joe and Claire's, her hands felt steady on the wheel and she was glad she had not cancelled. Pretending to be calm for J.D. might help her actually feel calmer.

Forty-five minutes later, she sat down with him in the Patriot Center of George Mason University. In the middle ring, a bear danced with a man. The look of pleasure on J.D.'s face removed any doubts that she had done the right thing. He'd been so sweet when she finally pulled up at Joe and Claire's, forgiving her instantly. He was such a good kid.

'Geez,' J.D. said, looking up at her. 'How do they get him to do that?'

'The bear probably gives him marshmallows.'

J.D. gave her a pained smile. 'No, I mean how do they get the *bear* to dance? It stays right on the beat of the music.'

'Watch the man,' Suzannah said. 'He's making little motions with his hand. The bear sees that and hops. The training method was developed by the Russians.'

J.D. gave her a sidelong glance. 'I'm impressed. You really know your bears.'

'I've always loved them. I read everything I can get on them. Incidentally, the polar bears are back at the National Zoo.'

'How do you know?'

'The new *Smithsonian* has an article on it. Remember how they had to rebuild the polar bear grotto because they'd put it too much in the sun?'

J.D. nodded.

'Well, they're done now. The article has a lot of pictures on the construction. The new grotto's really neat. They brought the bears back from Philly last week. Want to go see them in their new habitat?'

'Kind of cold for the zoo,' J.D. said doubtfully.

'Chicken.' Suzannah thought of Juli standing in the cold shower at the POAC. Clearly, her son was not so stoic.

J.D. leaned forward, gazing raptly at the dancing bear. Suzannah thought about what had happened at the POAC. With the comforting presence of the crowd all around her, the gunman was not quite so terrifying. The detective was probably right; it was a flasher who had turned violent.

On the other hand, how easy would it be for someone to borrow a modus operandi? It would be the perfect way to make her killing look random.

Lancaster?

He must be furious at her for going to the FDA. But she could not believe he would try to have her killed.

She thought of the man who had broken into Dr Munley's office, and the one in the blue Ford outside Andrew's house. Juli had said the CIA kept a fleet of blue Fords. But surely no federal agency would put a hit out on an innocent US citizen. It just didn't add up. Why try and kill her at a public place like the POAC? Why not just slip into her house and shoot her in her bed?

*Because someone is watching your house, and the killer knows it.*

A chill went through Suzannah.

'Look, Aunt Suze!'

She felt J.D. nudging her. The tightrope walkers were at work now, gorgeous men and women in white tights. A big man with thick muscular legs balanced on the rope. Another man stood on his shoulders. A woman stood atop the second man. The spotlights held them in a dazzling corona high above the Patriot Center floor. The huge acrobat gripped the long pole across his stomach, inching forward above the abyss, the net out of sight in the darkness below. His concentration was obvious in every line of his body, every small calculated step.

Suzannah watched the acrobat inch across the tightrope. We have a lot in common, she thought.

On the way home, J.D. gazed out the car window at the dark Virginia countryside. He seemed quieter than usual, and Suzannah remembered what Juli had said about his maybe having a problem. 'So, how's school?'

'OK.'

Uh-huh, Suzannah thought. 'Just OK? I thought you liked it.'

'I do.' He turned from the window. 'Our class president got kicked out.'

'Kicked out?' Suzannah glanced at him in surprise. 'That's pretty strong, even for a private school. What'd he do?'

'Drugs,' J.D. said.

'Damn.'

'Yeah.'

'You were friends?'

'Not really.' J.D. looked out the window again.

Suzannah tried to put together what was bothering him. 'You think he got a raw deal?'

'He got what he deserved.'

Try again. 'So who's going to be the president now?'

J.D. gave her a long look. 'I was thinking of running.'

'Great! I think you'd be terrific.'

'Yeah, but what if I lose?' His voice cracked comically on the last word. Though she could not see it in the darkness of the car, she knew he was blushing. Her heart went out to him.

'That would be rough,' she said.

'The other guy who's gonna' run – Gregory – he's a big guy, a jock. I'm something of a twerp, in case you hadn't noticed.'

'A very smart twerp with a great sense of humour.'

J.D. groaned, but she could tell he was smiling. 'You don't have to agree with me.'

'Listen, J.D., you think the girls all like jocks? They don't. And neither do the guys.'

'Gregory's pretty smart, too. And he's got red hair. Lola Munson think he looks like Van Cliburn.'

'So? You look like Robert Redford.'

'I'll bet.'

'Except your hair's kind of messed up.'

J.D. reached into his hip pocket for his comb. And reached, and reached. Suddenly he turned on her with an accusing stare. 'Aunt Suzannah, did you steal my comb?'

Laughing, she pulled it from the pocket of his coat and handed it to him.

He grinned. 'I never felt a thing. When did you lift it?'

'In the crowd, coming out.'

'I'm proud of you.'

'Thanks . . . I think you could win that election.'

'Yeah, but what if I . . . lose.' He kept the emotion out of the word this time, and his voice didn't crack.

Suzannah thought suddenly of Tricia. 'What if you had a

vision, and in that vision you saw yourself winning. What if you knew your vision was correct, that it would come true and you would win?'

'That would be great.'

'Would it?'

J.D. turned on the seat towards her. 'You bet it would. I wouldn't get butterflies in my stomach every time I thought about it. I wouldn't have to worry about looking like the freak of the week for getting stomped in an election by some jock.'

Suzannah glanced at him, troubled. 'Think about it, J.D. Suppose I'm not joking and you really could have that vision and know it was true. In your vision, three days before the election, you see them counting the ballots and announcing that you won. Then the day actually comes and they're counting the ballots up front. You're sitting there watching it. How do you feel?'

'Real calm.'

'Where's the fun in that?'

J.D. looked out the window again. 'I see what you're saying. But I just want to win, Aunt Suze.'

And then, hearing the longing in her nephew's voice, a longing to see the future, Suzannah understood why Andrew Dugan hadn't gone to the press about the microchip. She felt a dawning horror. I have to find him, she thought. Andrew, where are you?

# 19

Andrew Dugan stared at the blank canvas, wishing he did not know what to paint. Instead, he saw in every detail the painting he could do: the carefully plotted greens, drab to iridescent, the gnarled twining of supportive browns, the baleful slash of yellow that would form a sort of horizon. At the top centre floated the eye, present now in most of his imaginings. A lidless eye, incapable of sleep, unable even to blink.

Repulsed, he turned away. Suddenly, he felt the chill of the room along his skin, smelled the kerosene heater, a faint unpleasant odour, like spoiled margarine. He stepped to the window. The sky was grey, with flat, listless clouds. The south light had paled into a weak square on the floor, barely lighter than the surrounding planks.

It did not matter. He would not be painting anyway.

Today was what, Saturday. He'd been gone from home for four days. He felt an overpowering desire to give it up, to stop hiding, to go back to the city and call Suzannah –

No, he must not. Andrew's throat tightened. He felt a horrible sense of loss. He'd seen her only three times, but the pain of knowing there must never be a fourth meeting was nearly unbearable. But he would have to bear it, for her sake. That day in the art store, he'd *seen* the men coming after him. Men led by another like himself, a man who *saw* – and who knew he could see too. They could have learned this from Lancaster, though he had not yet seen whether Lancaster was one of them. If they catch me, Andrew thought, I'll have a simple choice: join them or die. If they connect Suzannah with me, they'll go after her, too.

Andrew realized he had crossed over from his visions to his fears. No matter. Logic still counted for something, and logic said they were determined to keep the side effect secret. Suzannah had already caught them watching her. Perhaps it was only a precaution, since she'd helped develop the chip. But if they saw him with her, they'd assume he'd told her about the side effect and she would be in great danger. So he must harden his heart, forget Suzannah, stop tormenting himself about her.

Andrew heard a car droning up the long gradient on the highway at the south border of the property. Uneasy, he stepped away from the window, then edged back until he could see the split-rail fence and the road, seventy yards away. A blue late-model Ford had slowed almost to a stop beyond the fence. Andrew's anxiety sharpened. It was just the sort of car feds would use.

The Ford picked up speed and rolled on past, vanishing behind the high bank at the west end of the farm. Dark smudges of oil-tainted exhaust hung in its wake. Andrew let out a long breath, relieved. No respectable shadow would use an oil-burning clunker like that, not when they could just grab another from the motor pool. Relax, Andrew told himself. They aren't on to this place yet.

He felt the chill again, working its way into his bones despite the heater. He took another sweater from his suitcase and pulled it on. Seeing the rest of the suitcase's contents, he had to laugh at himself. Toothbrush, soap, towels – what had he been thinking of? Clearly, he needed more practice at being on the run. He should have thought of the fact that there would be no working plumbing in an old farmhouse that had sat empty for four years. Poor old house, too far beyond the suburbs, too dilapidated and architecturally undistinguished to interest Washington yuppies looking for a weekend place in the country. Their loss was his gain.

Andrew looked at the bottle of Evian sitting under the window sill and laughed at himself again. Yuppies, indeed. He took a long swig and looked around him, remembering his friend Everett's courage as he lay in the sagging bed that used to be beside this window. Everett, coughing out tall tales with his life. He and Myra and I laughed a lot, Andrew thought, even though we all knew he was dying. Ironic. We would never have been so close at the end if my marriage hadn't been breaking up and I was hiding out from my troubles. Being with them, losing Darcy didn't seem as bad.

He remembered Darcy grabbing his shirt when he was in the middle of painting *Engine Joe*. She'd pinched some chest hairs in with his shirt, and it had really hurt. She'd yelled, 'Are you listening to me?' And he'd said yes, but she'd been sure he wasn't. She was probably right. He wanted to listen, he was no doubt looking at her attentively and responding at all the right points, but his mind was a thousand miles away, trying to sort out some problem with the painting. She knew that, understood it, and yet she could not help but resent it.

Perversely, those struggles to drag out a painting that he just couldn't *see* were his fondest memories now. He'd scuff around the studio with the brush clamped in his teeth, pulling at his hair as if he could drag the painting out with the roots. Sometimes he would get nowhere for weeks. He would feel the damned thing hiding down deep in his unconscious, a shimmer of colour, a suggestion of shape that faded before he could get it down. He would go to bed exhausted when he hadn't painted a stroke all day. Black despair would grip him. He would believe he was through as an artist, would never paint again. Then morning would come, and some small aspect of the painting might be there, delivered while he slept. He'd rush to the canvas and get it down – usually wrong. But he would keep at it, trying again, again, until the colour, the shape on the canvas mirrored the thing that hid deep inside his brain. When he finally got it, he would stalk around the studio, grinning, feeling like a god.

He could never have appreciated it at the time, but now, too late, he knew it had been the effort, the weeks of slow, gruelling work that made him love painting. The long safaris in his unconscious, hunting shadows.

Andrew found himself standing at his easel again. He picked up a brush, dipped it in the burnt sienna on his palette, mixed in a bare trace of burnt umber, and made the twisting stroke up from the bottom of the canvas.

It was perfect.

He turned away with fresh despair. The hunt was over. All that was left was shooting fish in a barrel, effortless – and pointless.

Andrew threw the brush against the window, leaving a splotch of dark paint, ugly as a wound.

Retrieving the brush, he cleaned it. He broke the easel down and put it, the brush, and his paints back into their case.

He weighed the water bottle in his hand, dismayed at its lightness. He'd thought three bottles would last him a while. The cheese and nuts were holding up fine, but he'd drunk all but a cup of the Evian. Maybe he could drop some stones into the well, break the ice, and pull up some water. If not, he'd have to go to the barn, brush the mountain of straw off his car, and go in search of a convenience store.

Which would only put off the real decision: where he would go to hide permanently. Odd that he had not already seen what he was going to do.

The realization gave Andrew a twinge of hope. Could the ability be fading?

No. How long would he go on hoping for that to happen only to be bitterly disappointed? Hoping was a curse, tearing the same wound open over and over, giving it no chance to scar over. He would *not* hope. He would soon see what he would do. There was no escaping the movie that would roll in his head.

Meanwhile, he could enjoy not knowing. If he were smart, he would head west and keep going. Find a place in Phoenix or Tulsa, put the cash he'd stowed at the bottom of the suitcase in a bank, and take up life under a new name.

The sadness engulfed him again. If only he could see Suzannah one more time before he left.

I could be extremely careful, he thought. I could follow her at a distance. They're probably following her too, but I could rent a car, so they won't recognize mine. I could wait for her to go to a grocery store or a movie. Slip in and see her one last time . . .

And then he did see her. He pressed his fists against his eyes in a vain attempt to stop it. He saw himself in the bathroom of a strange house, holding Suzannah Lord in his arms, kissing her. 'Stop!' he shouted. 'Stop, damn it. I don't want to *see* my life, I WANT TO LIVE IT.'

But the movie kept rolling in his head.


Suzannah sat beside Jay Mallernee at the microfilm viewer on the second floor of the *Washington Post*. The work room stretched away in all directions. Dividers rose to eye level, partitioning the vast space into cramped office cubbyholes. Though it was Saturday afternoon, a good many of the spaces were occupied. Heads kept popping up comically above the partitions to peer into neighbouring domains. Suzannah wondered if it was to talk or to snoop. Snooping was certainly in these people's blood. She hoped Jay would be a very good snoop today.

She watched him at the microfilm machine. His cowboy shirt stretched tight across his broad back as he bent over the viewer. He looked very relaxed, very much in his element. Remembering last night, she had a very warm feeling. She'd taken J.D. back to Juli, then headed straight to Jay and spent the night cocooned in his strong arms.

Watching him twist the knob on the side of the viewer, she worried that she might be leading him into danger. They were safe enough in here with all the people around them, but what about afterward?

Suzannah remembered her talk with J.D. last night. *I just want to win. Aunt Suze.* If it became known that the microchip gave certain people the ability to see into the future, how many would feel the way J.D. did? People with innocent motives and others whose desire to see the future was not so innocent. The more she thought about it, the more sure she was that it was why Andrew hadn't gone public. The side effect of the microchip was explosive, as unstable as nitroglycerine. Perhaps Andrew had even seen a vision – a horrifying prophetic vision of apocalypse in a world craving the microchip, paying any price to get it.

Suzannah shuddered. She leaned over Jay's shoulder. 'Is there some way I can help?'

'Thanks, but the system's so screwy it would take longer to teach it to you than to keep plugging myself. By the way, why didn't you tell me how handsome this Dugan character is?'

'Is he?'

'Come on. I just found a photo of him. I don't know if I want to help you find him or not.' He flashed a smile at her to show he was joking, but she could see in his eyes that he wasn't, not entirely. It troubled her. Jay had never displayed even the slightest jealousy before. It was one of the things she found so attractive about him.

There is nothing between Andrew and me, she thought.

But she knew that wasn't true either.

Oh, what did it matter? True or not, they had to find him.

She paced away along the row of viewers, past other *Post* staffers busily working the machines. When she turned back, she saw a man and a woman talking to Jay. She waited, watching. Obviously, Jay knew them well. The woman was Hispanic, very pretty. The man was older, balding, with the indefinable look of an editor about him. He looked vaguely familiar to Suzannah. Snatches of their conversation caught her ear:

'. . . coming back?'

'. . . couple more months on this book . . .'

'Miss you . . .'

'Strange as it seems.'

All three broke out laughing but Suzannah could see that Jay was tense, looking past the two at her, as if he was worried that she'd join them. Maybe he was afraid she'd take up their refrain and gang up on him about his stalled manuscript.

She waited until the two moved on, then rejoined Jay. 'Anything?'

He sat back with a sigh. 'Well, there have been some references to his ex-wife Darcy, the divorce and so on, most of them in the Style section. Seems the divorce was fairly rough for both of them. She remarried – a rock star – and moved to England. We can try tracking her down and calling her if you want, but I wouldn't put much priority on it.'

Suzannah remembered the picture on his bed table. She had thought of trying to reach Darcy then decided Andrew was unlikely to go to his ex-wife. If he no longer loved her, he would want to stay clear of her. And if he still loved her, she was the last person he would put in danger.

'What about friends?'

'Well, I did find a short paragraph buried near the end of one article about a couple he stayed with briefly while his marriage broke up. He'd been good buddies with the man in college. The guy was a dealer in old books who lived on a farm outside Washington.'

'Was?'

'Yeah, I thought maybe it was a decent lead, but I cross-checked and found the guy again – in our obits. Poor devil died of cancer. So I don't think Andrew could be with him. Least, I hope not.'

Suzannah ignored the gallows humour. 'Where was the farm?'

'The article didn't say – other than that it's out in Virginia, fifty or so miles. Are you thinking maybe Andrew went to hide out with his friend's wife?'

'Could be,' Suzannah said. 'Do you think you could find the address?'

Jay gave her a reproving look. 'Bite your tongue, doc. You happen to be dealing with a cracked investigative reporter.'

Suzannah mustered a laugh at his pun and watched as he quickly located a drawer of microfilm spools for area phone books. The spools dated back to 1965. In the 1987 listings, Jay found Everett Cook, the friend of Andrew's named in the article. Jay dialled the number. A 7-Eleven in Chantilly answered. Presumably, Myra Cook had moved out after her husband died. A quick call to a local real estate agent settled the matter; the farm and house were empty at present – and for sale. Would they like to see it?

Jay told the woman no thanks.

'Empty at present,' Suzannah said. 'Hmmmm.'

Jay looked sceptical. 'It's a long shot, a tin can at two hundred paces.'

'Sure, but the house was a refuge for Andrew once. Maybe it is again. And what else have we got?'

'True.'

Suzannah tried to hold the map so that it and her head would bounce together.

'Sorry,' Jay said, swerving to miss a pothole the size of a dinosaur's footprint. He did miss, but he hit a bump instead, jiggling the map again. 'We just passed Hickory Corners, right?'

'Right.'

'So it's another five miles to our turnoff.'

'Right.'

She looked at him. 'If you know that already, why am I trying to read this map?'

'Take your mind off the bumps?'

She put the map down. It was hard to be amused when she felt this horrible sense of urgency. If she and Jay could dig the location of the farmhouse out of an old newspaper and a phone book, so could the people with the blue cars. Andrew Dugan was a famous person. The article had appeared quite some time ago, but if the wrong person had read it and remembered . . .

She gazed out of the window. The day mirrored her urgent mood. The sky boiled like molten lead, paling to a sullen white around the cauldron of the sun. Patches of snow, grimy as fallen tombstones, dotted the raw brown fields. Along the margins of the fields, rows of naked trees clawed at the sky like the exposed arms of buried giants.

It would make a powerful painting, Suzannah thought.

She wondered if Andrew, while he was staying at the farm, might have had the same thought, might have painted to take his mind off his divorce. The brief mention in the article said nothing about that. But if he had done some paintings there, the place would draw him all the more powerfully now that he was blocked.

Be there, Andrew! she thought fervently.

'Take a look behind us,' Jay said.

Turning, she saw a white sedan about a hundred yards back. She tensed, feeling suddenly anxious. 'Is it following us?'

'Too early to say. He just now showed up in my rearview mirror. Probably nothing. We'll see after the turnoff.'

She watched the car, thinking of the man at the athletics centre, hearing the flat, horrid sound of the silenced pistol as the door frame splintered beside her face. The white car fell further and further back and finally disappeared as Jay rounded a curve. She felt only a small relief. 'If they show up again, maybe we should break this off,' she said. 'I don't want to make you a target, too.'

'I've let myself be shot at for crusty old editors, I can surely do it for you.'

His voice was matter-of-fact, free of bravado. She hoped he really understood the danger. She'd done all she could to make it clear. Before asking him to help her at the *Post*, she'd told him about the man in the POAC. A strange light had come into his eyes. He had gazed at her with a sudden fierce concentration, and she'd realized it was fury. It had made her feel good in a perverse way, this evidence of how much she meant to him. But she didn't want his fury to get him killed.

'You were shot at in the Gulf?' she said as casually as she could. He had never mentioned it before.

'Once or twice. Fortunately, the Iraqis are lousy shots.' His jaw tightened, and she knew he did not want to talk about it. But maybe he needed to.

'I imagine you saw some people killed, too.'

'Yes.'

'That must have been hard.'

'Yes, it was.'

'Could it be why you're depressed now?' she said gently. 'Why you can't get started on the book?'

He glanced at her. 'What makes you think I'm depressed?'

'It's a hard thing for a man to say, I guess.'

'I have no *right* to say it – or to be it.' His voice was soft, but she could feel the tension radiating from him like a heat wave distorting the air between them. 'I watched the Kurds walk up into freezing mountains,' he said, 'with everything they owned strapped to their backs. I saw old men, Shiite Muslims, who'd had every rib in their chests cracked by Iraqi boots. I saw whole compounds of women whose menfolk had been dragged or marched away and were not coming back. I watched those women in the camps hold up pictures of their men – sun-faded photographs in cheap frames – and weep their hearts out. Compared to that, what is writer's block? You tell me.'

'I see. Only those who have suffered more than you have a right to suffer.'

'Can we stop this?'

'If you like.'

'Please. Let's just drop it.'

'All right.' She felt the frustration again, the disappointment. She had come close, just then. But he wouldn't let her in.

'If you won't let me help you,' she said, 'how about talking with Sharon Harrad?'

'Suzannah.' His voice rose warningly on the last syllable. He leaned forward, slowing the car. 'There – isn't that our turn?'

'Yes. Turn left.'

Jay slowed. 'Is that car still with us?'

She turned around, amazed that she could have forgotten. There was a car way back, but it was a different colour, a bright red sports car of some sort. 'No, they're gone.'

Jay made the turn and drove along the wooded road, slowing whenever there was a break in the trees. They passed several farmhouses, but the numbers on the boxes didn't match up. Then the trees cleared again, revealing a sloping front lawn. Jay read the number off the rusting mailbox. 'I guess this is it.'

Between the patches of snow, more dirt showed than grass. Peeling paint covered the farmhouse at the crest of the rise. The windows on the lower storey were boarded up. The barn behind the house leaned precariously.

Jay pulled off the road into the dirt driveway. Suzannah looked for tyre tracks, but the drive was so full of ruts she couldn't be sure what she was seeing. The only car in sight was the rusted chassis of an old Rambler beside the barn. She saw a sign on the side of the house: NO TRESPASSING.

Jay drove up to the barn. The door hung on a rusted overhead runner. He jumped out and leaned on the edge of the door. Rusted metal screeched as it slid open. Jumping back into the Jeep, Jay drove into the dark sanctuary of the barn, hopped out again, and pulled the door closed. Shafts of grey light shone down through holes in the roof.

'Why are we hiding the Jeep?' Suzannah asked.

'Because professionals don't just follow you with one car,' Jay said. 'They use relays.'

'The red sports car! You think it was following us?'

'I think maybe it was.'

He seemed very calm. Suzannah remembered the time on TV when the scuds had been raining in and Jay hadn't batted an eye. She began to be afraid.

# 20

Suzannah got out of the Jeep, still afraid but wondering, too – would anyone really use a red sports car as part of a tailing operation?

Holding a finger to his lips, Jay waved her over to the barn door. She pressed an ear against a crack. The road, about fifty yards away, was quiet. Her anxiety eased. It was getting cold. She pulled her coat tighter. It could be worse – the weathered walls of the barn screened out most of the wind.

'Do you think it's safe yet?' she asked.

'Let's just wait a bit to be sure,' Jay whispered.

A bird flapped in a high dim corner of the barn. The burst of sound startled her but she did not jump – and felt rather proud of it. She became aware of the mildewy smell of damp straw. Several bales had been pulled down from the loft and piles of it lay strewn about, as if someone had been tossing it around.

She looked at Jay. He stood very still, leaning his back against the barn door. His eyes were distant, his jaw set. She wondered what he was thinking.

Jay wondered if Suzannah realized what a storm she'd stirred up in him back on the road. He hoped not, or she'd surely press it. Her intentions were only the best, but he did not need to remember seeing people killed, *a boy being murdered*. He would never forget the terror on the Palestinian boy's face, the pathetic thinness of his arms inside the clenching fists of the two Kuwaitis. If only the Kuwaiti soldiers had not already been inflamed by the blood on the walls, the stories of Iraqi atrocities against their women and children. If only the tall blue-eyed man in the Arab clothes – the man from the underground – had not been there . . .

If only *I* had stopped them.

Looking at the boy, Jay could feel the blue eyes of the man in the *keffiyeh* burning coldly into the side of his face. The man hadn't even turned when they'd brought the boy in, as though he'd expected it. The two men holding the boy began talking rapidly to the Kuwaiti sergeant. The sergeant scowled at the quivering teenager.

'What are they saying?' Jay asked.

The sergeant brought his pistol to the boy's forehead.

'Stop!' Jay shouted. 'He's just a child.'

'This man is a Palestinian collaborator. He informed on Kuwaitis.'

The boy's legs collapsed. He hung between the grip of his captors, crying and blubbering. The sergeant thumbed the safety off.

Horrified, Jay yelled, 'Don't do it!'

The boy gazed at him, a new spark of hope in his eyes.

'Let me speak to the boy,' said the underground man. Jay felt a physical relief at having the cold blue gaze removed from him at last. But he was puzzled, too. So the man *did* speak English. In fact, he seemed to have a southern accent, such as you might hear in Virginia. Why had he tried to hide it earlier?

The man took the youth by the shoulders, gazed into his eyes, and spoke soothingly in Arabic. The boy answered in a low, submissive voice. They spoke for several minutes. Then the underground man turned to the Iraqi sergeant and gave an order. The sergeant nodded and put his gun to the boy's temple again.

'Wait!' Jay shouted, shocked.

'Best y'all stay out of this,' the underground man said. Now his accent sounded Texan, as though he'd made a guess about Jay's background and was showing off.

'I can't stay out of it,' Jay said. 'This boy –'

'This *traitor*,' the underground man said, 'has washed away his boyhood in Kuwaiti blood.'

'You can't know that.'

The terrible blue eyes gazed at him. 'It's you who cain't know.'

Before Jay could move, the Iraqi sergeant shot the boy in the head.

'No!'

Suzannah heard Jay gasp it. She stepped closer, taking him by the arm. His face was pale. Concern knifed through her. 'Jay? What's wrong?'

He blinked and looked at her; blew out a breath. He gave her a sheepish smile. 'Just daydreaming.'

'Your expression – you scared me.'

'Sorry.'

She held on to his arm. Slowly, the colour returned to his face. He wasn't daydreaming, Suzannah thought. He was having a nightmare, a waking nightmare.

Something slithered suddenly in the hayloft, and this time Suzannah did jump. Turning, she looked up into the loft, but she couldn't see anything in the dimness. 'Andrew?' she called softly.

'Probably a rat,' Jay said.

206

'*Euggh.*'

'Never mind. Let's go check the house now.'

She turned back to him. 'Jay –'

But he had already slipped out of the barn door.

She followed him. We'll talk about this later, she thought.

The back door of the house was securely boarded up. 'I'll see if I can find a loose window,' Jay said.

'I'll check the front,' she said.

'Be careful. That car might still be around, cruising the neighbourhood.'

Suzannah nodded. Listening for sounds on the road, she hurried around to the front. The porch sagged and creaked under her. The front door had not been boarded up, but it was locked with a good dead bolt. A car engine rumbled in the distance. Suzannah dropped flat onto the porch. The rumble drew nearer, ripples of loud and soft, modulated by the line of trees along the roadway. She pressed herself into the boards, smelling the weathered wood and the damp earth beneath. The car slowed to a halt as it drew level with the house. The engine idled beyond the property's front bank in a patient but hungry way, like a large panting animal. Inching her head around, Suzannah saw the top of the car, a sliver of red just visible over the front edge of the porch. A chill went through her.

Where was Jay? Had he got out of sight in time?

The car pulled away, picking up speed. Suzannah scrambled in the opposite direction, dropping off the side of the porch, peeking back over the edge as the car rose into view beyond the house. It slowed again, and she realized its occupants could see the back of the house now, too. *Jay, where are you?*

The car accelerated again, pulling over the rise and disappearing. Suzannah blew out a huge breath. Close. She hurried to the rear of the house and found Jay working his way along the small basement windows, trying each one.

'I don't think they saw me,' she said. 'Any luck?'

He gave the basement window a last tug and it opened with a screech. 'Yes.' He stuck his feet into the dark opening, scooted his rear onto the sill, then turned over onto his stomach, as easily as if he'd done it a hundred times. With a little wave, he slid backward out of sight into the basement. She imitated his moves, thinking of the night she'd broken into Andrew's house. She slid through quickly. Jay caught her feet and eased her down. Dim metallic light from the window wells showed a floor of bare packed dirt. A noxious coldness rose from it, tinged with the smell of fuel oil and rotting potatoes.

Upstairs, they entered what had once been a big farm kitchen. Old linoleum curled at the corners of the floor. The sink was stained with rust. The stale odour of cigarette smoke oozed from the yellowing wallpaper. The room stirred a sense of melancholy in Suzannah. She could imagine people sitting in this kitchen, laughing and talking as a Thanksgiving turkey roasted in the oven. The burners of the stove were thick with spider webs now, the cabinets and counters empty and abandoned.

She sniffed.

'What is it?' Jay said.

'Linseed oil. Artists use it. Come on.' Her hopes reviving, Suzannah hurried out of the kitchen. She ran up the steps in the centre of the house, following her nose. The smell drew her into a bedroom that looked out over the road.

The room was empty, like the rest of the house. 'He's gone,' she said, disappointed.

Jay gave her an assessing look. 'You have a lot in common with this guy, don't you?'

'What do you mean?'

'I'd never have known that was linseed oil, but you do because you paint.'

She laughed. 'I paint, but he's an artist.'

'Would you like to be, if you had the talent?'

She looked at him, mystified. 'I'm happy being a surgeon. I love art, of course –'

'Especially Dugan's stuff.'

'Stuff?'

'Paintings, sorry.'

'Jay . . .' She trailed off, uncertain. Had that been resentment in his voice? Even if it had, now was hardly the time or place to make an issue of it. Jay gazed at her. His steady blue eyes made her a bit uncomfortable. She turned away to the window.

'So you think he was here?' Jay asked.

'Yes. Remember all that loose straw in the barn? He probably used it to cover his car.'

Jay frowned. 'I should have thought of that. This damned book is making me dull.' He said the second part half under his breath.

Suzannah saw an odd smudge on the window glass. She leaned close to inspect it. 'Burnt umber,' she said. 'And burnt sienna. Oil pigments.'

'He tried to paint the window?' Jay asked sarcastically.

'He threw his brush at it.' She felt a stab of sympathy for Andrew, imagining the rest of it: the blank canvas set up in the middle of the room; Andrew trying to paint, failing, and in his anguish hurling his brush against this window.

And now he had fled this place in frustration.

*Andrew, where are you?*

With a finger, Suzannah wiped the paint off the cold windowpane and looked for a place to hide it. The room had a

209

small closet. She ran her finger down the wall inside the doorjamb, getting rid of the paint.

'What are you doing?' Jay asked.

'The people in that car are going to end up back here,' she said. 'If we can find an old article in the *Post*, so can they – especially now we've given them reason to think this area is important.'

'I wonder why he moved on,' Jay said.

'He came here because the place held important memories for him. He wanted to recapture some of what he felt here once, and he couldn't, so he left before his disappointment could write over the old memories.'

'People shouldn't try and live in the past,' Jay said. 'They ought to forget it and move on.'

At first, Suzannah thought he was criticizing Andrew, then she realized he might be talking about himself. The Gulf War was a disproportionately huge part of his past. What terrible things he had seen – and was probably still seeing, when he closed his eyes or looked at the ceiling or walked away from his word processor. He'd been there the day after Allied warplanes had strafed and bombed the fleeing Iraqi army on the highway out of Kuwait City. He had seen the blackened corpses, frozen into stiff sculpted poses, not by ice but by fire. He had poked his head into the gym where two Kuwaiti schoolgirls had been hanged with wires by Iraqi soldiers. And, as horrific as that was, she was beginning to think he had seen worse: something so bad he simply could not talk about it. Suzannah's heart went out to him. He needed so much to escape that past but he could not seem to, either by pulling it out with words or by pushing it deeper.

And meanwhile, Andrew could not escape the future, playing out on the screen of his mind.

Suzannah went to Jay and gave him a hug.

'Let's get out of here,' he said.

'Fine by me.'

Outside, she headed for the barn.

'There's a field over there,' Jay said. 'It's out of sight of the road. Want to take a short walk, burn off some of that frustration?'

Suzannah wanted to say no but she hesitated, conscious of the quiet appeal in his voice. The red sports car was out there somewhere. They should get out of here. But something was definitely on Jay's mind. She looked up at the sky. Still some daylight left. 'Sounds good,' she agreed.

The field, unploughed for many years, was still frozen despite today's warmer weather. Suzannah tested the crust. Her heels punched down an inch or so, but it seemed hard enough to bear her weight. The wind had died down somewhat, leaving the air heavy and cold. Jay slogged along beside her in his cowboy boots. 'To know the future,' he said. 'It seems impossible. If anyone but you had told me, I'd still be laughing.'

'It's no laughing matter.'

'No.'

Suzannah saw the look in his eyes. His Texas tan had, again, gone a shade paler. She stepped closer, put her hand on his arm. 'What are you thinking?'

'Nothing.'

'Jay.'

He gave her a fleeting smile and patted her hand. 'I was recollecting a time when I was in Kuwait and might have liked to know the future. But it wouldn't have helped.'

'Tell me.'

Jay looked off across the field again. 'We went to meet the leader of a Kuwaiti resistance group one night. A very strange man. We crossed paths in Kuwait City. Lots of terrible things happened over there. He was just one of them.'

'Jay, look at me.'

He turned back to her, his expression hard and a little desperate.

'Tell me about the Kuwaiti resistance leader.'

'Tall. He dressed like an Arab and had a deep tan, but he also had these ... striking blue eyes. He spoke perfect English.' Jay shuddered. 'No,' he said softly. 'I can't.'

Suzannah was suddenly frightened for him. She was wrong to press this. If he shattered now, came apart, what could she do? She was a surgeon, not a psychiatrist. And even if she were a psychiatrist, her feelings for Jay might well hinder rather than help him. She was one step from being in over both their heads.

She squeezed his hands. 'It's all right. Just relax. We won't talk about it.'

He took a deep breath, expelled it.

'When we get back,' she said, 'I want you to go and see Sharon Harrad.'

'I can't do that.'

'Why not?'

'I'm just not the type who goes to a shrink and spills his guts. Especially one I know.'

'Then we'll find one you don't know.'

'Forget it, Suzannah.'

She tried to think what else to say. *She* would go to a psychiatrist.

Wouldn't she?

'Maybe Andrew's back in town by now,' she said. 'We could take a turn by his house.'

'Are you sure you have to find him?' Jay said.

Suzannah looked at him sharply. 'Yes, if we can. We discussed all this last night.'

'Yes, but maybe you could find some other proof.'

'Like what?'

Jay spread his hands in an exasperated gesture. 'I don't know.'

'What is it, Jay?'

He looked at her. 'I guess I'm just wondering if the microchip is your only concern here.'

'What do you mean?'

'You had dinner with him while I was gone.'

Suzannah flushed, caught by surprise. 'Yes, I did.'

'And in all your talking about this, with his playing a central role, you somehow forgot to mention it.' Jay's voice was not accusing, but there was no escaping the meaning. She wanted to ask him how he knew she'd been to dinner with Andrew, but that would sound like a guilty counterattack.

All at once, she realized how he knew. Those two staffers at the *Post* talking to Jay today – the bald man had seemed familiar. It was because she had seen him that night in the restaurant. Not knowing him, she'd taken no notice. Obviously he had seen her and Andrew too – and remembered her when Jay had walked into the newsroom with her. He must have said something. Reporters were, in fact, born snoops.

'I didn't mention it,' she said, 'because I didn't think it was important.'

'What do you think now?'

'You seem to be making it important.'

'Suzannah, I realize you have admired this man for years, and he's handsome as the devil. You go to dinner in a romantic restaurant with him and keep it from me. What am I supposed to think?'

'Whatever it is, you could come out with it right away and not wait to ambush me,' she said, annoyed.

'I wasn't meaning to ambush you. I told myself it was nothing. I already knew you were talking to him, and the dinner was just a natural part of that.'

'It was.'

'But then I watched your face while you hunted through the farmhouse for him. You seem to know what he's thinking, what's in his heart. I have to ask myself why that even enters your mind.'

She knew she should say something. But she did not want to lie to Jay. Andrew did mean more to her than just a piece of evidence. What did Jay see in my face? she wondered. The question both fascinated and worried her.

She said, 'What I feel or don't feel about Andrew is irrelevant.'

'Not to me.'

'The point is, I have no choice but to go after him. Your worrying about what I might feel for him only makes the whole thing harder, and it's hard enough already. We've got to find him. He's the key to all this. With Tricia still unconscious, he's the only one who can stop approval. We've got to get him to tell his story to the FDA. Now, are you going to help me or not?'

'I'm going to help you,' Jay said. He sounded weary, dejected. It cut her to the bone. He started to turn away from her.

'Jay – all right. I am attracted to Andrew. And I admire him. But I *love* you.'

He stopped, looked down at the ground. 'And I love you. I

don't want anything to happen to that.'

She pulled him to her and held him. 'Oh, Jay. Neither do I.'

# 21

Driving home from Jay's, Suzannah tried not to worry. Everything had seemed all right when she'd said goodbye, but was it really? They'd stood outside his apartment, between his Jeep and her Chevy, their breath steaming in the cold night air, mingling with a sad, ghostly intimacy. He hadn't asked her up.

But then, they had agreed earlier that she'd spend the night at home.

'Call me tomorrow,' he'd said.

'I will. I love you.'

They'd kissed. It was not quite the same as their usual kiss, everything suddenly out of focus – or too much in focus.

She started to park in the street, then realized Juli's Porsche was already there. Saturday, she thought. I get the garage this week. She pressed her garage door opener and pulled in. Her headlights bathed the rakes and hoes that leaned along the back wall of the garage. Jay and I will find our way through this, she thought. Right now I have to find Andrew.

She killed the blazing headlights and got out of the car, hurrying in through the furnace room, the TV room, and upstairs. A light shone in the den. Juli's purse was not in its usual place beside the couch. Instead, Suzannah found a note:

> Suze,
> Joe and Claire took J.D. and me to a flick at
> Skyline. Back around eleven.
>
> Love, Juli

Suzannah was disappointed. She wanted to talk to Juli, to find out if any of the intelligence services were showing an interest in the microchip. She checked her watch. Only ten. Sheba walked into the den, tail high. Suzannah scooped the cat up and hugged her, needing the contact. She carried Sheba downstairs into the bedroom and turned on the light. The cat started to squirm, wriggling more and more frantically until Suzannah had to let her jump down. Sheba ran to the doorway, then stopped dead. She stared past the foot of the stairs at the furnace room door, ears pointed in concentration. Suddenly her tail puffed out and she scooted back upstairs as if the furies were after her.

'What's got into you?' Suzannah said. She glanced across the TV room. The door to the furnace room stood slightly ajar. The sight made her instantly uneasy. She must have forgotten to shut it. In fact, she could not remember shutting the garage door, either.

She hurried through to check. The garage door yawned wide open.

Her uneasiness deepened. She'd been preoccupied coming in. With Juli's car out front and her mind full of Jay and Andrew, she'd given no thought to being alone. She must be more careful.

Suzannah pushed the button to bring the door grinding

down. She locked the furnace room door and hurried back into the house. Back in her bedroom, she closed the curtains on the small ground-level windows and dialled the rheostat on full, so the recessed lights blazed with sunny brilliance. With the world shut out, she felt better.

She sat down on her bed and dialled Andrew's number. On the eleventh ring, she gave up and replaced the receiver.

She felt an ache in the middle of her chest. Andrew, Andrew.

Going to her bookshelf, she pulled out her folio-sized book of his prints, feeling the well-worn edges of the pages as she thumbed through. She stopped at the one he called *Sol*. The field of blazing yellow soothed her. Its strange polyhedral shapes suggested sunbeams refracted through a tear-blurred eye. How had he known to make them just like that? One false line, one clean edge where a blur was needed, and the radiant energy would drain from the composition. Even the yellow of the field itself was psychologically pure and perfect, the source from which the dancing polyhedrons drew their enchantment. Had he, in some burst of inspiration, dashed the colours straight onto the canvas? Or had he schemed, analysed, experimented?

Wondering about it made her want to paint.

She went to the corner cabinet where she kept her painting gear. She got it out, spreading the plastic tablecloth on her desk, setting up the mini-easel. She centred her half-finished canvas on it, surprised to find the paint dry to her touch. Had it been that long since she'd worked on it? She stood back and stared critically at the canvas: an apple in a bowl.

It was awful.

Oh, well, she'd just view it as a challenge, try to think what would make it better. An apple was red, yes, but there were many other colours in it, too. How could she know this and still not be able to tease them out with her eyes? Their subtle presence was essential to make the apple look real.

Suzannah squeezed some alizarin crimson and some light green onto her palette, savouring the oily burst of scent. She applied some fresh red to the apple and then tried dappling one side of it with the green. The result was muddy.

She stood back, aggravated.

She attacked again, working on the bowl, trying to get it to look rounder. Seen side on and slightly from above, it looked like a half moon lying on its back. The shape was right, but she could not quite capture the way light and shadow slid over the curving surface.

She looked at Andrew's painting again, wishing she could do something like that; Andrew Dugan had gone so far beyond basic shapes and colours to an understanding of what lay behind them. He knew how to make his paintings reflect emotions, using colours and objects to create a mental landscape. She could feel all this when she looked at his paintings, just as she could identify the feelings in herself that she wanted to pour into her work. But an immense chasm stood between her feelings and what actually showed up on canvas.

She couldn't even make an apple look edible.

She worked for half an hour, and then her enthusiasm left her. She put her paints away and washed her hands. Holding her left thumb under the streaming tap, she scrubbed at a patch of red, hoping she could get it off without resorting to turpentine.

Suddenly she noticed a note lying beside the sink.

*Suzannah*
*Don't say anything while you read this or*
*afterwards. Your silence is absolutely vital. I*

*am standing in your shower right now.*
*DON'T SAY ANYTHING!*

*Andrew*

Suzannah stared at the note, stunned, feeling her heart race as its message sank in. She dried her hands on the towel and flipped on the shower light. A dark form stood behind the frosted Plexiglas. Her scalp prickled. She yanked the shower door open and there stood Andrew, a finger to his lips.

My God, Suzannah thought. I've been looking for him all over creation and here he is. And I can't say a word?

He pointed to the bathroom door, leading her back into her bedroom. She saw that he was pointing up under her lampshade. Even before she looked, she knew what it must be. Yes, there it was, a tiny brass-coloured disc stuck against the brass socket. It looked as if it belonged there. She stared at it, outraged. Someone had bugged her room.

How had Andrew known it was there?

She reached for it but he caught her wrist and shook his head urgently.

He went to her desk, pausing for a minute to look at her painting. Her face burned with mortification. She would rather he'd caught her naked than see that dreadful thing. Much rather. He must have been in the bathroom all the time she was painting. Even if he couldn't see her, he'd have smelled the paints. She remembered she had hummed while she painted. She couldn't carry a tune, either.

I'm going to die of embarrassment, she thought.

Andrew motioned her over, pointing to the phone.

He was telling her that it was bugged too. She nodded.

He scribbled on her memo pad and handed the sheet to her. *Turn on your shower*, it said.

She went back into the bathroom, her mind still reeling.

Andrew here, her room bugged. She thought of the house across the back yard, the man – or men – who must still be sitting up in the darkened room, and was glad she'd pulled her curtains. She turned the shower on. Andrew took her by the shoulders, positioning both of them just outside the open shower door.

He whispered something. The hiss of the streaming water drowned it out. She leaned her ear close to his mouth. 'We can talk for a minute,' he whispered, 'if we're quiet.'

She nodded. 'You scared me.'

'I'm sorry. I had to sneak in. They're still watching your house.'

'Did you see them?'

He hesitated. 'In a way.'

She realized he meant that he had seen them in a vision. A sense of unreality filled her.

'You must assume that every room, even the garage, is bugged,' he said. 'I rented a car. I parked up the street and waited for you to come home. You shouldn't leave your garage door open.'

'I know,' she whispered. 'I was out looking for you.'

He moved closer to her, taking her elbow. She could smell him, a faint hint of cologne. The black lion's mane of hair stood up slightly, as though charged.

'We can't talk long this way,' he said. 'Can you meet me tomorrow?'

She hesitated. Was he just going to promise to talk and then disappear again? No. He'd risked a lot to come here and set it up. Still, she did not want to wait. She wanted to talk to him *now*.

She remembered Juli and J.D. They'd be home in minutes. If J.D. came down and saw her and Andrew standing there he'd surely say something, and the men listening to the bugs would move in.

Even standing near the running shower was too dangerous, more dangerous than Andrew probably realized. Juli had come home one day enthusing about Naval Intelligence's new toy – the latest generation of listening device. It was incredibly sensitive. The receiver was integrated with a computer, which could screen out noise, leaving only the signal, much the way the microchip did.

Andrew squeezed her arm, raising an eyebrow, waiting for her answer. 'Where?' She mouthed the word.

'Somewhere outside, with people around.'

'How about the zoo?' Suzannah said. 'The polar bears are back. There should be lots of people trying to see them.'

'Fine. Five o'clock.'

'Why so late?'

'Dusk is safer for us.'

Suzannah felt a chill. 'All right But don't be late. The zoo closes at dark.' She became aware of Andrew's hand, gently holding her elbow. The beautiful, intense eyes gazed into hers.

'Are you all right?' he asked.

She nodded.

'I didn't know the polar bears were gone.' Andrew's eyes held the hint of a smile.

'I like bears.'

'I like your painting.'

She flushed. 'You can't. It's horrible.'

'You struggle.'

She smiled. 'You've got that right.'

She saw tears in his eyes. He leaned toward her and kissed her on the lips. This time it was not the brief kiss of the art store but a lingering one, full of passion. When at last he broke it off, she drew a deep breath, her head spinning.

'Tomorrow,' he said.

'Just you be there,' she heard herself whisper.

'If they don't get to me first. They may be about to close in on you, too. Be careful.'

'Who is *they*?'

Andrew's eyes went distant. 'They call themselves Adepts. I believe they are from the CIA.'

She gazed at him, stunned. He turned and slipped from her bedroom and was gone. She became aware again of the water pounding beside her. Reaching into the shower, she shut it off.

CIA.

It made sense. Who would value seeing the future more than intelligence experts?

Adepts. The word had an ugly sound. Whoever they were, these men thought they were superior.

Suzannah's dread grew as she remembered the man in the POAC, the gargoyle face behind the nylon stocking, the murdered John Stockwell. Had someone in the United States Government decided that, for the good of the country, Andrew and she must die?

# 22

At 3 a.m., Archer Montross took his usual walk. A moment on his balcony told him the air was heavy and moist, cool but not freezing. The break in the Arctic front the forecasters had been talking about for days must be finally under way. He put on his greatcoat and trod softly down the five flights from his apartment, careful not to disturb the other tenants. He went through the back parking lot, turned left, and walked down the middle of the street until he passed the end of Prospect House, the long, ritzy high rise that blocked the view from his own apartment. The short sacrosanct preserve of Fourteenth Street fell away at his feet, yielding an unobstructed view of the city.

As always, the grand panorama made him catch his breath. A hundred yards away, the giant marines of Iwo Jima raised the flag in floodlit glory. Beyond the Marine Memorial wound the Potomac, black in the night, and then the federal city. The gleaming white shaft of the Washington Monument dominated the near distance; beyond it, only slightly out of line, rose the beautiful elongated dome of the US capitol, bathed in its own pure white light. Even this late, a few cars, tiny with distance, crept along Constitution Avenue. But back here on the hill next to Arlington Cemetery the night hovered at its peak, still and silent. Normal humans were asleep.

Archer felt almost drunk with what he was seeing. Laid out before him was the most powerful city in the world. The decisions made here affected millions upon millions of people. The enemies of America were changing, things were in flux. The danger to America now was not careful old men in Russia and China but the fanatics, the Husseins and Gaddafis with their bloody hands, their vicious minds, their nuclear and chemical warfare programs. To know what America's enemies were doing, what they intended, where and how they would strike next, was more important and more difficult than it had ever been. America needed a new edge. And America was getting it.

Me, Archer thought.

He inhaled the cool wet air, his head filled with pride. He was glad to be awake, glad to stand here in the silent street while other men slept.

What a strange creature he had become. Some nights, he felt like a vampire out here, powerful but alien and alone. Even vampires slept. But he could not – not any more. When the visions started, the dreaming had stopped and, soon after, the sleep. His body did not care. He did not need sleep any more. Rest was just as good.

Archer remembered his uneasiness when the dreams had first stopped. He'd gone back to his grad school psych texts, hoping they might suggest an explanation. He'd found himself rereading Freud with growing fascination. Freud had believed that hunches and dreams and certain other glimmerings at the edges of consciousness were actually windows into the unconscious mind. And what did these windows suggest? That the unconscious was not logical and rational. Hunches often didn't pan out. Dreams were crazy mixed up visions in which faceless people chased you through dim landscapes, or you were back in school and suddenly you were walking around in your underwear hoping no one would notice. *No comprende*, said the conscious mind. *Ich verstehe sie nicht.*

And so Freud, and other major theorists, had concluded that the unconscious mind worked at a lower and more disorganized level than the conscious mind. In evolutionary terms, the unconscious mind was seen as the older and more primitive, the primordial ooze from which the conscious mind had arisen.

The theorists were wrong.

Archer smiled, full of the knowledge that he alone possessed. Freud had been right to consider dreams the window into the unconscious. He had been daring to try to interpret them despite their scrambled disorder. But his efforts had been doomed, *because he and everyone he studied were asleep when dreams came*. It was so simple, really. Dreams seemed irrational and distorted, all right, but not because the unconscious projected them that way. In normal humans, the conscious mind was always busy, hopping with neural traffic and 'noise'. Only when that traffic quieted in sleep could the images of the unconscious break through. Ironically, at that point, consciousness was too dim to receive them properly. If a man dozed off in front of the TV, he would hear dull currents of sound, see an occasional meaningless image through a slitted eye, but it was not the TV that was distorted.

As for hunches, they were simply dreams trying to break through when the conscious mind was awake. They often failed or were garbled because, when awake, the conscious mind drowned them out with a ceaseless flow of its own information, both visual and verbal.

The truth was that the unconscious was not irrational or illogical. It knew everything that passed through consciousness and a thousand times more. It forgot nothing. It saw from the centre of the eye and its corner at the same time. It heard the murmured conversations at the next table, smelled the fear in an angry man, remembered the face of the mugger that the conscious mind repressed. It monitored everything a friend – or an enemy – had done for years and computed what the person would do next.

The bottom line: the unconscious mind was not the primordial ooze from which higher consciousness had risen. Consciousness was the ooze. The 'unconscious' mind was the next step in the evolution of the brain.

And I am there now, Archer thought, thanks to the microchip. I am awake when my unconscious speaks. Its images reach me through the microchip, clear and with no distortion. That's why I don't dream anymore. I *see* my dreams, my hunches. And they are always right.

Archer felt the pride again. Let humanity stumble along, following its penlight beam of consciousness through the dark. He, Archer Montross, was the new man. As the visions came more and more frequently, his metamorphosis would complete itself. He would be as high above man as man was above the apes.

The city wavered and disappeared.

Archer rocked back on his heels, clutching for balance, then steadied himself as he realized a vision had struck. He was in George Pederson's office at Station Three. As always, the office was dim, lit only by its green banker's lamp. Pederson was sitting in the same chair he'd sat in during their meeting. He was talking to someone in the corner, hidden in shadow. Archer tried to make out the man's face and couldn't. Then the man stepped forward, into the lamplight.

Ellis Grayburn.

Archer's mouth went dry. Ellis Grayburn, the infamous Deputy Director for Operations. He had never actually met the DDO, just seen him in the halls a few times. In fact, hadn't he passed Ellis Grayburn when he'd left Pederson's office the other day? He'd been too preoccupied to notice fully, but it seemed now that he had.

From the invisible vantage point in his vision, Archer gazed at Grayburn, a short man with a narrow hard face, thinning hair, and coal black eyes. As DDO, Ellis Grayburn was technically parallel to George Pederson. But in reality his position was not parallel, could never be parallel, because one of Grayburn's responsibilities was 'special operations'. Ellis Grayburn took care of the 'wet work'. The killing.

Archer listened to Grayburn and Pederson.

'This has gone far enough,' Grayburn said. His voice was flat and cold. 'We know from Lancaster that Andrew Dugan is having visions. As long as he stays outside the fold, he can ruin us. You've had days to find him. You've had men watching everything Dr Lord does. She was in Dugan's house, but that doesn't mean she has any real idea where he is. In fact, it probably means she *doesn't* know. Your men followed her and her reporter friend out into the country. They went inside that farmhouse and came out without Dugan. You searched the house. Nothing, dead end. She hasn't got a clue. It's time to give up.'

A farmhouse, Archer thought. That was what my vision showed me – Suzannah and Jay walking in the field.

'You're missing one thing,' Pederson said to Grayburn. 'Even if Dr Lord can't find Dugan, *he* can find *her*. If she's dead, he won't come to her, will he.'

*Dead?* Archer felt suddenly sick to his stomach.

'He's not going to come to her.'

'You can't know that.'

'Damn it, he's an artist. He's impulsive. If he were going to seek her out again, he'd have done it by now.'

'He *was* an artist,' Pederson said. 'Now we're not sure what he is. Remember, he has the same ability as our Adepts. If he didn't, we wouldn't have to chase him down in the first place. And you're forgetting something else. Even if Dr Lord doesn't lead us to Dugan, we need her.'

'She'll never co-operate. If you bring her in, you'll only be arming her with more information about Adept.'

'So what? If she won't co-operate, you can have her. Then she won't be telling anyone.'

No! Archer thought with alarm. You can't give her to Grayburn. She's mine.

'It's too risky,' Grayburn said. 'Suppose you bring her in and she escapes?'

Pederson made a throw-away gesture. 'This is pointless. We're just speculating.'

'My men will find Dugan,' Grayburn said. 'We don't need Dr Lord for that – or anything else.'

'So far you haven't done any better than we have,' Pederson said. 'And we have an edge you don't have: Archer Montross.'

Archer, feeling the implications of what was unfolding before him, shivered. He did not want his name mentioned to Ellis Grayburn.

'Fortunately, your man missed her in the POAC on Friday,' Pederson said. 'I want no more attempts on her life.'

Archer groaned. They had *already* tried to kill her!

Ellis Grayburn folded his arms across his chest. 'I don't like you giving me orders, Pederson.'

'I run this operation, we agreed on that.'

'As long as you run it right.'

'I insist we keep to our agreement.'

'Or you'll what?' Grayburn said coldly. 'Tell the DCI? Get me fired?'

Pederson looked at him without speaking, and Archer could see the fear in his face.

'Give her another day,' Pederson said at last, his voice low and urgent. 'You've scared her -- fine. If Andrew Dugan has seen it, maybe it'll bring him out.'

Grayburn paced back into the shadows, stayed there for a minute. 'A day,' he said. 'We'll give it one day. Then we do it my way. You can protect her in her house, but you can't follow her everywhere. The POAC proves that.'

The vision winked out, leaving Archer staring at the distant Washington Monument. He felt cold.

Ellis Grayburn wants to kill Suzannah. He's already tried once. If he succeeds, I won't have my chance with her. I want her; she's mine!

A wild fury filled Archer. Somehow, he would have to get to Suzannah before Ellis.

# 23

Suzannah arrived at the zoo at a quarter to five and headed straight for the bear pens. The setting sun poured long bands of rosy light and shadow up the grand slope of the zoo. A cold wind, heavy with the gamey smell of the monkey house, chilled her face. A single polar bear was ambling along the sculpted cement crest of the new grotto. She watched it, captivated. It was a magnificent animal. The white ruff of fur at its neck swung as it made a rearing turn. The bear sauntered down toward its pool . . . and her. Suzannah leaned over the rail to follow its progress. Its shoulders rotated like two massive cams beneath the rippling white pelt. She noticed that the ice in the centre of the pool had been broken open. The bear must have taken a swim not too long ago.

The thought of plunging into that frigid water made Suzannah shiver. She turned her collar up, savouring the warmth of thick wool against her cheeks as she watched the bear prod at the hay bales below her. It sorted through the creases between the bales, looking for goodies hidden by its keeper. It pleased Suzannah that the zoo cared enough about the bear's mental health to hide its food. According to the *Smithsonian* article, when zoo bears get to forage, it greatly reduces their sad, repetitive pacing.

The animal gave up on the straw and ambled back up to the

moulded concrete rocks above the pool. It looked lazy and laid back, but Suzannah knew the polar was the most dangerous of all the bears, a real killer under all that simon-pure fur.

She turned away and leaned against the rail. She realized suddenly that no one was around but her. And she'd told Andrew the place would be crowded. Surely she wasn't the only person in Washington who loved bears. Maybe it was too cold. Or too late – the sky was dimming to a deep translucent sapphire as the sun went down. Dusk was almost here. In only a few minutes, the zoo would close. Where was Andrew? Had the people chasing him caught him? Not if he could see their moves ahead of time. But maybe he had seen nothing, one way or the other, about this meeting. When he showed up, she would ask him.

There was so much she wanted to ask him.

She peered anxiously up and down the path. She could only see a few yards in either direction. The zoo trails here were hilly and serpentine, flanked with trees and bushes as they wound through the bear grottoes. Not only was there no sign of Andrew, there was no sign of anyone at all. The few people she'd seen earlier must be heading for the exits, their toes cold, thoughts of hot chocolate filling their minds.

He's around the next curve, she told herself. He'll come any second. She stared at the bend, the mountain of ersatz rock that made up the next pen. No one appeared. Frustrated, she turned back and was surprised to see the polar bear directly below her again, its wise catlike head swinging away from her. Goosebumps rippled on her arms. It's watching me, she thought. It wants to eat me for dinner.

'Shame on you,' she said to the bear.

Come on, Andrew, come on!

Keeping her eye on the bear as it padded away, she thought

about Andrew. She had so many questions. First she must hear from him if all the speculations she'd piled up from reading Tricia's file were correct. Was he seeing the future? Was that why the Agency was after him?

She replayed last night's kiss in her mind, savouring the warm echoes it roused. She felt a mixture of guilt and excitement. Her feelings for Jay hadn't changed one bit, but she was powerfully attracted to Andrew, too. If Andrew pressed her, what would she do? She groaned.

On the other hand, if she had to have a problem, choosing between these two men wasn't bad –

With relief she heard the scuff of a shoe behind her. As she turned, something smashed into the side of her head.

She awoke to a fierce pounding headache. The dusty smell of hay filled her nose. She realized she was terribly cold, and her whole body ached. She lay on some firm matted surface. Water lapped softly nearby. I'm in the polar bear pen, she thought. A wave of terror swept through her, banishing the pain to a distant part of her brain. She held still, afraid at first even to open her eyes.

A moment passed. Hearing nothing, she eased her eyes open. It was night. The only light came from security lamp poles in the distance along the zoo path. In the dimness she could make out the bear's pool a few feet from the edge of the bales she was lying across. Beyond the pool, the moulded concrete rose thirty feet to the crest that hid the bear's outdoor cave. She remembered from the *Smithsonian* article that the pen had a steel door in the back of that cave. She prayed that, while she was unconscious, someone had opened that door to let the bear inside.

Lying absolutely still, she listened. She could feel her heart pounding through the thickness of her coat, so hard it seemed to lift her body a fraction with each beat. She could hear the slosh of water, the chunks of ice tapping together.

Why was the water moving?

The bear is in the pool, she thought. Now's my chance.

She gathered herself to spring up, then thought better of it. The bear might not be in the pool. It might have got out already. It could be standing behind her right now, looking at her, wondering what she was. If she moved or made a sound, it would know what she was: prey.

Holding herself still, Suzannah scanned what she could see of the pen, ignoring the pain each movement of her eyes sent shooting through her head. She fought panic. She was trapped, and freezing. The pen had been designed to contain a huge strong animal, one much bigger and more agile than she or any other human.

She looked again at the side walls of the pen, squinting in the near darkness, searching for a blacker crevasse. The article had noted that the builders of the new grotto had included a bolt hole, a deep fissure in the concrete where a keeper could hide if trapped in the pen with a bear.

The bear burst up from the centre of the pool, snorting, shaking its head. Suzannah froze in terror. Only ten feet away, the animal looked as mammoth as a prehistoric monster. The ice chunks beat together around it, splashing a scrim of water beneath the bales. She kept her eyes on the bear as it broke its way through the ice at the margin of the pool and clambered out, shaking itself like a dog. Icy droplets stung her face.

The bear circled the pool, its claws ticking on the cement, fading, then growing louder again as it drew up at her feet and stopped. She closed her eyes, willing herself to lie still. She could smell it suddenly, a fishy odour, growing stronger—

Something struck her hip hard, rolling her onto her side on the straw. Terrified, she held on to her will, letting her arms flop back to stillness. *Oh God Jesus please help me.*

The bear snuffled her face, its whiskers, stiff and big as soda straws, raking her cheek. It prodded her again, rolling her onto her back. She lay on the straw, paralysed with fear, eyes slitted, seeing the awful head weave above her. The bear pushed its forepaw into her belly, pressing her down into the hay. She couldn't breathe. She fought the urge to struggle. It would only excite the bear. Her lungs ached. Her vision went dim from lack of air. She knew in seconds she would pass out.

The bear lifted its paw and walked past her.

She drew in a slow huge gasp, let it out and drew another as the animal lumbered away up the rise to the top ledge of its pen. A spasm of shivering hit her. Her teeth chattered. As if it heard her, the bear wheeled toward her atop its ledge.

Go! she told herself. She pushed up from the straw and sprinted toward the wall. The bear lunged into motion on the ledge above her, bounding down to cut her off. She felt its weight hammering through the cement. She plunged a shoulder into the nearest fissure. The cement stopped her – *too shallow.* Pulling back out, she screamed and ran to the next black crease. She could see the bear closing on her. As she plunged into the shadowy fissure, she felt the bear's shoulder slam into the rock at her back. She burrowed deeper, panicked. Jamming herself through a slight turn, she broke through into a larger cul-de-sac inside the cement. She felt the muscles of her throat burning and realized she was still screaming. The bear crashed against the opening behind her. Her head rang from the impact.

Suzannah groped the rounded walls of the cul-de-sac, hoping for a door. Instead, she felt a button. She hammered it and heard the muffled clamour of an alarm from somewhere above. As if maddened by the sound, the bear roared and smashed against the opening again. She could smell its breath, a meaty stench that made her stomach lurch. Her legs gave out and she slid down the wall. She clutched her knees up to her chest. She couldn't think what to do next. So cold. The alarm yammered on and on, then stopped. The bear snorted, its head in the entry only a few feet from her. She heard a distant crack, like a gunshot.

She felt numb. Her eyes started to close and she jerked them open again. Mustn't drift off in here; she'd freeze to death and they wouldn't find her for days. She butted her head back against the stone, bracing herself with the pain. She moved her arms and legs and flexed her fingers.

'Hello? Hello in there?'

Suzannah pushed up, her head pounding from the sudden movement. 'I'm here!'

A light shone into the crevice. 'You can come out.'

'Where's the bear?' Her voice sounded very high.

'He's here, but he's unconscious. We tranquillized him. You can come out, lady.'

Suzannah edged to the opening. A light shone for an instant in her face; then the man tilted his flash up so she could see his face. He was an older man, sober, concerned. She thought he was the most wonderful man she'd ever seen. Behind him, she could make out the moving silhouettes of other people. A slice of light fell across the bear's flank.

Suzannah let the zoo keeper take her hand, help her through the narrow opening. She watched the bear, turning her head to keep an eye on it as they led her up and around to the top ledge. Her knees felt weak as jelly. She was shaking and realized she must be cold, though she could not feel it. The men gathered around her.

'How did you get down there?' the keeper asked.

'Someone p-pushed me.' Suzannah felt the weight of a thick blanket being draped around her shoulders. Her heart hammered as though she were running in full stride. A hand on the back of her neck guided her down and through the low portal into the warm dim enclosure of the bear house. She smelled straw and manure.

'Do you know who pushed you?' one of the men asked.

'No. Do you have any more of that tranquillizer?'

The men all laughed.

# 24

A police detective from the Washington PD arrived first. On his heels came the paramedics, and then reporters from the *Post* and *Times*, and then a camera crew from the local CBS affiliate. The zoo keepers had called the paramedics. Everyone else had evidently been monitoring the police on their radios.

The paramedics found bumps and contusions. Clearly, Suzannah had suffered at least a mild concussion. But her head felt clear and she had no trouble seeing, so she refused a ride to the hospital. After the lonely terror of the bear pit, she savoured the babble of voices, the camera lights, the people crowding around her. Wrapped in blankets, drinking hot coffee, she talked first with the detective, then with the reporters. Yes, someone had hit her and dumped her into the bear pit. No, she didn't see who it was, couldn't even say if it was a man or a woman. She didn't know if the assailant had taken her purse.

The bear? She'd played dead with him, then run like hell and screamed her head off.

The police found her purse down the path. Her cash was gone. The detective did not ask why someone would want to push her into the bear pit. In a town that every year produces more senseless murders than days, the surprise would have been if the mugger *hadn't* pushed her in.

Suzannah was glad the detective did not ask. If the assault on her was connected with the microchip, it could be dangerous if the press or police dug out the truth.

One other thought kept going through her mind. If Jay didn't see her on TV tonight, he would surely see her face in the *Post* tomorrow. It was too juicy a story to pass up: SURGEON FOILS BEAR. Jay was going to ask her what she was doing at the zoo. She must either tell him she'd gone to meet Andrew or lie.

She did not know which she dreaded more.

The police drove her home, one of the officers following in her car. Juli, alerted by a call from the detective, met her at the door with a long wordless hug. She had started a big fire in the fireplace. Suzannah settled with her back against the couch, her feet inches from the flames. She ached in a dozen places. The knot behind her ear throbbed. The wonderful heat almost made up for it. She scrunched around a little so she could see Juli. 'Where's J.D.?'

'He's over at Cindy Markbright's making posters. He's decided to run for class president.'

'Cindy Markbright? I didn't know he was starting to notice girls.'

'More that they're starting to notice him. He got three calls tonight and took the best offer. When he learns he missed you driving up with a police escort, he'll be devastated.' Juli shook her head. 'I'm a little blown away myself. My kid sister, attacked by a polar bear in the middle of Washington, DC.'

'Great-grandma Thompson would love it,' Suzannah agreed. 'But when she told people the story, she'd leave out that the bear was in a zoo.' Suzannah tried to smile, but it wouldn't come. 'I'm going to need your help,' she said.

'I kind of figured that. But first you have to tell me exactly what's going on.'

'Are you sure you've got all the bugs?'

'I'm sure. I spent most of the day sweeping. They were the latest in high tech. Whoever did it stuck pretty close to the manual. Fortunately, I've seen that manual too. I could have found most of them even without using electronics. Most of them were in your room. Two in here, one in the kitchen.' Juli's voice was hard, and Suzannah realized how much the surveillance must be gnawing at her. For all the internecine squabbling between the intelligence services, whoever had bugged the house were still Juli's colleagues.

'Do you think we should get J.D. out of town for a while?' Suzannah asked.

'Where?'

'He could stay with Mom and Dad in Michigan.'

'What about school?'

'It shouldn't be for long.'

'They vote for class president next week, Suzannah. It means a lot to him.'

'I know. Damn.'

Juli bit at a thumbnail. 'Suze, you told me Andrew thinks the CIA is after both of you. Is that what you told the police?'

'No. I told them someone shoved me and I have no idea who.'

'Wise decision.' Juli looked troubled. 'I know a fair amount about the Agency, and in my experience they rarely kill. I think Andrew is wrong.'

'I'm not sure that's possible.'

'What do you mean? Anybody can be wrong –'

'When they are using logic, yes. Andrew was not using logic. He . . . had a vision.'

Juli rolled her eyes. 'Suzannah –'

'Hear me out. According to Tricia's medical file, she had visions of the future. Those visions were coming true. When I told you the microchip has a side effect, that's what I was talking about.'

Juli gave her an uncertain smile. 'You're kidding . . .' Her smile faded. 'You're not kidding. Suzannah, I'm sorry, but that's just too fantastic. In the POAC, when you told me the microchip has a dangerous side effect, I assumed it was headaches, strokes, something like that. I can believe the microchip causes hallucinations that seem like visions of the future, but they couldn't be accurate.'

'Then why is someone after Andrew – and now me? If all Andrew is doing is hallucinating, why would someone kill to keep it quiet? The only way it makes sense is if Andrew has something they really want – or really want to keep quiet. They're after him because they want to use him or silence him.'

Juli got up, walked around the couch, sat down again. 'We have analysts who've spent their *lives* trying to predict the future – specifically, enemy goals and actions. These are very bright people. And they're right for about a third of the time. I can believe you outsmarted a bear tonight. But don't ask me to believe people can see into the future.'

'Juli, I know this is hard for you. Hell, it's hard for me. But the best evidence I have is that the microchip has allowed – no, forced – two people to accurately foresee future events.'

'How could that be possible? People just don't have that kind of ability.'

Suzannah gripped her sister by the forearm, desperate to get through to her. 'Juli, when I was a second-year resident I had a very unusual patient. The old term for him was *idiot savant*. Fortunately, we've adopted more humane terms now. But you get the point, I'm sure. Even though he was thirty-four years old, he couldn't read. He could barely tie his shoes. But he could instantly tell you the square or cube of a four-digit number. No one knows how he and others like him do it, least of all the man himself. It appears the microchip has created two *genius-savants*. Above average to begin with, Tricia and Andrew now have an extraordinary new capability. They don't understand it any more than my patient did, but they *can*, in effect, see the future.'

Juli paled. 'If you're right,' she said, 'there would be people in the Agency willing to kill for that skill.'

'Which people? Would it come from the top?'

'The Director of Central Intelligence? I doubt it very much. From all I know about him, he's a decent, honourable man. Even if you set that aside, the DCI is too political to risk being involved in something like this. If there is a project to exploit the microchip side effect, it's more likely being run illicitly by a renegade, someone with enough clout to form his own tight little group. He sees a chance to greatly increase the power and effectiveness of intelligence gathering. He knows if it comes to light he'll be hung out to dry, but he's a powerful, confident player. He's sure he won't fail.'

'We've got to make him fail.'

Juli gazed at her uncertainly. 'Why? If the microchip really gives that kind of capability, maybe –'

'You saw Tricia hanging from a pipe. Maybe they did that to stop her from going public. That's a good enough reason to fight them. And if she did it to herself, it's even more important to stop this thing.'

Juli chewed her lip. 'I guess you're right. But, God, it would be so incredible. To see the future . . .'

Looking at her sister's dazzled expression, Suzannah had a sinking sensation. Even Juli didn't understand how dangerous it could be. She hasn't thought it through, Suzannah realized. If she'd seen Andrew's anguish, heard Tricia on the phone, she would know. 'Juli, whether you believe in God or evolution, there's a reason why a veil exists in our minds. We all can think of things we'd like to know about the future. But if we got our wish, it would poison us, destroy us.'

Juli still looked unconvinced.

'What would you do,' Suzannah said, 'if you saw J.D. in the White House and knew he was president? Not just of his class, of the country?'

'That would be pretty exciting.'

'And what if you saw him dying in an accident next year. I mean, you really *saw* it, perhaps over and over?'

'Suzannah!'

She reached for Juli's hand, squeezed it. 'I'm sorry.'

Juli pulled her hand away, then nodded. She took her glasses off, wiped them with a tissue. Her unfocused eyes made her look so vulnerable. Suzannah felt sorry. But I had to say it, she thought. Juli has to understand.

Juli put her glasses back on and leaned forward on the couch, rubbing at her forehead. 'All right, so our theory is that some renegades in the Agency want Andrew because he can see the future.'

'They call themselves Adepts,' Suzannah said.

'How would you know that?'

'Andrew . . . *saw* it.'

'The visions are that detailed?'

'Apparently.'

For the first time, Juli looked a little frightened. 'All right, let's assume for a minute that these . . . Adepts are trying to kill you, because they're afraid Andrew told you about the visions and you will expose them. There's still something I don't understand. If the Adepts let FDA approval go forward, won't the side effect become public anyway, when

243

other implant recipients start developing the ability?'

'I'm sure the Adepts want to stop FDA approval, just as I do. They also must know how careful they have to be. They must find a way to stop the microchip without letting the slightest hint slip out to the wrong people that it enables some implant recipients to see into the future.'

'Because certain people out there would want it anyway. People with the power to get it whether it's approved or not.'

'Exactly.'

'When is the FDA decision due?'

'It could be any time, but it's expected next week.'

'If the Adepts mean to stop it, they're cutting it awfully fine.'

'They may have already arranged for the microchip to be turned down. If they work for the CIA, they probably have pipelines into every other government agency, far above the level of that snide bureaucrat I talked to.'

'True,' Juli said. 'But why would they wait?'

'Because they're afraid to cross Roland Lancaster. He's a very arrogant man. I don't know if he is knowingly co-operating with them or not. It's more likely they're stringing him along, getting all the information they can out of him. Only two people out of fifty, that I know of, have experienced the effect. The Adepts would want to improve those odds if they mean to implant microchips in their own people. The best – and virtually the only – man able to help them would be Roland Lancaster. He knows more about the microchip than anyone else. If the Adepts are rogue CIA executives, they would be able to present themselves as legitimate govern-ment officials, possibly quite highly placed. By flattering Lancaster's vanity, they may be able to get quite a bit out of him.

'But he's no fool. The minute he realizes someone has killed approval of his magnificent gift to mankind, he'll put two and two together and go ballistic. The public worships Roland Lancaster. He would make a powerful enemy. And in the battle, the truth about the microchip might well slip out.'

Juli nodded. 'All right. But if the Adepts want approval denied, we don't really have to worry, do we?'

Suzannah contained her frustration. Juli wasn't dumb, but her daily immersion in intelligence work gave her a blind spot to its dangers. 'Juli, do you really want certain people in the US Government to be able, if they want, to see everything a citizen is going to do before he does it? To act against us on that knowledge if they see fit?'

'The CIA has no charter for domestic spying . . .' Juli trailed off.

'Right. Tell that to the people watching us from Sydecki's house. But there's an even greater danger: the Adepts obviously feel they can keep this all to themselves. But if they start sending out operatives who can see the future and acting on what they see, it will not stay a secret. A tiger this big can't be ridden. Juli, we have to stop this, for the public, the legitimate intelligence community, everyone. The sooner the better.'

Juli held up her hands. 'So what do we do?'

'Andrew is still the key. He's living proof of what the microchip can do. We can't stop it – discreetly or otherwise – without him.'

'And he's disappeared again.'

'The Adepts must have captured him.'

'Do you have proof of that?'

'Not directly. But Andrew told me yesterday that they were after him. He was afraid they would catch him before we could meet. So capture looks like our best guess. Is it possible they're holding him at Langley?'

'I doubt it. They'd be taking a huge risk, holding an unofficial prisoner right under the noses of the director and top CIA staff.'

'Unless Adept is being run from the top.'

'I just can't accept that,' Juli said. 'Movies and TV love to portray the CIA as bad guys. In real life, the vast majority of Agency people are decent, dedicated citizens just trying to do their job within the rules. The CIA has had the occasional bad director and made some rule-bending decisions over the years, but what we're talking about here goes beyond bending rules. The Adepts might have some very powerful backers, but the DCI isn't one of them.'

'I'm glad you're so sure.'

'I'm in the business,' Juli said stubbornly. 'I know how it works – and how it doesn't.'

Suzannah saw that Juli wasn't going to budge on this point. 'If you're right, where does that leave us?'

'Assuming the Adept people are Agency renegades and have taken Andrew prisoner, they could be holding him anywhere.' Juli hesitated. 'I hate to say this, but they . . . might not be holding him.'

The fear Suzannah had been holding at bay swelled inside her. Had they simply killed Andrew, as they'd tried to kill her? She thrust the thought aside with her own surge of stubbornness. 'I won't believe he's dead,' she said. 'And either way I'm going to find him.'

Juli smiled grimly. 'Take it easy. I believe you.'

'When I asked you to check for any link between the microchip and intelligence services, did you find anything?'

'No. You hadn't told me any of this, so I just checked for direct mention of the chip. But something this volatile will be very, very black, especially if it's being run outside Agency authority. No way will I find any mention of the microchip itself. But maybe these people are using a Company facility under cover of another project.'

'Good thinking,' Suzannah said. 'If their plan is to implant the microchip in their own people, they'd need access to a secure medical facility.'

'All right, I'll scan for any project of a biomedical nature the CIA is currently running. If I get even a hint of a connection, I can go to the director and get his co-operation in looking for Andrew, uncovering the project, and stopping it.'

'What if the DCI is in on it? You might not get out alive.'

'OK. The heck with it.'

Suzannah gave Juli a long hard look. Juli grinned. She went to the bay window. Pulling the drapes aside, she flipped two fingers off her chin toward the back of the Sydecki house.

Suzannah's neck tingled with alarm. 'Don't antagonize them, Juli.'

'I already did, when I took out their bugs. If they're going to be mad, they'll be mad about that. Tough.'

'I'm serious, big sister,' Suzannah said sternly. 'Just dig out whatever information you can find and then we'll talk over the next step.'

'I may not find anything,' Juli said. 'Andrew may be wrong; the people who are after him may have nothing to do with the Agency.'

Suzannah started to interrupt, but her sister held up a hand. 'My point is,' Juli said, 'even if this has no connection to the Agency, I think I should go to the director with it. If it's someone else, then it represents a huge threat to the Agency. And who is better equipped to quietly ferret it out and put a stop to it?'

'Do you think we could get the situation across to the director over the phone?'

Juli shook her head. 'No way. The DCI's office fields phone calls every day from paranoids convinced they have vital information "for the director's ears only". His staff screen all calls. In trying to get access by phone, you'd have to spill more than you want to underlings. The odds are they'd think you were just another crazy. And if the wrong staffer took you seriously, you could trigger the very thing you're trying to stop. You said it yourself: whoever stops the microchip has to play it as tight to the vest as possible. No, if I get something, I'm going to have to go in person, as an officer in Naval Intelligence, and win the director over step by step, face to face.'

Suzannah knew Juli was right. But she had a heavy sense of foreboding. 'It gives me a bad feeling to think of you delivering yourself right into their hands,' Suzannah said. 'It's like sticking your head in a lion's mouth and trusting him not to bite it off. I don't want you walking into Langley and never coming out again.'

'Sooner or later, I'll have to go in,' Juli said. 'Unless you have a better idea.'

I do, Suzannah thought. *I'll* go in.

But she didn't say it.

# 25

Eating a cheese-and-lettuce sandwich at her desk, Suzannah glanced out of her office window to check the weather. The sky shone blue and crystal clear. Sitting in the drowsy heat of the surgical wing, she could almost believe it was warm out. But it was freezing again.

She felt incredibly anxious. She had to find Andrew, but she didn't have much of a plan.

She took another bite of her sandwich. It wasn't bad. Leaving the salami out would be good for her cholesterol count. She remembered what Andrew Dugan had said at the restaurant when she'd asked him if he was a vegetarian: *Only when I eat*. The answer had amused her; now she could see how well it summed him up, his humour, his economy of thought, his utter lack of any impulse to proselytize. He would have made a horrible Jehovah's Witness.

On the other hand, she'd left the salami out, hadn't she?

Was Andrew locked in a cell right now – or worse?

I could call Jay, she thought. Maybe he knows someone at the Agency and could get me in.

No, she thought. I can't face Jay right now.

She put her sandwich down, her appetite gone. He'd been so wonderful this morning, rushing over to her house at 5 a.m., the *Post* still in his hand. Throwing his arms around her, holding her as if she was the most precious thing in the world to him. She was on the front page all right, but she'd got the headline wrong. It was BRAVE SURGEON FOILS BEAR. His arms still around her, Jay had started asking the questions. The most important one was, 'What were you *doing* out there?'

And she'd lied.

She'd told him she'd gone to see the new polar bear grotto. It was credible enough. He knew she loved bears, and the zoo was only a few blocks from Adams Memorial. She'd gone there several times before, after finishing with her afternoon office patients.

Jay had accepted it at once. She felt terrible.

But what was she supposed to tell him? Andrew was at my house late at night. We stood outside my shower. We agreed to meet at the zoo, and then we kissed.

It was the first time she had lied to Jay. If it was going to be the last, she'd have to avoid him the next few days. Besides, Jay would never let her go to Langley alone, and she didn't want him in danger any more than she did Juli.

She would have to do this alone.

But how? If she didn't come up with a decent plan soon, Juli would beat her to the punch. Suzannah thought of her sister. By now she was probably home in bed after working the entire night in the Pentagon. Or, if she'd found a solid lead, she might this very minute be on her way to Langley. She promised to check with me before she did anything, Suzannah thought, but she's at least as headstrong as I am. If she thought I'd try to stop her, she might just go for it.

Suzannah closed her eyes, concentrating. First she had to get through the gate at Langley. There were sure to be guards—

Her intercom buzzed. 'Dr Lord,' Marjory said, 'there's a

Mr Percy Jones out here. He'd like to see you at once. He says it's urgent.'

Suzannah checked her watch. Her first patient of the afternoon was scheduled in half an hour. She'd been operating all morning. This was her one little window of time to think in, and she needed it desperately today. 'I'm sorry, but he'll have to make an appointment.'

'He – um, he says he's from the CIA.'

Suzannah's heart began to pound. Was this an Agency killer, come to do what the bullets and the bear had not? No, she thought. Not and announce himself to Marjory first. All the same, she'd better have some back-up ready. 'Tell him I'll be with him in two minutes.'

She dialled Sharon Harrad's private office line, praying she'd be sitting at her own desk eating her usual bagel and apple.

'Sharon Harrad.'

'Sharon, thank God you're there. Can you spare Curtis and Jack down here? I may have a problem.'

'Sure, it's a slow day in mental health heaven. You going to drum me up some business?'

Suzannah forced a laugh. 'No, but I might need a little muscle for a few minutes.'

'No problem. I'll send them right down.'

'Tell them to wait at Marjory's desk.'

'You all right?'

'Fine. You're a pal.'

As soon as Sharon hung up, Suzannah went to meet Percy Jones. The knob of her office door slipped in her hand. She dried her palm on her medical coat. Jones stood at Marjory's desk, his eyes already centred on her door. 'Thank you for seeing me, Dr Lord.' He looked about fifty, a stoop-shouldered man in a grey suit. Longish hair curled over his ears. Wire-rimmed glasses added a professorial touch to his innocuous smile.

He held out an ID. It said he was Percy Jones of the Central Intelligence Agency. It looked authentic.

'Percy *Jones*,' she repeated.

He gave an easy laugh. 'Yes, everyone comments on that. But Percy is my real name, I assure you.'

Suzannah could not find a smile. 'Come into my office,' she said. She walked behind her desk, pointed to the chair. He remained standing; so did she.

'What can I do for you, Mr Jones?'

'It's not what you can do for me that brings me here, Dr Lord, it's what you can do for your country.'

'And that is?'

'Stay away from everyone who took part in Dr Lancaster's pilot study. Keep any opinions you may have about the microchip and the study strictly to yourself. In two words, forget it.'

'Please don't beat around the bush.'

Percy Jones smiled.

'You bugged my house. You've been watching me. You've tried to kill me twice, and now you come here –'

'Wait a minute,' Jones said sharply. 'Back up. We didn't try to kill you.'

'You expect me to believe that?'

'*Someone* is trying to kill you, yes. But not . . . us.'

She noticed the hesitation before 'us'. It did nothing to reassure her. What had hung him up? Some hair-line distinction between his own section and someone else's?

'If it's not you, who is it?'

'Someone we can take care of – if you will stop trying to stir things up.'

Did she detect a false ring to his certainty, an extra force in

252

his voice, as though he was trying to convince himself? If they can't even call off their own killers, Suzannah thought, I'm in trouble. Her knees felt suddenly weak. She walked around her desk and sat down, pointing to the chair across the desk again. Jones looked like he wanted to decline, then sat, crossing his legs. Her impression of a slightly flaky college professor deepened.

'Why do you care what I think of the microchip?'

Jones raised a hand. 'I'm not here to discuss the microchip. I will say only that, despite what you think, it will harm no one. And it may do even greater good than you realize.'

'What about Tricia Fiore?' Suzannah said. 'Is that the greater good you're talking about? She's in a coma now. Did she hang herself, or did you people do that for her?'

Jones gave a weary sigh. 'Doctor, I am a simple government worker, a public servant. We do not go around killing people, despite what you've seen in the movies.'

'Don't patronize me.'

'Forget the microchip, doctor.' His tone turned flat, edged with menace.

Even though she was afraid, she felt a flash of resentment. Simple, no; a public servant, yes – and he had no right to talk to her like this. 'And if I don't?'

'If you go public with any misgivings about the Lancaster procedure, I guarantee you'll be discredited. We will see that everyone knows you are a hysterical woman who threw herself sexually at a great and noble man, a medical genius greater than Jonas Salk or Christiaan Barnard. When Dr Lancaster gently and tactfully turned aside your advances, you reacted with the fury of a woman scorned, plotting his downfall. Believe me, Dr Lord, you will have spoken up for nothing, and you will be severely embarrassed.'

Suzannah struggled to contain her anger. She had already

faced this threat, didn't he realize it? You hypocrite, she thought. You're not afraid I'll stop the Lancaster procedure. You're afraid I'll let the wrong people know what it does. Then you couldn't keep it for your own little toy. With an effort she controlled her voice. 'Is Roland Lancaster co-operating with you?'

Percy Jones smiled smugly and said nothing.

'What have you done with Andrew Dugan?'

'Not a thing.'

'I want to see him – *before* I make any deals.'

'Dr Lord, what makes you think we have any idea where he is?'

'You've been after him. Now you've caught him.'

Jones looked at her, as if weighing which answer would best serve his needs. 'I resent your implication that we would hold any US citizen against his will, and I deny it categorically. Before you say that in public, be ready for everything I've warned you about.'

They do have him, Suzannah thought. They caught him because he came to my house. That's probably why they were watching me in the first place – hoping Andrew would try to contact me. They heard us over the sound of the shower, even though we whispered. And now that they have Andrew, they don't need to keep back from me any more; which is why Mr Jones is here now.

She stood. 'I'm tired of your threats, Mr Jones.'

He stood, too. 'I like making them even less than you like hearing them, but I'm deadly serious. We will drag your name through the mud?'

'Get out of my office.'

Jones gave her a reproachful look. 'I can see that you have not taken our little talk seriously.'

'I want you out of here *now*.'

'Let's both go,' Jones said quietly.

'What does that mean?'

'In the interests of national security, Dr Lord, I have been authorized to bring you to my superiors if you refuse to co-operate.'

Suzannah felt the fear again, a moth brushing at the walls of her stomach. 'You have no authority to arrest me.'

'I can be back here inside half an hour with an Arlington police lieutenant who does have that authority.'

'On what charge?'

'Breaking and entering, stealing the confidential patient files of Dr Vincent Munley.'

Suzannah looked at him, stunned. The man in the stocking mask, she thought. But how did he know I was there? He never saw Jay and me. And we didn't steal the records, we only looked at them.

Maybe they came back, found the hidden room, and stole the file themselves. That must be it.

But how did they know I was there? Did someone – one of their people – see it in a vision? She felt a deep chill at the thought. 'You can't make a charge like that stick.'

'You'd be surprised what we can make stick. And you did, in fact, break into Munley's office. Even if you don't get a jail sentence, you'll be finished as a physician.'

He's right, Suzannah thought with a sick feeling. I couldn't even pass a lie detector test on Munley.

Or is he bluffing? That business about the police lieutenant. If the Adepts are renegades doing their own thing within the CIA, how many strings can they pull without alerting the director and exposing themselves? I could try to call his bluff. But if I'm wrong –

'What's it to be, doctor? A nice quiet chat with my superiors or the humiliation of being arrested in front of your colleagues and patients?'

An idea struck Suzannah.

No, she thought, it's outrageous.

And I've got to try it. 'All right, I'll go with you.'

'Now you're being reasonable,' Jones said.

'But first I need a moment in there.' She pointed to the door of her office bathroom.

Jones got up and opened the door. When he turned back, his face was pink. 'By all means.'

She slipped inside, shut the door and sat on the toilet seat. Picking up the phone, she dialled Marjory.

'I'm calling you from my bathroom,' Suzannah said. 'Don't be alarmed, but the man in my office is definitely not from the CIA. He's paranoid and irrational and I think he's probably violent.'

'Dear God –'

'Are Curtis and Jack there?'

'Yes, they're right here.'

'Tell them what I just told you. We're going to commit Mr Jones. I want them to wait thirty seconds and then come in. They are to take him back to the psychiatric ward and put him in seclusion. Warn them that he'll probably put up a fight. Don't forget, they're to wait thirty seconds.'

'Will you be all right?'

'Yes.' Suzannah hung up her phone. She leaned against the wall, her heart banging against her ribs. This was insane. But she couldn't let him take her in. Then she would disappear, just like Andrew, and they could do whatever they wanted.

Suzannah flushed the toilet and stepped back into her office.

Percy Jones rose. 'All set?'

She nodded. 'But I'd like to see your ID one more time, please,' she said.

'Certainly.' Jones handed it to her.

She pored over it, not seeing it at all, feeling the panic build. She was acutely aware of Jones watching her. She wondered suddenly if he had a microchip in his brain?

No. Why would he wear glasses?

To put her off guard?

*Come* on, *Curtis.*

A light rap on the door.

Relief rushed through her. 'Come.'

Curtis and Jack walked in, two towering hulks. Suzannah slipped Jones's ID into her coat, turning to him.

'Mr Jones,' she said, 'we have a nice room for you.'

'What?' He looked at the two orderlies. His face paled.

'Don't be alarmed,' Suzannah said.

'Wait – take your hands off me.'

She watched as Jack and Curtis took Mr Jones by the arms and started him towards the door. Jones tried to tear free.

'Just take it easy, sir,' Curtis said in his soothing professional voice.

'I'm a government agent,' Jones said in a loud, outraged voice. 'She has my ID – just a minute, wait a minute, damn you. She has my ID. Just look at my ID –'

'Yes, sir,' Jack said, in a tone much like Curtis's.

They marched Percy Jones through the door. He tried to stop them by spreading his legs, planting a foot on either jamb. They pulled him through easily.

'You'll pay for this, all of you!' Jones yelled.

He went on yelling all the way down the hall.

I'm sorry, Suzannah thought, but you really should have left me a way out.

# 26

'You say you want it cut short, hon?'

'As much like this as you can.' Suzannah held up three close-up photos she'd taken of Juli during the summer at Ocean City. One was a profile and the other two were full-face.

The chief hairdresser at the Arlington Forest Beauty Salon, a plump woman named Bonny with a red bouffant, shuffled through the photos with a critical squint. The powerful musty-fruit stench of perming solution drifted down from the next chair, where one of Bonny's assistants was fixing lots of little blue curls onto the head of an elderly woman. 'OK,' Bonny said, 'a bob, but leave long bangs in front, right?'

'And dye it blonde.'

'You got it.' Bonny handed the photos back and gave her a sympathetic look. 'Boyfriend troubles?'

Suzannah forced a laugh, thinking of Jay. Those, too, she thought. 'I just need a change.'

'Don't we all.' Bonny moved around behind her, patting her hair dry with a towel. Suzannah listened to the steely snip of the scissors, felt the disfiguring tugs. Snippets of her hair fell down the cloth in waves. She watched it stoically. It would grow back.

If she was lucky.

She could not believe she was being so calm about this. Usually, every time she had her hair cut, she had to take a Valium – and that was when she stayed with the same style. Nothing like sticking your neck under the axe to put a haircut in perspective. She only hoped Bonny was fast. Even if she was, this was going to take at least two and a half hours. It was only a matter of time before Percy Jones or whatever his name was got control of himself and convinced Sharon he was really from the CIA. If Sharon had given him a shot to calm him down, it might be tomorrow before he could talk himself out of seclusion and off the ward.

But I can't count on it, Suzannah thought.

She felt terrible, using Sharon this way. She hadn't even dared hint to her that Jones wasn't really crazy. Sharon is one of my best friends, she thought. Maybe I should have told her that Jones wasn't really crazy but was threatening me. That I was in trouble and needed him held for a day. She probably would have done it.

But then she'd have been in deep trouble just like me.

No, I *had* to lie to her to protect her.

Suzannah put Sharon and Percy Jones from her mind. She must work on her plan. Juli's uniform coat, cap, and spare glasses were tucked away in the car. Fortunately, Juli slept like the dead, especially after an all-nighter at the Pentagon. Even when she woke up, she wouldn't miss the badge until the next time she got ready for work.

All right, Suzannah thought. Assume I get past the gate as Commander Lord. What then? How do I get to see the Director of Central Intelligence, what did Juli call him? – the DCI?

Suzannah's heart sank. It was crazy. A commander in naval intelligence might be able to bluff her way to the DCI's office, but if the director had approved a microchip project, she would end up right where Percy Jones had wanted her from the start.

No negative thoughts, Suzannah told herself firmly. You're going to do this, so stop arguing with yourself.

She worked on what she was going to say. Assuming the DCI did not know about the Adepts, what did she want him to do? First, make sure he stopped FDA approval and second, make sure he didn't decide the Agency could get away with using the microchip. The first sounded easy enough, especially if the Adept people already had an FDA plan in the works. The second might be much harder, if Juli's reaction when she'd learned what the microchip could do was any indication.

Suzannah imagined herself in the DCI's office, talking to him. She would begin by making it clear that she was an expert on the microchip, that she had helped Roland Lancaster develop it.

She worked out her plan while Bonny snipped and dyed.

The warm blast of the blow drier surprised her. Almost finished. The time had gone by like lightning. Bonny worked on her with a brush for a minute. Suzannah gathered her nerve.

'There, hon.' Bonny swung her chair around. Suzannah stared with shock at the blonde woman in the mirror. She squinted and tilted her head. She did not look like Suzannah Lord anymore. But did she look like Juli? Her confidence plummeted. I'm never going to fool them, she thought.

Driving out the George Washington Parkway towards Langley, with Juli's uniform jacket on and the funky cap perched on her head, she felt a little more positive. She shrugged inside the uniform jacket. It was a bit large in the shoulders, but the shoulder pads she'd put under her white blouse were helping. As for her facial resemblance to Juli, it wasn't bad. One did not just see, one *learned* to see, and she had learned all the small differences between her face and Juli's. The guard at the gate had no such practice. The glasses were the key. Round and dark-rimmed, they were a prominent feature of Juli's appearance. When she put them on, the resemblance between her and the photo was quite striking.

There was only one problem. When she put them on, she could barely see.

Anxious, Suzannah picked up the glasses, then put them back on the seat. She needed practice seeing through them, but not while she was driving.

Rounding a curve on the parkway, she got a quick view down through the trees at the Potomac below. The river looked dead, its grey water still as a lake. She realized the river was frozen over all the way across. She could not remember the last time a cold snap had lasted long enough to do that. She wished the cold would end, the ice melt, the air ease back into the moderate forties and low fifties Washington usually boasted in the winter. It was as though a curse had been put upon them, a withdrawing of warmth by some angry god. Perhaps it was the god of visions, angry because man had invaded a place he did not belong.

Suddenly Suzannah felt alone and afraid. She wished Jay were here beside her, just to hold her hand and give her moral support.

Suzannah saw the sign for the CIA and turned off, following the winding road through winter-bare trees. A sign instructed all visitors to keep right. She did, drawing alongside a strange object that looked like a square trash can about four feet high. In its side she saw a panel of dark glass and a speaker like the ones in the drive-through at

McDonald's. Ahead, a guarded gate blocked the way. Suzannah stopped and rolled her window down.

Nothing happened.

I'll have a shake and fries, she thought, and if you're holding Andrew, I'll have him, too. She wondered if the speaker was broken. Despite the chill air pouring through the window, she started to sweat.

A disembodied voice asked her identity and purpose.

She noticed a camera behind the dark glass. Slipping on her glasses, she faced the camera. 'Commander Juli Lord, USN, here for a meeting at fifteen hundred.'

'What is your SSN?' the voice asked.

My what? she thought. Oh, my social security number. *No not mine – Juli's.* For a moment, she froze. Was it on the badge? No. Sweat prickled on her forehead. Then she remembered the joint account she kept with Juli for household expenses. She must have forged Juli's signature and social security number at least a hundred times – whenever she needed to make a withdrawal and Juli wasn't around. What was it? Her mind blocked for a second. God, they'd think she'd had a stroke. The number came to her suddenly and she blurted it out.

After another pause, the voice droned, 'You may drive up to the gate for the ID check.'

Suzannah's heart pounded. Her mouth was dry. She tried to swallow and couldn't. She inched the car forward to the gate. This is it, she thought.

'Good afternoon, commander.' The guard held out his hand.

'Afternoon.' She handed Juli's badge to him and sat, intensely aware of his gaze on her face. She had no idea whether she should look straight at him or be more casual. She settled for glancing at him, then at her dashboard, as though there was something interesting there. Her eyes started to water. She resisted the urge to take the glasses off.

'Thank you.'

She nodded, taking the badge back, waiting for the gate to rise. It did not. Instead, the guard shoved a small clipboard through the open window. 'Sign in, please.'

Her heart sank as she looked at the blurred grid of lines and indecipherable writing. She would have to take off Juli's glasses. She did, bending over the board, writing in the required squares, signing Juli's name. The guard took the clipboard back, but stayed leaning on the window, watching her as she put her glasses back on.

'Since you don't have a sticker,' he said, 'you'll have to park over there in visitor parking.'

'Fine.'

The gate opened at last and she drove through, feeling a surge of exhilaration. Made it! she thought – then reminded herself it was only step one. She parked and headed toward the main building, taking her glasses off long enough to get a look at it. It was a long fortress-like building of seven or so storeys, built in the stark style of the sixties. The entry was shielded by a saw-toothed concrete portico. Windows, tight upon one another, each recessed in concrete, marched in inscrutable rows above the portico. CIA headquarters had none of the charm of the federal buildings along Constitution Avenue, no graceful pillars, no noble statues. Juli had told her there was a statue of Nathan Hale off to the side among some trees, but she couldn't see it.

Approaching the door, she slid Juli's glasses back on in case there was another checkpoint inside. The lenses turned the building into a grey, shimmery blur. Her eyes began to water badly; she must look like she was crying! She felt the beginning of a headache. Wiping her eyes with her fingers, she stumbled on the first step, then recovered herself. A man in an air force uniform walked out. She realized with dismay that one of them was supposed to salute the other. She saw a blurry glint of gold on his shoulder. Her mind raced. Gold could only be a second lieutenant or a major; both ranked below a commander. The man should salute her first. She kept her arm down and he saluted. Returning the salute the way she'd seen Juli do it, she passed him and walked inside into a huge lobby walled in polished marble. Another guard motioned her to his table, viewed her pass, and gave it back, after only a quick look at her face.

'Do you have an access card?'

Suzannah had another sinking feeling. 'Sorry?'

The guard smiled. 'You don't have an access card, which means you'll need an escort. Who have you come to see?'

'The Director.'

She thought the guard raised his eyebrows, but she couldn't be sure through the glasses. A pain, fierce as migraine, stabbed from behind her ear. She felt another desperate urge to take the glasses off and realized it would be all right to do so. She took them off. For a second, her vision stayed blurred; then she could see. The relief was immense, her headache easing at once. She watched the guard dial a phone on his desk. He did not look at her but mumbled a few words into the phone. Suzannah had another attack of nerves. This would never work.

The guard hung up. 'You can wait at the gate there,' he said.

She eased a breath out and walked to the turnstile halfway into the lobby, standing aside to let two men through. They inserted their cards, and the gate lifted for them. She looked around, trying to appear nonchalant. On the marble wall beside her, a message had been carved: YE SHALL KNOW THE

TRUTH, AND THE TRUTH SHALL MAKE YOU FREE.

Good words. But now someone in this building was trying to substitute 'future' for 'truth', and that would make no one free.

'Commander Lord?'

She turned to see tall blond man in a grey suit standing on the other side of the gate. He had a handsome, even smile and a thick crewcut. He said his name was Marty Grainger. She gave him a return smile and shook hands. He slipped a card into the gate and it rose for her. She had her speech about national security all ready, but Grainger didn't ask. He just said 'Follow me', and she followed, with a sense of wonder. This was going well. She had expected to be challenged – What do you want with the director? and so on. Grainger turned left down a long hall and then into a stairwell. She started for the stair leading up.

'No, this way,' the man said.

She felt a twinge of unease. 'The Director's office is in the basement?'

Grainger laughed. 'Hardly. The DCI's in the library right now, Commander Lord. He can see you for a minute down there.'

Suzannah followed Grainger down, beginning to feel alarmed. This was *too* easy. He should have asked if she had an appointment, some questions about the nature of her business. Three-star admirals might walk straight in on the director of the CIA without explanation, but not mere commanders.

What should she do, run back upstairs? But then what? She had no idea where the Director's office was. And the minute she ran, she was dead.

The basement corridor was empty. Her alarm deepened. Then a door at the far end opened. A delivery man came through, pushing a hand truck. Suzannah felt a little better. Grainger couldn't try anything now. As the delivery man drew nearer, Suzannah debated whether she should stop him, ask for help. She had a very bad feeling about Grainger.

The delivery man drew even with her. 'Excuse me,' she said.

He stopped, letting the hand truck come to rest, steadying the large box on it with one hand. 'Yes, lady?'

'Do you mind if I walk along with you?' She was acutely conscious of Grainger, standing beside her.

'I'll do better than that,' the delivery man said. 'You can ride.'

Suzannah turned just in time to see Grainger pull a strange-looking gun from his coat.

'Sorry,' he said and pulled the trigger.

A massive shock flamed along her nerves, snapping her muscles rigid. She felt herself toppling stiffly forward. The delivery man caught her and eased her down. Every nerve in her body prickled fiercely, like a foot that has gone to sleep. With a fierce effort she sucked in a breath. The two men turned her over. She saw them tip the box towards her and open the top. She tried to scream but nothing came out. The box blurred. Everything began to seem unreal. She felt them sliding her into it. She tried to fight them, but her arms and legs would not move. Please, she thought, someone help me.

And then everything went dark.


Jay Mallernee sat in his apartment, working at his word processor. He felt good, exhilarated. The words were starting to come now. He'd done six pages since he had returned from Suzannah's early this morning. Not much by his normal standard, but an explosion of words compared to the last six months. Odd, how it was starting to come now.

Even though he had not been able to tell Suzannah about seeing the Palestinian boy shot, just coming close seemed to have helped.

The room brightened slightly and he glanced at the window above his computer. Sunlight blazed in molten streaks along the edges of the miniblind. Too dark in here, he thought. He stood and opened the blinds. The heat of the floor felt good against his bare feet. He ought to turn the thermostat down, but he was so tired of this endless cold weather. A little summer in the apartment wouldn't break his budget.

He stood in the flood of sunlight, eyes closed, basking. He could see the light in pinkish swirls on his lids. I'm working again, he thought.

Suzannah is all right. The bear didn't get her.

He felt his stomach tighten. What a harrowing experience. She'd been so brave, so matter-of-fact about it. Hadn't called him last night, because she didn't want to worry him. So I see it in the paper this morning, he thought, and almost swallow my tongue.

He felt a surge of anger at the nameless mugger – or whoever he had been. He'd taken her money and left her purse, but a pro might do that to confuse the issue. The zoo was usually a very safe place. You rarely read of anyone being attacked or mugged there.

And it was highly unlikely that two 'random' attacks on Suzannah would occur so close together, first the POAC and then the zoo.

Jay had the sudden urge to talk to her, make sure she was all right. It was four o'clock. She'd still be seeing patients. Maybe he'd get lucky and she'd have a minute free.

He picked up the phone by his computer and dialled.

'Dr Lord's office.'

'Hi, Marjory, this is Jay. Is she busy?'

'She went home sick, Jay. Cancelled her appointments.'

'OK, thanks. I'll call her there.' Jay hung up the phone, unsettled. He saw Suzannah in his mind as she had looked standing in the field, her cheeks pink with the cold, her thick brown hair blowing to one side in the wind. She had gazed at him with those beautiful warm eyes, brimming with energy. In the five months they'd been dating, he had never seen her sick. He could not imagine her sick, did not want to.

He touched the button on his phone console where her home number was programmed. He listened to the phone ring and ring. Finally the answering machine picked up. 'Hi, this is Suzannah. Can't come to the phone right now, but if you'll leave your name and number, I'll get back to you as soon as I can.'

She's not sick, Jay thought. She's up to something. Did she get a lead on Dugan and take off on her own? He groaned, feeling a mixture of jealousy and alarm. Suzannah, Suzannah. He pulled his boots and leather jacket on, grabbed the keys to his Jeep and, on the way out, his Orioles cap. When he got to Suzannah's, he pounded for half a minute before Juli came to the door, dressed in her bathrobe.

'Jay,' she mumbled, rubbing her eyes.

He realized she'd been sleeping. 'Sorry to wake you, Juli,' he said. 'Suzannah's office said she came home sick, but no one answered the phone.'

'What can I be thinking,' Juli said, 'keeping you standing there in the cold. Come in, come in.'

He followed her inside.

'Hang on,' Juli said. 'I'll check her room.'

She loped away, disappearing into the den. Already she'd shaken off sleep. Jay was impressed by her energy, a lot like her sister's.

Juli walked back in through the den. 'She's not in her room. Strange.'

Jay's stomach knotted. I knew it, he thought.

'Wait a minute,' Juli said. 'She came home around lunchtime. I heard her tiptoeing around in my bedroom. I only woke up partway. I figured she was just borrowing one of my scarves or something. Hold on another minute.' Juli ran up the stairs, two at a time. Jay stood in the living room, rolling his hat around and around, trying to think where Suzannah might be. He heard an explosive curse from upstairs. Juli ran back down and into the den again, ignoring him now, rummaging through a purse that sat on an end table.

Jay heard her swear again in the den and smiled in spite of himself. Women back in Texas sometimes swore like that, though never in public. Governor Ann Richards was reputed to hold her own with the most colourful men in her cabinet. It was refreshing to hear a woman let go a little. 'What is it?' he asked.

Juli walked back in. 'Do you know what she's been involved in lately?'

'Yes.'

Juli shook her head, looking baffled. 'I can't believe this. She took my spare glasses, my DoD badge, and one of my uniforms. Damn!'

'What?'

'She's gone out to Langley, the idiot. She's trying to pass herself off as me. She thinks they have Andrew.' Juli groaned and pressed a hand into her forehead. 'I should have seen this coming.'

Jay felt a stab of dismay. Langley! 'Thanks,' he said. He turned to go.

'Wait. What are you going to do?'

'I'm going out there.'

'You can't get in. Come to think of it, neither can I – she's got my damned pass.'

'Is there some way you can get another?'

'Yes, they'll make me a temporary if I say I lost it. But it'll take time.'

'How much time?'

'A couple of hours, if I really push it.'

'Then let's really push it.'

# 27

Suzannah drifted back to consciousness. She became aware that she was sitting in a hard chair, her chin pressing into her chest. Her neck hurt. Opening her eyes a crack, she saw she was still dressed in Juli's uniform jacket and skirt. She raised her head. The room was small and windowless. Across from her, a man sat behind a small desk. Another man stood beside him, tall and handsome, with a crewcut. She had no idea who either of them was. *What happened to me?*

'Hello, there,' said the tall man.

She sat up straighter; her muscles seemed stiff and a little clumsy. She could remember parking her car in the CIA visitors' lot and walking to the main building. An air force major had saluted her. After that, nothing.

'Where am I?' she asked. 'Who are you?'

The two men exchanged knowing glances. 'I'm Marty Grainger,' said the tall man. 'This is Joe Davidlourian. I'm afraid you passed out . . . commander.'

The name Grainger seemed familiar suddenly, as did his face. But she still could not place him.

Grainger said, 'You wanted to see Andrew Dugan, so that's where we brought you.'

Suzannah's head swam with confusion. She gripped the arms of the chair, trying to make sense of Grainger's words.

Surely she had not asked these men to take her to Andrew; that had not been the plan. Why couldn't she remember?

*I didn't pass out. They did something to me.*

She was suddenly very afraid. She kept her face calm. The man had called her commander. If they didn't know who she really was, there was still hope.

She pushed up from the chair. 'I don't know what you're talking about,' she said. 'I asked to see the Director. What's going on here?'

Grainger walked past the desk and unlocked a door, pulling it open. On the other side stood Andrew. He looked at her for only a second, then turned to Grainger. 'This isn't my lawyer.'

'You're not going to get a lawyer, Mr Dugan. I think you know that.' Grainger didn't even look at him; instead, he was watching Suzannah expectantly.

'Mr Grainger,' she said sternly, 'I don't know what you think the situation is, but obviously you're confused. I am Commander Julia Lord of Naval Intelligence. My office sent me over with a Special Mission for the Director. Now, please take me to his office at once!'

For the first time, Grainger looked uncertain. 'May I see your badge, please?' he said. She handed it to him, her hopes rising.

Grainger studied the picture on the badge. 'You're not wearing your glasses, commander.'

Suzannah took Juli's glasses from the pocket of her blouse and put them on. Grainger melted into a blurry, wax figure. The man at the desk – Davidlourian – dissolved into a vague smear of colours.

'Would you mind reading this for me, please?'

She realized Grainger had picked something up from the desk. It looked like a paperback book, but she could barely

272

make it out, even though it couldn't be more than six feet away.

'Just the title, please. You can do that, can't you, commander?'

The cover swam before her eyes, an indecipherable mix of blurred colours.

Then she heard both men laughing and realized they were only toying with her.

'Leave her alone, you bastards,' Andrew said hotly.

She took the glasses off, blinking away tears, not just from the lenses but from the casual cruelty.

'Sorry, Dr Lord,' Grainger said. 'But you shouldn't try to fool us. It was a nice try. You do look a lot like your sister – especially with the glasses on. But, as it turns out, we've been expecting you, blonde hair and all.'

A chill went through her. Someone here had a vision about me, she thought. Was it Andrew?

No, he would not have told them – ever.

Grainger said, 'Why don't you join your friend, Mr Dugan, here.' He pointed into Andrew's cell. She walked in and heard the door close softly behind her.

Andrew took her hands. 'I'm sorry.'

'It's my own fault,' she said. 'I thought there was a chance. But they *knew* I was coming.'

'You risked a lot to try and help me.' He pulled her into a hug. The hard strength in his arms surprised her. Suzannah hugged him in return, feeling a powerful yearning well up inside her. If she could just stand with him like this, she could forget the world of trouble they were both in.

'Where are we?' she murmured into his ear.

'I was hoping you could tell me.'

'Did they knock you out, too?'

'Yes. The last thing I remember before I woke up here was

walking up the zoo path to the bear pens.'

Reaching up, she probed his head for bumps. There were none. She did the same to herself with the same results. 'Maybe they shot us with a taser,' she said. 'But that doesn't explain the amnesia – unless they injected us with something right afterwards. Versed would probably do the trick.' As she looked over his shoulder, the room registered and she felt a rising indignation. These smug men in grey suits had no conception of who and what they had trapped in this ugly cell. Andrew Dugan, who had struggled to show the world to itself, had been given only a sink, a cot, and a toilet to look at. A single bulb in the ceiling, sealed away behind dusty Plexiglas, cast a dingy, eye-starving light.

Andrew released her and stepped back, still holding her shoulders, inspecting her hair. 'Suzannah, Suzannah. What have you done to yourself?'

'I thought blondes had more fun. I was wrong.' She felt a stab of despondency over her lost hair. She had cut it off for nothing. I don't want to be buried this way, she thought.

'I'm sorry I didn't make our meeting at the zoo,' Andrew said. 'What must you have thought of me?'

'I didn't have much time for thinking. They threw me into the bear pit. The polar bear almost ate me.'

Andrew paled. 'They tried to kill you? I don't believe it! Why didn't I see . . . think of that?' He turned away, pacing to the door, hitting the jamb with the heel of his hand.

'It's all right. I wasn't hurt.'

'I should never have agreed to the zoo,' Andrew said. 'After I left you, I thought of the perfect place, but then it was too late.'

'Where?'

His face softened. 'The Washington Monument. They keep it lighted all night. It's in full view of the cars on

Constitution Avenue. And it's...' He hesitated, blushing slightly.

'What?'

'It's always been lucky for me. I'd take the elevator up when I got stuck painting. It's a hell of a view from the top. I got the idea for *Sol* up there.'

Suzannah thought of the print of *Sol* hanging on her wall. Her favourite. And now she knew where it had first come into Andrew's mind. She felt a small thrill. There was so much she wanted to ask him – about himself, his painting. If we get out of this, she thought.

'Andrew, we've got to –'

He raised a cautioning hand. 'This room is one giant listening device.'

'Did you *see* that?'

He gave her a sharp look. 'You know?'

'Yes. But I thought you saw only the future.'

'I see whatever my brain decides to send me. I can't control it.' He gazed at her with wonder. 'How did you know about the visions?'

'There are two of you from the pilot study. I read the psychiatric file of the other one. Her name is Tricia Fiore, a teacher. Andrew, why did they bring you here? Do they want you to work for them?'

'Yes. But most of all, they don't want me talking to anyone about the microchip. I have to correct something you just said. There aren't two of us from the pilot study, there are three. The teacher, myself, and one of the Agency's own. You probably remember him from the implant phase of the pilot study. He'd be a hard man to forget. His name is Archer Montross.'

'Arch?' Suzannah looked at him, shocked. 'Arch is working for them?'

'So you do know him.'

'Not just from the study,' Suzannah said. 'We were good friends in college.' She shook her head, stunned. Arch, working for the Agency? He'd gone to grad school, become a psychologist. He'd always hungered to heal himself inside, to believe he was all right despite his disfigured face. When he'd been accepted for the pilot study, he'd told her he was working for AID, the Agency for International Development. Suzannah remembered Juli telling her that AID provided cover for some intelligence operatives.

'That's how they knew I was coming,' she said wonderingly. 'Archer *saw* it and told them. He betrayed me. I don't believe it.'

'If it's any comfort,' Andrew said, 'Archer has been changed in ways beyond his control.'

She heard the sad note in his voice and realized that, despite the danger Archer represented, Andrew felt a sympathetic bond with him. They were like two angels, Lucifer and Gabriel, dark and light, both possessed of an awesome power that bound them together above mere mortals. For Andrew, it was a cruel power, stripping away the most important thing in his life.

'Andrew,' she said, 'why has the microchip blocked your ability to paint?'

'It hasn't. I can paint any time I want. I no longer want to.'

'But why?'

'Because I *see* every painting, now, before I can even pick up a brush.'

'Dear God,' Suzannah said, appalled. 'It would be like doing a paint-by-the-numbers kit.'

'Exactly.' Andrew's flat voice held a universe of pain.

'Then the world has lost you forever.' The horror of it

struck her fully, overwhelming her. 'When Lancaster gave you your eyes, he took away your soul. And I helped.'

'Now, stop it, Suzannah. You didn't know what you were doing – either of you.'

She could find no words. She hugged him. He patted and soothed her in return, as if trying to forgive her with his touch. 'I should never have drawn you back into this,' he said. 'Once I understood you'd dropped out of it, I tried to stay away, but I couldn't.' He stood off, touching her shoulder as though she were a sculpture, a work of art. His wonderful dark eyes held her.

'Andrew, I –'

He motioned fiercely at the walls.

She nodded. But her mind spun. How could she love two men at the same time? She did love Jay. And she knew she could love Andrew, too; it was already happening. What was she going to do?

Get out of here, or she wouldn't have either one of them.

Andrew rubbed his forehead, the long elegant fingers probing as if to sense the tiny piece of metal buried only inches away. 'I must warn you, Suzannah. They want you even more than they want me. They hope I'll pitch in here, conjure up visions for them. But you! You have the power to create dozens more like me. They want you to implant microchips.'

'They can just forget it.' Suzannah said hotly. She shook her head. 'It doesn't make sense. If they want to use me, why did they try to kill me – twice?'

'Evidently there are two factions of the Agency working at cross-purposes here. One feels you and I are too dangerous to use. The other, the men who put us in this cell, feel they can persuade us –'

Andrew stopped as the door opened.

Archer Montross walked in. He seemed bigger than Suzannah remembered, thicker through the shoulders. She saw that the burned side of his face had undergone another skin graft since the implant. It had gained him little. The graft area was smooth where, before, the burned skin had been pitted. But it was too pink, and the scar tissue pinched the corner of one eye upward, making him look half alien. As he now had become.

'Hello, Suzannah.'

'Hello, Arch.'

'You look very nice in that uniform.'

'Go to hell, Arch.'

The unscarred side of his face reddened. 'Yes, I knew you'd say that.'

'That's your basic problem, isn't it? You know too much.'

His gaze hardened. 'It's not a problem, it's a gift, a talent. Andrew is right. We *do* want you. We never told him that, but he saw it anyway. Was that knowing too much?'

'Yes,' Andrew said. 'It was.'

Archer ignored him. 'Come with me, and we'll talk.'

'I prefer to stay here.'

Archer sighed. 'Please, Suzannah. We'll just talk a few minutes, then I'll bring you right back.'

'Let her go,' Andrew said. 'If you do, I'll work with you. I'll do anything you want.'

Archer looked coldly at him. 'How noble.'

'Unlike you,' Suzannah said.

Archer closed his eyes for a second. 'You're being spiteful now, Suzannah. I understand. But couldn't you at least wait until you hear my side of the story? We were friends once. Maybe, when you understand it all, we can be friends again.'

278

Suzannah walked past him. Her shoulder brushed his chest, and she realized he'd stepped forward ever so slightly to cause the contact. The little nuance alarmed her. She would have to be careful with him.

The room down the hall was much nicer than Andrew's cell. It had a low coffee table, comfortable armchairs, a soft earth-tone carpet, and innocuous prints on the walls. A small sideboard on one wall held cups and a coffee dispenser.

The door, however, was just as locked.

Suzannah sat across the low table from Archer. He poured a cup of coffee and handed it to her. Suddenly, coffee was just what she wanted. Her veins clamoured for the caffeine. But she held the cup out to Archer. 'You first.'

He looked blank for a second, then smiled. 'Of course.' He took a swallow from the cup and handed it back. Picking up one of the napkins he'd laid out, she wiped the rim all around. 'Suzannah, you have nothing to fear from me.'

'Really? So you have nothing to do with the men who've tried twice to kill me?'

'That's right.'

'And what about John Stockwell? I suppose you had nothing to do with that either.'

'He was a loose cannon, Suzannah. We had recruited him for a microchip implant. We gave him the chance of a lifetime, and he turned it down. He was going to use you to go public with the microchip side effect. By now you must see how dangerous that would be.'

'You are the loose cannons,' Suzannah said. 'You Adepts.'

Archer's eyes widened. 'Where did you hear that term?'

She said nothing.

'Dugan,' Archer said. 'Amazing. It makes perfect sense that he would see us in a vision. But to know what we call

279

ourselves? A number of terms would fit just as well.'

'Maybe you're more predictable than you think,' Suzannah said.

Archer smiled. 'All of us are, dear. All of us are.'

'Does Adept go all the way to the top of the Agency?'

'We won't discuss that just yet,' Archer said.

'I tried to save Mr Stockwell,' she said. 'I held his heart in my hands, saw the blood run out of him, watched him die. That's what you are a part of, Archer.'

'I regret that he had to die,' Archer said. 'But he knew what he was risking. The stakes here are very high.'

She gazed across the table at him, feeling for the first time a deep sadness. He *had* been her friend: laughing with her across other tables in the campus restaurant, lifting her spirits when she was down, always willing to sit and talk. And not just talk. He had not been full of himself. He had had the gift of listening, refreshing after dating guys who seemed to be interested only in themselves.

What was she to do with those memories now?

Archer tipped his own cup back, then set it down. 'It's so strange to see you a blonde.'

'Why? You've already seen it.'

'Yes. The vision was very real. But you can't converse with people you see in visions – or, if you do, they don't answer.' He sighed and sat back, taking something from his trouser pocket. She saw it was the cigarette lighter she'd given him back in college, during his brief infatuation with cigars. Gold plated, it was engraved with the words *To Arch from Suze*. He drummed the butt of the lighter on the table a few times. Though he did it in an absentminded way, she had the impression the gesture was a deliberate rebuke. Again, she did not respond. He slipped the lighter back in his pocket.

'All I ask,' he said, 'is that you hear me out before you decide. Will you do that?'

'I'm listening.'

'Good. Think back a few years. Back before a hundred and fifty burning oil wells in Kuwait turned the sky black. Before the dead birds washed up on the Gulf beaches. Before a hundred thousand Iraqi soldiers, most of them kids in rags, were sent to their deaths by Saddam Hussein.' Archer paused dramatically.

Instead, Suzannah thought of Jay. What Archer was describing so melodramatically, Jay had lived. Had Archer been there? Jay had, and his memories were nearly paralyzing him. She was so glad, now, that she had not asked his help today. *Dear Jay: Miss you, glad you're not here.*

'Before all that happened,' Archer went on, apparently satisfied with the look on her face, 'one man in US intelligence told his superiors that Saddam Hussein would, despite all his avowals to the contrary, invade Kuwait. No one much listened to this man. Saddam did invade. He ran clear through Kuwait, setting up a huge force of arms, tanks, and men just across the border from Saudi Arabia. The President and all the politicians despaired. If we tried to put a force in there now, it would be smashed before we could build it up – the first wave and the next, thousands of our young men. Then this same man told them not to worry; we could put our troops into Saudi Arabia. Saddam would vacillate, he would dither, he wouldn't attack, even though it would take weeks to get enough US forces into Saudi Arabia to fend off such an attack. Because it was the same man who had sworn that Saddam would invade Kuwait, the Deputy Director of Intelligence for the CIA took the recommendation to the Director in the strongest possible terms. The DDI convinced the Director and the Director convinced the President – without telling him the source, of course. The President started sending the troops in. The rest you know. Most people never realized what a hideous gamble it was. If Saddam had struck during the first few weeks, we would, without question, have been overrun and our liberation of Kuwait and its oil would have demanded a terrible cost in American blood.'

'What's your point, Archer?'

He looked incredulous, then smiled. 'You always did have a sense of humour. Sorry if I got long-winded.'

'I suppose this man you've been talking about was you,' she said.

'As a matter of fact, it was. I had been studying Iraq at the time I joined your pilot group at NIH. I had written several position papers on the Gulf countries. Suddenly, about a year after the implantation, I began to *see* what Saddam would do. That's where all this started. We quickly did a microchip implant on our best agent in Kuwait, an Arab American, and another Iraq expert has just recently undergone implantation. This man will be particularly good because he actually lived there for a while. But I started it all. I was the accident, like Tricia Fiore and Andrew Dugan. The microchip placement was slightly differently positioned in our brains from the other forty-seven test subjects. Only a few microns, but enough. We have since discovered that moving it a bit more makes the effect show up within weeks.'

Suzannah felt a deep alarm. They were further along than she'd feared. They knew how to create the effect at will. It was no longer a side effect, it was the main effect!

Archer took a sip of coffee, set the cup down again. 'Suzannah, we need you. Mike Fachet is already with us. He agreed with our assessment of the enormous potential of the effect.'

'What about Roland Lancaster?'

Archer eyed her slyly. 'If you join us, you won't have to have anything to do with him.'

'That's not what I asked. Is he part of this?'

Archer hesitated. 'Let's leave that aside for the moment. The point is, we need more Adepts.' Archer hesitated, looking uncomfortable. 'To be candid, Fachet isn't having the success record we would like. Incredible precision is required. You have the hands, the nerve, and the steel that Fachet lacks.'

'Archer, cut the bull.'

'It's not bull. Sadly, more than half the people Dr Fachet has operated on didn't develop the side effect. People we recruit for surgery from within the Agency are our best, our leading experts in various areas of intelligence. When one of them is squandered by Dr Fachet, it represents an irredeemable loss. Fachet insists we can't move the microchip once it's implanted for fear of blinding the subject.'

'That's right.'

Archer gave her a cold half smile. 'Now, Suzannah. It's right for Fachet. But you were Lancaster's best student. You took part in forty of the fifty pilot implantations. We are confident that you would have a high success rate in removing the chip without blinding the subject. If you can do that, you can also reinsert it, and we could turn some of our most disappointing failures into successes.'

Suzannah could not believe what she was hearing. 'Archer, would you risk a substantial chance of being blinded?'

'To have the power, yes. These are very dedicated people.'

Suzannah felt a chill. *The power.*

Archer sighed. 'I've been spending time with Fachet lately, and I've seen that he'll never be any better. Why, I do not know – not consciously. What I do know is that you would do much better.'

Suzannah was surprised to find a part of herself rising to his bait. The temptation was powerful, seductive. To do neurosurgery again –

She caught herself, dismayed. Dear God, what was she thinking?

'If you know that I would be better than Mike,' she said, 'then you must also have seen that I will not do it.'

'That is not true,' Archer said. 'I haven't seen what you will do either way. It could mean that my brain simply hasn't decided to show me anything on that yet. But it could also mean that you are right on the razor's edge, with equal chances that we could persuade you and that we couldn't.'

'That's absurd,' she said, but she felt a stir of dread. Could he be right? Did she know herself so poorly?

'Suzannah, you must understand. What I have now is a great gift.'

'It's a curse. Look at yourself, at what you've become.'

Archer put his cup down. 'And what is that, Suzannah?' Suddenly he was very still.

'The Archer I knew would never have betrayed me.'

'The Archer you knew? I was never the Archer you knew. Did you ever stop to think I might have wanted more from you, from us?'

His voice was choked with bitterness. Suzannah stared at him, stunned. 'Archer, I would have welcomed a chance to get closer to you, but you never allowed –'

'Stop it, Suzannah. I was a big, ugly kid with thick glasses. I knew it and you knew it. Do you know that before my parents and I went out for a drive that day, I was handsome?

284

Thirteen years old. Lots of girls had crushes on me.'

Suzannah thought of J.D. Thirteen, but it seemed impossible that this man could ever have been like him.

'Then the pickup broadsided us,' Archer went on. 'I didn't just lose my parents. I lost . . . the capacity to be loved. I lay in that stinking hospital for months, crying for my parents, hoping the skin grafts would take, imagining that I would be all right some day. But I never was. Can you look at me now and feel anything but revulsion?'

Suzannah heard the pain in his voice and was touched by it, despite herself. 'Your face never repelled me,' she said softly. 'What you've become repels me.'

'Admit it, Suzannah. There was no way you could ever see me as a man, before or now.' Archer's low, choked voice frightened her. He pushed up from the table, glaring at her.

'Archer, take it easy,' she said, alarmed.

'Shut up.' Stepping around the table, he grabbed her arm.

Terror sprang up in her. 'Archer, let go, you're hurting me.'

He jerked her to her feet and slapped her hard in the face. 'Stupid woman. I'm a god, and you don't even know it.'

For a second, she nearly fell; then she pushed at him, trying to wrest her arm free. He held on, pulling her to him, his huge muscular chest pressing against her breasts. His hand gripped the back of her neck, forcing her face into his. She tried to turn her face aside but could not. He pressed his mouth on hers, forcing her lips apart.

Terrified, she jammed a knee up into his groin; twisting, he avoided most of the blow. He slapped her again, then ripped the front of her blouse.

'Help!' she screamed, fighting with all her strength. But she knew there was no one here to help her.

# 28

Terrified, Suzannah tried to grab Archer's arm. He shoved her back; her heel caught on the edge of the coffee table, and she sat down hard. She lunged forward, determined to fight him. Archer shoved her against the wall. He pinned her arms with his huge hands. Letting go of one arm, he grabbed her hair. She screamed again.

'That won't do you any good,' he said. 'Even if someone hears you, I'm the main man around here. No one would dare cross Archer.'

Behind him, the lock blew inward with an explosive bang and the door slammed open. 'Freeze!'

Juli! Suzannah thought, overjoyed.

Archer froze, a dumbfounded expression wiping the lust from his face. Suzannah knocked his hand away from her hair and pulled free, scrambling along the wall away from him. She saw her sister standing right behind Archer, her feet spread, a gun jammed into the nape of his neck. The weapon looked odd – plastic. Suzannah realized it was one of the new guns designed to defeat metal detectors. Juli was in uniform but she looked savage, her teeth bared in rage. Beside her stood Marty Grainger, his suit coat pulled back and down around his elbows to pinion his arms. His face was very pale. 'Don't shoot him!' Grainger said. 'Whatever you do, don't shoot!'

'Shut up and get over there in the corner,' Juli shouted, keeping her eyes on the back of Archer's head. Grainger complied at once, edging around, jamming himself into a back corner of the room.

*How did she find me?* Suzannah wondered.

'I *ought* to kill you,' Juli said into Archer's neck.

Archer let out a long breath. 'But you won't.'

'For God's sake, don't push her,' Grainger shouted.

'Shut up,' Juli snapped at Grainger. 'And you – you'd better listen to your buddy, you nauseating piece of filth.'

Suzannah's mind started working again as the fear and fighting rage drained out of her. 'Archer will make a good hostage,' she told Juli. 'He *is* the main man around here.'

Archer glared at her.

Juli jabbed the gun into the meat of his neck. 'All right, pig face. I want you to walk into the hall, nice and slow. I'm going to keep this gun right in your neck. Remember, I want very much to pull the trigger.'

Suzannah straightened her blouse. He'd ripped two buttons off, but three still held. 'We have to get Andrew, too,' she told Juli. 'He's just down the hall.' Her heart was beating very fast. She saw every detail of the room in a scorched, adrenaline focus.

'You!' Juli said, jerking her head toward Grainger. 'Go out in front of Archer. Be sure the way is clear for us, or he dies.'

'Yes, fine, just don't hurt him.' Grainger edged out in the hall. Looking down the hallway, he held his palms out as high as his pulled-down jacket would allow. 'Back off!' he yelled.

'What is it?' Juli said.

'Security. I'll handle it.' Into the hallway, he yelled again, 'Put your guns down. She has a hostage. Damn it, that's an *order*!'

Juli got behind Archer, holding his shirt collar with one hand as the other forced the gun into his thick neck. Suzannah could see the flesh bulging around the barrel. She felt no pity for him, none at all.

'Have they put down their guns?' Juli said to Grainger.

'Yes. You can come out.'

'First I want you to understand something. I am not a terrorist or a criminal. I am an officer of the United States Navy. You know damned well that you have no right to hold my sister or Andrew Dugan. I'm going to take them out of here. If you make sure that happens, I give you my word of honour as a naval officer that I'll release Archer as soon as possible, unhurt. If you cross me, I have nothing to lose. This man was about to rape my sister. I *will* kill him.'

'Understood,' Grainger said. 'I'll get you out.'

She marched Archer into the hall. Going out behind her, Suzannah saw four people in dark blue uniforms. Their guns lay on the carpet.

'Down on the floor,' Juli said to the guards. 'All of you. Now.'

They got down on their knees and lay gingerly on their stomachs. Suzannah followed Juli and Archer, stopping them when they drew even with the door to Andrew's cell. 'Is your friend still in there?' she said to Grainger.

'Davidlourian? Yes.'

'Go in and let Andrew out. Tell Davidlourian to stay right where he is.'

Grainger nodded. Moving awkwardly, he unlocked the hall door and went in, emerging a moment later with Andrew. Andrew showed no surprise when he saw them.

'Help me get these guns,' Suzannah said.

Andrew nodded. When they had gathered up the weapons, Suzannah told the guards to stay as they were for fifteen minutes.

'Do as she says,' Grainger said. 'I don't care what your normal procedure is. I am ordering it. I take full responsibility. These people are to be allowed to leave.'

'I could almost like you,' Juli said to Grainger.

'Just don't hurt Archer.'

They went to the end of the hall together, passing a desk that looked like a guard station. The desk was untended; the guard lay behind it, his eyes closed. His nightstick lay beside him and Suzannah saw a darkening bruise on his forehead. Juli pushed a button behind the desk and the door slid open. Beyond it stood a grove of pine trees lit by a fading, rosy twilight. Suzannah followed Juli out, fighting a sense of disorientation.

'This way,' Juli said, prodding Archer with her gun.

They followed a trail through the grove of trees to a high fence. The gate stood open. In the guard shack, a man lay on the floor, bound and gagged. Suzannah felt a surge of admiration for her sister. Looking across a grassy field, she saw a building larger than the one they'd left behind. It looked like a hospital. Beside it was a parking lot. She could not remember seeing any of it before.

Juli raised an arm, waving at the lot. Headlights poured suddenly across the small snowy field, pinning them in the beams. Seconds later, the headlights switched off and the car accelerated out of the lot toward them, racing across the field. No, not a car, a Jeep – *Jay!* Suzannah's heart leapt with anticipation. She looked behind to see if anyone had followed them to the gate. If they had, they were keeping out of sight among the trees. The Jeep swerved to a stop beside them.

289

'Get in,' Juli said to Archer.

'You promised to let him go,' Grainger said.

'As soon as possible. If I release him now, you'll follow us. Move, you!'

Prodded by Juli's gun, Archer climbed into the back seat. Juli slid in beside him, followed by Andrew. Suzannah could see Archer staring out the window at her. She did not want to get in the car. She turned back to Grainger. 'If you're looking for Percy Jones, he's locked up in isolation at the Adams Memorial MHU.'

'Not any more,' Grainger said stiffly. 'A Veterans Administration doctor was kind enough to sign him out into our custody.'

'I won't press charges if you won't.'

Grainger gave her a thin smile.

'Suzannah!' Juli said.

Suzannah got up front with Jay. 'Go!' Juli said as soon as the door closed.

Jay gunned the Jeep back across the field and into the lot, then out a long winding driveway. Suzannah looked at him. His face was grim in the fading light, but he flashed her a quick smile, then concentrated on merging onto a highway. Suzannah recognized it as the George Washington Parkway. At last she got her bearings. They were not at Langley, but they couldn't be more than a few miles away. Suzannah could smell Archer in the back seat, a sour, sweaty odour that made her want to gag. She breathed shallowly, through her mouth. He can't hurt me now, she told herself.

For several miles, no one spoke. We're *all* afraid of him, Suzannah realized. He looks human, even with the burns, but he's not, not entirely, and they all sense it.

Jay glanced at Suzannah. 'Damn, but you *do* look different with blonde hair.' He noticed her torn blouse. In the glow from the instrument panel, she saw his expression harden.

'It's nothing,' she said. She crossed her arms to hide her trembling hands.

'Did that bastard do that to you?'

'He didn't get anywhere.'

Cursing, Jay braked the Jeep.

'No!' Juli shouted. Suzannah felt a blast of cold air on her neck and turned to see Juli reaching out the open door, a look of shock on her face.

Archer was gone.

Juli fired a shot into the bushes at the roadside, but Archer had plunged out of sight. Jay flung his door open and started to lunge out. Suzannah grabbed him, hanging on with desperate strength. 'No, Jay, *stop it!*'

'Give me one of those guns!' Jay said through clenched teeth.

'I'll handle this,' Juli said. She stared into the dark tangle of underbrush just beyond the shoulder. The wooded bank dropped away steeply to the Potomac River, hundreds of feet below. 'I don't see him,' she said. 'I don't know if I hit him or not.' She started to climb out of the Jeep.

'Juli, don't do it,' Suzannah said. 'He's in the bushes now. Even if you wounded him, he's very strong, very clever.'

'And he can see in a way you don't,' Andrew added.

'All right,' Juli said grudgingly. But Suzannah could see she was relieved, too. 'Let's go.'

Jay pulled away, gunning the Jeep in obvious fury. 'I'm sorry,' he said. 'If I hadn't braked –'

'I was the one holding a gun on him,' Juli said. 'I can't believe how fast he moved.'

'That bastard,' Jay growled. 'I want to kill him.'

'So do I,' Andrew said in a very quiet voice.

Suzannah said, 'Forget Archer, both of you. I'm all right.'

Jay gave a low curse, tempering it by reaching up and giving her hand a quick squeeze. With Archer gone, Suzannah felt almost giddy with relief. 'I didn't think I'd ever have the pleasure of riding in this kidney puncher again,' she said. 'How on earth did you two find me?'

'Mr Dugan,' Juli said, 'will you keep watch out the rear window for me while I talk with my sister? If they know we've lost Archer, they'll move in.'

'Right.'

Juli leaned forward, putting a hand on Suzannah's shoulder. 'We tried Langley first. When I checked to see if you'd signed in, the front desk guard thought he remembered you. But when he tried to verify it on his clipboard, a sign-in sheet was missing. Right then, I knew they'd grabbed you. But where had they taken you? Langley is strictly an administrative headquarters. There are no holding cells or anything like that; the Agency has always handled the messy part of its work away from the home nest. In any case, I knew these were probably Agency renegades, who wouldn't risk holding you right under the Director's nose. Last night, snooping at the Pentagon, I found out the Agency has a secret medical facility under cover of a US fisheries station. They call it Station Three. The project they are supposed to be running there is top secret. I couldn't find out much, but apparently it has to do with electrocortical stimulation of the brain to recover memory in agents who have been drugged or brainwashed. That set off alarms for me. I don't know much about electrocortical stimulation, but clearly the facility would be equipped for neurosurgery. Knowing the Agency and the budget process as I do, I could believe a study like that might still be running even though the cold war is over. Or they might be doing a different kind of neurosurgery there. It looked like a good setup for the Adepts. They could give the chairman of the Senate Intelligence Committee a guided tour and he wouldn't know if they were tapping memories or implanting microchips.'

Suzannah's admiration of Juli deepened. 'You did good, sis.'

'Where shall I drive us?' Jay asked.

'The *Post*,' Juli answered.

'We can't tell the press!' Andrew and Suzannah said at the same time.

'I know that. But can you think of any place safer than the middle of a newsroom right now? No one will dare try and grab us there. Jay can pretend he's showing us around.'

'Good plan,' Jay said.

'All right,' Suzannah said, 'but what then? We've got to keep the pressure on, make them stop.' She was beginning to feel calmer now that Archer was gone. She focused on the calm, imagining that it was a bubble in her mind. She made the bubble grow larger until it surrounded her and eased away the tremour in her hands. She had to think. This wasn't over by a long shot.

Juli said, 'What if we could get the DCI to run a surprise inspection of the facility? He might uncover something – especially if we tell him exactly what to look for.'

'He might,' Suzannah said, 'but how do we get to him? I had a pretty fair plan today, and look what happened. Clearly the Adepts have him covered; they might even have people on his staff.'

'True,' Juli said reluctantly.

'What about the Pentagon?' Suzannah said. 'Do you know anyone there who could help us?'

Juli laughed. 'If I were buddies with the Secretary of Defense . . .' She cocked her head. 'Suze, you might have something there. I'm not in the same high circles as Secretary

Hastings, but we might be able to get a few minutes with him if I pull out all the stops.'

'Does he have authority over the CIA?'

'Technically, no – or rather, not directly. On the flow charts, the DCI is in charge of all intelligence services. But in practical terms, Army, Navy and Defense Intelligence, as well as the CIA, all exist to meet the Defense Department's needs and priorities. The Secretary of Defense effectively controls nine-tenths of the intelligence budget, which means he controls the Agency and to hell with the flow charts. But assuming we could manage to get an appointment with Secretary Hastings, how would we convince him this is really going on?'

'I'll go in with you,' Andrew said.

'And do what?' Juli said. 'Predict the Secretary's future? Sorry, Mr Dugan, I didn't mean to sound snide. In fact, that might be exactly the thing to do – except he wouldn't know your prediction is right until later, will he?'

'I can't control my visions,' Andrew said.

'Damn.'

'What kind of man is the secretary?' Suzannah asked. 'I realize you don't know him personally, Juli, but there must be a general sense of him around the Pentagon.'

'What are you getting at?'

'She wants to know if the Secretary would shut down the Adepts,' Andrew said quietly, 'or take over the project himself.'

Suzannah glanced back at him. He did not turn, keeping his eyes on the back window. You're right, she thought. Exactly right.

'I don't know how to answer that,' Juli said. 'John Hastings seems like an intelligent man. He has a good grasp of defence issues and he's decent to his staff. Every year, he drops by the women's professional group Christmas party. I was photographed with him the year I was president of the group. Beyond that, you probably know as much about him as I do. Jay, you interviewed him during the Gulf War.'

'I must have forgotten to ask him how he'd feel if he could see the future,' Jay said.

'I think we might have trouble,' Andrew said.

Something in his voice made Suzannah turn again. His face lightened in a wash of headlights. A car behind them was rushing up very fast.

'Can you step on it, Jay?' Juli said. 'Damn. Look out!'

Suzannah felt a shock in her back as the car rammed them. The Jeep fishtailed along the shoulder of the parkway. Suzannah sucked in a breath, shocked. If the car pushed them over the bank, it was a long steep slide down to kill us!'

'What the hell are they doing?' Juli shouted. 'They'll kill us!'

The car rammed them again. Suzannah's stomach flipped as the Jeep spun around. Jay fought the wheel, skating along the shoulder. For a second it looked as though he would regain control.

Then they slid over the edge of the bank.

Suzannah set her feet on the dashboard, fighting to stay off the windshield. Dark trees flashed past. Metal screeched. The Jeep took a hard blow, spinning around. For a second, Suzannah felt her back pressing into the roof. Panic filled her. She could hear branches snapping like gunshots.

Then the sound and the light stopped and there was nothing.

# 29

The pain was horrible. Commander Julia Lord gritted her teeth against the searing waves, clinging desperately to consciousness. A whining hum gradually descended in pitch – one of the Jeep's tyres spinning to a stop. Gathering her courage, she looked down at her right leg. In the green glow of the instrument panel, she could see it was bent. Yes, she had felt the shin snap.

Blackness lapped at her. She looked away from the leg and cursed through clenched teeth until the blackness receded.

She realized she was lying on top of Jay. He was not moving. Crying out in pain, she slid off him and eased over, bracing her back against the dash. In the green glow of the instrument panel, she saw her sister sitting in the back seat, gazing vacantly at her. 'Suzannah! Are you all right?'

Suzannah smiled vaguely but did not answer. Her eyes looked out of focus. Concussion, Juli thought. She must have hit her head on the roof when she was thrown into the back seat.

Beside Suzannah, Andrew reared up, rubbing his shoulder. He glanced at Juli, then turned to Suzannah, gently cradling her face in his hands. Suzannah returned his gaze as if he were a total stranger.

Wonderful, Juli thought.

Andrew turned back to her. He saw her leg and reached for it.

'Don't touch it,' Juli shouted, and he jerked his hand back.

He said, 'I think you're going to need a splint before you can move.'

'Don't worry about me. Check Jay.'

Andrew picked up Jay's wrist. 'Good pulse. Maybe he's just knocked out. Suzannah has a lump on top of her head.'

'How about you?' Juli asked.

He felt his shoulder again. 'I'm all right. Just bruises, I think.'

'You've got to get out of here right now, go for help.'

'I can't leave you.' Andrew looked at Suzannah again.

Another wave of pain swept Juli. She fought it off. 'Listen to me,' she said. 'They *will* come down after us. They're probably on their way right now. If they find all of us here together, they may well kill us. If one of us has got away, there will be a potential witness against them and they may decide to take us alive. Suzannah might be able to walk, but she's too out of it from the blow to her head. You're our only chance. You've got to go.'

'All right, commander.'

He tried the rear door. It resisted. Planting a foot against it, he forced it open with a shriek of tortured metal. Juli groped along the floor, finding one of the guns she'd taken from the guards. 'Here, take this with you. I've still got mine.'

He looked at it as if it were a loathsome slug. 'No.'

'Dammit, take the gun. Our lives depend on you. Take it, but stay the hell away from them. They know how to shoot and you don't. There are some houses uphill on the other side of the highway. Try to get to one of them and call for help. But most of all, *do not get caught!*'

297

'Right.' Andrew took the gun. With a last lingering look at Suzannah, he slipped away. The accident had smashed out the glass in the rear window. With her back braced against the dash, Juli had a decent if restricted view up the dark slope that rose beyond the back window. She pulled the plastic gun from her jacket and steadied it on her good knee.

'What?' Suzannah said dreamily.

'Shhhh.'

Several minutes passed. Juli wondered how Andrew was doing. She hoped fervently that he would make it. She became aware of the cold. It was heavy and damp, pouring into the Jeep through the smashed rear window. The tyre had stopped spinning outside. She heard a distant, steady crunch from above. Footsteps, drawing closer.

'Come on, you bastards,' she murmured. 'Come on.'

The rear window framed one of them about forty yards up the hill, a faint image painted red by the Jeep's tail lights. He held his gun in the air as he descended carefully towards them.

Aiming carefully, Juli squeezed the trigger. In the corner of her eye, she saw Suzannah jump as the gun went off. Dirt sprayed at the man's feet and he scrambled backwards.

Suzannah clambered across the back seat, her hands pressed into her ears. Juli tried to grab her, but she slithered out through the door Andrew had left open.

'Suzannah – come back!'

Suzannah wandered away from the Jeep, her hands still clamped to her ears. Juli fired at the man up the slope again. He dodged away, disappearing from the window. A helpless sense of horror filled Juli as she realized he would now head down to cut Suzannah off.

Suzannah had the suspicion that she was dreaming. The air

298

seemed thick as molasses. She felt mired in confusion, unable to think straight. Things kept getting sharper, then duller again. A vague fear gripped her. In her dream, someone had shot off a gun. She hated guns.

Below her she could see the river, glowing in the moonlight. She liked the river. It had ice on it. She didn't have her skates, but she could walk out on the ice and look up at the moon, like she used to do in Michigan.

She heard a noise in the trees above her. She looked up the slope. A dark shadow moved down towards her. It scared her, but only a little. Focusing on the river again, she took another step, stumbled, and fell. She rolled over a few times, then stopped herself by grabbing a root. Looking up again, she could see the shadow man was closer. She worked her way backwards down the steep hillside, feeling her way with her feet, grabbing roots and stones to keep from sliding. The ground felt cool under her. She would like to lie here and sleep, let go of the dream, but it wouldn't let go of her.

She heard feet crunching down the slope toward her. Letting herself go, she slid and rolled down the last few feet to the edge of the river.

'There she is!' cried a voice above her.

Suzannah felt a pang of resentment. They were going to stop her from walking on the ice. She hurried onto the frozen river. The ice glowed like spilled milk, enchanting her. She walked out further.

Her feet slipped and she went down to one knee. Glancing back, she saw two men stepping onto the ice behind her, one on either side.

'Come back,' one of them said. 'It's dangerous.'

She did not like the harsh sound of his voice. She walked further out onto the ice. She heard footsteps running behind her. Someone grabbed her arm. She yanked it free and pushed the man. He slipped and went down with a curse. She ran out further. Glancing over her shoulder, she saw the second man hurry towards her with small, rapid steps. She heard her feet sloshing; at the same instant the cold wetness of her toes registered. She began to feel uneasy. Why was there water on the ice?

She looked over her shoulder and saw the second man closing in, only ten yards away now. She angled away from him, hurrying into the middle of the river. Alarms went off in the back of her mind. What if the ice wasn't safe? She could fall through!

At that instant, she heard a booming crack and felt the ice shift beneath her. She tried to stop, but skidded, then tumbled onto the ice. Rolling onto her shoulder, she saw a crack shoot past her face, a black line that zigzagged away to the middle of the river. The ice boomed again. Frightened, she rolled onto her back and saw the man who had been chasing her. He had fallen to his hands and knees, about three yards away. He stared not at her but at the ice beneath him. His face was terrified. And then she realized that he was not on his hands and knees – one of his legs had punched through the ice.

She watched with dull horror as the ice jerked under him, breaking loose in a jagged circle. One end of the circle rose up, and he disappeared with a harsh curse into a black hole of water.

Suzannah twisted around. She felt the ice crack right beneath her. She held very still, pressing her cheek into the film of water. It was freezing cold. But she must stay as flat as possible.

'Dr Lord.'

The voice came from another direction. Staying flat on her

stomach, she spun herself carefully on the slick cracked surface until she could see him.

The man seemed to be someone she knew. He was about thirty feet away, on his stomach too. 'Come to me,' he said. 'I'll pull you to shore.'

For some reason she did not believe him. She felt her teeth chatter.

He inched towards her, stopping when the ice rumbled. 'I won't hurt you,' he said. 'If you don't let me help you, you'll die.'

Suzannah considered it and realized he was right. She pulled her leg up and pushed towards him a few inches. The ice was so slick, she could not get a grip with the sides of her feet. She heard herself sobbing, seeing in her mind the horrible image of the other man disappearing into the blackness.

'Come on, that's right,' the man cajoled.

Grainger. His name was Grainger.

She heard a siren high above, faint, swelling rapidly.

Grainger cursed. She saw him backing away, abandoning her. Terror gripped her. 'Don't leave me!'

He scrambled backwards, pushing frantically with his hands. She tried to follow, but the ice was wetter here and she couldn't make any progress. Grainger dwindled to a black form on the ice, crouching now, running into the trees at the shoreline.

A strange peace settled over Suzannah. She saw the beauty of the pale ice, the distant black shore, and felt an odd sense of comfort. It was all so beautiful, so quiet, except for the sirens.

'Suzannah!'

The voice sounded very close. She rolled over and saw Jay, only a few yards away. He was flat on his belly, inching toward her. It looked like he was wearing a red mask. Then she realized it was blood.

'Take this,' he said. He whipped his arm along the ice, sliding the end of a thick rope towards her. Catching it, she saw it was a rolled-up blanket from the Jeep. 'Hold on,' he said.

'All right,' Suzannah said. 'Did you know your face is bleeding?'

He gazed at her. 'Yes,' he said, 'I knew that.'

# 30

Suzannah struggled not to blink while the albino fly crawled across the root of her eyeball.

'Hmmm,' Ed Gaspard said and switched his penlight to the other eye.

Hmmmm *what?* Suzannah thought, annoyed. She was running out of patience. What more did he want? She knew exactly where she was: the neurology ward at Adams Memorial Hospital. It was Monday night, 25 January, and she was Dr Suzannah Lord. I was locked up in a US Fisheries substation, she thought. Juli saved me from Archer. They followed us down the parkway and ran us over the embankment, and . . .

All right, so things were a little hazy after that. She had the gist of it.

Suddenly, a horrid memory popped into her mind, of the renegade agent disappearing with a curse into the cold black water. By now, his body must be far downriver, lost under the ice. She shivered. He had been after her, perhaps to kill her, but she knew the memory of his sinking through the ice would haunt her for the rest of her life.

As Ed shone the light around her eye, she became aware of the indelible hospital smells of disinfectant, soap, and lotion. As a surgeon, she rarely noticed them. But she was not a surgeon now, she was a patient.

She had to change that as quickly as possible.

She thought of Grainger, crawling across the ice towards her, then backing away when he heard the sirens. Grainger had not fallen through the ice. No doubt he had followed the ambulance. He and his men would be set up in the parking lot by now. If they knew anything about hospitals, they'd wait for the shift change. For ten or so minutes around midnight, the incoming and outgoing nurses would all converge on the station for the patient briefing. It would be the perfect moment to walk by her room, raise the silenced pistol . . .

Suzannah shuddered. What if I call the police? she thought. Explain that it wasn't an accident, that someone ran us off the road and we need a guard –

No. They've already threatened me with an Arlington police lieutenant. Even as a rogue operation, they may have some police in their pocket. I wouldn't know my police guard wasn't a hit man until it was too late. And if the police were legit, they'd want to know more. They'd investigate. They might get all the way to the microchip. Too many people know what it can do already.

Ed switched his light back to the first eye.

Suzannah wished he would stop it. She felt ridiculous lying here on the bed in the stupid hospital gown. Ed had said Jay and Juli were all right, but she wanted to see for herself. And Andrew – what happened to him? Someone had called the ambulance, but it could have been a motorist with a car phone who'd seen the Jeep run off the road. If Andrew had got away, he should lie low now. Even a phone call would be risky. But she would feel a lot better if she knew he was safe.

'Mmm-hmmm,' Ed said and clicked his light off.

'Is this really necessary?' Suzannah said.

'Oh, you think exams are for other people?' He was clearly enjoying this.

'Jay Mallernee is the one with the concussion.'

'You examined him, did you?'

'No.'

'Well, I did. He suffered some very nasty lacerations and, yes, a mild concussion, but he's all right now. Your concussion wasn't quite so mild. I'm going to keep you here on neuro for a day or two.'

'No way.' She tried to sit up in bed. Pain stabbed through her head. She eased back down. Looking past Ed, she saw that the hall glowed with the reduced lighting of late night. It must be getting close to midnight. 'What time is it?'

Ed checked his watch. 'Eleven-fifteen.'

She felt an icy rush of alarm. 'Ed, I can't stay here.'

'Why not?'

'I . . . I've got to help Juli.'

'I told you, your sister is fine. I just talked to her. They've set her leg and ankle and she's resting comfortably down on ortho.'

'But my nephew, J.D. –'

'Juli said to tell you he was all right. She called some neighbours and they've taken him for as long as necessary, until you or Juli get out of the hospital.'

Joe and Claire, Suzannah thought gratefully.

'Just worry about yourself,' Ed soothed.

Suzannah grabbed his wrist. 'I'm serious. I can't stay here.'

'Well, you're going to have to, for a day or so. First of all, your clothes were a total loss. I had them thrown away. Second, I've already called your chief of surgery and told him to have the staff cover your office patients and operations for

305

the rest of the week. Third, I don't think you could get out of that bed even if your life depended on it.'

It does, Suzannah thought. She tried to push up again. As she was about to make it, Ed put a gentle hand on her shoulder and eased her back.

'I want a shot of dex,' she said.

Ed frowned. 'Dexedrine?'

'Any amphetamine. I don't care. Just something to get me up and out of here.' She tried to keep her desperation out of her voice.

'Hell, Suzannah, that's the last thing I'd dream of doing. I'm going to give you a shot all right – Demerol for the pain.'

'I won't take it.'

He seemed baffled. 'Why not? I know you're hurting.'

'It will make me sleepy.'

'Which is just what you should be. You need to rest.'

Suzannah realized she was getting nowhere with Ed. She had to get out of here.

'Just twenty-five mg,' Ed said, 'to take away that headache and help you rest.'

'No.'

He began to look concerned. 'Uh, Suzannah, I'd like to call down someone from psychiatry, have them give you the once over, too.'

'Don't be ridiculous . . .' Suzannah hesitated. 'I'll see Dr Harrad. No one else.'

'I'll check if she's up there.' Ed headed for the door, shaking his head.

'Ed, wait. How is Tricia?'

He turned. 'Still unresponsive, I'm afraid. We'll start calling chronic care facilities tomorrow.'

As Ed walked out, Suzannah battled against despair. She

might as well face the fact that Tricia wasn't going to get better any time soon. She'd taken her down from the rope, and she was still alive, but only just. Andrew was out of reach again.

And I still have to stop the microchip, Suzannah thought. Getting out of here is not enough. I've got to get back after them.

She struggled to think: Juli and she had been discussing a plan in the car – going to the Secretary of Defense. But with Juli hurt, how could they hope to get in to see Secretary Hastings? And how could I convince him anyway? Suzannah wondered. Even if Andrew is still free and links up with us and tells his story, the Secretary might think he was crazy or lying.

Suzannah pushed and struggled until she sat up. Her head throbbed viciously. She found herself longing for the painkiller she had turned down. She looked at her watch. It wasn't on her arm. No clock in the room, either. Using the phone beside her bed, she called Time: 'At the tone the time will be . . . eleven-twenty, and twenty seconds.' She hung up before the tone could pierce her ear. Half an hour, and then they'd move in.

She straightened one leg, planting her foot on the warm tile. She stood, leaning her thighs against the bed. Her head throbbed, but it was not too bad. She could stand it.

'Hey! You are surely a sight for sore eyes.' Jay walked in, beaming, giving her a big hug. She squeezed back, glad to see him and tremendously relieved. His voice had its usual booming vigour. The stitches along the side of his forehead looked horrible, a railroad track dividing an orange desert of Betadine disinfectant, but she knew from experience it looked worse than it was. He was going to be fine.

As she let go of him, she staggered a step.

'Whoa – easy, *easy*,' he said. 'Come on, back to bed with you.'

She sat on the edge of the bed, and her dizziness cleared at once. She smiled at him. 'I'm fine.'

He sat next to her, putting an arm across her shoulders. 'Truthfully, now,' he said, 'how *are* you feeling?'

'Not bad, thanks to you. That was a very brave thing you did.'

'Not really,' he said. 'I love you. It wasn't brave, it was selfish. Without you, I'd be sorrier than a coyote with no howl. Of course, now that I saved your life, you have to do everything I say.'

Suzannah laughed, then gritted her teeth at the stab of pain.

'And right now I say you get back in bed.'

'I can't, Jay. They're out there. They'll move in.'

'I'll stay right here with you.'

'What good will that do if they have guns? They'll just kill you too. And besides, I'm not the only one who took a blow to the head tonight.'

'I'm fine.'

'So am I.'

Sharon Harrad walked in and stood, shaking her head. 'Two of my favourite head cases. What happened?'

'Car went off the road,' Jay said. 'Us too. What are you doing here so late?'

'I had an emergency readmission.' Sharon gave Suzannah a long second look. 'Since when are you a blonde?'

Suzannah patted Jay's knee. 'Would you excuse us a minute, Jay?'

Jay frowned, then said, 'I'll be right outside if you need me.' He ambled out. Suzannah watched him go, satisfying herself that he was moving all right. Clearly, at least he was up to leaving the hospital. She turned back to Sharon. 'I want to apologize about Percy Jones. It was a terrible position to put your best friend in.'

'That's all right. You can't help yourself. You're a surgeon.' She said it with the fondness of an indulgent aunt.

'What's that supposed to mean?'

'Nothing,' Sharon said, smiling. 'You're a born risk taker. You decided you had to do it, so you did it.'

'If there's any trouble with the licensing board, I'll tell them I lied to you about his mental state.'

'I know. There won't be any trouble.'

'Sharon, I need your help.'

'That's what Ed thought.'

'Not that kind of help.'

Sharon smiled. 'Why did I know you were going to say that?'

'Sorry. What I need right now is a shot of Dexedrine. Or if you have capsules, that would be fine, too.'

'Would it, now.'

'Can you finagle it with your meds nurse?'

Sharon gazed at her.

'Sharon, I'm not crazy. And I can't explain. But I have to get out of here right now.'

'Are you in danger?'

'Yes, I am.'

The green eyes never wavered. 'A VA doctor came for Percy Jones,' Sharon said. 'I signed his care over and they left. I know he wasn't crazy, but just tell me this: was he really CIA?'

'Yes.'

Sharon rubbed at her temples. Suzannah noticed that her thick raven-black hair had started to pull away from its barrettes. 'I was in the MHU here once,' Sharon said softly, her gaze going distant. 'Not as a doctor but as a patient. Did you know that?'

Suzannah looked at her, startled. 'No.'

'It's one of MHU's embarrassing little secrets. It was while Dr Valois was still head of psychiatry here. I was one of his residents. Someone slipped me a dose of angel dust and I flipped out. Next thing I knew, I was strapped to a bed in MHU. I couldn't convince Valois I wasn't psychotic.'

Suzannah shook her head, astonished. 'Who slipped you the PCP?'

Sharon's eyes focused on her again. 'It's a long story. Like yours, I suspect. Suzannah, if you're too weak or worn out, a hit of amphetamines could cause a heart attack.'

'I'm not too weak. I'll prove it. I'll walk up to MHU with you.'

Sharon sighed. 'All right, on one condition – when it's all over, you and I sit down and tell each other our stories.'

Suzannah hesitated.

'In strictest confidence, of course,' Sharon added.

'Deal. There's just one more thing.'

Sharon looked at her with resignation.

'I'm going to need your clothes.'

The cab was too warm. It was partly Sharon's thick overcoat, Suzannah knew, and partly the amphetamines. Suzannah could feel the dex burning through her veins, lifting her to a high, fidgety alertness. And Jay was holding six more, in case she needed another hit. *Bless you, Sharon.* Suzannah felt a surge of gratitude as she imagined her friend driving home, shivering in her white doctor's coat and slip. I'll make it up to her, Suzannah told herself – if I make it through this.

She glanced out of the back window, checking for any

following car. There didn't seem to be any. Slipping out through the hospital's administration wing appeared to have worked. She wondered if, even now, a man in scrubs or a doctor's white coat was walking down the hallway towards the room she'd left, a lethal syringe concealed under his coat. If so, he was about to shoot it into a mound of pillows.

'A pretty night,' Jay said, mistaking why she was staring out the window. Or perhaps he had not mistaken it. Either way, he was right. Bright moonlight gilded the Virginia countryside, turning the treetops crystalline with silvery brightness. She recognized a horse farm with a distinctive front gate. Only a few more miles to Roland Lancaster's house.

Her eagerness to get at him again surprised her. She had survived hit men, not just twice but probably tonight, too. Lancaster had nothing left to throw at her. She was going to learn where he stood in this, if she and her amphetamines had to shake it out of him.

'I keep thinking about Andrew Dugan,' Jay said.

Abandoning the rear window, Suzannah steeled herself. 'Thinking what?'

'Where is he?'

'Lying low, I hope.'

'Odd that he didn't call the hospital.'

'Maybe he didn't need to.'

'That's another thing,' Jay said. 'He's a, what did you call it? – an Adept.'

'He's not with them.'

'How can we be sure of that? He certainly has their abilities. How do we know he wasn't in that cell voluntarily as part of a ruse to persuade you to join them?'

Suzannah suppressed a stab of annoyance. There was some logic, after all, in what Jay was saying. But he was wrong.

311

'Andrew would not help them,' she said evenly.

'I know you want to believe that, but—'

'Jay, can we just drop it?'

He looked at her. She knew she should return his gaze, but she couldn't.

'I'm sorry,' Jay said. 'But if he's with them, we need to know it.'

'He's *not* with them, I'm telling you. I'm afraid he might be hurt or . . .' She swallowed. Fear welled up in her. She suppressed it. She could not think about that now.

Jay reached over, covered her hand with his own. 'If you think that much of him, I shouldn't be doubting him in front of you. I'm sorry.'

She realized what the words must have cost him. She took his hand, looking at him at last. 'It's all right,' she said. 'It's all right.'

They rode in silence a minute.

'Maybe you ought to tell me what you have in mind with Lancaster,' Jay said, 'so I can back your play.'

Suzannah glanced at the cabby. Security glass sealed him away from them. He looked oblivious in any case, bobbing his head in time to inaudible music flowing from his Walkman headset. She leaned towards Jay and kept her voice low. 'I don't think Lancaster is working with the Adepts. He's too arrogant and egotistical. He'd be appalled by anything that required his genius to be kept secret. If they pull strings at the FDA to get the microchip quietly stopped, he'll fight them. That could be very dangerous for him. If he plays to the press, which would be just like him, it will be very dangerous for the human race.'

Jay frowned. 'He would risk the side effect becoming known?'

'I don't think he believes the side effect exists. He sincerely believes that Tricia and Andrew are just crazy. It's logical, and he's got a talent for believing what he wants. We've got to try one more time to put him fully in the picture. You can tell him what they did to me at Langley. Maybe he'll listen to you. We want two things: First, to persuade him not to fight it when the FDA turns down the microchip. Second, to get him mad enough to help us make sure the Adept conspirators don't get the microchip either. I can't stand the bastard, but he'd be the most powerful ally we could hope for. He might even go to the Secretary of Defense with us just to strike back at the Adepts. That would be a real break. Lancaster is famous. Right now the whole world sees him as a giant of science. The Secretary would see him and the Secretary would listen to him.'

'It has potential,' Jay said admiringly. 'But what if we walk into that house and the doctor is working with them?'

'Then he'll probably pull out a pistol and hold us until they come.'

'No-o-o-o-kay.'

The cab slowed to a stop, and Suzannah realized they had reached the foot of Roland's long twisting driveway. His house sat on the hilltop, bathed in security lights, like a castle daring anyone to storm it. How would he like being wakened at four-thirty? Not much.

The cabby opened a port in the bulletproof shield. 'Hundert dollars,' he said.

'Wait for us,' Suzannah said. 'We'll be riding back with you.'

The cabby eyed her. 'A dollar every minute I wait.'

'Fine,' Suzannah said. Maybe some day Washington, DC, would put meters in its cabs like every other city. But right now she had more important things to think about.

She got out with Jay and stood at the foot of the driveway.

Released from the heat of the cab, she buttoned Sharon's coat against the chill. The three-quarter moon, rimmed in a glowing corona, lit the woods around Roland's house. Up the hill, the young maples that screened the front portico in summer yielded a decent view through bare, tangled branches of the sprawling house and three-car garage. Seeing the place again brought back memories of the monthly staff parties back when she was Lancaster's resident. She'd spent hours in the half-finished basement rec room, drinking Hearty Burgundy and trading morbid hospital jokes with the other residents. Gallow's humour, they'd called it. How golden the world had seemed then, how unlimited her possibilities! She would be a neurosurgeon. She would push the envelope, be the best neurosurgeon ever.

Tonight she would settle for averting catastrophe.

'I have a bad feeling about this,' Jay murmured.

'You, too?'

'There's not even any smoke from the chimney.'

'Maybe he turned the furnace back for the evening.'

'Maybe. Shall we go wake the great man up?'

'Please. I'm feeling nauseated enough as it is.' She strode up the steep driveway, the artificial vigour of the amphetamines powering her legs. There would be hell to pay later, but right now she'd take any edge she could get.

At the front door, she noticed that the shrubs hadn't been trimmed in years. Mrs Lancaster – Martha – used to do that, before she got fed up and divorced Lancaster. One of life's golden moments, Suzannah thought. She grabbed the cast-iron knocker, relishing the thought of startling Lancaster awake. At the first blow, the door swung inward an inch. She started to push it further, but Jay grabbed her wrist.

'Now I really don't like this,' he said.

She eased the door open another few inches. The tinny

music of a radio drifted from the left – the kitchen, Suzannah remembered. '*We all live in a yellow submarine . . .*' Lancaster must be working late. Except he was an opera buff who despised any music written after the nineteenth century.

'Dr Lancaster?' she said.

No answer. She pushed the door wide and walked through the foyer into the kitchen, feeling Jay right behind her. The house was quite cool, the heat clearly shut off. She reached for the kitchen lights, her hand finding the switch by memory. A sea of white tile and oak cabinets winked in, out, then blazed coldly under the fluorescents. On the counter next to the refrigerator, a small radio continued to spin out the Beatles lyric.

The door to the basement stood open.

'Suzannah,' Jay cautioned as she went over and looked down the steps. Lancaster lay at the bottom on his back, his legs sprawled apart on the lower steps. He stared up into a bare light bulb of the still unfinished rec room. She felt a cold shock in her stomach and stepped back. Jay moved around her and swore. 'We're getting out of here, now.'

'No. He might be alive.'

Suzannah started down the steps, halted by Jay's hand on her arm. He went down ahead of her, stopping astride Lancaster's body, staring left, then right. 'All right.'

She hurried down and knelt beside Lancaster, feeling for a pulse at the angle of his jaw. Nothing. His skin was cool. Seeing his blind, staring eyes, she felt a strange sense of release. In a very real way, this was a tragedy, a great loss to science. But she could feel no sorrow, only a vast relief, filling her like a deep breath taken after a very long wait.

I don't have to hate him any more, she thought.

She closed his eyes. 'I guess he wasn't working with them,' she said.

'This could have been an accident.'

'That's what the papers will say. And it might well have been. I have a feeling the moment of truth came. He found out they were going to stop FDA approval. He got angry, threatened to fight them. Maybe he even struggled physically with them. Or they tried to restrain him and things got out of control.' Suzannah thought of John Stockwell, bleeding his life out in Emergency; of Archer's statement: *The stakes are very high.* 'If they became convinced it was the only way to save themselves, they'd kill him,' she said. 'Murder or accident, they caused it.'

She got up and went to the filing cabinets in the corner of the basement. Locked. Returning to the body, she slipped her hand into his pocket and retrieved his keys. She unlocked the top drawer. Empty. So were the other two.

'Damn!' she said, feeling cold.

'I take it he kept his research notes in those files,' Jay said.

'Yes, all his raw notes on the development of the microchip, the computer printouts of the visual codes, his protocols for surgical implantation – everything. He kept a microfilm version in the safe at work and this as a backup. His notes have been stolen. It proves he didn't fall down those steps without help, accidental or otherwise. Maybe they think the notes will help them improve their "success" rate with the side effect. Or they just don't want anyone else to have them.'

'Correct on all counts,' said a voice from the top of the stairs.

Suzannah's heart sank. She looked up the steps. Archer Montross was not holding a gun. But the two men with him were.

# 31

Suzannah felt a desperate urge to run as Archer and the two gunmen descended towards them. But there was nowhere to go. The only way out was up the stairs.

Archer stepped carefully over Lancaster's sprawled body, an expression of distaste on his face.

'Why did you kill him?' Suzannah asked.

'I didn't kill him. He slipped. Admit it, Suzannah – you're glad the arrogant bastard is dead.' Archer gazed at her with a smugness that infuriated, then chilled her. He *saw* me coming here, she thought, despairing. How can I hope to defeat or even outwit such a man?

'Are we about to slip too, Archer?'

He looked genuinely upset. 'Suzannah, we don't want you dead.'

'Some of you do. You can't even control your own people. The traitors have their own traitors.'

Archer shook his head. 'We disagree about you, yes. But there are no traitors among us. We care very deeply for our country. Don't force me to join those who want to kill you, Suzannah. None of us will put a determined surgeon and a nosy reporter ahead of the millions of other Americans we must protect. The microchip will make America safer than it has ever been in history.'

'From whom?'

'You scoff. But when the next Saddam Hussein decides to smuggle the parts of a nuclear bomb into this country and explode it under Constitution Avenue, I want us to know about it ahead of time, not afterwards.' Archer's face was red. He took a deep breath. 'I think it's time we were on our way. We have a car waiting in Dr Lancaster's garage. I believe you know the way.'

One of the gunmen started back up the stairs. The other motioned her and Jay into line, falling in behind them. Suzannah gathered her nerve as she climbed the steps. She had to do something. Once they got into the car it would be much harder to escape.

The lead gunman walked through the door above her and turned to help cover them. The butt of a gun swung down from behind the door, smashing the back of his head. The man's eyes went blank and his knees buckled. From behind the door, a hand pulled him out of sight. Astonished, Suzannah listened for a shout behind her, then realized she was blocking everyone's view up the steps. Keep walking, she thought. She turned right through the door, followed by Jay. The gun butt descended again as the second guard cleared the door. It made a soft, sickening thud as it connected with the top of his head. He crashed down like a poleaxed steer.

Before Archer could react, Andrew Dugan stepped around from behind the door and pointed the gun at him. Suzannah wanted to shout for joy.

Archer stopped on the last step, looking resigned. 'So you saw her coming here, too.'

'That's right.'

A calculating look crossed Archer's face. 'The question is,

would you really shoot me? As it happens, I've already seen that you are not a killer.'

Jay snatched the gun from Andrew and pointed it at Archer's forehead. 'Maybe he wouldn't shoot you, but I sure as hell would. Get down on the floor.'

Archer got down on the floor.

'Andrew,' Jay said, 'see if there's some clothesline in one of those kitchen drawers.'

Andrew rummaged for a moment and came up with a bicycle chain and padlock.

'Better yet,' Jay said. 'Wrap that around his neck, nice and tight, and padlock him to the refrigerator door.'

Andrew did it. Archer, sitting on the kitchen floor, stared straight ahead, not looking at any of them.

'Do you have a car?' Jay said to Andrew.

Andrew nodded. 'But I had to park it a mile from here and come in the back way, in case they had the place staked out.'

'You don't know?'

'I don't see everything,' Andrew said softly. 'Not yet.'

'Archer said their car is in the garage,' Suzannah said. 'We can take that.'

Jay bent and took keys from the pocket of one of the fallen men.

'Come on,' Suzannah said, leading the way to the garage. The door was open. A blue Ford sat in the nearest bay, one door already open, waiting for them. Jay slid behind the wheel. Andrew got in back. His face was still ashen. Suzannah got in beside Jay. The dash looked like a police car's, complete with a CB radio. She hoped it was fast.

'Where to?' Jay asked.

'Anywhere but here,' Suzannah said.

Jay gunned the car down the curving driveway to the road,

passing the cab. 'If Archer's crew doesn't kill us,' he said, 'our cabby will when he realizes we stiffed him for the fare.'

Andrew groaned. 'I never hit anyone before in my life,' he said. 'I never want to again.'

Suzannah reached back, giving his hand a squeeze. 'You saved us.'

Jay glanced at him in the rearview mirror. 'We weren't properly introduced last night,' he said. 'I'm Jay Mallernee.'

Andrew's eyes focused on his in the mirror, and Suzannah could see the two men sizing each other up in the glass. 'Andrew Dugan.'

'I know. Since you seem to have the same ... abilities as Archer, maybe we should turn the leadership of this little group over to you. What do we do now?'

'I don't know.'

Jay eyed him again in the mirror and Suzannah glanced back.

'Sorry. I don't choose my visions, unfortunately. If something relevant comes, I'll let you know.'

'Oh-oh,' Jay said, still looking in the mirror.

Suzannah saw with alarm that another blue Ford was on their tail, accelerating fast.

'Hold on to your seats,' Jay said, wheeling the car onto a side road. 'It looks like they *did* have a backup team.'

Jay wheeled around another corner, throwing Andrew to the side. The headlights swept across a wooded hillside then steadied up on a dirt road.

'Where did you learn to drive like that?' Andrew gasped.

'Kuwait.'

'We've got to split up,' Suzannah said.

'No way.'

'We'll triple our chances of getting away from them. At least one of us has to. If one drives on and the other two of us

320

get out and head in opposite directions –'

'I can beat them into town,' Jay said.

'No, you can't,' Andrew said. 'They're sending helicopters.'

'How the hell do you know that?'

'I see it.'

'Christ,' Jay murmured.

Suzannah realized that Andrew had probably seen the CB on the dash too without necessarily noticing it. It had been enough to start his unconscious mind rolling. The trailing car, with its own CB, must have radioed for air support as soon as they'd seen Jay career out of the driveway.

'All right,' Jay said, 'we *do* have to split up. And since I'm the best driver, I'll stay with the car.' He wheeled around another corner and slammed on the brakes. Suzannah saw in the side wash of the headlights that they were surrounded on both sides by woods. Deep gullies, rivers of black shadow, flanked the road on both sides.

'Jay!'

'Andrew, get her out of here. I'll ditch the car in another mile.'

Andrew jumped out of the back door. Suzannah sat, frozen in indecision. Jay opened her door and gave her shoulder a gentle shove. 'For God's sake, get going!' Andrew grabbed her arm and pulled her with him, slamming the door. Jay accelerated with a screech of tyres.

'Quickly!' Andrew said, pulling her down into the gully, pressing her flat against the bank as the pursuing car roared past. She tried to get up, but he held her down a moment longer, a hand on her neck. When the sound of the two cars had died completely, he let her up. She wiped a glob of grass and thawing mud from her nose. Sharon's cashmere coat was now filthy. 'Andrew –'

'Come on!' He pulled her away from the road, into the woods. Moonlight filtered down through the branches, strong enough to cast soft shadows. She heard the low, distant *thok-thok* of a helicopter. Fear burst in her legs, driving her past Andrew. They dodged through the trees together, running up a gentle incline. She slipped and fell on some wet leaves and leapt up again, panic hammering at her as the sound of the chopper swelled. Andrew caught up with her, steering her into a copse of pine trees. 'Down,' he said, then grabbed her arm and pulled her down with him, rolling under the protective cover of a big pine. The sweet fragrance of old pine needles filled her nostrils. The ground was almost dry under the thick branches.

The helicopter swooped overhead, sweeping the ground with its searchlight. A blazing circle of light flickered through the nearby trees and vanished. Suzannah looked at Andrew. His face, pale in the moonlight, seemed distant. His blank expression sent a chill through her. It was the glassy look of an amnesiac or stroke victim. He's having a vision, she realized. She grabbed his hands, squeezing gently. His blank expression did not change. The thrashing of the helicopter faded away over the treetops.

Suddenly Andrew gave her hands a return squeeze.

'That was close!' He laughed, his voice vibrant with exhilaration.

'You certainly seem to be having fun,' she said crossly.

'I haven't seen what's happening now,' he said.

'Just how much do you see?' she asked, afraid of his answer.

'More and more. The visions are coming with increasing frequency. I can't stop them.'

She understood the terrible weight of his burden then. No wonder he had asked her to remove the chip. Would a time

322

come when he would see everything in his mind and nothing around him? Under the onslaught of the future, would he lose his grip on the present? It would be enough to drive anyone insane. Even blindness would be preferable to lying in some locked ward, catatonic, fed by tubes as he stared at movies of the future rolling on and on inside his mind.

'Oh, Andrew.'

'If we get out of this, will you take the chip out of my brain?'

'Yes. But right now we have to split up –'

'In a minute. We'll be all right here for a minute. Swear to me you'll do it.'

'It's more than just me, Andrew. It would take a well-equipped OR, a surgical team, and special permission for a general surgeon to operate on your brain. Even if by some miracle we got that, there's a thirty per cent chance I'd blind you. It could be more. We've only tried it with monkeys. The best you could hope for is that you'd see as badly as before the microchip, probably worse.'

'I'll take the risk. You must help me.'

'Of course I will.'

Tears flooded his eyes. Putting his arms around her, he pulled her to him on the soft bed of pine needles. Above them, she heard the sweet cry of a whippoorwill. 'There's so little time,' he said. She saw the pain in his eyes, the desperation. She felt him pulling her closer.

'You're worried about Jay,' he said, his voice sympathetic. 'Don't. They won't get him.'

'But . . .' She heard echoes of something else in his voice. 'That's what you saw a minute ago, isn't it?'

He nodded.

Relief flooded her. 'We should split up now.'

'Another minute.'

323

She watched his mouth, the fine expressive lips, until they blurred and she felt them on her own, questing, moulding themselves to her. Andrew's arms enfolded her, drew her close. She felt the whole length of him against her. She opened her mouth to him, feeling the heat of his tongue, gripping him to her as he gripped her. His kiss lingered on and on, making her dizzy. Breaking it off at last, he slid his face past hers, his cheek on hers, his breath moist and warm against her ear. 'I love you, Suzannah Lord. I have loved you from the moment when you and I went to the coffee shop that night.'

'And I love you, Andrew. In a way, I've loved you for years. How many hours have I spent looking at the man inside you? Every one of your paintings, so honest, so beautiful.'

Andrew held her by the shoulders. His dark eyes burned into her, as if they could see into her soul. They can, Suzannah thought. Or they will. She looked at him, thrilled and mystified. His face, softened by moonlight, looked as fully at peace as she had ever seen it. She did not know what was going to happen next. Life was terrifying, and sweet.

Andrew took her wrist, his expression suddenly grim. 'This was your idea, wasn't it? – getting out of the car.'

'Yes.' She felt a sudden, horrified understanding. 'Archer!'

'They've probably found him chained to the refrigerator by now. There's a good chance he will have *seen* you getting out.'

At that moment, the sound of the chopper became audible again, a low thumping that raised the hairs on her neck.

'Come on,' she said, pulling him up with her. 'We can't let them catch us both. As long as one of us is on the loose, they'll dare a lot less. You go down that way. I'll head uphill. Try to find a house. Phone the police. When they come, tell them anything you want about who's after us – except the truth, of course. When you get back to the city, go straight to the *Post* newsroom and tell them. You say Jay will get away; I believe he'll go there, since we talked about it earlier. I'll meet you both there.'

His eyes held hers. He nodded.

She kissed him again as the chopper flew nearer. Pulling away, she ran up the hill into the moonlit forest.

# 32

Suzannah heard a sound behind her and froze, listening. A branch crackling under someone's foot? She tried to see back down the slope, but the setting moon cast long twisting shadows among the trees, confusing her eye, making it hard to be sure what she was seeing. She heard the helicopter searching in the distance, its rotors chopping, then fading. It was a disheartening sound. The Adepts might be a renegade group, but clearly they could bring powerful resources to bear. Whoever was running the operation must be close to the top of the Agency.

She continued staring downslope. Someone was there, she could feel it. Andrew? No, he should be far away by now. She listened a moment longer. The *thrum* of the helicopter faded completely. A soft breeze rattled the branches together. An owl hooted in the distance. Nothing else. Her tension eased. Maybe it had just been a branch falling.

She continued working her way up the long hill. If she could just find a highway, or a house, get away and meet Jay and Andrew at the *Post* ...

And then what?

She battled a sense of hopelessness. The Adepts had headed her off at the Agency and at Lancaster's house. What made her think Archer wouldn't *see* through her again and stop her?

Suzannah realized with surprise that tears were running down her cheeks. Must be the amphetamines. She tried to stop crying and couldn't. The flood of tears exasperated her. I want to be back at Adams Memorial, she thought. I want to take out a gall bladder or an appendix and feel good because somebody's pain will be gone. What am I doing out here, stumbling around a dark forest at night, like a convict trying to escape? I just want to have a normal life. Instead, I got my sister's leg – and possibly her career – broken. I got Sharon into trouble. I put Jay's life in danger.

And I'll probably be dead before I can make any of it right.

She pressed on up the hill, wiping her face, feeling the grit on her palms mix with her tears. God, she must look a sight.

Stumbling suddenly from the woods, she pulled up short, her stomach plunging. In the darkness, she had almost stepped over a cliff! A yard from her, the ground ended. Over the edge, she could see a field about a hundred feet below. A river divided it, a black ribbon of water glinting in the last slanting moonbeams. From this height, the river seemed barely to crawl.

A limb snapped behind her, much closer than last time.

She suppressed the panicky urge to run, easing into a crouch instead. She heard the brittle rustle of a bush about fifty yards back. Homing on the sound, she saw a soft flicker of shadow and light through the trees: a man, making his way straight towards her. A terrible urgency filled her. She must get moving or he'd be on her in seconds.

Quickly, she looked to either side. The path along the cliff bent back out of sight in either direction. She crawled towards the bend that was further away, keeping low until it was safe to stand up and run. Just before she rounded the bend, she looked back. No one was behind her. She felt a huge relief. When the man got to the cliff, he would naturally assume she had run around the nearer bend. Now all she had to do was keep heading in the opposite direction.

She made her way as quickly as she could, careful not to step too close to the cliff.

Archer stepped from the trees, directly in front of her. 'Hello, Suzannah.'

A shock went through her. She looked at the edge of the cliff. Jump off, she thought. Now! But she could not make herself do it.

Suzannah came awake slowly, aching, feeling hung over. Raising her head, she saw she was in a hospital bed. A dead TV screen stared down at her from a pastel wall. Where was this, Adams Memorial?

*Archer.*

Shuddering, she remembered. Once again, Archer had blocked her move. She remembered the horrible smug silence he'd kept as he led her back down through the woods to his car.

At least he had not tried to touch her.

She swung her legs out of bed, feeling the warm air along her back where the skimpy hospital gown parted. The orderly had taken her clothes. She was back at the secret facility, what had Juli called it? – Station Three.

What did they plan to do with her?

She heard a key turning in the door and got back in bed. Archer walked in.

'Good morning,' he said.

'Don't be insipid, Archer.'

'I'm glad you had a chance to rest. I know you must be

hungry. We'll take care of that as soon as we can.'

She realized she had not eaten for a long time, but she did not want food. She wanted to get out of here. Wherever 'here' was. 'What time is it?' she asked.

'Ten o'clock. Tuesday morning.'

Good. She'd slept only a few hours. That, and her lack of hunger, meant the amphetamines were not totally out of her system yet. She could tell by the gritty feeling around her eyeballs that she was headed for a crash, but not yet, not yet. 'What are you going to do with me?'

'I'm going to reason with you.'

'Why? I won't work for them. Not ever.'

Archer looked pained. 'Listen to me, Suzannah. A year ago two members of Saddam Hussein's secret police came into the United States through Mexico, crossing the border at a remote point. With them they had a SAM, a surface-to-air missile. They drove across the southern part of the country to a field not far from Andrews Air Force Base. They set the SAM up in the field. They were right on the flight path for Air Force One. The next day, the President was to fly to London for a meeting with the Prime Minister.

'The men with the SAM missile never fired it because I saw it. We caught the men and . . . stopped them.'

'What do you want me to say? That I'm impressed? Of course I am, but—'

'But nothing. If I had not been an Adept, the President of the United States would be dead now. You cannot go on pretending that the microchip is a bad thing.'

'I *know* it's a bad thing.'

'Do you?' Archer smiled, a secret, knowing smile. It sent a shiver up her spine. 'I could tell you something about Andrew Dugan and you, something very important—'

'Shut up, Archer!' she said, furious.

He gazed at her. 'You have to adjust to this, Suzannah.'

'Tell me, Archer, how does it feel to know what's going to happen?'

'It feels very powerful.'

'Andrew can't control his visions. I assume that's the case for you, too.'

Archer shrugged. 'I can't *consciously* control them, no. I might have to wait to see something I want to see. But sooner or later, my unconscious has shown me most of what I've wanted to know.'

'And some things you haven't wanted to know?'

Archer remained silent.

'Have the visions increased in frequency since they first started?'

'Oh, yes. That's just it, I'm seeing more and more, and seeing it sooner. I'm getting much more powerful.'

'More powerful? Maybe at the moment. But where will it end? Will you get to the point where you will feel no anticipation any more? No hope, because you know everything that's going to happen? You used to love the movies. What happens when you start seeing how they'll end? How long before the visions start coming to you every hour, then every minute, until you don't know whether you're living something or *seeing* it? How long before you go catatonic or turn into a machine, Archer?'

She stopped. His face had paled. He has at least *imagined* what I'm saying, she thought. And he's afraid I might be right. Despite herself, she felt sorry for him. 'Archer, listen. You must help me stop this. The people you work for might have wanted to shut Tricia up, but she beat them to it, didn't she. She hanged herself, Archer, a teacher who loved life, loved her students. How long before you feel like she did?

330

Have you already seen yourself putting a rope around your neck, a gun to your head?'

'You shut up,' Archer snapped. 'Instead of fighting this, why don't you help us? With you on our side, we could straighten out these problems.'

'I won't help you.'

'You will when the microchip is in you.'

She stared at him, horrified. 'No, Archer. You don't mean that.'

'We had hoped Dr Fachet would fill this role, but we see now that he has no real understanding of the microchip. You are a brilliant woman, a scientist in the true sense of the word. We don't just want you to do more implants for us, we need you to help us understand this thing. I won't lie to you. None of us has yet seen the future of the microchip. Think of it. You will be the neurosurgeon you always longed to be. And you will be awakened to a part of your own mind a hundred times more powerful than the most brilliant human minds around you. You're afraid now. I understand that. But your fear will go away. You will be like a goddess, Suzannah.'

Suzannah's mind reeled in horror. She felt short of breath. 'Don't do this, Archer.'

'You can't fight us, Suzannah. Dr Fachet is preparing right now to do the surgery.'

Panic welled up in her. 'No, Archer! You have to have my co-operation in placing the microchip. I won't give it.'

'Yes, you will. Otherwise, there might be worse damage to your brain. You might be blinded.'

'I would rather be blind,' she said, then felt the horror of the words. I have to get out of here, she thought. Please, God. She tried to still her panic and think. Instead, she jumped from the table and ran for the locked door. Archer let her go, let her twist the knob until she came back to herself. Then he stepped forward and held her. She started to resist. A desperate idea formed in her mind. She leaned against him, trembling, feeling him stiffen in surprise. He put his arms around her, holding her against him. She shuddered, and then hugged him back. She squeezed hard, slipping one hand into his pocket as she did so, terrified he would feel it.

He patted her back. 'It will be all right, Suzannah. You'll see.'

The key, she thought. *The key!*

# 33

Suzannah stared with bitter disappointment at the cigarette lighter she'd picked from Archer's pocket. The man who would walk back through that door any minute was not the *Arch* engraved on the lighter. He was a man named Archer who had lost most of what made him human.

And he wanted to make her like him.

Suzannah's fist closed desperately around the lighter. Surely she could make some use of it. The very fact that Archer had not foreseen her taking it was, in itself, a small victory. He – or his unconscious – might know her well, but not totally. Archer didn't know that her nephew had taught her to pick pockets. J.D. hadn't even existed when she and Archer were friends. He's not God, Suzannah thought. He can be defeated.

Could she use the lighter to set her bedding on fire? Maybe, but she'd either asphyxiate herself with the smoke or they'd come and get her out and take her to surgery anyway.

Light it and stick it in Archer's face? It might get her past him. After what had happened to him, Archer must be terrified of fire.

She heard a trolley rumbling up to the door. Her heart sank. Even if Archer was out there, he had company. The dead bolt clicked open. She thrust the lighter in the waistband of her underpants, under the pocketless hospital gown.

Archer entered with two orderlies. 'It's time, Suzannah.'

The bigger orderly took her arm, holding on as she tried to break free. 'Archer?'

'That's all right, William,' Archer said to the orderly. 'She won't run. There's really nowhere to run, anyway.'

'I won't run,' Suzannah said. 'But I don't want to ride on that trolley either. May I walk, please?'

Archer gave a sympathetic grimace. 'Sorry.'

She climbed onto the trolley, sitting upright. William took her shoulder and firmly forced her down.

'I'll see you . . . after,' Archer said. His face was rigid, the unscarred half all the paler beside the pink graft tissue. He turned and walked away down the hall. William rolled her in the opposite direction, the other orderly walking alongside. She was so frightened she could barely think. The hall, empty of people, ended ahead in ominous wine-red doors. She concentrated on the lighter. One quick move and she'd have it in hand. To do what? The Operating Room would probably have a tank or two of oxygen. Oxygen would not ignite or burn on its own, but it would turn a small fire into a big one very fast. She needed something else, something volatile.

William rolled her through the red doors into a small OR with an observation balcony overhead. Mike Fachet stood beside the surgery table, gloved hands in the air, his eyes wide between the strip of mask and cap.

'Hello, Suzannah,' he said.

She felt a surge of contempt for him. He was supposed to be a physician. What had happened to the oath he had taken to do no harm? She wanted to say it, to throw the words in his face, but her throat was too dry to speak. She turned her head away, repulsed by the sight of him –

And saw the canister of ether.

Her heart raced. Ether – on the bottom shelf of the glassed-in instrument cabinet. She began to hope. Ether was highly flammable, one reason it was no longer used as anaesthesia. It was still found in many ORs because it was an excellent cleaner for surgical instruments. If she could get to it before William grabbed her . . .

Just as she was about to leap from the trolley, a nurse, capped and masked like Mike, stepped into her field of vision, picking something up from a tray on top of the cabinet – a syringe! Suzannah realized with alarm that they were about to inject her with a barbiturate. The nurse thumped a bubble from the syringe and walked towards her. Suzannah leapt up, grabbing the lighter from her waist as she sprang towards the cabinet. The nurse tried to stop her. She punched the woman in the stomach; the nurse gasped and sat down. Suzannah dodged around her. She heard one of the orderlies shout behind her. Sliding the cabinet open, she grabbed the flask of ether, spinning the cap off as she turned. William was striding toward her, not even running, his expression stern and confident. She held the ether in front of her and flicked the lighter. William hesitated, then took another step.

'I'll blow you up!' Suzannah shouted.

'William, *stop*!' Fachet yelled.

The orderly stopped, uncertainly. Suzannah smelled the sickly sweet scent of the ether.

'Suzannah,' Fachet said, 'the fumes. You've got to cover it up.'

She ignored him, looking for the oxygen. There, at the end

of the counter. She sidled over to it. Setting the ether on top
of the cabinet, she kept the lighter over it as she opened the
valve on the oxygen tank.

'No!' Fachet shouted as pure oxygen hissed into the room.
She brought the ether down into the cold stream.

'Suzannah,' Fachet screamed. 'For God's sake!'

The other orderly ran at her. She flicked the lighter and
splashed ether through the flame into the stream of oxygen. A
huge gout of fire leapt halfway across the OR, engulfing the
orderly. She heard herself scream in horror along with him as
flames leapt from his white jacket. Fachet ran to him and
rolled him on the floor. Suzannah saw William edging toward
her. She turned the tank of oxygen toward him and splashed
more ether through the lighter flame. He cursed and shrank
back as another gout of flame leapt out towards him.
Suzannah grabbed a pile of surgical towels, dumped them on
the floor, and doused them with the ether. She kicked the
whooshing oxygen tank onto it and tossed the lighter into the
middle. Flames roared up in a towering column almost to the
ceiling. Beyond the flames, she glimpsed William helping the
other orderly, whose white coat was still smoking, through
the exit. Fachet was already gone, leaving only the nurse,
who was struggling for breath, trying to get up. Suzannah ran
to her, feeling a strange, floating detachment. She pulled the
nurse's scrubs off, one yank for the top, two for the trousers,
and scrambled into them. She tore off the woman's surgical
cap and mask, dragged her to the door, and pushed her out.
Mike and William were waiting just outside the door. They
lunged at her, driving her back inside. A wall of heat seared
her face like a blast furnace. Black smoke swirled down from
the ceiling. In desperation, she turned back to the red doors,
but flames raced across, cutting her off.

The balcony – there must be an exit up there!

Fighting panic, she ran to the instrument cabinet, tipping it over. Surgical instruments clanged across the floor. Upending the cabinet, she used the divider jambs like rungs of a ladder and clambered up it until she could grab the rail of the balcony. Chinning herself, she threw her leg over the balcony rail. She could feel the flames surging up behind her as she pulled herself over the rail into the balcony. The smoke was thick up here, tearing at her lungs. She could barely see. She found an aisle and staggered up between the seats, trying to make out the door through the smoke. Her eyes burned and watered. There! Pulling the door open, she reeled into the hallway. The clean air tasted wonderful. She drew her surgical mask down and inhaled deeply. As her head cleared, her legs steadied up. The hall was empty, but she pulled the surgical mask back up in case someone came and ran toward the door at the end. Just as she got there, it opened. A man in a grey suit stood there, a gun in his hand.

'Dr Lord is in there,' Suzannah cried. 'The fire – I didn't dare –'

The man pushed past her, and she ran. She did not have to fake her panic. She found a stairway down into a floor-level corridor. A man and a woman stood in the hall. The woman was sniffing the air.

'There's a fire in the OR,' Suzannah yelled. 'Hit the alarm! Evacuate the building!'

The man turned to the wall and pulled a red switch down. An alarm began to clamour. Suzannah ran down the corridor toward the guard desk at the exit. The guard stood and held out a hand toward her.

'Wait a minute –'

'Get out, get out!' Suzannah shouted. 'There's a fire!' She reached over and hit the button on his desk, running past him and outside, praying that he wouldn't try and stop her. He

337

shouted after her. She ran down some steps and onto the path. The skin on her back crawled, anticipating a bullet. She made the protection of the pine grove and began to hope. Only one gate left. She ran along the path. As she neared the gate, the guard stepped from his booth, his hand on the butt of his pistol.

'Fire!' she shouted.

'Hold on – what?'

'There's a fire in the OR!'

The phone in his booth rang. He turned back to it, and she grabbed his gun from his holster. He turned back to her, his face stunned. 'Hey –'

'Open the gate!'

'No.' He grabbed the barrel of the gun, yanking it against her finger. It fired. The man went rigid and toppled over onto his back. She screamed, horrified. Bending over him, she saw that a strange double dart stuck out of his chest. A thin wire led from the base of one dart back to the barrel. The guard was still rigid, but his eyes tracked her. Confused, she looked at the weapon in her hand. The plug end of the wire ejected from the barrel as she watched, then another round popped up into the chamber. This is what they shot me with, she realized, the day I went to Langley. She looked at the man again. His eyes were still on her, but they looked drowsy now. One dart must have shocked him and the other was the anaesthetic that wiped out short-term memory.

Suzannah pulled herself up the doorjamb of the booth, hearing the alarm clamouring in the distance. The panel in the booth had five buttons. She felt a wave of frustration. It was a code sequence. Unless she got the numbers in the proper order, the gate wouldn't open. She rifled the papers on the guard's desk, looking for the number. Nothing. She heard shouts, coming from the woods between the building

338

and the gate. Desperately she knelt by the fallen guard, searching his shirt and pants pockets. The number code wasn't in any of them. She noticed something inked on his wrist.

Five numbers—

She heard footsteps drawing closer through the woods. She turned, holding the gun out.

Archer emerged from the woods. He stopped when he saw the gun.

'Suzannah, you've got to come back—'

She shot him in the chest. Archer went rigid. He wobbled towards her, his feet thumping heavily in the pine needles. 'Suze,' he wheezed. She read the numbers off the guard's wrist, punched the code into the box, and the gate slid aside. In the distance, she could hear sirens now.

'Suze,' Archer said, right behind her.

He stood weaving on his feet. His eyes rolled up and he flopped forward onto his face.

Suzannah stuck the pistol into the waistband of her scrubs and pulled the shirt down over the butt. She ran out the gate and away from the psychiatric building, skirting the pine grove until she found a deeper woods beyond. The ground felt cold and damp against her bare feet. The woods grew denser. Branches clawed at her face and hands.

She realized suddenly that she was making a mistake. The entire grounds might be fenced. She did not know what was waiting out here. They might even have dogs.

She turned around and ran back out of the woods, past the pine grove, toward the psychiatric hospital. At least there she knew the layout. She'd make a grotesque figure, barefoot and in surgical scrubs, but with luck she'd be able to run right past it. Then she could follow the road out.

She sprinted across the lot in front of the hospital. A man

in a suit was walking on an interception course with her as he headed for the parking lot. He slowed and stared at her, his mouth dropping open. 'Hi,' she said and ran past. She pounded out the access road, barely feeling the burn of pavement against her feet. In the distance she heard sirens. They grew louder and a fire engine appeared, barrelling down the entry road. She stood aside for it, then ran along the roadside.

They'll send a car after you, she thought. Veering away from the road, she headed into the woods. She ran on and on. A burning stitch started up in her side, a penalty for all the runs she'd missed lately. She ignored the pain. The ground was slippery and the hills were very steep. Twice she fell and got up again, her scrubs smeared with mud. The fashionable suburb of McLean was not far from here, she knew. If she could just keep going, find a house, she could call Jay. Even then, she would not be safe. They knew now she would never help them. They would hunt her and go on hunting until they found her. Then they would kill her.

# 34

Andrew Dugan sat alone at the front window of the crowded deli, feeling helpless. He didn't know where Suzannah was. When he'd found his way out of the woods last night, he'd hitched a ride straight to the *Post*. Jay had already been there, but no Suzannah.

Andrew grimaced around the rim of his coffee cup. It had been awkward, sitting there with the other man she loved. And then the *Post* staffer had recognized him and asked what the famous artist was doing sitting around in the newsroom. Before long, the Adepts would not have needed their special skills to know that Andrew Dugan was hiding out at the *Post*. Jay had seemed genuinely reluctant to let him leave. A good and decent man, Jay. But he needn't worry.

I'm not afraid of the wolves, Andrew thought. I'm one of them.

*Suzannah, where are you?*

Andrew reviewed his visions. He'd seen her in a cell at Station Three, and then he'd seen her escape and run across in front of the psychiatric building. He'd seen her clawing her way through the woods.

And nothing more.

Andrew sipped his coffee and watched the traffic on Dupont Circle. He scanned the trendy shops, looking for anyone watching him. He had not seen them watching or moving on him, but he did not see everything.

There was still some use left for his eyes.

He picked up the Nature Company shopping bag from the floor beside his chair and looked at the piece of sculpture inside. The only sculpture he'd ever done. It was supposed to be a pregnant woman, à la Henry Moore. Cobwebs clung to the ugly, misshapen figure. Why, after all these years, had he suddenly felt it so necessary to have the hideous thing that he'd gone by the self-storage place and got it out?

I'm going to give it to Suzannah, he thought.

He smiled. Yes. Let her see that she wasn't the only one who could struggle endlessly over a piece of art and never get it right.

He thought of her out in the woods, running, terrified. It pained him deeply. Maybe she would reach a place where she could call Jay. Maybe at this very moment she was calling him. But that was only speculation.

There's a phone booth right out there, Andrew thought. I could call Jay. Ask if he's heard from her.

Andrew started to get up, then sat down again. They probably had a tap on Jay's line. Tracing did not take minutes now. All you needed was the caller ID circuit, and you could do it at once.

And besides, if Jay *did* hear from her, he'd be out of the newsroom door the next second.

What's the matter with me? Andrew thought. Can't I think straight any more? Is the microchip taking that away, too? A cold sweat broke out on his forehead.

The deli window and street faded away. Andrew saw Suzannah and Jay running through broad hallways. They entered a narrower, plusher corridor. At the far end, ahead of them, he saw a marine in dress uniform standing at attention beside a dark ornate door. The door bore the seal of the Secretary of Defense.

The Pentagon, Andrew thought. We talked about it in the Jeep!

Behind Suzannah and Jay, men in blue uniforms ran in pursuit. The one in the lead had his gun out. 'Suzannah!' Andrew shouted, trying to warn her, then remembering that it was a vision. She could not hear him.

'Get out of the way!' the guard shouted.

Andrew watched, horrified, as the dozen or so people in the corridor parted, scurrying to the walls, giving the guard a clear shot at Suzannah and Jay.

'Stop or I'll shoot!' the guard shouted.

Suzannah and Jay did not stop. They were only a few yards from the door now. The marine guard at the door was drawing his sidearm. The guard in the blue uniform stopped, his gun out front in the classic two-handed grip, feet spread. He was aiming the gun straight at Suzannah's back.

'No!' Andrew groaned.

The gun fired and at the same instant the vision faded to black.

Andrew found himself sprawled across his small table, his coffee spilled on the tiles. The people around him were staring at him. He righted himself, ignoring them, appalled at what he had seen. It must not be. But he had seen it. The gun had fired ... just before everything went black.

That had never happened before, a vision fading so abruptly. Did it mean anything?

Andrew stared out of the window, watching a tour bus chug around Dupont Circle. He knew suddenly what it meant. He got up and went out to the phone booth inside the door of the deli. He dialled information. 'Give me the number of Pentagon Tours, please.' He was amazed at how calm his voice sounded.

# 35

Suzannah tried to contain her anxiety as she waited with Jay inside a south entrance of the Pentagon. Two-thirty: time was slipping by with frightening speed. First the forty minutes from the McLean barn to Jay's apartment. Thirty more, showering and dressing at Jay's – unavoidable if she was to have any hope of getting an appointment with the Secretary of Defense. Ten more minutes to drive here from Jay's, and another five had bled away just since she'd called Juli's boss on the phone at the guard desk. All together, from the time she'd run out the gate at Langley, it was over three hours. By now Archer Montross would be shaking off the tranquillizer.

He had seen so many other things, she must assume he'd see her coming here. The thought terrified her. She looked at Jay. He stood next to her, arms folded, leaning against the square pillar furthest from the guard desk. He looked as if he hadn't a care in the world.

Suzannah said, 'If we get to see the secretary, and he believes us, what will he do?'

'You mean, will he close down the Adepts?'

'I mean, will he take the project for himself?'

Jay took a deep breath. 'Now you're asking *me* to see the future. I have a sense John Hastings would feel a strong, gut opposition to the Adepts, but I'm not sure where that comes from. It may be something I knew about him and have forgotten, or it may be his nice smile. Or I could be dead wrong. The Adepts represent an awesome power, and John Hastings isn't Secretary of Defense because he hates power. It will come down to his character and his wisdom. Face it, Suzannah, we're gambling – and we have no choice.'

Suzannah could think of nothing more to say. Jay was right. It was like surgery. Once you'd decided you had to cut, you cut, and that was that.

'I thought only Texas barns had phones,' Jay said, his voice lighter. Obviously, he was trying to relax her. And she needed it. She could feel the chemical energy of the amphetamines surging through her. Right now, it was almost too much, making her jittery. But she'd be in worse trouble if the dose wore off too fast. Jay had been able to find only the two in his pocket from last night. When those wore off, she'd be near collapse. Just another hour, she thought. If we haven't got to the Secretary by then, the Adepts will have got to us.

'Suze?' Jay edged closer to her, looking concerned.

She found a smile for him. 'I just wish the barn had had a shower and a closet full of clothes, too. We could have saved half an hour.'

'I don't know. I like you in that dress.'

She knew he was being gallant. The dress, grey and full-skirted, was all right at best: rather plain, but not too out of place among the buttoned-down, suited women of the Pentagon who kept filing past the guard desk. And it was infinitely better than shorts and a halter, the only other clothes she'd left at Jay's.

'We should have gone to the closest entrance,' she muttered.

346

Jay gave her a reproachful look.

All right, she thought. I left it up to Jay for a good reason. If Archer *is* watching me now in his mind, the fewer choices I make the better.

But the furthest entrance from the Secretary's office? From here, it will take us at least another five minutes just to walk there.

And what if Archer sees me letting Jay make the decisions? That will go into the equation and we lose anyway. A chill ran up Suzannah's spine. They were playing paper/scissors/rock with a mind reader.

She watched people file in. Most of them passed the guard's desk with a nod and the flick of a badge. Two guards manned this station, intelligent-looking men in their late forties. Amazingly, they seemed to know by sight most of the hundreds of people filing in and out. One of them kept looking at her. Suzannah could almost feel his gaze, a slight heat along the side of her face. She glanced past him into the broad corridor, searching the crowd for Juli's boss. Where was he? If only they could get in without an escort —

There he was! She squeezed Jay's arm, alerting him, and watched Captain Milt Cochran's bald head bobbing towards her above the crowd. Milt was tall and thin, an Ichabod Crane figure, except for the smart navy uniform. She waved at him and, after a second, he waved back with a surprised expression. Suzannah realized it was her hair. He had not expected her to look like Juli. He came out past the guard's station, and she introduced him to Jay. Milt directed them to the airport-style metal detector in front of the guard desk. Suzannah walked through. Good thing the alarm could not be triggered by tension. When they were in the corridor, Milt said, 'On the phone, your sister mentioned something about you needing to see, uh, the Secretary?'

347

'That's right,' Suzannah said. 'He knows Jay – Jay interviewed him during the Gulf War. If you can just get us as far as one of his aides.'

'Juli was rather mysterious about it all,' Milt said, eyeing her, obviously wanting more of an explanation.

'Jay has been working on a story,' Suzannah said, 'and he discovered a highly sensitive piece of information. It concerns Secretary Hastings directly. That's all I can say. But I can assure you, the secretary will be glad if you help get us to him.'

'And you are coming along because . . . ?'

'I'm an eyewitness to part of the story.'

'Aha,' Milt said dubiously. He edged ahead of them, turning into a stairway and going up one flight. Suzannah and Jay fell in behind him, letting him navigate through the people in the corridors, trying not to feel intimidated by the sheer size of the place. Even the hallways were huge – there must be fifty of the Pentagon's twenty-five thousand employees walking around them right now, but the size of the hall made them seem fewer. Every few yards, it seemed, there was a bathroom, a trash room, or a branching side corridor. The tiles and walls were beige and yet they seemed to eat light, leaving the huge space dim and cavern-like.

'Mr Mallernee,' Milt said over his shoulder, 'you're a well-known reporter. I guess I'm wondering why you didn't go through normal channels. Public Affairs would be the best way for you to get an appointment with the Secretary.'

'The information is such that we need to avoid normal channels on this one, captain.'

'Aha. Well, I'm not sure how much influence I have. No way can I get you all the way to Secretary Hastings. But there's a slim chance I can get you in to see his military assistant, General Southfield, for a minute some time today.'

Suzannah remembered Juli speaking admiringly of General Southfield. Apparently he was a nice man, young for a general and certain, as a result of his present position, to get that second star. Colin Powell, the last chairman of the Joint Chiefs of Staff, had done a turn as the Secretary's chief aide when he was a brigadier. Suzannah's throat was suddenly dry. If we get in, she thought, do I have enough to convince him?

Milt turned down a side corridor. There were fewer people here and more light. He stopped at the door to his office suite and pushed a sequence of buttons beside the lock. The door opened and he led them past some offices. Passing Juli's little office, Suzannah noticed distractedly that the dieffenbachia was wilting. Milt's office was much bigger than Juli's, with a couch, a conference table, and a big desk. 'Why don't you two have a seat, there,' Milt said. 'I'll –'

His phone rang, interrupting him. 'Excuse me.'

Suzannah sank into the low couch to the side of Milt's desk. Jay remained standing, studying the map of Europe that took up one wall of the office.

Settling behind his desk, Milt snatched up his phone. 'Yes?' he snapped.

Suzannah saw his hand tighten on the receiver. He sat up straighter in his chair. She felt a sudden sharp uneasiness.

'Yes, *sir* . . . Yes.' His voice was suddenly much quieter. 'That will be fine.' He replaced the receiver gently and gave Suzannah a ghost of a smile. 'Sorry about that. I'll just call the general now.'

She leaned forward to watch Milt dial, but he defeated her by turning his chair away and putting the phone on his lap. Who just called you? she wondered. Her imagination served up an image of Archer Montross sitting in the office of a high official at Langley, telling him to call Juli Lord's supervisor and instruct him to hold Suzannah and Jay in his office until

349

Agency counter-intelligence people could get there.

'Yes,' Milt said. 'I'll call back then.' He swung back to her, hanging up the phone. 'Well, doctor, the good news is that both the general and the secretary are in today. But I'm afraid they're in conference right now. The general may be free in fifteen minutes. I'll call him then.'

Fifteen minutes. Suzannah felt a surge of impatience. But she made herself smile. 'Great!'

Archer Montross sat in George Pederson's office, feeling faintly sick. He watched Ellis Grayburn hang up Pederson's phone.

Pederson sat forward, his hands clenched together on his desktop. He looked up at Grayburn, entreaty in his eyes. 'Do you think this Captain Cochran can hold them?'

Grayburn shrugged. 'You've got your prime Adept here. Ask him.'

Pederson glanced at Archer, then away, out of the window.

Do I look that bad? Archer wondered.

Then the office shimmered and faded around him. He saw Suzannah and Jay running through a broad hallway of the Pentagon. At the far end, ahead of them, he saw a marine in dress uniform standing at attention beside a dark ornate door. On that door was the seal of the Secretary of Defense. Behind Suzannah and Jay, men in blue uniforms ran in pursuit. The one in the lead had his gun out. Archer felt his muscles go rigid. No! He thought.

'Get out of the way!' the guard shouted.

The dozen or so people in the corridor parted, scurrying to the walls, giving the guard a clear shot at Suzannah and Jay.

'Stop or I'll shoot!' the guard shouted.

Suzannah and Jay did not stop. They were only a few yards

from the door now. The marine guard at the door was drawing his sidearm. The guard in the blue uniform stopped, his gun out front in the classic two-handed grip, feet spread. He was aiming the gun straight at Suzannah's back.

'No!' Archer yelled. He stood up, clawing at his eyes, feeling the wall of the office smash his shoulder as the gun fired.

Suzannah sat in Milt Cochran's office, trying to contain her impatience. Jay turned from the map and glanced at her. Her unease deepened.

'So how's your sister doing?' Milt asked.

'I haven't talked to her today,' Suzannah said. 'But yesterday she was doing all right. It's a fairly bad break, but they think she'll recover fully.' Fifteen minutes, she thought. Too short for us to consider trying another channel. Plenty long enough for Pentagon Security to close in on this office and hold us.

She hesitated, torn by indecision. If she was wrong, if Milt was really trying to help her and Jay see Secretary Hastings, she was about to throw away the best chance she had.

She pushed up from the clinging couch. 'Thank you, Milt, but Mr Mallernee and I can't wait fifteen minutes.'

Jay raised an eyebrow, then headed for the door.

Milt stood, his face furrowing into alarm. 'Wait. I'll walk you out. Technically, you have to stay with me.'

Suzannah walked quickly out of the office suite and down the hall behind Jay. She heard Milt yelling behind her, running after them. She put a hand in Jay's back. 'Run!'

He broke into a trot, turning left into a short hallway. She followed.

'Stop!' Milt shouted.

Jay turned right into another cross corridor. Suzannah

followed. Behind her, she heard Milt's voice, muffled by a corner in the hallway. 'They went that way!' he shouted.

She heard people running behind her, their shoes slapping the tile. Glancing back, she saw four men in the dark blue uniforms of the Federal Protective Service. Adrenaline slammed into her. She ran around a corner. She saw a man in a sailor's uniform leaving a room up ahead. He carried a thick stack of papers. A copy room? She surged past Jay and ran in, pulling him with her. The room was empty. Two huge copy machines took up one wall. Reams of paper formed a wall stacked nearly to the ceiling. She ran behind them and squatted down. Jay crouched beside her. In the cramped dimness she could smell a ripe banana peel. Cobwebs swept her face.

The door banged back.

Suzannah clenched Jay's arm. He found her hand and gripped it tightly. Closing her eyes, she could see the security man in her mind. Would he just stick his head in or make a more thorough search?

Feet clattered out of the room and the door banged again.

Her shoulders sagged.

'Let's go,' Jay whispered. 'If they think they've lost us, they may just head for the Secretary's office. Other security people are probably headed there now anyway.'

She followed him out of the copy room. They walked quickly down the corridor. Suzannah resisted the urge to break into a run.

'This way,' Jay said. 'We can cut through and back to the E-ring further down.'

'Right.' She followed him, walking as fast as she could, like a harried mid-level manager, late to a meeting. She passed bulletin boards with photos of smiling officers pinning medals to other smiling officers. Posters, done in the crude style of World War II propaganda, warned against 'loose lips sinking ships'. A petty officer pushed a hand truck loaded with bound reports.

'Up ahead,' Jay said. 'E-ring again. We go right.'

Suzannah saw they were now on the opposite side of the building from where they'd entered. The broad hall wasn't nearly as crowded so close to the Secretary's office – a few civilians and five or six military.

'There they are!' someone shouted behind them.

Suzannah's heart sank. She broke into a run. 'Hurry, Jay!' she said.

'It's just up there!' Jay said, pointing as he ran.

She saw the tile ahead giving way to rich blue carpet. A marine in dress uniform guarded an ornate door framed in dark wood. Beyond him, more blue-uniformed FPS men ran toward the Secretary's office.

Suzannah heard the security guard behind her shouting, 'Get out of the way, get out of the way!' Dread surged in her as she saw the people ahead of her scatter to the walls; she knew they must be doing the same behind her. A memory flashed in her mind. Three or four years ago, a mental patient had run past guards at an entrance and headed for the Secretary's office. A guard had shot him dead.

The Secretary's door was only a few yards away now, the marine guard turning to them, reaching for his sidearm.

'Stop or I'll shoot!' yelled the security man behind them.

I can make it, Suzannah thought. As she sprinted towards the door, she heard the gun fire. A woman screamed, a terrible sound, raking Suzannah's nerves. She saw the marine freeze, his gun halfway out, looking beyond her. The horror in his face made her stop and turn. Behind her, she saw a fallen man sprawled on the tile between her and the FPS guards. The man was wearing dark clothes. He had a thick mane of black hair.

*God, no!* Suzannah's throat closed in horror.

She ran back, ignoring Jay's shout. The security guards stood around the fallen bystander, their faces transfixed with horror. The one who'd shot him looked sick, his gun hand hanging at his side.

Not a bystander, Suzannah thought.

She knelt beside Andrew, horrified at the spurting blood on his chest. The wound made a horrid sucking sound. She realized he was dying. She planted her hands over the wound, applying pressure until the sucking noise stopped. Andrew grabbed her wrist, his grip appallingly weak. He gazed at her, his face white as chalk.

'Don't be sorry,' he said. 'It was the only way.'

'Lady, freeze. You're under arrest.'

'I'm a doctor,' she said.

'A doctor? No, they said you . . .'

'Shut up, damn you!'

The security man stood back, his face uncertain.

She leaned down to Andrew, crying in anguish. 'Andrew, Andrew.'

'I don't think I could have lived being blind,' he said. 'My eyes have been the world to me.'

'I know.'

'But I couldn't bear this either. Before long I would have known everything you were going to say before you said it. Everything you would do . . .' He stopped, closing his eyes in a grimace, then looked at her again. 'I have already loved you as much as any human can.'

'Andrew, I love you, I love you!'

'I know. But it's good to hear it.' He smiled at her, and

then the life left his eyes. She felt his chest go still under her hands. Bending over him, Suzannah wept.

# 36

Suzannah lifted her hands and stared at them. They were bright with Andrew's blood. Tears poured down her cheeks. She felt as if her heart would break. She stood and looked at the security men all around her. Their weapons were still drawn, but pointing down at the floor.

'What have you done?' she said.

A tall man in a grey suit stepped forward, showing an ID to the security men. Suzannah realized it was Grainger. 'Arrest those two,' he said.

'Wait,' another voice called.

Suzannah looked up into the eyes of a tall man in an army uniform. On his shoulder was a single silver star.

'General Southfield,' Jay said. 'I'm Jay Mallernee from the *Washington Post*. This is Dr Suzannah Lord. We must see the Secretary at once. National security is at stake.'

'Mallernee. You reported on the Gulf War. Damned fine job.'

'Thank you, sir.'

The exchange sounded slightly unreal to Suzannah, as though she were hearing the words over a tinny tape recorder. Her hands felt numb. She realized she was slipping into shock. She took deep breaths. As the numbness dropped away the grief rushed in again, a crushing weight around her heart. I have to be strong now, she thought. Jay can't do this alone.

She met General Southfield's gaze. 'You can arrest us afterwards,' she said, 'if you still want to. Right now, millions of lives depend on your getting us into that office.'

Southfield's face revealed nothing, but he motioned and one of the FPS guards came over. 'We need to check you for weapons,' he explained. The guard frisked them. Then Southfield said, 'Follow me.'

Suzannah was dimly aware of passing over deep beige carpet through a vestibule. The image of Andrew Dugan, sprawled on the bloodstained tile, burned in her brain. Andrew stepped into the path of that bullet, she thought, to save my life. And to prove to the Secretary that the future can be seen. Now I will make it count. Later, I will mourn for Andrew. Tears welled up, threatening to spill. With a fierce effort, she held them back.

The Honourable John Hastings sat behind a vast desk writing. A grouping of chairs in front of the desk surrounded a low table set with a silver coffee service. Suzannah could smell the coffee.

At last Hastings looked up. 'The shooting?' he asked.

Southfield explained and made the introductions. Hastings stood and came around his desk, motioning them to seats around the low table. General Southfield stood behind and slightly to the right of Hastings's wingback chair. The Secretary leaned forward, poured a steaming cup, and handed it to her. She was impressed by the kindness of his face. He peered at her, his head slightly to the side. He had the manner of a man who was once shy and, despite his power, might still be. She sipped from the cup. The coffee was strong and black.

General Southfield said, 'Andrew Dugan – the man who

was shot out there – was a national resource. I have two of his paintings. He signed up for the Pentagon tour today, then gave the tour guide the slip. Can you tell us anything about that, Dr Lord?'

A lump rose in Suzannah's throat. She waited until she could control her voice. 'More than you want to know,' she said.

Secretary Hastings looked at her for a long moment, then transferred his gaze to Jay. He gave a wry, almost diffident smile. 'All right, you have my interest. What's up?'

Jay glanced at Suzannah.

'I'll take it,' she said, surprised at how strong her voice sounded. She set the cup down, forcing the horrible images of Andrew from her mind. 'Mr Secretary, are you aware that a group working for the CIA has a radical new form of intelligence gathering?'

John Hastings pursed his lips. 'Radical? No. I'm not aware of anything that would fit that description.'

'Are you familiar with the Lancaster microchip?'

'I don't know about familiar, but I did read the recent *Newsweek* feature on it. What does that have to do with the CIA?'

Suzannah told him. She told him everything.

The Secretary listened politely. He did not interrupt her once. She knew it was a bad sign.

'I'm sorry,' he said, 'but this is just too incredible.'

'Only if you think we know more about the human brain than we do.'

The Secretary gazed at her. 'You are saying Andrew Dugan came here today because he saw that the security guard would shoot at you. That he knew just where to stand to step out and take the bullet?'

'That is correct. And before you write it off, consider the

likelihood of its happening any other way.'

The Secretary glanced at General Southfield again. 'Go on, doctor.'

She told him about how Adepts had contributed to the Gulf War.

The Secretary sat back with a sigh. 'Doctor, you are obviously an intelligent woman. And we certainly did get some remarkable humintel at key points in the Gulf War. But again, this is simply too much to believe.'

*Humintel*. Suzannah remembered the word from discussions with Juli: intelligence from a human source. 'Before the war,' she said, 'you were shown an analysis that predicted Saddam Hussein would invade Kuwait. You ignored it. It was the same source who said you could establish Desert Shield in Saudi Arabia without taking casualties even though every sensible analyst would have said otherwise. That time, you listened.'

'I don't acknowledge any of this,' the Secretary said, 'but where did you hear it?'

'From a man named Archer Montross. He is one of the Adepts. He and I were once friends. He had very poor vision, and I got him into Dr Lancaster's pilot study. He was the first to experience the side effect. He started using it in his analyses at the Agency.'

The Secretary turned to the general. 'Do we have anything on this man?'

'I'll see.' The general walked out of the big office into an adjoining room. Instead of asking her questions, the Secretary sipped his coffee and glanced out of his window at the stark tree line where the Potomac River wound its way south to Alexandria. Several minutes passed. I'm losing him, Suzannah thought.

'Mr Secretary,' she said, 'the CIA recently foiled a plot on the President's life. They intercepted two men in a field near Andrews Air Force Base. They were getting ready to fire a SAM at Air Force One.'

The Secretary put his coffee down, stood, and paced around behind his chair. He leaned on the back of it, looking down at her. 'Dr Lord, that information – everything you've been telling me – is deeply classified. You could not have known it. And yet, clearly, you do.'

The general came back into the room. 'There is an Archer Montross at CIA,' he said. 'And he *is* one of the pilot subjects for the Lancaster implant.' The general hesitated, looking at Suzannah and Jay.

'Go on,' the Secretary said.

'There is a surgical facility under cover of a US Fisheries toxicology station. They were conducting electrocortical stimulation of the brain to aid in recall. The project had approval from Congress's joint oversight panel. The facility burned down a few hours ago.'

'Thank you, General.'

Suzannah saw a new respect in Hastings's eyes and knew she had struck home at last.

'Dr Lord, you say these intelligence coups are due to the implant. Let's say, subject to my own investigation, that I become convinced you are telling the truth, fantastic as it seems. Why are you coming to me now?'

'Because the Adept project must be stopped.'

'Please explain. I understand why this could not be approved for the public, but if what you say is true, we have an inconceivably powerful new source of intelligence.'

'Mr Secretary, if our intelligence people could have this ability and use it strictly to protect national interests – and keep it an absolute secret from anyone else who might abuse it – some might consider it worth the human cost. But that will never happen. And the human cost is terrible, even to the Adepts themselves. These people cannot control what they see, any more than you can control your dreams. The unconscious is in control. As the conscious mind adapts to the microchip, the visions take the place of thinking. In the end, many Adepts may not be able to tell their visions from reality. Which means they won't know the present from the future. Some of them may become lost in permanent catatonia if they do not kill themselves first. Remember, they are capable of seeing their own futures, too. Of the fifty people in Dr Lancaster's pilot study, three that I'm aware of have had these visions. One is in a coma now after trying to hang herself. A second, Andrew Dugan, died today, not just to save me but to stop the microchip without spilling its secret. Andrew was so desperate he asked me to take the chip out, even though he knew it would leave him virtually or totally blind and take away the most important sense a painter has. In the end, he too chose death. Unlike Tricia, he got it . . . out there in the hall today.' Suzannah felt Jay's hand on her shoulder.

'What about Archer Montross?' the Secretary asked.

Suzannah hesitated. It was the question she had been dreading. 'It is possible that he will lose his grip on reality,' she said. 'But if he does not, and if he is not stopped, Archer Montross will see more and more of the future. He will help the Agency – or whoever employs him – turn that future against the present. Armed with his special abilities, he might become head of the Agency or almost anything else he chooses.'

The Secretary raised an eyebrow. 'You are telling me that a certain percentage of these Adepts can remain effective – the most powerful humintel source we could ever hope for.'

'Or dread.'

'Would it be so wrong for our enemies to dread us?'

'How long could we be clairvoyant with our enemies before they learned how we do it? When we dropped the bomb on Hiroshima, we were guaranteeing that our enemies would soon have it, too. This "secret weapon" will be no different. Mr Secretary, you used the word *humintel*. It will not be long before the only thing human about Archer Montross will be his body. Adepts can see into our lives. They can see what we have done and what we will do. I can't imagine a more total loss of the most basic human right: privacy. If this weapon is allowed to exist and proliferate, the future of all of us will be controlled by beings that are no longer human.'

The Secretary of Defense nodded, ever so slightly. She did not think he was even aware of it. He sat for a long moment, looking at her.

Jay said, 'Mr Hastings, Dr Lord is in danger. People involved with the Adept project have made several attempts on her life.'

'Well, that shouldn't be a problem now.' The Secretary glanced at the general, who nodded and disappeared again into the next room.

Suzannah said, 'FDA must not approve the microchip. And no one must know why. All use of the microchip side effect has to be ended. Archer Montross and any other Agency Adepts must be taken to a secure facility where the microchip can be removed.'

'Who would do the surgery? These people aren't supposed to even have the microchip. If we bring in a neurosurgeon, word might get out.'

Suzannah was encouraged. The question showed that the Secretary was thinking along with her, that he might be leaning her way. 'I'm a surgeon and I completed part of a residency in neurosurgery. I can remove the chip.'

'From what you say about Montross, he won't willingly co-operate.'

'No. And you will have to move quickly, before he *sees* that you will order it and takes countermeasures.'

The Secretary paled slightly. A chill went through Suzannah. Archer may already have seen this, she realized. What will he do?

Hastings stood. 'I want to thank you, doctor, and you, Jay, for bringing this to my attention. As incredible as it seems, you know too much to be ignored. The general will take down any and all details you can add. If it checks out, I will call the Director of CIA. If necessary, I will include the President.' He looked at Jay. 'I know you are a reporter, but you must not, under any circumstances, let any of this out to the public.'

'Quite right, sir. And, if you'll forgive me, neither must you or the general.'

The Secretary gave a small, grim smile. 'I do understand, Jay.'

Do you? Suzannah wondered as she rose from the couch. Will you put an end to this? Will you make it as if it has never been? Or do you think you can ride this tiger and not be devoured? She looked into the Secretary's eyes, hoping to find an answer. But she was not Archer. She could not see the future.

# 37

Suzannah sat at Tricia Fiore's bedside, watching her sleep. The sun poured through the window, warming the pastel walls. Surrounded by light and colour, Suzannah felt only the greyness of life.

Tears welled up, and she felt her nose start to run again. How am I going to make it through the funeral tomorrow? she wondered.

She became aware of the TV droning from its perch high up the wall: Phil Donahue interviewing a priest who claimed to have done exorcisms. She started to get up and turn it off, then realized that Ed Gaspard probably wanted it on. A day had passed since Tricia – on the verge of transfer to a long-term care facility – had awakened. But people did not pop straight out of comas; while Tricia had crossed the border out of darkness, she was still disoriented and prone to sleep. The stimulation from the TV set would help her ease back into the world.

Suzannah got up and straightened the blanket around Tricia's shoulders. The bruise around her neck was healing nicely, fading to a mild greenish ring. But what about Tricia's mind? What would happen when she had the strength to get up on that stool again?

The question oppressed Suzannah. Nothing seemed under control. She did not and could not know whether Tricia would try to kill herself again; whether the Honourable John Hastings would really put aside the most powerful weapon ever tapped or if he would feel that an Adept's mind was a terrible thing to waste. All she knew for sure was that, even though a microchip could show her how things would turn out, this way was better.

Bad as it was.

She walked to the window, looking down on the frozen grey courtyard of the hospital. Where is Archer? she wondered. He must know Hastings will launch a manhunt for him; they'll want him under their control whether or not they really mean to shut down the project. He's probably on the run, maybe even in another country by now.

'Hello,' Tricia said.

Suzannah turned, hurried back to the bedside. 'How are you, Miss Fiore?'

Tricia peered at her, recognition dawning slowly. 'You're Dr Lord. You helped run the pilot study.'

'That's right.'

'You called me the night I . . .'

'Yes.'

'Dr Gaspard told me you cut me down.'

Dread welled up in Suzannah. She nodded.

For a long moment Tricia said nothing. Then she sighed. 'I've seen terrible things.'

Suzannah took her hand. 'Yes.'

On the television, Suzannah heard the hourly newsbreak begin. The lead story this time was the same as it had been an hour ago. 'The FDA said today that it is denying approval to the Lancaster procedure,' the anchor intoned solemnly. 'While the widely hailed procedure was proven to greatly improve the eyesight of people with severe visual impairment, recent findings – on the eve of FDA approval – indicate that the surgical implant also leads, in time, to severe hallucinations and mental illness in some patients. This is disappointing news to the thousands of people with serious visual impairment who had hoped to benefit from the surgery. With the accidental death three days ago of the procedure's creator, Dr Roland Lancaster, it is unclear whether the newly discovered defects in the process can be corrected.

'On the economic front–' Suzannah turned off the TV.

'Hallucinations,' Tricia said, but she was smiling. 'Dr Lord, will you take it out of my brain?'

Her voice held such entreaty that Suzannah felt tears coming again. 'You would very likely be blind or almost blind.'

'I don't care,' Tricia said. 'I can teach if I'm blind. I could teach blind children. I would be all right again, too. I . . . I can't live this way. I don't want to *see* my life. I want to live it. You wanted to save my life, save it now. Please. Please!'

'Yes,' Suzannah said. 'I'll do it.'

Tricia began to cry. 'Thank you, doctor.'

Suzannah leaned over and hugged her. Tricia hugged back with fierce strength. For the first time that day, Suzannah knew a moment of happiness. She felt Tricia's fingers tighten on her arms. She pulled back and looked into the woman's eyes and saw she was having a vision. Suzannah felt a helpless horror. She shook Tricia's shoulders, but her eyes remained blank. Then they focused again. Tricia gave her a wan smile.

'I'll be all right,' Tricia said. 'If you take it out, everything will be all right.'

Suzannah nodded. She wished she could share Tricia's

optimism. I'll know everything is all right, she thought, when the Secretary of Defense asks me to remove the microchip from Archer's brain.

She patted Tricia's hand. 'I've got to go, but I'll see you tomorrow.'

'I want it out as soon as possible.' Tricia tried to sit up in bed. Too weak, she fell back.

'As soon as you're strong enough. I promise.'

Out in the corridor, Suzannah hesitated, unsure whether she wanted to go home or stop by her office. The time off Ed Gaspard had arranged for her because of her concussion did not expire until tomorrow, after Andrew's funeral. It might be nice, though, just to sit in her office, start reclaiming a sense of normalcy.

In the surgery wing, Suzannah walked through the bustling ORs before letting herself into her office. The office was quiet, the outer desk empty. In her own office, her desk was strewn with memos and notes from Marjory. She sat down and riffled through them, then set them aside. The sculpture Andrew had given her drew her gaze. General Southfield had found it in the shopping bag beside Andrew's body at the Pentagon and given it to her, along with the note:

> *My dear Suzannah, Don't ever tell anyone this is a Dugan. And don't ever give up on your apple. Realizing it is wrong is the beginning of wisdom.*
>
> *Love, Andrew*

Suzannah traced the sculpture with her fingers. Lumpy and misshapen, it was truly awful, and in its awfulness it comforted her. It *is* just like my apple, she thought. She picked it up, feeling the weight of the plaster, tracing the awkward contours. What had Andrew meant this to be? A human head? It looked more like a big cheese ball caught out in a hailstorm. How much frustration Andrew must have felt as he fought this unruly shape. How much pleasure.

Suzannah jogged up the long walkway towards the Washington Monument, savouring the wet snowflakes on her face. Inside the ring of floodlights, the massive stone base of the monument blazed white against the night. The flags planted all around the base hung limp. A man and two kids in bulky coats turned from the monument to gawk at her. Probably tourists from Florida who never jogged. Actually, at thirty-one degrees and slight wind, sweatpants and shirt were all she needed. Anything more, and the inner burn of exertion would overheat her. She waved at the tourists, glad for their company. A couple of times around the building ought to make three miles, and then she could trot back to her car. Suzannah leaned into the slight grade, pushing herself, feeling the sweat soak into her headband. Her blood raced, scouring her brain, moving out some of the sludge of grief and dread she felt at facing the funeral tomorrow.

It would be all right. Jay would be there with her. She would get through it.

She ran off the paved path into the soft snow-dusted grass, circling the monument, thinking of Andrew. He'd said this place was lucky for him. She glanced up at the pointed top, far above, and felt a dizzy second of vertigo. The clean edges of the building softened a bit in the snow mists overhead. Up there, Andrew had been inspired to paint *Sol*. How had it felt to gaze out over the city at the moment of artistic breakthrough? Like a god, she was sure.

She wondered if some part of Andrew might be up there now, looking down at her; knowing why she'd come.

She veered in closer to the giant doors at the base of the building. The monument was closed for the night, of course, but if anything was left of Andrew, doors would no longer stop him.

Suzannah saw with surprise that one of the doors was slightly ajar. An eerie thrill went through her. She knew her grief was making her foolish. Not Andrew, no; just a park police officer or monument caretaker making rounds.

An idea struck her. Maybe she could get in, wheedle a quick ride to the top of the building. Right now, there was no place in the world she would rather be. Maybe, for a second or two, she could see the city, the world, through Andrew Dugan's eyes.

She checked to make sure the tourists weren't looking, then headed for the door and slipped inside. Faint smells of dust and mildew met her. In front of her stood another wall of white stone, the central elevator shaft. The doors of the elevator were closed. To either side, corridors led back.

'Hello?' she said.

No answer. She pushed the elevator button just to see what would happen. The doors remained closed. Oh, well. She wasn't about to go up alone anyway. She trotted to the side and looked down one of the corridors. In front of her, steps rose along the wall to a landing above. A chain blocked off the steps. No one was allowed to walk up any more. The steps and landing were empty.

The outer door of the monument clanged shut behind her.

Suzannah whirled, feeling a rush of goose bumps. He stood beside the door. 'I knew you'd come,' he said with a cold smile.

'Archer,' she whispered. She wanted to scream, but the muscles of her throat would not obey her. She felt weak with terror. She thought of the tourists, the bright lights, the bustling traffic on Constitution Avenue. Only a few yards away, but it might as well be a thousand miles.

'Looking for Andrew's ghost?' Archer asked. His smile faded. The look of hatred in his eyes froze her blood. The stairs! she thought. No, too far up – a sure trap. Archer was much stronger. He would catch her before she got far, and then she would be too winded to fight him.

'I asked you a question,' Archer said.

She stared at him, petrified. How had he known that this was a haunt of Andrew's?

Because he told me when we were locked together in the bugged cell. Archer heard it then.

But to know I'd come here, tonight . . .

*He didn't know it. He saw it.* Her head spun with horror. Had he seen himself killing her, too?

'Come here, Suzannah.'

She stayed where she was.

'If you make me come after you, I'll hurt you worse.'

She realized it might be better to go to him. That way, she'd be closer to the door. She might be able to get past him and out.

She walked slowly to him, stopping a few feet away.

'That's a good girl. Take off your sweatshirt.'

She pulled it off, shivering in her bra.

The unscarred side of Archer's face flushed. The look in his eyes filled her with dread. She feinted left, then dodged back, trying to get past him. He grabbed her and pulled her against him. His arms tightened, flattening her lungs. She couldn't breathe. He stared into her eyes. She gasped desperately, trying to suck a breath. He lifted her. She kicked at his shins, but he only laughed. Spots swam in front of her eyes. For a few seconds everything went dim; then she felt the cold floor pressing into her back. She gasped, filling her lungs. Her vision returned, filled with Archer's face above her. She could feel his hands clawing at her sweatpants. She tried to squirm away. He banged her head on the floor.

Her vision went grey again. No, she thought, hang on, hang on.

When she could see again, she realized Archer was staring down at her – no, *through* her. His face was rapt, his body perfectly still. He's having a vision! she realized. Hope flooded her. She tried to slither away, but his legs tightened, locking her in. She realized that even if he couldn't see her he could still feel her. She pounded on his chest. It was like hitting the stone of the monument. His expression never changed. I have to get loose, she thought desperately. Now, before his vision passes.

Gritting her teeth, she plunged her thumbs into Archer's eyes.

He jerked back with a howl of pain. With a fierce effort, she slithered free, but he rose and planted his back against the door, blocking her escape. He covered his eyes with one hand, his teeth bared in pain. She saw his other hand groping for the bank of light switches beside the door.

Everything went black.

A choking horror filled Suzannah. The darkness was absolute. Now she was blind, too. She backed away, keeping her feet pointed toward her last image of the door. She could feel her heart hammering in her chest. At least Archer had lost physical contact with her. All she had to do was keep away from him, wait this out, until morning if she had to. Someone would come.

Archer groaned. 'You *bitch*. I'll kill you.'

She said nothing, hoping he would keep talking. That way, she would know where he was. She continued, slowly, to back away from him, glad for the silent soles of her running shoes. A wall nudged her back; feeling behind her, she eased along it until she came to the corner.

All right, now she knew exactly where she was.

Suddenly Archer chuckled. The sound sent a chill up her spine.

'I see you,' he said in a cloying, sing-song voice. 'Oh, this is beautiful. You are standing with your back against the corner. Your left hand is on the wall.'

The hackles on Suzannah's neck rose. She remembered running from Archer through the dark woods, making the turn she'd thought would fool him, only to have him step out in front of her. And he was seeing her now, in his mind, something in that mind knowing her so well that he could even see which hand she had put on the wall.

She heard the rush of his feet and ducked, blind, feeling his hand swipe her shoulder. She tried to run past him. He grabbed her hair, spinning her around in circles. She jerked away and ran, feeling a distant pain in her scalp. Something caught her thighs – the chain blocking the stairway. She stepped over it, then stumbled against the bottom stair, falling forward. The sharp edges of steps slapped her palms. Scrambling to her feet, she ran up the stairs. Her foot swiped hard through empty air, then she connected with the landing. Turning right, she dragged one hand along the wall to find the rail. She ran on, holding the other hand out front. Her palm slapped a wall and she turned again. Behind her, Archer laughed. She could hear his footsteps coming after her, unhurried and relentless, regular as a metronome. She stumbled up and up, rounding the corners.

'You can't get away,' Archer said. 'I see you plain as day. My eyes hurt, Suzannah. I think they're bleeding. Maybe you'd like to know how that feels.'

Suzannah ran up another flight, and another, another, losing count. Her legs burned with exertion, her breath tearing at her lungs. The sharp, gritty scuff of Archer's shoes pursued her with the persistence of nightmare. He told her the things he was going to do to her. She wanted to scream, to make the voice stop.

And then, suddenly, just below her, it did stop.

So did the footsteps.

She stopped too, hardly daring to hope. Had the vision ended? Was he blind now, too?

She tried to gauge where he was. The darkness wrapped her like a shroud. She could almost feel it pressing against her eyeballs, down her throat. Her eyes, straining to see, began to water and sting. She willed herself to calmness. His voice had been very close – only a few feet away and slightly to her left.

'I see you,' Archer said. But his voice was subtly different, uncertain. She kicked out at him, putting all her body into it. Her foot connected. He gasped. And then she heard the sound of something heavy falling, down and down, the crack of bone, the most horrible and yet beautiful sound she had ever heard. She ran down after him, tripping over a leg – or arm. Hanging on to the rail, she regained her balance and resumed her blind plunge downwards. She started to scream. She did not stop until she stood outside in the wonderful white light.

# Epilogue

**Columbia Gardens Cemetery, 29 January 1993:**

Suzannah stood with Jay, down the slope a good distance
from the grave side. Her hands hurt where the stone steps of
the Washington Monument had scraped them. The back of
her head throbbed where it had hit the floor. But she felt
a vast relief. Archer was dead, his neck broken in the
fall.

She would not go to his funeral.

A dusting of snow drifted down from a grey sky, whitening
the bare oak branches. Through a blur of tears, she watched
the small group still lingering under the tent by Andrew's
grave. There was Grace Gorkachova, his agent. The older
woman who looked so much like Andrew must be his
mother. His ex-wife, Darcy, stood with a number of his
friends. Their heads were bowed in grief.

Suzannah became conscious of the black dress under her
coat. Would Andrew have preferred her to wear a colour to
his funeral today? One of the bright yellows or mysterious
earthy orange-browns from his paintings, perhaps? She
could not say. Unlike him, she had not sped through decades
of deepening love in a single week. She could not say what he
would have liked for dinner, whether he hated hot weather or
loved it, preferred *MacNeil/Lehrer* or *Cheers*. She knew
none of the things the microchip had shown him about
her.

She did know that he himself had liked to wear black and that she had fallen in love with him.

Jay squeezed her shoulder. 'I am very sorry, Suzannah. He was a good man, a brave man.'

She leaned against him, smelling his clean sandalwood smell. He looked strange in dark pinstripes and starched white shirt, with only the cowboy boots to mark his normal persona. Strange, but good.

'You look so handsome,' she said.

'Don't get too used to it.'

'Dr Lord, Mr Mallernee?'

Suzannah turned. She was surprised to see John Hastings, Secretary of Defense. Behind him, on the cemetery road, a black government car idled. The rear door stood open, the driver at the wheel.

'I'm sorry to intrude,' Hastings said. 'I thought I might find you here.'

'That's all right.'

'Dr Fachet has turned informer. With his help, we've uncovered those involved with the project at CIA. It was a rogue operation. We'll have to make some sort of deal with the renegades, of course, in return for their silence, but the project is over and all Agency personnel involved are retired as of now. Dr Fachet has given us the names of all Adepts and agreed to surrender his medical licence in return for a change of identity under the federal witness protection programme. It seems he is terrified of Archer Montross.'

'But—'

'We didn't tell him Montross is dead,' the Secretary said with a slight smile.

Suzannah nodded.

'We'll want you to operate on the Adepts to remove the microchips. According to Fachet, you are very good. Maybe you can save the vision of some of them. Of course, whatever the risks, it has to be done.'

'I'll do my best, Mr Secretary.'

'I know you will. We owe you a lot, doctor. I'll be in touch.' The Secretary walked back to his waiting car and the black limo glided off, tyres hissing on the new-fallen snow.

Above, on the hill, the mourners started to drift away. Jay did not move. 'Ironic,' he said. 'I saw a lot of dead people during the Gulf War. I saw lots of burials. But I never saw a funeral. Funerals are important. They tell you it happened. They tell you it's over.'

'Is that what your book is supposed to be? A funeral?'

He looked at her. 'Yes. I've started writing – really writing. Did I mention that?'

She squeezed his arm, pleased. 'No, you didn't, you big goof.'

'We were kind of busy.'

'Yes.'

'I let them kill a boy.' His blue eyes were suddenly shiny.

She looked at him, startled, then took his hand in both of hers. 'Tell me.'

He told her. When he had finished, she felt the tears welling up again, this time for Jay. She said, 'The blue-eyed man in Arab clothes who ordered him shot –'

'An Adept,' Jay said. 'Yes, I've figured that out. It doesn't matter. I should have been able to save him. He was just a boy.'

Suzannah held his hands tightly.

'Big brave reporter,' he said, his voice hoarse and broken. 'I was . . . afraid they'd kill me, too. What do you think, Suzannah? Should I put that in my book?'

'Jay, listen to me. Being afraid has nothing to do with it. If

376

it had been humanly possible to save that boy, you would have done it.'

'How can I know that? How can I ever know that?'

'By knowing yourself the way I do.'

He looked away. 'I did try to save him. I should have tried harder.'

She heard a new note in his voice -- release. It was enough. He had told her something he'd thought he could never say. He'd said it and the sky hadn't fallen. Now she could help him forgive himself.

He was letting her in, at last.